ONE WEEK LOAN

British Women Writers and the French Revolution

Palgrave Studies in the Enlightenment, Romanticism and Cultures of Print

General Editors: **Professor Anne K. Mellor** and **Professor Clifford Siskin**

Editorial Board: **Isobel Armstrong**, Birkbeck; **John Bender**, Stanford; **Alan Bewell**, Toronto; **Peter de Bolla**, Cambridge; **Robert Miles**, Stirling; **Claudia L. Johnson**, Princeton; **Saree Makdisi**, UCLA; **Felicity Nussbaum**, UCLA; **Mary Poovey**, NYU; **Janet Todd**, Glasgow

Palgrave Studies in the Enlightenment, Romanticism and Cultures of Print will feature work that does not fit comfortably within established boundaries – whether between periods or between disciplines. Uniquely, it will combine efforts to engage the power and materiality of print with explorations of gender, race and class. By attending as well to intersections of literature with the visual arts, medicine, law and science, the series will enable a large-scale rethinking of the origins of modernity.

Titles include:

E. J. Clery
THE FEMINIZATION DEBATE IN 18TH-CENTURY ENGLAND
Literature, Commerce and Luxury

Adriana Craciun
BRITISH WOMEN WRITERS AND THE FRENCH REVOLUTION
Citizens of the World

Peter de Bolla, Nigel Leask and David Simpson (*editors*)
LAND, NATION AND CULTURE, 1740–1840
Thinking the Republic of Taste

Mary Waters
BRITISH WOMEN WRITERS AND THE PROFESSION OF LITERARY CRITICISM, 1789–1832

Forthcoming titles in the series:

Brycchan Carey
BRITISH ABOLITIONISM AND THE RHETORIC OF SENSIBILITY

Ian Haywood
BLOODY ROMANTICISM

Anthony Jarrells
BRITAIN'S BLOODLESS REVOLUTIONS

**Palgrave Studies in the Enlightenment, Romanticism and Cultures of Print
Series Standing Order ISBN 1–4039–3408–8 (hardback) 1–4039–3409–6
(paperback)** (*outside North America only*)

You can receive future titles in this series as they are published by placing a standing order. Please contact your bookseller or, in case of difficulty, write to us at the address below with your name and address, the title of the series and an ISBN quoted above.

Customer Services Department, Macmillan Distribution Ltd, Houndmills, Basingstoke, Hampshire RG21 6XS, England

---

British Women Writers and the French Revolution

Citizens of the World

Adriana Craciun

First published 2005 by
PALGRAVE MACMILLAN
Houndmills, Basingstoke, Hampshire RG21 6XS and
175 Fifth Avenue, New York, N.Y. 10010
Companies and representatives throughout the world

PALGRAVE MACMILLAN is the global academic imprint of the Palgrave Macmillan division of St. Martin's Press, LLC and of Palgrave Macmillan Ltd. Macmillan® is a registered trademark in the United States, United Kingdom and other countries. Palgrave is a registered trademark in the European Union and other countries.

ISBN-13: 978–1–4039–0235–1
ISBN-10: 1–4039–0235–6

This book is printed on paper suitable for recycling and made from fully managed and sustained forest sources.

A catalogue record for this book is available from the British Library.

Library of Congress Cataloging-in-Publication Data
Craciun, Adriana, 1967–
    British women writers and the French Revolution : citizens of the world / Adriana Craciun.
        p.   cm. — (Palgrave studies in the Enlightenment, romanticism, and cultures of print)
    Includes bibliographical references and index.
    ISBN 1–4039–0235–6 (hardback)
    1. English literature—Women authors—History and criticism.
    2. France—History—Revolution, 1789–1799—Literature and the revolution.   3. France—History—Revolution, 1789–1799—Foreign public opinion, British.   4. Women and literature—Great Britain— History—18th century.   5. English literature—18th century—History and criticism.   6. Revolutionary literature, English—History and criticism.
    7. Public opinion—Great Britain—History—18th century.
    8. English literature—French influences.   I. Title.   II. Series.
    PR129.F8C73 2005
    820.9′358—dc22   2004054895

10   9   8   7   6   5   4   3   2
14   13   12   11   10   09   08   07   06   05

Printed and bound in Great Britain by
Antony Rowe Ltd, Chippenham and Eastbourne

For John and River
the violets are blueing in the green

Contents

List of Illustrations

Acknowledgements

The idea for writing *Citizens of the World* originated in my positive experience of editing *Rebellious Hearts: British Women Writers and the French Revolution* (2001) with Kari Lokke. The book's cosmopolitan focus no doubt also drew inspiration from my peripatetic last few years: I spent my sabbatical leave at UCLA and the University of Washington, while working at the University of Nottingham and now at Birkbeck, University of London. Thanks to a research grant from the University of Nottingham, I was able to spend a good amount of time in four Parisian archives: Archives de Paris, Archives de Ministère des Affaires Étrangères, Archives Nationales, and the Bibliothèque Nationale. While in Paris, I benefited from the hospitality and conversation of Stéphan Vincent-Lancrin and Marianne Lemaire, and also John Nally, my companion to Montmorency on Bastille Day. I spent a productive month in residence at the Helen Riaboff Whiteley Center in Friday Harbor, an oasis of scholarly tranquility, and wrote large portions of this book while at the Center for Seventeenth and Eighteenth-Century Studies at UCLA, with sabbatical funding from the University of Nottingham and the Arts and Humanities Research Board. Thanks to Sally Ledger and my new colleagues at Birkbeck, I had an additional period of leave allowing me to complete the manuscript in time. At Palgrave, Emily Rosser and Paula Kennedy were patient and efficient editors – I am grateful to them, to the series editors, and to the anonymous readers of my manuscript for helping me see the project through to completion.

For their comments on drafts of individual chapters I am very grateful to Markman Ellis, John Logan, Kari Lokke, Máire ní Fhlathúin, and especially John Barrell for his immensely helpful feedback: their collective efforts have materially improved this book, and the faults that remain are of course my own.

For their diverse support of my work, I wish also to thank Isobel Armstrong, C. M. Baumer, Oliver B. Butt, Stuart Curran, Janette Dillon, Joanna Dodd, Dana Frank, Tracy Hargreaves, Anne Janowitz, Steve Jones, Deborah Kennedy, Jon Klancher, Mark Kozelek, Nancy Kushigian, Anne Mellor, Louise Millar, Felicity Nussbaum, Marvin O'Gravel, Judith Pascoe, Mary Peace, Seth Schein, Wil Verhoeven and David West. Jerome McGann and Duncan Wu were, as ever, indefatigable sources of encouragement. My ongoing conversations with Kari Lokke regarding British women and the French Revolution, and in particular Charlotte Smith, have played an important part in my thinking through the years; being able to count on Kari's enthusiasm and many acts of kindness always made life better.

Citizens of the World was composed under difficult personal circumstances, and without the help of friends and family its completion would have been impossible. To Dr Ulrich Batzdorf and his team at UCLA I owe my husband's recovery. To my family, especially my mother, and Nan and Bruce Parker, I owe the emotional wherewithal to muddle through. Mark and Dana in California, and Máire in England, were also especially generous with their time and support. This book is dedicated to John and River, with all my love.

ADRIANA CRACIUN

Frontispiece 'Don Dismallo Running the Literary Gauntlet' (1790). Copyright British Museum

Introduction

You will not suspect that I was an indifferent witness of such a scene. Oh no! this was not a time in which the distinctions of country were remembered. It was a triumph of human kind; it was man asserting the noblest privileges of his nature; and it required but the common feelings of humanity to become in that moment a citizen of the world.

Helen Maria Williams, referring to the Fête de la Fédération in Paris, *Letters Written in France* (1790)

Patriotic attachment forms a marked feature in the character of those worthies of old who are recorded in holy writ. And the Saviour of the World, by condescending to imbibe this predilection for the soil in which he was born and suffered, has most effectively rescued the genuine feelings of the patriot from the undeserved reproach of prejudice and narrowness of soul. The citizen of the world... affects to despise distinctions which the Lord of Life has sanctioned.

Jane West, *Letters to a Young Lady* (1799)

Women and revolutionary cosmopolitanism

Helen Maria Williams's enthusiastic identification with the 'citizen of the world' ideal in her *Letters Written in France* (1790), and Jane West's loyalist dismissal of this ideal as literally unChristian in her *Letters to a Young Lady* (1799), represent the full range of British representations of this cosmopolitan ideal in the 1790s. Building on the growing body of scholarly work that has restored women writers to the centre of Romantic-period studies,[1] my aim in *Citizens of the World* is to illuminate the underappreciated extent to which Romantic-period British women writers cultivated a radicalized cosmopolitanism through their engagement with French revolutionary politics. British women were drawn to France for both its *ancien régime* associations as 'the paradise of lady wits' (to quote Fanny Burney, *Journals* 1: 197), and its revolutionary politics that extended across gender and national lines. Most visible in the 1790s, yet persisting through the rise and fall of Napoleon in the writings of Francophiles like Anne Plumptre and Lady Morgan, revolutionary cosmopolitanism flourished in women's writings of the Romantic era.

Anticipating the Peace of Amiens of 1802, Anna Laetitia Barbauld mused in 1801 that 'now France lies like a huge loadstone [*sic*] on the other side of the Channel, and will draw every mother's child of us to it. Those who know French are refreshing their memories, – those who do not, are learning it; and every one is planning in some way or other to get a sight of the promised land' (*Works* 2: 119–20). Long deprived of their Grand Tour and Parisian pleasures, British elites flocked to France during this brief respite from the war, as did writers like Fanny Burney, Anne Plumptre, Amelia Opie and Maria Edgeworth. Members of the aristocracy and the leisured classes traditionally had a high regard for French culture and used the French language as the international language of the privileged; together with the formative experience of the Grand Tour, this Francophilia served as a means of educating the international ruling classes on how to rule. Earlier in the eighteenth century, aristocrats like Lady Mary Wortley Montagu and Tory 'civilised gentlemen' like Dryden cultivated distinct cosmopolitanisms, in both commercialized and anticommercial forms, and often with a Francophilic core.[2] Shaftesbury's humanism likewise centred on the 'citizen of the world' as the ideal political and aesthetic subject – an enfranchised male property owner, because as John Lucas has elaborated, 'only those who are enfranchised can be truly disinterested in desiring the best for the state, and they will use their freedom to the best advantage if they have the faculty for judgment which is based on wide and deep knowledge of other states' (26). It is not this eighteenth-century elite cosmopolitanism that interests me here, but rather the revolutionary turns that a specifically Francophilic cosmopolitanism took among predominantly middle-class British women writers during and after the 1790s, when the franchise's relationship to property (and sexual) rights came under intense scrutiny.

Critical studies of cosmopolitanism enjoyed a renaissance in the 1990s, particularly among political and social theorists who reformulated it as a contested tradition central to contemporary debates on globalization and its discontents.[3] Enlightenment cosmopolitanism is a crucial aspect of twentieth-century notions of this tradition, exemplified by figures like Voltaire, Diderot, Goldsmith, Hume and Kant. Goldsmith's popular essay series, *The Citizen of the World* (1760–62), continued the tradition established by Montesquieu's *Lettres Persanes* (1721), in which a *faux-naif* narrator (in Goldsmith's case, a Chinese visitor to Britain) satirizes the national prejudices of his contemporaries. Written and set during the Seven Years War between France and Britain, *Citizen of the World* condemns the historic hostility between these two nations as the result of greed and ignorance. As an alternative to this destructive nationalism, Goldsmith offers the ideal of the 'citizen of the world' (the literal translation of a cosmopolitan/cosmopolite) in the tradition of Confucius, long regarded by Sinophiles like Voltaire as an exemplary cosmopolite.

Enlightenment cosmopolitanism on both sides of the channel flourished despite (and in response to) the eighteenth century's numerous military and colonial conflicts, particularly between France and Britain. Linda Colley has catalogued the intermittent wars between the two nations, which according to her argument in *Britons* were instrumental in cementing a British identity in opposition to a French 'Other'. Britain and France

> were at war between 1689 and 1697 . . . between 1702 and 1713, 1743 and 1748, 1756 and 1783, 1778 and 1783, 1793 and 1802, and, finally, between 1803 and the Battle of Waterloo in 1815. And even in the interludes of token peace, the two powers repeatedly plotted against and spied on each other. Their settlers and armed forces jostled for space and dominance in North America, the West Indies, Africa, Asia and Europe. (Colley 1)

According to Colley, British nationalism was forged via an intensifying Francophobia, which Gerald Newman has described as 'a loose cannon on a rolling deck' (234), used widely by prerevolutionary radicals, 1790s loyalists, and early nineteenth-century evangelicals with equal fervour in their different political struggles. Despite the internationalism and universalism traditionally associated with the rise of democratic movements at the end of the eighteenth century, Newman's *The Rise of English Nationalism* articulates a growing consensus regarding the formative impact of (in his case, English) nationalism:[4]

> In its philosophical soul, this Age [of Democratic Revolution] was not the realization but the repudiation of cosmopolitan ideals; it was the beginning of the new era of democratic nationalism. It was not so much 'the rights of man' as the rights of Englishmen, Frenchmen, and other nationals, that was to bring whole peoples into the streets. (224)

Cosmopolitanism, meanwhile, is thought to have retreated along with the Francophilic aristocratic ascendancy, eclipsed by the increasingly nationalist mercantilism that fuelled Britain's colonial and military expansion, its uneven cultural consolidation after the 1707 Act of Union, and its burgeoning reform movements from the 1770s onwards.

And yet in this same era of intensifying nationalisms, political theorists, reformers and philosophers also responded to the revolutionary crisis by radicalizing cosmopolitanism, developing doctrines of universal human rights, and resisting national 'prejudices' through the idealized power of universal reason or universal benevolence. In Immanuel Kant's 1795 pamphlet, *Toward Perpetual Peace*, 'along with the civil law of states and in place of international law', Kant introduced, as Jürgen Habermas has argued, 'an innovation with broad implications: the idea of a cosmopolitan law based on the rights of the world citizen' (Habermas 113). Kant's concept of an association of republican states, all respecting the rights of citizens of the world, was forged in the decade of revolutionary wars in which the classical cosmopolitan ideal took on new significance, in light of the contradictions regarding how 'universal' human rights were, and were not, put into practice. In Britain as on the continent, transnational approaches to social conflict were also on the rise, from abolition to constitutional reform, all in this era of nationalism.

The particular charges available to anticosmopolitan critiques have remained remarkably consistent from cosmopolitanism's origins in the philosophy of the Cynics and Stoics, through the revolutionary period, and into the twenty-first century's heated debates surrounding globalization, international law and human rights. One of cosmopolitanism's most articulate modern critics, Craig Calhoun, has isolated two such central objections to the cosmopolitan ideal; first,

> much cosmopolitanism misrecognizes its own social foundations, assuming these to be universal when in fact they are representative of particular social relations. Cosmopolitanism is, too often, the class consciousness of frequent travelers. Second... appeals to universal similarities and universalistic moral obligations are too thin a basis to support either cosmopolitanism or democracy.[5]

Calhoun sharpened this critique of cosmopolitanism's limitations in several post-September 11, 2001 essays, where he argued that while 'the cosmopolitan ideals articulated during the 1990s seem all the more attractive... their realization [is] much less immanent' because of cosmopolitanism's failure to account adequately for local solidarity and communitarianism ('Class' 870). Calhoun is acutely aware of how his critique of 1990s cosmopolitanism (for example, that of Habermas and Martha Nussbaum) is historically situated (after the intensifying xenophobias following September 11). However, his twin objections to the cosmopolitan ideal – its denial of its own situatedness, and its abstract universalism – shared by numerous modern critics, underestimate the historical diversity among earlier cosmopolitanisms.

Certainly, the Enlightenment cosmopolitan ideals on which French revolutionaries drew were partial, in both senses of the word, in their articulation of the local and the universal.[6] Combining an aristocratic ideal of an international elite, with free market capitalism and classical and Enlightenment philosophy, eighteenth-century cosmopolitanisms owe their 'universalism' to a contradictory, exclusionary set of beliefs and practices envisioned by elite European men. Furthermore, Enlightenment cosmopolitanism was indebted to, even when highly critical of (for example in Diderot's, Kant's and Goldsmith's cases) the colonial and commercial expansion that brought Europeans into contact with diverse cultures. And nationalists like Edmund

Burke and Hannah More would have agreed with Calhoun's second point (though not with his politics), that universalism is an inadequate basis for a just society. Yet it is misleading to suggest that in the revolutionary era (or in the Enlightenment) 'there could be only one kind of cosmopolitanism', characterized by an abstract and disembodied universalism, while 'like nations, cosmopolitanisms are now plural and particular'.[7] Bruce Robbins implies this in the recent volume *Cosmopolitics* when he clarifies 'that cosmopolitanism is located and embodied' in modern models, citing examples like Mitchell Cohen's 'rooted cosmopolitanism', Homi Bhabha's 'vernacular cosmopolitanism', and Benita Parry's 'emergent postcolonial cosmopolitanism' as evidence of this modern correction of what is assumed to be an eighteenth-century abstraction (Robbins, 2–3).

Today's debates on cosmopolitanism, and in particular the Marxist association of cosmopolitanism with global capitalism, should not obscure the radical potential of this tradition in the Romantic period. In calling for 'embodied and located' cosmopolitanisms, Calhoun and the editors of *Cosmopolitics* ironically echo the terms in which the archloyalist Jane West dismissed cosmopolitanism as an impractical abstraction in 1799:

> Whatever the pretended cosmopolites may boast of the effects of universal philanthropy and general benevolence, we must embody those indefinite ideas, and combine them with some strong tie of nature or of choice. (*Letters* 1: 40–1)

As we shall see in Chapter 1, West's dismissal of 'pretended cosmopolites' is typical of counterrevolutionary writers of the 1790s, who consistently represented 'modern philosophy' as an unwieldy set of universalist abstractions without ties to nature, interest or tradition.

Jean-Jacques Rousseau, a perpetual exile, embodied this reviled cosmopolitanism that professed universal benevolence while neglecting local and familial responsibilities. As Burke complained in 1791, Rousseau

> melts with tenderness for those only who touch him by the remotest relation, and then, without one natural pang, casts away, as a sort of offal and excrement, the spawn of his disgustful amours, and sends his children to the hospital of foundlings.... Thousands admire the sentimental writer; the affectionate father is hardly known in his parish. (*A Letter* 35)

I highlight this consistency in critiques of cosmopolitanism's limitations (among critics with radically different politics, in different contexts) not to dismiss them in our twenty-first-century contexts, but, rather, to ensure that our present-day vantage points do not inadvertently obscure the complexity found in those of the past. The 'suspicion of closed horizons' (Mehta 621) that unites all cosmopolitanisms today, while derided by Calhoun as 'the class consciousness of frequent travelers', was in 1790s Britain a dangerous, even a criminal, outlook.

In the revolutionary debates that are my focus in *Citizens of the World*, British women writers were drawn to a radicalized cosmopolitanism that had at its core a Francophilia (corresponding to an 'Anglomania' in its French Enlightenment precedent) increasingly dangerous to maintain in Francophobic Britain, thereby situating their cosmopolitanism, historically and geographically, as a deliberately oppositional strategy. They shared this Francophilia and cosmopolitanism with male radical writers and activists who, as Anna Clark argued in *The Struggle for the Breeches*, generally went on to embrace a nationalistic and gender-exclusive strategy for political reform. As I will argue throughout this study, this revolutionary cosmopolitanism is particularized in origin and intent: looking to the continent (especially France), not to the British nation, for political and cultural inspiration; militantly pacifist when pacifism was unpatriotic at best; often argued from secular and philosophical, not religious and moralistic, perspectives; and usually overtly feminist in attempting to carve out new 'rights of women' based on transformed Enlightenment ideals. As with modern cosmopolitanisms, these Romantic-era visions were of course riddled with contradictions (chiefly those regarding class and race) that are inseparable from their ideals. Helen Maria Williams, for example, was either unable or unwilling to extend her vision of 'citizen of the world' to include the working classes that made up a large part of her Jacobin rivals' supporters. Charlotte Smith's citizen of the world ideal likewise stopped short of universalism by remaining ambivalent towards the colonial slavery on which her family wealth depended. While attending to these important historical limitations throughout this study, I will redirect our attention to the conditions of possibility in which this revolutionary cosmopolitanism was forged. The revolutionary nature of this cosmopolitanism becomes visible once we consider the hostile reception that 'Eurocentrism' in particular received in a xenophobic Britain that understood this 'limitation' (according to twenty-first-century perspectives) as an unlimited threat to national and natural order.

We are accustomed, and with good reason, to associate the Romantic period with growing nationalism, and women with playing a central role in shaping diverse visions of British national identity. Women writers in particular are also associated with the claims of the local, the quotidian and the domestic. Yet I suggest that revolutionary cosmopolitanism remains central to the works and thinking of Romantic women writers in Britain, and, moreover, that this cosmopolitanism can serve as a productive axis around which to reconsider the ideological and aesthetic innovations that these writers introduced. Rather than conservative versus liberal, or feminist versus antifeminist, we can envision a continuum of cosmopolitan through loyalist allegiances to reassess women writers' participation in debates that transcended national borders. Before sketching the outlines of revolutionary cosmopolitanism in Helen

Maria Williams, Charlotte Smith, Mary Robinson and Mary Wollstonecraft, I will look first at their formidable loyalist counterparts, who rejected both the 'citizen of the world' ideal and its female advocates.

The modern controversy surrounding cosmopolitanism's contradictions is not new. Loyalists like Hannah More and Jane West dismissed the cosmopolitan ideal as a pernicious doctrine that contributed to the neglect of local and national traditions. Yet More, in addition to being an indefatigable abolitionist, also supported a charitable effort on behalf of the French émigré clergy in 1793, overcoming her antiCatholicism and Francophobia in an effort to help fellow Christians. More's critique of the British empire's inhumane practices, and her support of Christian foreigners, share with Kant's stance in *Perpetual Peace* a critique of colonialism and emphasis on the right to hospitality (a universal right, in Kant's formulation), but they do not share Kant's cosmopolitanism. More's Christian nationalism informed all her charitable efforts, whether on behalf of African slaves or French clergy.

In her 1808 didactic novel *Coelebs in Search of a Wife*, More used the previous decade's debate regarding British aid to the émigré French clergy to contrast cosmopolitan, patriotic and Christian nationalist perspectives. The Amazonian spinster feminist Miss Sparkes, who styles herself a 'citizen of the world' (192) and holds ancient republican virtue in higher regard than the contemporary British version, exemplifies a fashionable cosmopolitanism devoid of Christianity. The patriotic but unreligious Mr Flam, on the other hand, sees Britain's treatment of the émigrés as exemplary of superior national character: 'Tell me, Madam, did your Athens, or your Sparta, or your Rome, ever take in seven thousand starving priests, driven from a country with which they were at war; a country they had reason to hate, of a religion they detested?' (192). But the pious patriarch Mr Stanley correctly judges that the British national character is inseparable from the national religion: 'I should be inclined', said Mr Stanley, 'to set down that noble deed to the account of our national religion, as well as of our national generosity' (192). National religion and national character are together, for More, the foundation of the virtuous society, Britain's being the envy of the world. So fervently did More hold to her Christian nationalism that she wished never to leave Britain, even though she was recommended to go abroad for her health: 'I hold it to be a much better thing to be sick, or even to die in this country, than to be alive and well in most others', she wrote.[8]

How utterly unlike her peripatetic Francophile contemporaries, Helen Maria Williams and Mary Wollstonecraft, who travelled to France during the Revolution, immersed themselves in reading and translating continental writers, and found continental culture and politics a welcome change from British provincialism. Or Charlotte Smith and Mary Robinson, who only managed brief visits to the continent, but dreamed of emigrating to France, Italy or Switzerland, and set their revolution-era novels in these countries. These four outspokenly feminist writers participated in radical circles in

Britain and France, and shared a cosmopolitanism that places them in sharp relief against nationalist contemporaries like More, West, and even the more moderate Amelia Opie.

Opie's ambivalent retrospective on Wollstonecraft and Godwin considered the problem of Enlightenment cosmopolitanism more subtly than did ideologues like More and West. In *Adeline Mowbray* (1805), Opie identified the chief contradiction conservatives and nationalists perceived in cosmopolitanism: its supposed neglect of the particular and the local. Thus, like Rousseau, the self-absorbed Mrs Mowbray styles herself a citizen of the world at the expense of being a good parent:

> Nor had she even leisure to observe, that while she was feeling all the generous anxiety of a citizen of the world for the sons and daughters of American independence, her own child was imbibing, through her means, opinions dangerous to her well-being as a member of any civilized society.

The cosmopolite is, at best, neglectful of the local, and at worst a traitor to the nation.

Burke's *Reflections on the Revolution in France* (1790) offers an example of the latter usage, wherein he is careful to emphasize that private citizens of a particular nation are wrong to correspond publicly with foreign governments, as Richard Price and the Society for Constitutional Information (SCI) had done in congratulating the National Assembly:

> I certainly take my full share, along with the rest of the world, in my individual and private capacity, in speculating on what has been done, or is doing, on the public stage, in any place ancient or modern...but having no general apostolical mission, being *a citizen of a particular state*, and being bound up, in a considerable degree, by its public will, I should think it at least improper and irregular for me to open a formal public correspondence with the actual government of a foreign nation, without the express authority of the government under which I live. (*Reflections* 7, emphasis added)

Price and the SCI's Francophilia was for Burke the result of centuries of promiscuous Anglo–French contact, as he warned in February 1790 during Parliamentary debate: 'Our friendship and our intercourse with that nation had once been, and might again become more dangerous to us than their worst hostility' (quoted in Conor Cruise O'Brien, 397). In this decade of repressive laws and Treason trials, the centuries-old suspicion that the citizen of the world was a traitor to her or his nation became codified in a pervasive antiFrench prejudice that was increasingly difficult to resist as the war continued. Modern 'conservatism' originated in this counterrevolutionary agenda, as historian William Doyle explains:

Before 1789, conservatism, as a positive, self-conscious political outlook, was unknown. No established order was under the comprehensive threat that the French Revolution later posed. By 1793, however, a new, revolutionary ideology had led to attacks on all the principal pillars of stability – property, social hierarchy, religion, monarchy. (*Oxford* 422)

For British ideologues like More and Burke, the crux of this emergent conservatism remained their opposition to French-style (especially Jacobin) political revolution and the ideals behind it; it is these changing British conceptions of French revolutionary politics that orient my argument throughout this study.

Lacking civil and political rights as British subjects, prorevolutionary women writers were inspired by both the political and aesthetic promise of the citizen of the world ideal. Helen Maria Williams is the best-known example of such 'a persistently cosmopolitan character in an era of literary and economic nationalism' (Keane, *Women* 55): she immigrated to France in 1790, remained a stalwart republican through successive revolutionary regimes, ran a salon that included all major revolutionary figures and foreign visitors to the capital, and became a naturalized French citizen. Although she was briefly jailed during the Terror along with other foreigners, Williams otherwise enjoyed relative safety and prosperity in postThermidorean Paris as a *salonnière* and owner of a profitable printing press. Arriving in Paris in time to witness the Fête de la Federation in 1790, she enthused in her *Letters from France* that 'it required but the common feelings of humanity, to become in that moment a citizen of the world' (1:1: 14). As Chapter 3 demonstrates, Williams's relationship to French politics was more vexed than is generally appreciated, particularly in her rhetorical rivalry with Robespierre. Yet Williams remains the most stalwart and visible example of a British woman Romantic writer embracing the citizen of the world ideal.

Williams's revolutionary cosmopolitanism is precisely what Laetitia Matilda Hawkins objected to in her two-volume response, *Letters on the Female Mind...With Particular Reference to the Dangerous Opinions Contained in the Writings of Miss. H. M. Williams* (1793). Rather than becoming citizens of the world, English women were uniquely suited, according to Hawkins, to remain sheltered within the domestic bounds of national character: 'The whole world might be at war, and yet not the rumor of it reach the ear of an Englishwoman – empires might be lost, and states overthrown, and still she might pursue the peaceful occupations of her home' (2: 194). In contrast, cosmopolitans embraced the historical reality that invalidated Hawkins's isolationism, as Kant wrote in *Perpetual Peace*: 'The intercourse...which has been everywhere steadily increasing between the nations of the earth, has now extended so enormously that a violation of right in one part of the world is felt all over it' (142).

For Hawkins and other counterrevolutionary writers, this revolutionary intercourse of ideas opened up a particularly dangerous new social role for

English women, that of the 'female philosopher' or female politician. 'Every female politician is a hearsay politician' (1: 23), wrote Hawkins regarding Williams's involvement in French politics. Indeed, the unmarried Hawkins insisted that even female patriotism is impossible, given that as a *femme couvert*, a married Englishwoman has no country: 'In this age of female heroism, I shall gain no credit by avowing myself inimical to the idea of female patriotism; but in truth, I know no such virtue. A woman's country is . . . that which her protector chuses for her' (2: 197). Similarly, the 'petticoat philosophist', according to Jane West, 'seeks for eminence and distinction in infidelity and skepticism, or in the equally more monstrous extravagancies of German morality' (*Letters* 1: 27). Lacking the 'detachment' of (male property-owning) citizens of the public sphere, women enter the public political fray for all the wrong reasons, deficient in the resources needed to make accurate judgments for the benefit of Britain. Part of the gender panic that accompanied the revolutionary crisis, such female interventions into public politics were nervously dismissed not only as sexually suspect, but as foreign: sometimes via 'German metaphysics' (West's 'German morality'), but most often via 'the French disease', as Steven Blakemore has elaborated, drawing on Burke's syphilitic metaphor for such 'Gallicization'.

Like Williams and Kant (and disapproving counterrevolutionaries like More), Mary Robinson believed that the revolutionary crisis made possible new forms of cosmopolitan identities and politics. A lifelong Francophile, Robinson wrote controversial poetry, essays and novels in the 1790s critiquing British nationalist and sexual politics. Her political prose in particular remains an unmined source for expanding our notions of women writers' engagement with radical print culture. As Chapter 2 demonstrates, these unknown or little-known uncollected writings reveal how this lauded lyric poet was radicalized specifically through her French connections. Robinson's revolutionary cosmopolitanism also emerged throughout her novels; for example, *Hubert de Sevrac* (1796) chronicles the conversion of an aristocratic French émigré family into enlightened citizens of the world, thereby demonstrating the historical radicalization of this earlier aristocratic tradition. The novel's female protagonist extols the cosmopolitan ideal at the heart of Robinson's vision of how British subjects, like the French, might be transformed: 'to become a perfect citizen of the world, every minute particle of creation should be deemed worthy of investigation' (1: 296). Critical scrutiny of institutions hitherto grounded in national tradition, and international travel (and exile), make possible for Robinson this desirable transformation from national subjects to world citizens.

Charlotte Smith's entire range of work, from the novels and poetry, to the letters and translations, reveals a committed cosmopolite and Francophile, one who, like Robinson, grew more radical as her career progressed, as well as more disillusioned with England. 'I have neither naturally nor artificially the least partiality for my native country', she wrote to Joseph Cooper Walker in 1794, 'which has neither protected my property by its boasted laws, & where, if the laws are not good, I know nothing that is, for the climate does not agree with me, who am another creature in France' (*Collected Letters*, 105). In the Preface to her most radical novel, *Desmond* (1792), Smith claimed that the novel's inspiration was 'drawn from conversations to which I have been a witness, in England, and France, during the last twelve months'. As I discuss in the final chapter, there may be new evidence that she did make this visit to revolutionary Paris in 1791. Smith continued to dream, and occasionally scheme, about immigrating to the continent permanently: 'I dont love England to tell you the truth, & have always meditated flying away from it if my fetters or any part of them should fall off' (*Collected Letters*, 96). But those fetters (supporting her nine living children) proved insoluble, and instead Smith channelled this cosmopolitanism into her revolutionary novels, and specifically into her heroes, self-identified as 'citizens of the world'. While revolution awakens Smith's protagonists to their status as 'citizens of the world' in earlier novels like *Desmond* (1792), in *The Young Philosopher* (1798) her protagonists, female and male, are effectively born 'citizens of the world' through their complex international pedigrees and serial exiles. The increasing geographic sweep of Smith's novels reflects the author's unwillingness to abandon the cosmopolitan ideal despite the bleak state of revolutionary Europe, a humanitarian optimism nevertheless inseparable from the legacies of colonialism and slavery that shadowed her cosmopolitanism.

Admired by Smith, Williams and Robinson, Mary Wollstonecraft shares with these fellow travellers a cosmopolitan feminism imbibed through revolutionary ideals. While in writings like *A Vindication of the Rights of Woman* (1792) and *Historical and Moral View of the French Revolution* (1794) Wollstonecraft echoed British stereotypes of the French as artificial and effeminate, she did so in part to illustrate how national character, like sexual character, is constructed through institutions like political absolutism and patriarchy. As Jan Wellington has argued, Wollstonecraft's 1795 Scandinavian travels after her French sojourn of 1792–94 enabled her to reevaluate her earlier prejudice against French exuberance and sexual freedom. Preparing to embark on this final voyage from England, Wollstonecraft, echoing the sentiments of Robinson and Smith, wrote to her American lover Gilbert Imlay describing England as 'a country, that has not merely lost all charms for me, but for which I feel a repugnance that almost amounts to horror' (*Letters* 280). Like Smith and Robinson, Wollstonecraft also contemplated emigrating for good (to America with Imlay), but instead remained and faced increasing hostility to the 'Gallicized' sexual politics of her writings and personal life.

In moving against the current of nationalism, Smith, Robinson, Wollstonecraft and Williams challenge our emerging picture of a nationalistic, counterrevolutionary British culture, itself a reaction against an earlier critical overprivileging of the radical aspects of the Romantic era. In literary studies, Franco Moretti's *Atlas of the European Novel* situates the British novel at the turn of the nineteenth century as the 'new symbolic form' uniquely able to represent and reinforce this new sense of nationalism (17). Jane Austen is his paradigmatic Romantic-era novelist, of course, and through her vision of England, Moretti argues that 'the novel is truly the symbolic form of the nation-state' (45). Yet Austen's radical predecessors like Smith, Robinson, Wollstonecraft, and even the more moderate Opie, resist precisely this ideologically reassuring vision of England as 'home land' that Moretti posits as representative. Opie's *Adeline Mowbray* features a tragic heroine who travels far beyond the provincial contours of Austen's England: such a narrative 'certainly cannot turn the nation into a symbolic home', concludes Moretti (20). Neither does Opie want to – as a Dissenter, abolitionist and later a Quaker, Opie shares with feminist cosmopolitans like Wollstonecraft, Robinson and Smith a resistance to the palliating notion of Britain as 'home land', placing Austen's paradigmatic status in question, and her canonization in clearer focus. Opie's novel concludes with an all-woman and interracial refuge in the English countryside, an 'imperfect . . . harbinger of feminist collectivity' that, as Felicity Nussbaum has argued, 'forges connections among all the women of empire', not just of the English nation (*Torrid Zones* 46).

The cosmopolitan writings of Williams, Smith, Robinson and others contributed to a transnational and feminist project to imagine communities that 'specifically transgress and replace those of kinship and nation', as April Alliston has suggested in an important challenge to Benedict Anderson's and Franco Moretti's alliance of nation and print culture (134). The novel was an international invention, typically the product of an Anglo–French dialogue, Margaret Cohen reminds us in *The Literary Channel*, and it was specifically the sentimental novel that according to Cohen produced the 'first modern imagined communities' of transnational sympathy (123). In women's nineteenth-century sentimental fiction, according to Alliston, these imagined communities typically *'decentralize the nation-state geographically'* and linguistically (being 'located on the margins of the nation-state'), and also 'deliberately imagine the crossing of racial boundaries', incorporating 'racial hybridization' to resist national consolidation (143, orig. emphasis).[9] The utopian alternatives that Alliston outlines in the fiction of Germaine de Staël, George Sand and Emily Brontë are not present in the earlier French revolutionary writings that I examine here, although Smith's cosmopolitan 'circle of friends' comes close. The revolutionary and Napoleonic wars, imperial struggles, exodus of émigrés, stalled abolition efforts and other social crises unique to these revolutionary decades tested the limits of these imagined cosmopolitan communities, in both political and aesthetic spheres. As subsequent chapters will show, the contradictions within such revolutionary ideals proved inescapable, and institutionalized nationalism insurmountable, in both aesthetic and political realms. Yet the innovative responses of Smith, Robinson, Williams and others to these crises are invaluable to our understanding of how cosmopolitanism persisted well into and after the age of nationalism.

Women, nation and nationalism

The war with France in 1793 had impelled the British across the political spectrum to embrace nationalism more vocally and visibly than ever before. As Anna Clark, John Barrell and others have demonstrated, British radicals during the revolutionary period increasingly drew upon the patriotic traditions of the free-born Briton and ancient Anglo-Saxon liberties in their reform strategies. The nostalgia central to this radical patriotism, as Stephen Behrendt has argued, offered little to radical women writers: 'there could be little solace in the Radical yearning for a return to the Anglo-Saxon ideal that had no more place for them than the contemporary socio-political structure seemed to have' (85). Despite contrasting Scottish Enlightenment accounts in which substantial women's rights were seen as an important component of Anglo-Saxon liberties,[10] post-1789 radical women writers did not for the most part look backward for these liberties, but forward and across the channel.

Yet women's roles in the British nation inspired and authorized their participation in a wide range of social, aesthetic and political enterprises, from the patriotic war efforts that Colley has chronicled, to the female-led philanthropic, educational and moral reform movements institutionalized in the nineteenth century. Women's involvement in this turn of the century nationalism has thus attracted much scholarly attention, part of a growing consensus regarding the revision of this 'age of revolution' into the 'age of nationalism'. Along with historians, anthropologists and social scientists who have developed this shared vision of modernity's relationship to the rise of nationalism, literary scholars have recognized Romantic-period women writers' contributions to the discourse of nationhood in the British Isles in generic innovations like the 'national tale' and 'bardic' nationalism.[11] National tales refigured romance in order to dramatize national consolidation as the courtship and union of two nations, whether reassuringly as in Walter Scott, or more uneasily as in Maria Edgeworth, Lady Morgan and Germaine de Staël. In addition to romance, other feminized genres like the letter and travel writings have also proved central to our understanding Romantic women's shaping of national literary traditions – for example Mary Favret's and Nicola Watson's books on epistolary fiction, Elizabeth Bohls's work on Williams's travel writings, Steven Blakemore's work on Williams' rewriting of history using tragedy and romance, and Gary Kelly's study of the 'gendering of written discourse' in the writings of Elizabeth Hamilton, Williams and Hays (11).

Alongside feminized genres like romance and the letter, discourses of maternity also prove central to understanding women's public literary roles within the nation. Rousseau's seminal model of woman's sequestration in the ostensibly 'private' realm as wife and mother shaped subsequent practices of 'republican motherhood' in France and America, a formulation rejected by British radical feminists like Wollstonecraft as unacceptable both in theory and practice. Yet such 'maternal nationalism', to use Elizabeth Fay's term, also played an important role in British women writers' contributions to national politics (see Fay 50–106). Anne Mellor's *Mothers of the Nation* (2000) focuses on the literal and metaphorical impact of the maternal in British public politics, arguing that writers like Hannah More and Lucy Aikin used a discourse of motherhood to expand radically women's influence in national politics: 'the values of the private sphere associated primarily with women – moral virtue and an ethic of care', writes Mellor, 'infiltrat[ed] and finally dominat[ed] the discursive public sphere during the Romantic era' (*Mothers* 11). Departing from traditional accounts of 'republican motherhood' in which mothers influence national politics privately, through their husbands and sons, *Mothers of the Nation* locates an essential difference in maternity and femaleness through which women sought publicly to ameliorate some of the worst excesses and disparities in Britain.

Providing a different picture of a similar group of writers, Angela Keane's *Women Writers and the English Nation* charts a wide range of women's approaches to English nationhood during the 1790s. Contrasting 'the affective, organic and often biological discourse that characterizes nationalism – particularly Romantic nationalism' (5) with the 'rationalist discourse of the public sphere', Keane argues that, for Smith, Wollstonecraft, Williams, More and Radcliffe,

> it is the discourse of the public sphere, not of the nation, which allows them to imagine themselves as participating citizens. It is the discourse of nationhood not rationality that turns them into exiles, by naturalizing a patriarchal social contract and putting it beyond rational enquiry. (6–7)

Considering these two important studies together, we can say that Mellor takes up as empowering what Keane considered as a gender-specific limitation of nationalistic discourse: that is, its 'restricting female subjectivity to maternal reproduction' (Keane 5). Keane's public sphere rationalism and Mellor's essentialist maternalism help illuminate the continuum of Romantic approaches to questions of gender's role in national and public politics. By focusing specifically on the operations of revolutionary politics within this continuum, I aim to bring into sharper focus the significance of a distinctly French influence in British women's writings on national and international politics.

As the 'paradise of lady wits' (*précieuses*), *ancien régime* France was associated with effeminacy, artificiality and aristocracy in the eighteenth-century British imagination. According to republican feminists like Wollstonecraft and Macaulay, Burke's *Reflections on the Revolution in France* (1790) was a reactionary product of this *ancien régime* sensibility (particularly in Burke's sensationalized account of Marie Antoinette's flight from her boudoir in October 1789).

Wollstonecraft's *A Vindication of the Rights of Men* (1790) and Macaulay's *Observations on the Reflections of the Right Hon. Edmund Burke* (1790) brought to bear on Burke's effeminized sentimentalism a rationalist republican critique that Tom Paine would also use in *Rights of Man* (1791–92), reversing the gendered terms of contemporary political discourse in one stroke. Loyalists like Jane West tried to restore Burke's 'manly' opposition to the Revolution, but could not escape the effeminized associations of chivalry, even in such patriotic works as West's *Elegy on the Death of . . . Edmund Burke* (1797):

> Daughters of Britain! let the grateful tear
> Of kindred worth your Champion's Ashes dew;
> His Breast, like your's [sic], impassion'd and sincere,
> Glow'd with the Virtues he rever'd in you. (15)

Despite West's efforts to the contrary, the exaggerated sensibility and virtues that Britain's daughters shared with Burke were consistently associated with *ancien régime* effeminacy in the 1790s, in part thanks to the prolific critiques of radical feminists.

The extent and energy of such women's published responses to the revolutionary crisis became an object of conservative concern, more evidence of the degeneration of sexual and social hierarchies inspired by the Revolution. British popular prints staged this gender panic as a violent, sometimes pornographic, confrontation between revolutionary women and their opponents. In an anonymous satirical print published in December 1790, this political and sexual world-turned-upside-down is embodied by Burke himself as 'Don Dismallo Running the Literary Gauntlet' (Frontispiece). Depicted as a bare-chested fool, a terrified Burke flees before the cat-o-nine tails brandished by Helen Maria Williams, Anna Barbauld and Catherine Macaulay. Appealing fruitlessly to Sheridan for mercy, Burke does not stand a chance against these dominatrixes straight out of revolutionary pornography. Barbauld is next to strike in the gauntlet, declaring that 'The most incorrigible street Urchin in my School never felt from my hands what this Assassin of Liberty shall now feel!' Macaulay waits her turn, suggestively boasting that 'I am determined to tickle to some tune with this instrument in my hands!' Liberty too is phallicized, thrusting a sword against Burke's ribs while men like Horne Tooke stand passively by with their weapons lowered. The unmistakable sexual jests, visual and verbal, make this print a wonderful example of British revolutionary pornography (albeit clothed), illustrating the conflation of Gallicization and sexualization in the 1790s, and the inadequacy of (radical and counterrevolutionary) male responses to contain women's revolutionary fervour.

'Don Dismallo Running the Literary Gauntlet' was one of several in a series, among them 'Don Dismallo Among the Grasshoppers in France'.[12] Here we see Burke being led to the scaffold by a mob of French women enraged by his *Reflections*. In France as in England, women lead the revolutionary charge, and Burke is their prime target because of his seminal role in discrediting the Revolution so early and so effectively. Burke's own demonization of the women leading the march on Versailles as 'the furies of hell' in *Reflections*, along with his apotheosis of Marie Antoinette and his florid rhetoric, permanently associated that text with female excess, be it working-class or aristocratic. His sexualization of the revolutionary crisis became the key rhetorical register of all such political debates, whether visual or verbal.

'A Representation of the horrid Barbarities practised upon the NUNS by the FISH-WOMEN, on breaking into the Nunneries in France' (1792), like the Don Dismallo prints, sensationalizes women's revolutionary activities for salacious as well as political ends (Illustration 1). This infamous incident, also the subject of French pornographic prints, also had lessons for Britain, as this London print declared: 'This Print is dedicated to the FAIR SEX of GREAT BRITAIN & intended to point out the very dangerous effects which may arise as to *Themselves* if they do not exert their influence to hinder the "Majesty of the People" from getting the possession of the Executive Power'. French fish-women (*poissardes*) and British women writers are alike unable to wield the masculine instruments of 'executive power' with restraint.[13] The British 'fair sex' meanwhile, distinguished from these unfeminine extremes, are in this print urged to identify with the sheltered and sacred femininity associated with nuns.

These British satirical and pornographic prints illustrate the intensified resistance that women's increasingly public political activities inspired, be they in print or in the streets, in Britain or in France. The pamphlet war that Don Dismallo undergoes as a 'literary gauntlet' allowed women unprecedented access to public roles like polemicist, philosopher and historian, without *requiring* them to claim motives of distinctly religious, maternal or feminine sentiment. Anna Laetitia Barbauld is exemplary in this regard, because her impressive rhetorical range and authorial identities spanned this entire continuum. Barbauld could appear as both 'a dangerously radical virago', argues Harriet Guest, and the 'timid creature' (236) whose feminine verse Wollstonecraft rebuked in *Rights of Woman*. My concern here is with Barbauld's 1790s polemics, in which she crafted a rationalist and distinctly ungendered political voice that does not depend on religious or feminine sentiment for authority, and implies 'that the rights claimed for men are also those of women' (Guest 236). Barbauld assumed the role of an ungendered, 'active citizen' in her 1790s prose writings, maintaining a deeply-held connection to the British nation, yet thwarting a xenophobic nationalism at every rhetorical turn through her simultaneous allegiance to French revolutionary principles and universalist rhetoric. She is an ideal example of how French revolutionary politics inspired radicalized visions of citizenship for British women, whether as active citizens of a reformed British nation, in Barbauld's case, or as citizens of the world, for Williams, Smith and Robinson. Comparing

Illustration 1 'A Representation of the Horrid Barbarities Practised upon the Nuns by the Fish-Women, on Breaking into the Nunneries in France', Anon. (1792). Copyright British Museum

her to the counterrevolutionary nationalist More, moreover, illuminates the radicalized potential of what Angela Keane termed 'national belonging' for women like Barbauld who extended French revolutionary principles to domestic reform.

A Unitarian rational Dissenter, poet, teacher and educational writer associated with the Warrington Academy, Barbauld wrote openly in opposition to the war against France in works like *Sins of Government, Sins of the Nation* (1793), *Reasons for National Penitence* (1794), and *Eighteen Hundred and Eleven* (1812), all published by Joseph Johnson. Married to a French Huguenot descendant and once rumoured to have been romantically linked to a young Jean-Paul Marat while he taught French at the Academy, Barbauld had travelled widely throughout France in 1785–86, and remained a lifelong Francophile. Shown in the act of striking Burke in the first Don Dismallo print, Barbauld boldly entered the Revolution controversy, which she termed a 'word war':

> Of late years, indeed, we have known none of the calamities of war in our own country but the wasteful expence of it...we have calmly voted slaughter and merchandized destruction... We should, therefore, do well to *translate* this word war into language more intelligible to us. When we pay our army and our navy estimates, let us set down – so much for killing, so much for maiming, so much for making widows and orphans, so much for bringing famine upon a district, so much for corrupting citizens and subjects into spies and traitors... We shall by this means know what we have paid our money for, whether we have made a good bargain. (*Sins* 312–13, orig. emphasis)

In a classic exercise of radical demystification, Barbauld links the actual war against the French and its human costs, to the rhetorical war her government conducted in order to sustain these military efforts. Writing with cool irony, she enters this word war extolling cherished republican values like transparency, rationalism and clarity, and all in a Dissenting sermon (*Sins of Government, Sins of the Nation*) on the government's abuse of faith for unChristian ends.

In *Sins of Government, Sins of the Nation*, Barbauld defies the government-sponsored fast day, in which all British subjects were directed to pray for God's help in victory against the French republic, on the grounds that 'an unjust war is in itself so bad a thing, that there is only one way of making it worse, and that is, by mixing religion with it' (315). Barbauld's critique of nationalism and militarism, indebted to the universalism of rational Dissent, rejects utterly the Evangelical tradition (exemplified by More) in which 'We nourish our pride by fondly fancying that we are the only nation for whom the providence of God exerts itself' (*Sins* 311). While no country is perfect, 'we come nearer to it than any country in the world ever did', wrote More the previous year in *Village Politics* (352). Such a providential national pride, whether secular or Christian, is unacceptable to Barbauld.

Yet Barbauld responded strongly to struggling nations threatened by imperial domination, as in her poem 'Corsica' (1773), celebrating the ill-fated Corsican nationalist struggle against Genoese and French control.[14] When the young French republic was under attack by the Duke of Brunswick's counterrevolutionary armies, she also praised France in 'To a Great Nation' (comp. 1792): Barbauld celebrated the French republic as a democratic 'mighty nation' unified by a 'great spirit' (*Selected Poetry* 133), so that as Laura Mandell argues, '[s]he wants her readers to imagine and become a Nation animated by the only "spirit" capable of unifying the diverse intentions of many people: "the spirit of equality"' (41). In this poem as in *Sins of Government*, Barbauld crafts a progressive, ecumenical and distinctly Francophilic (republican, in this context) understanding of nation, a radical departure from Burke's xenophobic and familial model of the British nation. Barbauld's cosmopolitanism is congruent with, not in conflict with, her sense of nationalism, an illustration of Karen O'Brien's important argument that in the eighteenth century 'it was… possible to fashion an image of national selfhood which derived, not from an idea of the "other", but from the interplay of likeness and difference within the family of Christian churches and nations' (4). While my focus in this study will be on 'citizens of the world' like Williams and Smith, it is important to consider the revolutionary legacy that they shared with similarly antinationalist writers like Barbauld who were committed to radicalizing a distinctly British nation.[15]

Barbauld's progressive understanding of an egalitarian nation emerges throughout her 1790s works, from the *Civic Sermons to the People* (urging 'poor people' to become 'active citizens'), to her antiwar children's stories in *Evenings at Home* (published by Johnson 1792–98), to the anti-imperialist *Eighteen Hundred and Eleven*. The latter poem addresses the English nation with the same warmth as the embattled France of 1792: 'O my Country, name beloved, revered' (*Selected Poetry* 163). And yet even this great nation must share in the horrors of the war it pursued: 'Thou who hast shared the guilt must share the woe' (*ibid.*). Barbauld's nation and government are thus always subjected to the judgment of its citizens and of history, and always within an international framework.

Barbauld wrote consistently in opposition to the war against the French. In *Sins of Government, Sins of the Nation, or a Discourse on the Fast, appointed on April 19, 1793*, Barbauld critiques the very idea of a national day of repentance in support of the war, by asking 'a serious question: How far, as individuals, are we really answerable for the guilt of national sins?' (315). Government, Nation and Individual are three distinct entities with distinct duties, the latter's being to exercise rational ethical judgment on the nation and its government. Barbauld contends that war is equivalent to mass murder, and that this ought to be the true subject for repentance on this fast day. Given the gravity of the situation, even the least powerful citizens, women included implicitly, are required to consider either consenting or remonstrating:

the more strictly we are bound to acquiesce, the more it is incumbent on us to remonstrate. Every good man owes it to his country and to his own character, to lift his voice against a ruinous war, an unequal tax, or an edict of persecution: and to oppose them, temperately, but firmly, by all the means in his power. (*Sins* 317)

Nation and individual stand apart from the unilateral and unjust actions of the government, even while the latter claims the rhetoric of nationalism. Laura Mandell's conclusion regarding's Barbauld's 'To a Great Nation' can apply as well to *Sins of Government*: 'Barbauld is not advocating nationalism as we know it' (41). In contrast to oppositional notions of aggressive nationalism, 'the vivifying kind of identification proposed by Barbauld will produce a community of active, responsible citizens' (Mandell 41).

In *Letters to a Young Lady* (1799), Jane West echoed Barbauld directly in her patriotic defence of the war as God's will:

It is most certain, from holy writ, that war, famine, pestilence... are all means which the Almighty employs to correct the wickedness of offending nations... National sins, therefore, do not mean the sins of our governors, as some most perversely misrepresent; but the collective offences of individuals. (2: 481–2)

Barbauld's understanding of nation is thus utterly at odds with that of loyalists like West, Burke and More. Rather, it is an important example of the radical nationalism (typically evoking lost traditions of native, masculine liberties) that emerged in the 1770s and 1780s, and is in Barbauld's unusual case available to men as well as women and children. 'You need not chide away your children' when discussing such important issues, Barbauld wrote in *Civic Sermons to the People*, for 'they will give a spirit and edge to your meditations' (*Civic* I: 20). Barbauld's egalitarianism cut across the familial hierarchies that Burke, West and More enforced, because as Marlon Ross has noted, for Barbauld 'the greatest national states are educated in exactly the same way as children in a domestic setting' ('Configurations' 98).

In her two *Civic Sermons to the People* (Joseph Johnson, 1792), Barbauld explained the functions and limits of government to a popular audience, insisting that it is the duty of all 'citizens' to 'enquire what [their] rights and liberties are' (*Civic* I: 15). She addressed 'poor people, or those who work to maintain themselves' in a language recognizable as that of French republicanism: 'Citizens, expand your minds to take in these ideas! Let your country occupy a large space in your minds!' (*Civic* I: 4; *Civic* II: 20). In 'Thoughts on the Inequality of Conditions' (*c.* 1800), Barbauld called for even more radical reforms: 'Let every man know what it is to have property, and you will soon awaken in him a sense of honesty. Make him a citizen, and he will love the constitution to which he belongs, and obey the laws he has helped make'

(*Selected Poetry* 355). While she echoed the classical formulation that family 'is the root of every other society' (*Civic* II: 6), Barbauld did not draw on patriarchal or matriarchal authority for her model of national subjects: her readers are not addressed as children of the paternalistic king or state, or fathers and mothers of the future Britain, and neither is her narrator's voice identifiable as that of father or mother, male or female. Instead, she drew on the language of radical republicanism for her ungendered model of 'active citizens' (*Civic* II: 22). Even Barbauld's formulation of motherhood is social, not biological, argue William McCarthy and Elizabeth Kraft, conceived 'as a civic, or citizenly, role', as it was for Wollstonecraft (26).

Wollstonecraft specifically addressed her female readers as citizens first, and mothers and wives second. In *Rights of Woman*, published in the same year as *Civic Sermons*, Wollstonecraft insisted that a wife is 'also an active citizen' and that if you 'take away natural rights...duties become null' (144). Wollstonecraft made it quite clear what relation rights and duties bear to one another:

> The being who discharges the duties of its station is independent; and, speaking of women at large, their first duty is to themselves as rational creatures, and the next, in point of importance, as citizens, is that, which includes so many, of a mother. (*Rights of Woman* 145)

Maternal duties are therefore one part of the many '*human duties*' (51) of an active citizen, and they are inseparable from the rights of citizens as conceived by contemporary male republicans. Like Wollstonecraft, Barbauld conceived of the revolutionary crisis, and her public role within it, in terms of citizenship and civic duty, not in the familial and biological terms of loyal subjects – father, mother, child – preferred by Burke, West and More. Marlon Ross and Penny Mahon have each noted that Barbauld's political writings eschew an identifiably 'feminine' discourse, audience or perspective. Barbauld's unfeminized political rhetoric is related to her unwillingness to be associated with sexualized and scandalous radical feminist Dissenters like Wollstonecraft and Hays, and with 'The Rights of Woman' in general, as her poem by that name demonstrates.[16] But in her universalist and antinationalist insistence on the British becoming 'active citizens', Barbauld relied on the same rhetoric as these more radical contemporaries in their outspoken claims of citizenship for women.

The strength of Barbauld's republicanism is also evident when we compare her prose to More's tracts, to which Barbauld directly responded.[17] While More's *Village Politics* (1792) and *Cheap Repository Tracts* (1795–98) addressed the working classes as loyal subjects and taught them how their humility, economy and subservience were God's will, Barbauld's *Civic Sermons to the People* urged a similar audience to enlarge the earthly scope of their enquiries and desires, beyond their humble lot. 'Many seem to think that poor people' lack the faculty of reason, she begins her first *Civic Sermon*, and therefore 'have nothing to do with Government; that you are like sheep, who ought to follow the shepherd; like the feet and the hands, which ought to obey the head' (7). More's preferred analogies of organic order are here evoked and dismissed, and along with them More's central argument in *Village Politics* that 'the poor have as much share in the government as they well know how to manage', that is, none (354). One of More's didactic fables in *Village Politics* warned that, one day,

> The hands said, I won't work any longer to feed this lazy belly, who sits in state like a Lord and does nothing. Said the feet, I won't walk and tire myself to carry him about; let him shift for himself; so said all the members; just as your levellers and republicans do now. (352)

The results of defying this symbiotic relationship between the different classes of society are of course disastrous, because to quarrel with this governing organic hierarchy is to 'quarrel with Providence. For the woman is below her husband, and the children are below their mother, and the servant is below his master' (*Village* 354).

More's analogies are illogical, counters Barbauld, for sheep and shepherd, like feet and hands, are 'by Nature formed quite differently from each other', whereas all people are born equal: 'the son of a king [is] born into the world the same naked, helpless, ignorant creature that your own children are', and therefore 'it is proper to enquire *why* some men are set over and govern other men' (*Civic* I: 8–9, orig. emphasis). In contrast, More's most popular *Cheap Repository* tract, *The Shepherd of Salisbury Plain* (1795), presented the genteel author's idealized vision of the poor's meek submission to their misfortunes, through which the Shepherd found 'great joy and delight...from thinking how God has honoured poverty!' (*Tales* 35). The honour will come in the afterlife, of course, for as her virtuous blacksmith says in *Village Politics*, 'I...look forward to a treasure in Heaven', not to the earthly equality in France, which in any case is 'all a lye [sic]...'Tis all murder and nakedness, and hunger...These are your *democrats*!' (*Village Politics* 361, orig. emphasis). Barbauld's countervision of civic politics insisted on the treasure of *earthly* equality: 'we want the happiness of all; for this plain reason, that all have an equal desire to be happy, and an equal right to be so' (*Civic* II: 25–6).

The consequences of a government unresponsive to the majority of the population are disastrous according to Barbauld, who in her prophetic poem, *Eighteen Hundred and Eleven*, imagined the destruction of Britain's commercial and cultural dominion as a direct result of the ruinous war. Perhaps in the distant future, imagines Barbauld's poet, 'England, the seat of arts, be only known/ By the grey ruin and the mouldering stone', a ruined landscape visited by North American tourists on a new Grand Tour (*Selected Poetry* 165). Always forward-thinking, Barbauld had welcomed the French Revolution with a regenerative optimism that by 1811 was nearly extinguished by the expanding Napoleonic wars. As she wrote to her brother in 1791,

> I cannot help thinking that the revolution in France will introduce there an entire revolution in education; and particularly be the ruin of classical learning, the importance of which must be lessening every day; while other sciences, particularly that of politics and government, must rise in value, afford an immediate introduction to active life, and be necessary in some degree to everybody. (*Works* 2: 158–9)

This hopeful vision of French regeneration is linked to Barbauld's struggle throughout the 1790s to convince her British readers that the 'sciences...of politics and government...[are] necessary in some degree to everybody'. But Britain's commercial and cultural 'progress' is inseparable from its military ambition and political repression, hence Britain's glimpsed destruction in Barbauld's sobering poem. Looking back in an 1818 letter, Barbauld enthused over the Revolution's lasting impact, moving quickly over the conquests of monarchy, to the 'fresh and opening' promise found in North America, as in *Eighteen Hundred and Eleven*: 'How much less interesting since the French Revolution are the glories and conquests of Louis XIV! What is the whole field of ancient history, which knew no sea but the Mediterranean, to the vast continent of America, with its fresh and opening glories!' (*Works* 2: 100).

Barbauld's bold opposition to the war and to its authorizing spirit of nationalism, in her 1790s works and in *Eighteen Hundred and Eleven*, drew much conservative criticism. John Wilson Croker's vicious review in the *Quarterly Review* depicted Barbauld with green spectacles (like Robespierre famously wore) and knitting needles, slyly associating her 'confident sense of commanding talents' with the Reign of Terror (v. 16 (1812): 309). The most extensive response to Barbauld's radical critique of British imperial ambition was Anne Grant's epic *Eighteen Hundred and Thirteen* (1814), a triumphalist vision of 'highly favoured Britain': 'Well may Britannia boast alike the praise/ Of warlike laurels and poetic bays' (95). A catalogue of British military victories over France, Grant's poem explicitly rejects Barbauld's equation of war with murder by evoking God's will: 'Now cannon thundering through th'untroubled air/ Heaven's blessing on our glorious cause declare' (141). Even 'he who mourns the son untimely slain' should be grateful, for he 'died to purchase honourable peace' (142). For Grant, all claims of domestic affection are subservient to the militaristic (yet feminized) state, 'the chosen minister of Fate': 'To her the best, the holiest power is given/ For noblest purposes, derived from Heaven' (145).

The Anglican Jane West similarly dismissed the 'objections to war' raised by 'maternal tenderness', restricting maternal influence to 'fortifying the young volunteer against those temptations to excess and licentiousness' (*Letters* 2: 490–1). In 1799 poems like 'The Spartan Matron' and 'The British Mother',

West glorifies mothers who send their sons to war with a warning that if they refuse to go, 'No safety from the mother claim' ('Spartan Matron', *Poems* 3: 174). Death in battle, West reminds anxious loved ones in *Letters to a Young Lady*, only robs young men of 'a few years', sparing them the sinfulness of earthly life. Christian motherhood remains English women's highest calling in such a fallen world: 'though we are not entitled to a place in the senate, we become *legislators* in the most important sense of the word', that is, through moral influence (*Letters* 1: 64–5, orig. emphasis). Yet West's maternal militarism would have it both ways – mothers are both unacknowledged legislators of their nation, and subservient sinners before 'the *providential* government of God' (*Letters* 2: 483, orig. emphasis). This contradiction illustrates the difficulties of women's political empowerment as maternal and moral 'legislators' (especially through a 'national' religion), and explains the urgency with which radical writers, including Dissenting Christians like Barbauld and Wollstonecraft, pursued secular and civil alternatives.

Grant and West's providential patriotism and militarism dominated mainstream media in wartime Britain from 1793 onwards. Women writers in evangelical and prophetic traditions, like Sarah Trimmer, Joanna Southcott and More, while in other ways oppositional to mainstream British politics, also wrote firmly in support of the war against France (and the class hierarchy at home) and justified this war in terms of Britain's providential Christian mission (which Barbauld considered absurd, since 'as God is no respecter of persons, so neither is he of nations' (*Sins*: 311)). Reviewing Barbauld's 'Things by their Right Name' (1794), described by Penny Mahon as 'the first antiwar story written specifically for children' ('Things' 168), the evangelical Sarah Trimmer attacked Barbauld's equation of war with murder, and defended the war as both 'lawful and necessary' in a fallen world (*Guardian of Education* 2 (1803): 345). Evangelicals like Trimmer and More stressed earthly obedience and heavenly reward, and as Mahon argues, '[t]his fundamental distinction between qualities of peace – as a spiritual and as a temporal reality – clearly separated the evangelicals from the dissenting radicals and characterized the discourse of each' ('Things' 172).

When considering women's writings on revolutionary politics (war and nationalism, in this case) we need to keep in mind the myriad of interests that divided women writers within diverse Christian traditions. Barbauld herself famously wrote to Maria Edgeworth that '[t]here is no bond of union among literary women, any more than among literary men... Mrs Hannah More would not write along with you or me, and we should probably hesitate at joining Miss Hays, or if she were living, Mrs Godwin'. And yet Barbauld, like More and Southcott, and the feminist Hays and Wollstonecraft, had to endure misogynist criticism that objected to women's political agency, regardless of the vastly different uses which it served. Barbauld's *Eighteen Hundred and Eleven* shocked Tory critics because a woman had dared to speak so critically of British imperial ambitions during a military crisis. More's Sunday schools, in which the poor were taught to read the Bible, respect their superiors, and shun reform, came under misogynist attack during the Blagdon Controversy (1801–03) because of clerics' suspicion that More and her sisters' unregulated religious activities could inadvertently spread dissent (see Keane, 'Anxiety'). Southcott fared the worst of all three, pilloried in the press for prophesying that she was pregnant with the Messiah, but also attacked for boldly claiming public authority as in her numerous publications on international and national politics (see Binfield).

Barbauld's revolutionary writings were not explicitly feminist (that is, they did not advocate the 'rights of woman') or feminine, but neither were they written in a consciously 'masculine voice'. Wollstonecraft, Hays and Robinson had claimed the rights of citizens most boldly for women, while counterrevolutionaries like Hannah More and Anne Grant, who emphasized the moral value of enlarging women's educations, firmly restricted women's roles within patriarchal hierarchies. Barbauld, careful to avoid a 'bond of union' with either of these polarized camps, wrote radical polemics with a cool, ironic rationalism that evoked the detachment characteristic of a citizen of the public sphere – traditionally a male citizen, yet in the 1790s word war, increasingly accessible to women in radical traditions.

Barbauld's 1790s pamphlets do share some affinities with contemporary 'feminized' discourses on war, which as Stephen Behrendt, Mary Favret and others have argued, emphasized the effects of war on the domestic sphere, women and children. Charlotte Smith's *The Emigrants* (1793), Mary Robinson's 'The Camp' (1800), Elizabeth Moody's 'Anna's Complaint; Or the Miseries of War' (1795), and Amelia Opie's 'The Soldier's Return' (1806) are examples of a popular tradition (to which male writers also contributed) lamenting war's destructive effects on families, and as such serve as a counterpart to the Christian militarism of More, West and Grant, and the radical rationalism of Barbauld. Yet Barbauld had offered a brilliant take on the gendering of military conflict in *Sins of Government*:

> We must fix our eyes, not on the hero returning with conquest, nor yet on the gallant officer dying in the bed of honour, the subject of picture and of song, but on the private soldier, forced into the service, exhausted by camp-sickness and fatigue; pale, emaciated, crawling to an hospital with the prospect of life, perhaps a long life, blasted, useless and suffering. We must think of the uncounted tears of her who weeps alone, because the only being who shared her sentiments is taken from her; no martial music sounds in unison with her feelings; the long day passes and he returns not. (*Sins* 313)

In post-Waterloo Britain, Felicia Hemans would become the most successful poet to give (feminine) voice to the victims of such (masculine) violence that threatens all social and affective relationships. In 1793, it was Barbauld who brought both male and female war victims together into an integrated vision of an entire nation plunged into war against its will and interests. '[N]o martial music sounds in unison with' the widow's feelings, and similarly, no patriotic songs welcome the press-ganged and wounded common soldier. Both are victims of a war that Barbauld urges 'active citizens' to remonstrate against in *Sins of Government*, a pamphlet second to none in its exacting critique of domestic political coercion. While later she positioned herself against both Wollstonecraft and More, in the 1790s Barbauld forged an original voice in her prose works, neither masculine nor feminine, that was in fact closest to those 'female philosophers' and fellow rational Dissenters, Hays, Williams and Wollstonecraft.

Addressing the entire nation, resorting to neither xenophobia nor nostalgia, Barbauld situated herself uniquely as an 'active citizen' of a British nation always conceived with reference to its internal disparities and external relations. Thus, Barbauld's radicalized nationalism shares much with the revolutionary cosmopolitanism of Robinson, Williams and Wollstonecraft, and similarly rejects the loyalist implication that the international and political concerns of citizenship are incompatible with local and moral duties. She did not ally herself with these sexually suspect 'female philosophers' whom she resembled, but like them she found in the revolutionary crisis an unparalleled opportunity to assume a public role on an international stage. Even nationalists like More, Hawkins, Grant and West found themselves publicly agitating on international matters like war, foreign policy and refugees, despite their stated antipathy toward women's public political intervention (except when religiously sanctioned). Ironically, the French revolutionary crisis impelled even these loyalists to become in effect citizens of the world, if only to combat the spread of this pernicious ideal by promoting in its place the 'Saviour of the World', as West insisted in my epigraph to this Introduction (West, *Letters* 2: 478). As Steven Blakemore has chronicled, in 'Revolution and the French Disease', the 'French disease' thoroughly infected British aesthetic and political discourse, across all social divides. It is this unique historical crisis that compelled so many women writers of the Romantic period to experiment with the untried possibilities found in the citizen of the world.

1
Female Philosophers: Women and the 'Word War' of the 1790s

> Start not, readers, at the idea I have suggested, of a female philosopher.
> I know it is a character, which the world has been hitherto in the
> habit of considering as a sort of eccentricity of nature, very fit to be
> shown about as a sight, but not to be imitated. But, thanks to the
> improved state of knowledge in these times, we may hope that in a
> short time the character will become so common, that it will no longer
> be looked on as a prodigy, or shunned as a bane, but nourished as a
> plant of the most balsamic influence.
>
> Anne Plumptre, *Antoinette Percival. A Novel* (1800)

Perhaps the most far-reaching legacy of the French revolutionary crisis for
British women writers is also one of its least studied phenomena – the emergence of the 'Female Philosopher' as a public political role for women with
international ambitions. Counterrevolutionary writers like Richard Polwhele,
Hannah More and Jane West helped create the category of the Female Philosopher, but unlike other hostile formulations such as 'unsex'd females' or
'English Jacobins' that have remained current in modern scholarship, the Female
Philosopher has received little attention. This is regrettable because, unlike
these other oppositional categories, the Female Philosopher retains some
potential value to Romantic women writers, some of whom identified themselves as philosophers and wrote in defence of the 'rights of woman', a
1790s struggle that we recognize as an important origin of modern Western
feminism. John Thelwall famously lamented that he and his radical allies must
reluctantly endure the epithet 'Jacobin' as if it were a stigma akin to the
mark of Cain, since after the Reign of Terror during the short-lived Jacobin
Republic (1793–94), virtually no British radical would willingly associate themselves with this discredited group.[1] But as Anne Plumptre suggested in the
epigraph from her novel above, 'Female Philosopher' opened up as much
progressive and feminist potential as it invited misogynist invective.

In order to appreciate the revolutionary goals embodied in the Female
Philosopher phenomenon, both in the eyes of its counterrevolutionary critics

and its feminist adherents, we need first to situate this emergent political identity in the nationalist cultural terrain of 1790s Britain. Loyalist writers like More and West worked hard to demonize Female Philosophers as unnatural and unBritish, a fate shared by the Citizens of the World, as I argued in the Introduction. As the first half of this chapter outlines, counterrevolutionary writers discredited Female Philosophers like Wollstonecraft and Hays through three strategies: by associating them with Rousseau's radical politics and sexual transgressions, implicitly comparing them to the 'philosopher whores' of pornography, and literally demonizing them as Satanic. Loyalists in turn offered British women a restricted range of alternatives – as 'loyal subjects' and 'good Christians' – designed to combat the dangerously secular, politicized and international outlook of Female Philosophers. The second half of this chapter thus examines the repercussions of the 1790s Female Philosopher phenomenon in counterrevolutionary retrospective accounts by novelists like Elizabeth Hamilton, Amelia Opie and others. These early nineteenth-century critiques of the Female Philosopher sought in particular to discredit the secular and civic roles that Female Philosophers had claimed from the French revolutionary tradition, a conservative ideological victory with far-reaching repercussions for modern feminism.

The empress of Female Philosophers

Wollstonecraft was the preeminent example of the Female Philosopher, a self-identified philosopher who advocated the rights of woman as a logical extension of the revolutionary rights of man. Her controversial 1798 posthumous works (Godwin's *Memoirs* of her life and her unfinished novel, *The Wrongs of Woman*) shaped the career of Female Philosophers as a whole, and indeed the subsequent history of feminism. Richard Polwhele's *The Unsex'd Females* is a notorious example of the often hysterical misogyny of 1790s attacks on Wollstonecraft, and while its prominence in modern literary studies is out of proportion with its contemporary significance, it remains valuable because of the politicized demarcations it established between appropriate and inappropriate female intellectual pursuits. Published in 1798, *The Unsex'd Females* uses the recent revelations of Wollstonecraft's affairs and suicide attempts in Godwin's publication of her *Memoirs* to illustrate the fatal consequences of women acting on forbidden (because unnatural) intellectual, sexual and, most of all, political desires.

Given Barbauld's radical 1790s pamphlets, it is not surprising that she is the first such 'Unsex'd Female' that Polwhele names as a victim of Wollstonecraft's example. Barbauld's poetry is 'chaste and elegant', yet she is now 'classed with such females as a Wollstonecraft' because of her recent political prose: 'Mrs. B[arbauld] has lately published several political tracts which, if not discreditable to her talents and virtues, can by no means add to her reputation'(16). The pattern is the same for Charlotte Smith, Helen Maria Williams and Mary Robinson, praised for their appropriately feminine lyrical verse, yet each of them unsexed by their political prose in favour of the French Revolution, infected with the 'Gallic mania' (18, 15–20) introduced by Wollstonecraft. By 1798, radicalization and sexualization are identical to Gallicization, and Polwhele's goal is to recall these once-virtuous poets from their 'Gallic wanderings' in political prose, where they pursued the 'doctrines of Philosophism' and 'Gallic licentiousness' (20, 17, 19). Polwhele constructs a counterset of writers ('the obedient throng') assembled from Bluestockings and led by Hannah More, who write prose and poetry that does not advocate radical change or French revolutionary principles, and thus enjoys a 'vast…influence o'er the social ties' (32). Despite Polwhele's extremism, he did correctly identify the price that women writers would have to pay in order to continue to enjoy 'a nation's praise' (30) in a nineteenth-century literary and political culture increasingly intolerant of women's radicalization and Gallicization.

Barbauld's early reputation had been established by her critically acclaimed *Poems* (1773), Smith's by her celebrated *Elegiac Sonnets* (1784), Williams's by *Peru* (1784) and *Poems* (1786), and Robinson's by *Poems* (1791). While lyric and poetry of sensibility could always slip into dangerously erotic territory, it is the post-1789 prose of these writers that signals a unique cultural event. Aspiring to national and international audiences, and often arguing from untried positions of authority – not necessarily those of female sensibility, maternal concern, national interest or Christian morality, as in 'the obedient throng', but often as rational citizens and political agents – these Gallicized, secular radicals sought to influence the course of European events to an unprecedented extent. The distinctly Francophilic internationalism of Smith and Robinson, like that of Wollstonecraft, Macaulay and especially Williams, was the revolutionary, and historically unique, dimension of their status as Female Philosophers. Their counterrevolutionary opponents were at a loss as to how to classify such critiques, hence Polwhele's (in this respect representative) exasperation at these writers' failure to fit any 'sexed' model of writing.

The emergence of Female Philosophers as a cause for counterrevolutionary agitation coincides with Rousseau's transformation from sentimental seducer to dangerous republican philosopher. Sexualization and radicalization remain inseparable in the figure of Rousseau, who, though he died before 1789 and had been neither an atheist, feminist nor a democrat, profoundly influenced generations of French revolutionaries who then traced their political roots to the Citizen of Geneva. The 1789 Revolution and the publication of part two of Rousseau's *Confessions* that same year transformed Rousseau's British reception, and indeed his philosophy, beyond recognition. It was Burke who took the lead, and in *A Letter to a Member of the National Assembly* (1791), identified Rousseau as the Revolutionaries' 'holy writ' and 'standard figure of perfection' (31–2). The most dangerous text in Rousseau's canon, warned Burke, is that 'ferocious medley of pedantry and lewdness', *La Nouvelle Héloïse*: 'the false sympathies of the "Nouvelle Eloise"...subvert those principles of domestic trust and fidelity, which form the discipline of social life' (*ibid.*: 40). While that novel had enjoyed a wide appeal as a sentimental work since its English translation in 1761,[2] after the National Assembly erected a statue to Rousseau in December 1790, *Julie, ou La Nouvelle Héloïse* became the most poisonous French import in the late eighteenth-century culture wars. Much has been written about *La Nouvelle Héloïse*'s ongoing significance for British literature in the revolutionary decades, when, as Nicola Watson's exemplary study has shown, 'revolutionary politics were understood crucially in terms of sentimental fiction – and in particular the plot of a single novel, *La Nouvelle Héloïse*' (4).

Rousseau's privileging of virtue, sentiment and nature transformed him into the quintessential Modern Philosopher of radical sensibility according to British opponents of the Revolution. Rousseau's philosophy was distorted by loyalists like Reeve, More and Burke, so as to be unrecognizable: a 'return to nature' that these polemicists identified with libertinage, barbarism and a disregard for all social and domestic ties. In his *Confessions*, Rousseau had made shocking revelations of adultery, incestuous passion, homosexuality, masturbation and, most disturbing of all, the abandonment of his children to a foundling hospital. Burke ingeniously framed Rousseau's British reception as Modern Philosopher according to the contradictions between the sexual and philosophical, the private and public, the practical and theoretical, embodied in the philosopher's treatment of his children. 'Thousands admire the sentimental writer', wrote Burke, evoking that classic critique of cosmopolitanism's disregard for local ties, 'but the affectionate father is hardly known in his parish' (*Letter* 35). Identifying Rousseau's ruling passion as vanity, not virtue, Burke 'needs address himself neither to the substance of Rousseau's thought nor to the quality and sincerity of his intentions' (Duffy 41), a strategy successfully employed by all subsequent counterrevolutionary writers.

Rousseau had revolutionized philosophy by placing domestic and sexual critiques at the centre of philosophical enquiry, using sentimental and confessional genres. Writing novels like *La Nouvelle Héloïse*, the autobiographical *Confessions*, and essays like *Social Contract*, he located philosophical authority in the impassioned domestic dialogues of Julie, the interiority of Jean-Jacques, and the dispassionate analytical voice of the male law-giver. Sade represents the next dialectical turn in this philosophical tradition, likewise placing family and sexual politics at the heart of philosophical critique, but in the process reducing every Rousseauvian conceit of virtue into a materialist pursuit of pleasure and sensation. These antithetical philosophers were both demonized for their violations of philosophical decorum, religious orthodoxy and sexual propriety, Rousseau via sentimentality and confession, Sade via pornography. While Sade was virtually unknown in Britain, it is useful to consider how both these counterenlightenment writers help map the new outlines of French philosophy in the late eighteenth century, writing far outside the disciplinary and generic boundaries we associate with philosophical critique today.[3] It was the novel through which both Sade and Rousseau had greatest success in reaching a large audience, and it would likewise be the novel through which British Female Philosophers would continue these philosophical debates.

While the sentimental Rousseau was the quintessential Modern Philosopher according to counterrevolutionaries, rationalist English philosophers like Godwin and Paine, deeply indebted to the French enlightenment tradition (particularly materialists like d'Holbach and Helvétius) that Rousseau rejected, were also key figures in Modern Philosophy. Whether via sensibility or reason, Modern Philosophy left no tradition unexamined, threatening centuries of stability with a rage for reform in which accepted religion and morality had no place. 'Combining Pagan superstitions with the exploded reveries of irrational theorists', warned Jane West, modern philosophers 'place at the head of their world of chance a supine material God, whom they recognize by the name of Nature' (*Tale* 2: 273). Loyalist accounts of the modern philosophy had no interest in accurately characterizing or distinguishing the schools of thought that made up its diverse ranks, but instead, as Mathew Grenby has shown in *The Anti-Jacobin Novel*, combined heterogeneous elements like materialism, feminism, atheism, deism, pantheism, rationalism and sensibility into a nightmarish force intended to topple God's divine order. Opponents of reform like the government-funded Association for Preserving Liberty and Property (which helped distribute More's pamphlets) did not combat Modern Philosophy by directly disputing its principles, but rather by creating a climate of 'anti-intellectualism' (Olivia Smith 73) that was particularly hostile to Female Philosophers.

By the end of the 1790s, the Female Philosopher had emerged as one particularly dangerous disciple of the Modern Philosophy, and was above all identified with Mary Wollstonecraft as a politicized avatar of Rousseau's scandalous Julie. This cultural formation of 'Female Philosopher' joined Wollstonecraft's rationalist critique of marriage and her claims for women's equality via reason (in *Rights of Woman*), to her sexually transgressive 1798 *Memoirs* and *Wrongs of Woman*, and fashioned her vision of women's sexual and intellectual independence into one of sexual licence, akin to Julie's extramarital passion in *La Nouvelle Héloïse*. Wollstonecraft's own relationship to Rousseau was highly conflicted: she had described him as 'a strange inconsistent unhappy clever creature', and later in her life confessed to Imlay that 'I have always been half in love with him' (*Collected Letters*: 145, 263). He remained the most important touchstone throughout her intellectual development. The vehemence of her critique of Rousseau's novel of education, *Emile*, in *Rights of Woman*, reflects her disappointment over his views on women, given her admiration for his *Confessions* and *Reveries of a Solitary*

Walker.[4] Wollstonecraft felt an affinity towards the philosopher and his candid revelations of his struggle to balance passion and reason, yet rejected his essentialist view of women in *Emile*. In that influential novel, Rousseau asserted that men and women are essentially different, physically and intellectually, and that women are the inferior, passive counterparts of men, whose pleasure and comfort they should aim to promote via their sexual influence and sensibility.

Despite the criticism of radical English feminists like Wollstonecraft and Catherine Macaulay, Rousseau appealed strongly to women writers as *the* Romantic outcast, inviting their compassion and identification. Mary Seidman Trouille has demonstrated how a wide range of British and French women, from working-class, middle-class and aristocratic backgrounds

> viewed Rousseau as a superior soul, victim of a narrow-minded public incapable of understanding or appreciating him – as a scapegoat who aroused their compassion and symbolized their own frustrations as writers and public figures. (5)

Thus, both the working-class, monarchist feminist Olympe de Gouges and the bourgeois republican Madame Roland 'identified strongly with Rousseau's persona of persecuted virtue' in the *Confessions* and his 'ideal of enlightened domesticity' in the novels (Trouille 5, 26). Rousseau's *Confessions* and *La Nouvelle Héloïse* had been two of European Romanticism's most influential texts, and their influence was particularly controversial in 1790s British debates over women's involvement in the revolutionary crisis. In a 1795 letter, an enthusiastic Barbauld described Madame de Roland's *Memoirs* as

> surely the most singular book that has appeared since the Confessions of Rousseau; a book that none but a Frenchwoman *could* write, and wonderfully entertaining. I began it with a certain fear upon my mind – What is this woman going to tell me? Will it be any thing but what will lessen my esteem for her? If, however, we were to judge of the female and male mind by contrasting these confessions with those I just now mentioned, the advantage in purity, *comme de raison*, will be greatly on the side of our sex. (*Works* 2: 89, orig. emphasis)

Rousseau's unprecedented sexual revelations in the *Confessions* proved a dangerous example for women to emulate, hence Barbauld's reluctance to have her admiration for Roland tainted by any Rousseauvian transgressions.

It was above all Wollstonecraft, Williams and Hays who joined French republicans in translating Rousseau's political and moral vision into revolutionary agendas in the early 1790s. Their subsequent sexual scandals linked their philosophical achievements to *La Nouvelle Héloïse*'s narrative of philosophical seduction, creating the popular hybrid of 'female philosopher'.

Wollstonecraft's works of political philosophy were her *Vindication of the Rights of Men* (1790), *Vindication of the Rights of Woman* (1792), and *Historical and Moral View of the French Revolution* (1794), all part of the 1790s 'word war'. In *Rights of Men*, Wollstonecraft joined the republican historian Macaulay in condemning the 'effeminacy' and 'submissive flattery' characteristic of Burke's style and politics (Macaulay, *Observations* 8), and like Barbauld in her 1790s polemics, claimed the authority associated with disinterested citizens of the public sphere. Writing in these traditionally masculine genres of polemic and philosophical tract, and typically not signing their name to the first edition,[5] they deliberately avoided identifying themselves as women. In fact, they went to such lengths to attack Burke's 'unmanly' and 'effeminate' politics that Claudia Johnson has argued that 'Wollstonecraft is infinitely more disturbed by the permeability of the lines of sexual differentiation from the male side than outraged by insurmountable division between men and women' (30).

Regardless of whether these feminists adopted 'masculine' or 'feminine' authorial identities, issues widely debated in modern scholarship, it is clear that once their identities as female authors were known shortly after their first editions were published, their conservative contemporaries were alarmed by their trespass into these masculine realms. Seeking forbidden knowledge, in its political, intellectual and sexual senses, is what distinguishes these Female Philosophers from what Polwhele termed 'the obedient throng' – women like More who argued for changes like abolishing the slave trade and improving women's education, but did so within explicitly Christian limits that did not intentionally threaten class or sexual hierarchies, but sought to strengthen them by making them conform to evangelical understandings of propriety, sin and redemption. Grounding their polemics instead in the universalist rationalism associated with Enlightenment philosophy (and rational Dissent), Female Philosophers submitted everything to rational critique, a disturbing propensity for independent judgment that conservatives were quick to describe as everyway dangerous.

Wollstonecraft boldly identified herself as a philosopher early on in the *Rights of Woman*: 'As a philosopher, I read with indignation the plausible epithets which men use to soften their insults' against women (34). Her ambitious work of philosophical history, the 1794 *Historical and Moral View of the French Revolution*, further developed this identity as philosopher, as the book's reception demonstrates: she writes 'not like an annalist, but like a philosopher', enthused the *Monthly Review* (n.s. 16 (1795): 393). 'The *New Annual Register* similarly praised her "calm and philosophic eye" and her "variety of important reflections which merit the attention of politicians of every party, and statesmen of every country"'.[6] In this same year the ambivalent but finally disapproving Anne Grant acknowledged Wollstonecraft as 'the empress of female philosophers'.[7]

Macaulay, whom Wollstonecraft greatly admired, was 'the first historian in the eighteenth century to attempt a republican history of the seventeenth century' (the eight-volume *History of England*, 1763–83), and the author of important critiques of Rousseau (*Letters on Education*, 1790) and Burke (*Observations on the Reflections*, 1790) (Hill 250). A prominent Francophile, she was admired by future revolutionaries like Mirabeau, Brissot de Warville and Madame Roland, who declared she wished to be 'la Macaulay de son pays', as well as by American republicans (*ibid.*). Macaulay's 1779 marriage to William Graham when he was 21 and she 47, however, made her private life the object of misogynist ridicule. In the anonymous satirical poem *The Female Patriot* (1779), the 'Republican Heroine' Macaulay renounces her public role as patriotic intellectual for the erotic pleasures of the feminine heroine:

> When the bold hero to my ravish'd view
> Hid Godlike shape display'd so wondrous true;
> Stern patriotism ceas'd my Soul to move,
> And all the Heroine languish'd into love. (28)

And as we saw in 'Don Dismallo Running the Literary Gauntlet' (Frontispiece), Macaulay's later public censure of Burke's effeminate sentimentality was satirized as sexually perverse.

In 1796, Wollstonecraft's friend Mary Hays fictionalized the Female Philosopher in her semi-autobiographical *Memoirs of Emma Courtney*. A further turn in the dialectic of radical feminism, Hays's *Memoirs* featured a heroine who engaged in radical philosophical debates and violated sexual mores by voicing her desires for the unresponsive hero. The eponymous heroine is inspired by reading the first half of *La Nouvelle Héloïse*, in which Julie and Saint-Preux consummate their passion, but is forbidden to read the second half, ironically 'prevent[ing] Emma from reading its didactic warning against sexual transgression'.[8] Hereafter devoted to examining rationally all conventions, political and sexual, Emma is a radicalized Julie who cites English radicals like Wollstonecraft, Godwin and Holcroft, and French philosophers like Helvétius and Descartes, as influences. Once her 'curiosity was awakened to philosophic enquiries', in particular 'metaphysical enquiries', Emma, like Eve, endures a fortunate fall into knowledge (Hays, *Memoirs* 24, 25). The difficulties that unfold as a result of her pursuit of forbidden knowledge are so ambiguously and ingeniously framed by Hays that debate continues today as to the novel's overall effect and intent regarding its heroine.

Hays's unique contribution to the radical feminist debate surrounding the Female Philosophers is her insistence that passion and reason are equally important sources of virtue and truth. This radical valorization of (Rousseauvian) sensibility and passion is deliberately directed at Godwin (fictionalized as the philosopher Mr Francis) and to a lesser extent Wollstonecraft, for both had privileged reason in their liberatory manifestos (although Wollstonecraft's supposed rejection of passion and corporeality is consistently overemphasized by modern scholars).[9] 'I feel', writes Emma to Mr Francis, 'that I am neither a philosopher, nor a heroine – but a *woman, to whom education has given a sexual character*' (117, orig. emphasis). Both realms – philosophy and romance – are gendered, and because Emma wants to escape the 'barbarous and accursed laws of society' (143), neither of these mutually exclusive roles will do. Similarly, Robinson's *The False Friend* (1799) debated at length the claims of Godwin's philosophy given the realities of women's sexualization – 'We are philosophers in precept', insists her doomed heroine, 'but how often are we women in example!' (2: 94). Philosophy as conceived by Godwin diminishes the passions, and a heroine's life, as Wollstonecraft had argued, contains only passion, to the exclusion of the life of the mind that is equally desirable. The result for 'those who press forward' seeking access to both realms, that is Female Philosophers, is 'moral martyrdom' according to Hays (*Memoirs*: 195). Emma Courtney's 'moral martyrdom' deliberately echoed the self-aggrandizing rhetoric of martyrdom in Rousseau's *Confessions*, and became the standard conclusion to all subsequent tales of Female Philosophers, Robinson's included. Boldly allying herself with the 'illustrious name' of the recently deceased Wollstonecraft, Robinson's heroine in *The False Friend* is dismissed as a '*he–she* philosopher' by the villain (2: 77–8), and suffers a literal and 'moral martyrdom' for her misunderstood passion, effectively connecting Wollstonecraft's fate with Rousseau's (and Emma Courtney's).

Emma's correspondence with the philosopher Mr Francis had incorporated Hays's actual correspondence with William Godwin.[10] Godwin's widely-read anarchist manifesto, *An Enquiry Concerning Political Justice* (1793) and its companion novel, *Caleb Williams* (1794), combined with his publicized associations with women like Wollstonecraft and Hays, conspired to create in Godwin the home-grown Modern Philosopher counterpart to Rousseau. In the post-1793 conservative backlash, Godwin joined Rousseau as scapegoat for the Revolution, and his admirers joined Rousseau's in wishing a moral martyrdom: as Crabb Robinson wrote in 1795, *Political Justice* 'in effect directed the whole course of my life ... and I was willing even to become a martyr for it'.[11] Women like Wollstonecraft and Emma Courtney were in conservative eyes (im)moral martyrs for the radical cause, whose tragic lives or deaths were the direct results of putting Godwinian and Rousseauvian philosophy into practice.

This school of 'Modern Philosophy', led by Godwin, Paine, Rousseau and assorted *philosophes*, came to preoccupy counterrevolutionary novelists in the late 1790s who identified Modern Philosophy as a principal danger to British political stability. Female Philosophers featured prominently in these cautionary tales, either as victims of Rousseauvian and Godwininan libertines, or, more interestingly, as intellectual seducers in their own right. The destructive effects of women's moral martyrdom to revolutionary philosophy depicted in these novels directly reflected actual Female Philosophers' prolific and high-profile interventions in the French revolutionary crisis. These conservative works of misogynist propaganda, then, usefully indicate how the reception of actual Female Philosophers was significantly shaped by the internationalism inseparable from their sexual transgressions.

Philosopher whores

At the turn of the nineteenth century, Polwhele, Robert Mathias, William Beloe, Robert Bisset, Benjamin Silliman and Anne Grant all produced accounts of Wollstonecraft as a Female Philosopher destroyed by the contradictions embodied in that hybrid term. These conservative caricatures of the Female Philosopher as both unsexed and oversexed reflect the acute confusion over 'natural' sexual difference in the 1790s.[12] Termed an 'affective revolution' by Lynn Hunt and Margaret Jacob, the new revolutionary sexual and social possibilities opened up in 1790s radical circles also inspired an outright 'gender panic', visible in satires such as 'Don Dismallo Running the Literary Gauntlet' (Frontispiece).[13] Specifically, such misogynist attacks on these Female Philosophers evoke the contemporaneous pornographic tradition of the 'philosopher whore', revealing how by the end of the eighteenth century, this older enlightenment association of women with materialist philosophy had become untenable. French materialism had long been celebrated by philosopher whores, the embodied voice of a newly mechanized Nature, in such pornographic works as *Thérèse philosophe* (1748), *Julie philosophe* (1791), and Sade's *Histoire de Juliette*. These variations on the prostitute's confession tradition were typically antisentimental (unlike the similarly materialist *Fanny Hill*, 1748–49), amoralistic and featured philosopher whores who educated (sexually and philosophically) political and religious leaders, and men and women of different ranks, about the benefits of living according to nature's laws (above all, the pursuit of individual pleasure). As imagined by Enlightenment male *philosophes*, these public women are 'independent both financially and morally, intelligent, rational and responsible', and at the end of their autobiographical narratives find financial and social security (Norberg 240). Philosopher whores represent an important develop-ment not only in the history of pornography, but of women's ambiguous associations with Enlightenment individualism. Female philosophers like the sentimentalized Fanny Hill and the thoroughly *philosophe* Juliette articulated a materialism that according to Margaret Jacob 'offered the only philosophy of nature capable of addressing the individualism, the passions and the interests, the freedom and nonconformity, the disrespect and subversion to be found in the cities of Western Europe from early in the eighteenth century' ('Materialist' 192).

1790s Britain experienced these aspects of the radical Enlightenment as a cultural and literal invasion threat, with Female Philosophers like Wollstonecraft leading the way as avatars of this older (also male-authored) philosopher whore tradition. The philosopher whore became politically engaged in the revolutionary decade, with the post-1789 *Julie philosophe* and *Juliette* becoming radicalized republican *citoyennes*. It is with these radicalized philosopher whores in mind that we should read contemporaneous conservative British attacks on Female Philosophers as sexually corrupt and corrupting. 'Female materialist philosophers' were 'found easily on both sides of the channel', writes Jacob,

> and were relentlessly philosophical about the nature of the human order. By the late eighteenth century the female philosophers of the pornographic literature had become so commonplace as to be stock characters, and were generally depicted as enlightened prostitutes. For example, there is one routinely described in *Harris's List of Covent Garden Ladies; or, Man of Pleasure's Kalender* (1788)...She is listed as...'a comely woman, about forty...Indeed she has acquired great experience in the course of twenty years study, in *natural philosophy*, in the University of Portsmouth, where she was long the ornament of the back of the point'. ('Materialist' 174)

That women's pursuit of natural philosophy was linked to sexual transgression is well-known, for example, in studies of women's interest in botany and the 'loves of the plants'. '[H]ow the study of the sexual system of plants can accord with female modesty, I am not able to comprehend', despaired Polwhele of women who pursue 'bliss botanic' by examining the 'unhallow'd lust' and 'prostitution' rampant in the plant world (8).

Wollstonecraft, Hays and their fellow travellers belonged to this outlaw band of philosopher whores and natural philosophers, unacceptable under the increasingly hegemonic ideology of domesticated desire and complementary difference. This conservative conflation of feminist critiques of marriage with libertine celebrations of sexual licence found in contemporary pornography helps explain what seem like gratuitous overreactions by Polwhele and his *Anti-Jacobin* cohorts, who famously cross-referenced Wollstonecraft under 'prostitution' in their review of her *Memoirs*. Polwhele is representative of counterrevolutionary ideologues in their attempts to fit Wollstonecraft into the punitive narrative of the whore's progress as illustrated by Hogarth, in which her postpartum illness and death become the inevitable consequences of sin: 'she died a death that strongly marked the distinction of the sexes, by pointing out the destiny of women, and the diseases to which they are liable' (Polwhele 30). These female philosophers' works would then be confessions not in the Rousseauvian philosophical tradition admired by Wollstonecraft, Hays and Barbauld, but in the pornographic tradition of the prostitute's confession (exactly what Barbauld had feared before reading Mme Roland's 'confessions'). But even positive French philosopher whores like Juliette, Julie and Thérèse disappeared as Jacobin sexual politics closed off the public aspects of women's citizenship. Thus, in the conclusion to the prorevolutionary

Julie Philosophe, the philosopher whore 'becomes a devoted peasant wife, content to "give little citizens to the state"'.[14] Like their radical counterparts in Jacobin and Napoleonic France, British conservatives succeeded in demonizing as unpatriotic and sexually unnatural the most far-reaching demands for equality articulated by Female Philosophers, instead channelling these demands into a compensatory vision of complementary domesticity (in France, as 'republican motherhood').

Satanic Jacobins

Even more serious than the 'philosopher whore' associations linked to Wollstonecraft in particular were the religious transgressions associated with Modern Philosophy in general. As one of the Modern Philosophers, Wollstonecraft resembled what many would have scathingly referred to as the First Philosopher – Satan himself. This literal demonization of Female Philosophers illustrates the violence that British women writers' adoption of French revolutionary principles encountered in nationalist Britain. By the 1790s, the figure of Satan was 'widely employed as an ideological symbol, functioning as a vehicle of polarized political discourse' in both radical and conservative rhetoric (Schock 445). Eventually, Satan would come to represent Promethean genius in the 'Romantic Satanism' familiar to us in later writers like Byron, Mary Shelley and Percy Shelley. Yet in 1794, Anne Grant depicted a Satanic Wollstonecraft by connecting the counterrevolutionary associations of feminism with Satan's seduction of Eve. Grant observed that Wollstonecraft in *A Vindication of the Rights of Woman* 'speaks in such a strain of seeming piety, and quotes Scripture in a manner so applicable and emphatic that you are thrown off your guard'. Grant, like Eve before her, was intrigued:

> As to superiority of mental powers, Mrs. W[ollstonecraft] is doubtless the empress of female philosophers; yet what has she done for philosophy, or for the sex, but closed a ditch, to open a gulf? There is a degree of boldness in her conceptions, and masculine energy in her style, that is very imposing. There is a gloomy grandeur in her imagination, while she explores the regions of intellect without chart or compass, which gives one the idea of genius wandering through chaos...What, as I said before, has she done? shewed us all the miseries of our condition; robbed us of the only sure remedy for the evils of life, the sure hope of a blessed immortality.[15]

This ambivalently Romantic vision of Wollstonecraft as the wandering Satan traversing chaos, using both Scripture and reason to tempt other women with a spurious equality, is part of a larger 1790s phenomenon of reading both male and female philosophers as Satanic.

More similarly read Wollstonecraft in the role of Satanic tempter in her 'vindication for adultery', *The Wrongs of Woman*. In that novel, More writes, Wollstonecraft justifies 'French principles' like adultery and as such joins 'the most destructive class in the whole wide range of modern corrupters, who effect the most desperate work of the passions' through a cold-blooded rationalism, 'as in the infernal climate described by Milton' where '"frost performs th'effects of fire"' (*Strictures* 320, quoting *Paradise Lost* 2.595). Despite the points on which her arguments for women's education agreed with those of Wollstonecraft, More represented herself as locked in an epic struggle of good versus evil against the 'calculating, intellectual wickedness' of philosophers like Wollstonecraft (*Strictures* 320). In Eden as in wartime 1790s Britain, women were perceived as the weak link in the chain of domestic defence. In *Strictures on Female Education* (1799), More warned that 'the attacks of infidelity in Great Britain are at this moment principally directed at the female breast' (319). 'Conscious of the influence of women in civil society', she continued, these 'modern apostles of infidelity' now hold out 'the same allurement . . . which was employed by the first philosophist to the first sinner – Knowledge'.

France was merely the first to fall to such contagious 'Satanical ambition' for 'amazonian independence', warned Jane West:

> the state of manners in France itself, as far as related to our sex, had obtained such dreadful publicity, as allows us to ascribe the fall of that country in a great measure to the dissipated indelicate behaviour and loose morals of its women. Thus, though we are not entitled to a place in the senate, we become *legislators* in the most important sense of the word. (*Letters* 1: 213, 130, 64–5, orig. emphasis)

Such domesticization of women's public political agency would become hegemonic in the nineteenth century, partly through the efforts of polemicists like More and West. As unacknowledged legislators of the world, women in these restrictive visions were to enjoy a supposedly 'vast . . . influence o'er the social ties' (Polwhele 32) only by submitting to the literal demonization and radical curtailment of alternate (distinctly Gallicized) possibilities for women to 'legislate'.

Before this so-called 'domestic sphere' became inseparable from English female propriety, it was revolution-era novels like Jane West's *A Tale of the Times* (1799), Elizabeth Hamilton's *Memoirs of Modern Philosophers* (1800), Sophia King's *Waldorf, or the Dangers of Philosophy* (1798), and the anonymous *Dorothea, or a Ray of the New Light* (1801) that illustrated the perils of pursuing the alternate paths chosen by Female Philosophers. Working simultaneously against 'enlightenment' as a progressive ideal, and 'natural man' as a nostalgic ideal, these novels doggedly resisted French philosophical doctrines of experience, enlightenment and liberty, often evoking Wollstonecraft's recent death as a cautionary tale. Significantly, it is not only Satanic Gallicized libertines that seduce naïve English maidens in these narratives, but also Satanic Female Philosophers. In *Dorothea, or a Ray of the New Light*, the Modern Philosopher villain finds Dorothea happily married and seduces her by echoing Satan's appeal to Eve's independence: 'nor can the free agency of *my* spirit submit to such trammels, which, indeed, I blush and grieve to see have so much power over you. Are you the partner, or the slave of your husband?' (2: 56). Thus begins Dorothea's fall through intellectual pride along the trajectory already mapped out by Wollstonecraft, described in the novel as a 'genius clouded by pride, and lost, utterly lost, in the track of an unbridled imagination!' (1: 129). Unfortunately for Dorothea, writes the novelist, 'the posthumous works of Mary Woolstoncroft [*sic*] had not at that time presented this obvious comment on the prevailing doctrines' (1: 130). Orienting its narrative according to the unfolding catastrophe of Wollstonecraft's fall revealed in the 1798 *Memoirs*, *Dorothea* simultaneously evokes the Female Philosopher as an avatar of the Satanic wandering genius, endowed with a detectable frisson of intellectual glamour.

While it is the Modern Philosopher who performs the sexual seduction in these fictions, it is often the Female Philosopher who seduces intellectually. In *Dorothea*, it is a former servant and fallen woman, the aptly named Sophia, who is instrumental in Dorothea's undoing. Recalling Maria and Jemima in *Wrongs of Woman*, Dorothea forms an idealistic alliance with this plebeian fallen woman, putting into practice her notions of Godwinian reform. Yet Sophia is by now hopelessly bestialized and senses 'the Quixotic weakness of her benefactress', echoing Jemima's sentimental account of her own descent into predatory class warfare: 'her heart swelled with dreams of vengeance, she felt that she was an outcast, and...whilst society conspired to hunt her from its bounds, it gave birth to a natural desire of avenging her wrongs' (*Dorothea* 2: 13). *Dorothea* implies that the 'wrongs of woman' are in fact also Satan's, just as Female Philosophers' tempting promises of the 'rights of woman' are those that a naïve Eve believed. Thus the 'wretched Sophia' claims credit for destroying Dorothea's domestic paradise (by murdering her child and estranging her husband) with a Satanic flourish: 'It was *I* who, like the fiend in Paradise, poisoned your felicity: it was I who misled him, and tore you from each other' (2: 163, orig. emphasis).

By the next decade, the damning associations surrounding Wollstonecraftian feminism were so well-established that Charlotte Dacre could take the Satanic Female Philosopher to new narrative extremes. In *Zofloya, or the Moor* (1806), Dacre had shown an ambitious fifteenth-century heroine seduced by the pleasures and power promised to her by the Devil, embodied as an erotically irresistible Moorish servant. In her final novel, *The Passions* (1811), Dacre moved this drama to the contemporary crisis surrounding women's calls for 'bold independence' (1: 144), tracing the progress of *La Nouvelle Héloïse*'s forbidden knowledge as it is introduced by a Satanic feminist into a scene of domestic tranquility. 'You must taste of the tree of knowledge', says Dacre's villainess Appollonia to her victim Julia, for only knowledge can liberate women: 'that perceiving their equality in the scale of existence, they should (rebelling) throw off the iron yoke of slavery and never more consent to wear it!' (1: 169–70). As with Dorothea and Sophia, feminist Satanic seduction takes place entirely between women, an opportunity for homophobic associations as well: Appollonia boasts to the witless hero that it was '*I*, who seduced her heart...*I* bade her give the reins to loose illicit love and pleasure!' (*Passions* 4: 85, orig. emphasis). At once Satanic feminists and philosopher whores, Sophia and Appollonia attest to the conservative conflation of these traditions for misogynist ends.

Such antifeminist visions of a Satanic Wollstonecraft are examples of many Romantic-period associations (positive and hostile) of Milton's hero/ villain with the claims of both Female Philosophy and Modern Philosophy. But Wollstonecraft herself identified with Milton's Satan, part of an early unacknowledged tradition of a feminist Romantic Satanism that is visible in these conservative reflections, and continues through the nineteenth century in different guises.[16] Wollstonecraft's contempt for Milton's subordination of Eve is well-known in her *Rights of Woman*. There, it was with the Adversary himself that Wollstonecraft identified, against Milton and Eve: 'The domestic trifles of the day have afforded matters for cheerful converse', she writes regarding idealized visions of women's domesticity (*Rights of Woman*: 25). 'Similar feelings has Milton's pleasing picture of paradisiacal happiness ever raised in my mind', she continues. '[Y]et, instead of envying the lovely pair [Adam and Eve], I have with conscious dignity, or Satanic pride, turned to hell for sublimer objects'. Not Eve and the beautiful, but Satan and the sublime suit Wollstonecraft and her 'conscious dignity'. It is 'the contemplation of the noble struggles of suffering merit' – of 'an outcast of fortune, rising superior to passion and discontent' (at once Rousseauvian and Satanic) that wins her admiration. According to Polwhele, the transgressions of Female Philosophers sexualized them into fallen women, like Eve (they 'pluck forbidden fruit, with mother Eve' (8)). According to Female Philosophers like Wollstonecraft, Williams, Smith and Robinson, who also associated Satan's rebellion with feminist struggle, their ambitions elevated them to distinctly Romantic versions of the fallen but unrepentant Satan.[17] Allying themselves with the original Philosopher, as More saw him, these feminists demanded access to an expansive intellectual and political sphere made possible by the revolutionary crisis at home and abroad. Thus, even in face of widespread conservative demonization, the Female Philosopher's fortunate fall into forbidden knowledge, sexual and especially political, remained open to feminist redirection.

Embodying the Female Philosopher

Not all observers of this unfolding drama regarding women's interventions in the revolutionary crisis were as adamant in their condemnation of Female

Philosophers as were ideologues like More, West and Polwhele. Elizabeth Hamilton's *Memoirs of Modern Philosophers* (1800) and Amelia Opie's *Adeline Mowbray, or the Mother and Daughter* (1805) looked back to the 1790s controversies surrounding Hays and Wollstonecraft, and offered clear but qualified condemnations of the Female Philosophers, which avoided the extremes of the philosopher whore and Satanic Jacobin caricatures. Like their more conservative contemporaries, Hamilton and Opie maintained scrupulously asexual personal reputations, in part via their respective strict Christian faiths.[18] One of Hamilton's virtuous women in *Memoirs of Modern Philosophers* voices the author's conclusions regarding the appropriate scope of women's public political agency; lamenting the commodification of female sexuality that leads to so many impoverished fallen women, Mrs Fletcher proposes a solution:

> The government ought – but, alas! I cannot dictate to the government. I have not the power to influence the makers of our laws. But cannot I do something towards the relief of a few of these unhappy individuals?

Hamilton shows her virtuous Christian catching herself before committing the sin of pride that Female Philosophers consistently commit, in presuming to step out of their place and speak to government, of government. A far cry from Barbauld's insistence in 1792 that government 'is for YOURSELVES', and Wollstonecraft's call for female political representation that same year, Hamilton leaves government, philosophy and public politics to men of privilege, even while publicly urging that they submit to the doctrines of charitable Christianity. Her virtuous women like Mrs Fletcher and Harriet instead influence their world through a myriad of kinship and social relationships, largely charitable and domestic, and so contribute more to the general welfare than any of the novel's radical characters and their philosophy of 'general utility' and 'universal benevolence'.

These exemplary 'mothers of the nation', to use Mellor's formulation, stand in contrast to Hamilton's two Female Philosophers, Bridgetina Botherim and Julia Delmond, who rashly abandon the duties and joys of the 'domestic affections' for independence. Hamilton perceptively separates out two strands of the Female Philosopher phenomenon, according to their ability to fulfil the philosophical ur-romance of *La Nouvelle Héloïse*. The beautiful Julia inherits the sexualized liberation associated with *La Nouvelle Héloïse*, Wollstonecraft, and the seduced Eve. The ugly Bridgetina, physically unable to fulfil this philosophical romance, instead becomes a masculinized and oversexed spinster, associated with Mary Hays and Emma Courtney, whose sexual pursuit of the unresponsive hero Bridgetina parodies. In splitting Rousseau's Julie into two women – the eroticized beloved and the philosopher – Hamilton also wants to rule out the source of Julie's immense appeal (as an enlightened beloved) to generations of women readers and writers, making them choose (ideally the third choice, Harriet).

Bridgetina poisons Julia's mind with simplistic readings of Rousseau and Godwin, familiar tactics in 'Satanic Jacobin' narratives of the 1790s. And yet Hamilton is more sophisticated than many antiJacobin contemporaries, particularly in her understanding that sexualized beauty is a problematic element of the Female Philosopher controversy. The conclusion of *Memoirs of Modern Philosophers* presents us with a normatively patriarchal series of punishments and rewards for passion pursued and repressed: the sordid death of the fallen but repentant Julia, the gradual chastening of the ridiculous Bridgetina, and the idyllic marriage of the virtuous Harriet, the only one of the three who successfully repressed her sexual desires. After being seduced and abandoned by the Gallicized libertine Vallaton, Julia's death-bed repentance serves as object lesson for Bridgetina (and the female reader), according to the novel's sympathetic patriarch Mr Sydney. Mr Sydney warns Bridgetina that Julia's transformation from a beauty to a 'ghastly' wreck of her former self

> has been wrought...by the same delusive principles that have seduced you from the path of filial duty. Had nature bestowed upon you a form as beautiful, or a face as fair, you too would have been the prey of lust, and the victim of infamy. Be thankful that you have escaped a fate so dreadful. (364)

While Julia is a 'fair philosopher' seeking sexual independence from paternal control, Bridgetina is a 'female philosopher' who adapts the physical and intellectual habits of male philosophers like Godwin, and rejects all feminine duties (and ornament), to grotesque results (92, 202). Harriet, conversely, subordinates the mental accomplishments suitable to women – reading history and religious works – to domestic and religious duties, following More's prescriptions. Yet sexualized beauty remains central to all three heroines' varying abilities to fulfil the roles they pursue, and, in turn, to the appropriateness of each role.

Hamilton's forthright interest in sexuality and beauty as problematic elements, not only in the conventions of novel and romance but in the range of women's roles contested in the 1790s, illuminates the contradictions within her own domestic ideal, in ways that more ideologically rigid writers like More and West do not. *Memoirs of Modern Philosophers'* intriguing debate regarding Rousseau, Godwin and Wollstonecraft is unusual in its balanced assessment of the latter, resisting the temptation to caricature Wollstonecraft as a philosopher whore. Particularly significant is the novel's understanding of Wollstonecraft's critique of Rousseau, a careful political distinction among elements of the Modern Philosophy that most conservatives refused to grant, and one voiced by the novel's hero, Henry:

> 'I wonder', said Mrs Martha Goodwin, 'what Rousseau would have done with all the ordinary girls, for it is plain his system is adapted only

for beauties; and should any of these poor beauties fail in getting husbands, GOD help them, poor things, they would make very miserable old maids'.

'Beauty, madam', cried Bridgetina, 'is a consideration beneath the notice of a philosopher'... drawing up her long craggy neck so as to put the shriveled parchment-like skin which covered it upon the full stretch...'As to Rousseau, it is plain that he was a stranger to the rights of women.'

'The inconsistency and folly of his system', said Henry, 'was, perhaps, never better exposed than in the very ingenious publication which takes the Rights of Women for its title. Pity that the very sensible authoress has sometimes permitted her zeal to hurry her into expressions which have raised a prejudice against the whole. To superficial readers it appears to be her intention to unsex women entirely. But – '

'And why should there be any distinction of sex?' cried Bridgetina. (101)

Mrs Goodwin and Henry are sophisticated readers of Rousseau and Wollstonecraft; Bridgetina, on the other hand, is one of those 'superficial readers' who takes Wollstonecraft's critique too far. Thus Hamilton, in the politically polarized genre of counterrevolutionary novel, as Katherine Binhammer and Claire Grogan have each argued, makes a case for active reading; as Hamilton wrote in her own memoirs, 'It is only by the love of reading that the evils resulting from associating with little minds can be counteracted'.[19]

And yet behind this moderate appraisal of Wollstonecraft remains a consistent, and conventionally misogynist, association of Female Philosophy with unsexed and oversexed corporeality. Bridgetina and Julia both degenerate through their philosophical trespasses – a withered Bridgetina resembles the parchment she spends an inordinate amount of time with in her superficial studies, and Julia descends into poverty, abortion and self-destruction, marring her beauty in a classic dramatization of the wages of sin. Bridgetina abandons feminine adornment, decorum and even hygiene (consistent with earlier eighteenth-century caricatures of learned women)[20] in order to pose in 'the character of a female philosopher' (202). She also absurdly follows Godwin's (caricatured) system of 'mind over matter', putting into practice his precepts for the urban philosopher in *Political Justice* by walking long distances alone through city streets, with results both ridiculous and dangerous.

Beneath Bridgetina's superficiality and 'unsexed' behaviour lies the bedrock of immutable corporeal difference, an essential sexual difference that Hamilton connects to national and racial difference as well. The real lesson that Bridgetina fails to learn is not filial duty, as the narrator repeatedly complains, but that she is ugly. The Modern Philosophy she puts into practice is finally most absurd not because politically dangerous, but because stubbornly in denial of the 'nature' of (hetero)sexual attraction in modern, civilized and Christian England. The beautiful and consistently sympathetic Julia abandons herself to this 'natural' attraction through the feminist conviction that women should indulge their 'insatiable appetite for knowledge' (85). The pious Harriet sublimates her sexual desire into charitable duties. As for Bridgetina, 'she is neither *rich* nor *handsome*', and because of 'the deformity of her person' remains unmarried, unseducing and unseduced, neither a tragic nor a romantic heroine, and thus no type of English heroine at all (385, 255, orig. emphasis). Rather, Bridgetina's 'deformity' is both Gallicized and, as we shall see, Africanized, illustrating the degenerative effects of philosophy for Englishwomen.

This female Quixote's education consists in accepting lifelong celibacy, something she stubbornly resists. 'Regardless of the mere forms of matter', she reasons regarding her would-be lover,

> he would leave the unnatural admiration of beauty to the old, the dull, and the insensible; and seek for the object of his affections a discussing, reasoning, and an investigating mind. This is the true course of nature! This is the most sublime proof of the perfectibility of man! (218)

For Hamilton, a Female Philosopher like Bridgetina believing herself desirable to a romantic English hero is as absurd as the 'Hottentots' being mistaken for an enlightened civilization. 'Here is the Age of Reason exemplified' (142), enthuses Bridgetina after reading François LeVaillant's *Travels from the Cape of Good Hope* (1790), a French travel account of life among the indigenous people of the Cape, known to Europeans as Hottentots. Described as the inverse of British culture, the Hottentots naturally become the Philosophers' ideal destination in an emigration scheme. 'All our theory realized!' confirms one of the philosophers: 'Here is a whole nation of philosophers, all as wise as ourselves!...No man working for another! All alike! All equal! No laws! No government!...Take a wife today: leave her again tomorrow!' (141).

Deflating at once the Rousseauvian ideal of the noble savage and the enlightened self-image of Modern Philosophy as practised in republican France through this mutual displacement, Hamilton simultaneously aligns Bridgetina's denial of her physical ugliness with the Philosophers' denial of Hottentot barbarism. The narrative unfolds these painful lessons to both Bridgetina and the would-be emigrants, who are swindled out of their funds by a self-serving member of the French-style 'Hottentotian Committee' (161). Elevating the Hottentots to philosophers is shown to be absurd because their lives are utterly corporeal and beastlike, according to centuries of European and classical accounts. The Modern Philosophers' foolishness in seeing them as an 'enlightened race' (272) is a direct result of Godwinian Philosophy's disembodied, overrefined and impractical nature. '[H]ow nearly the extremes of barbarism and civilization are united', remarks a benevolent Christian patriarch later in the novel, comparing a dissipated 'modern fine gentleman' in a museum to the 'stupidity and indolence' of a 'savage' depicted in a painting (331–2). Bridgetina's resemblance to Hottentot femininity (characterized a decade later by the 'Hottentot Venus') and its unruly sexuality silently completes the comparison (of savage and overcivilized men) by extending it to women.

Within this racist morality lesson we have Bridgetina's refusal to accept the destiny to which her physical unattractiveness dooms her, in a novel ironically determined to correct Rousseau's sexualization of women. The parallels Hamilton draws between Hottentots, Modern Philosophers and the revolutionary French are distinctly gendered, for a key feature of these barbarisms is their shared failure to respect both private and sexual property, that is marriage, especially in its civilized British form. Hamilton's suggestive use of 'Hottentot' society to parody French-style republican utopias marshals the established racist associations of Hottentot representations for nationalist and antifeminist ends. English descriptions of the Cape people from the sixteenth century onwards played a significant role in the unresolved debates over the nature of racial and skin colour difference (whether the product of distinct creations, or of environmental differentiation from a common origin), and in burgeoning theories of national identity. By the seventeenth century, argues Linda Merians, 'both the people and the word [Hottentot] began to signify a racist ideology that stabilized the more crucial and complex fictions of England and of a superior English race' (140–1). Compared consistently in the seventeenth and eighteenth centuries to the native Irish and their increasingly racialized otherness that needed civilizing, moreover, 'Hottentot' by Hamilton's day signified a barbarism and sexual licence that verged on the inhuman, and one always implicitly contrasted to British nationalist self-identity.

Bridgetina's idealization of, and resemblance to, the people of the Cape connects her physical degeneration via Philosophy to Hottentot degeneration (via environment, according to many in the eighteenth century). Her sexualized grotesqueness thus mirrors Hottentot racialized grotesqueness, and raises the spectre of unbridled African female sexuality that had intrigued and horrified Europeans for centuries, culminating in the exhibition of Saartje Baartman, 'The Hottentot Venus', in England and France from 1810 to 1815. 'The antithesis of European sexual mores and beauty', according to Sander Gilman, the 'Hottentot Venus' became 'the central nineteenth-century icon for sexual difference between the European and the black' (212). In Hamilton's novel, then, the Female Philosopher embodies the antithesis of the civilized English woman, at once Gallicized and Africanized in her hypersexuality and 'deformity' (255), her vaunted intellect all but nonexistent.

Bridgetina's deformation also resembles that of French female republicans, as depicted in British satirical prints of the Terror. 'A Paris Belle' (1794) by Mary Stokes is typical of this ubiquitous British vision of French *sans culottes* women as both sexually and racially degenerate, taking on the physical characteristics associated with barbarity, and adorned with bloody daggers instead of the trappings of beauty (Illustration 2). 'A Republican Belle'

Des Tetes ! _ du Sang ! _ la Mort ! _ à la Lanterne ! _ à la Guillotine. _ point de Reine ! _ Je suis la Deesse de la Liberté ! _ l'egalite ! _ que Londres soit brulé ! _ que Paris soit Libre ! _ Vive la Guillotine ! _

Miss Mary Stokes delt.

A PARIS BELLE.

Pubd Febd 26th 1794, by H. Humphrey No. 18. Old Bond Street

Illustration 2 'A Paris Belle', Mary Stokes (1794). Copyright British Museum

of the same year similarly bestializes the female republican, situating her in a nightmarish France strewn with bones, where *sans culottes* play *pétanque* with skulls (Illustration 3). Callously shooting a fallen man, the Republican Belle looms larger than life in her muscular frame, distorted and dark facial features, and clawed feet, ornamented not with a cross and jewels, but with miniature guillotines. This vision of debased female agency would return to

Illustration 3   'A Republican Belle', Cruikshank (1794). Copyright British Museum

haunt the repentant illuminati Victor Frankenstein, causing him to destroy his female creature before she too could 'delight, for its own sake, in murder and wretchedness' and spawn 'a race of devils...who might make the very existence of the species of man a condition precarious and full of terror' (Shelley 160). As Malchow and Mellor have argued separately, *Frankenstein*'s racialized discourse of corporeal evil evokes distinct anxieties about miscegenation and empire.[21] And central to Frankenstein's vision, 'full of terror', of a race of female devils, are memories of *sans culottes* women in the Reign of Terror, whom Female Philosophers are in danger of resembling if they persist in emulating the French example.

A debased female corporeality thus links Modern Philosophers, barbarian Hottentots and French Jacobins. In other conservative 1790s novels, such false utopian visions of radical equality (France being the prime example) are also transposed onto primitive 'domestic others' like the Welsh, Irish and Scottish. For example, in *Dorothea*, the Female Philosopher rashly pursues her 'system' in a backward Wales, and the philosopher villain in Ireland, during the 1798 rebellion. Thus in 'Hamilton's fiction the "savage" state of the projected utopia confirms the "civilized" social and gender distinctions of the real one', as April London has argued (547). This aggressively 'politicized nationalism'(*ibid.*: 548) is consistently directed to and through women like Dorothea, Adelaide, Bridgetina and Julia, who follow French philosophical examples only to stray beyond the outer limits of English, European, female and finally white 'natural' identity, becoming versions of 'Republican Belles'. And as in other 1790s counterrevolutionary novels, the real target is the savage (because radically egalitarian) state of revolutionary France.

AntiJacobins eager to portray republican France as a dystopia also relied on the example provided by British ideological immigrants to revolutionary France like Tom Paine and the radical journalist Sampson Perry. These Modern Philosophers, like their Female Philosopher counterparts, provided anti-Jacobin novelists with a central plot device – the Gallicized English male radical who reaps the rewards of idealizing revolutionary utopia; that is, imprisonment, misery and (in fiction) the guillotine. Paine and Perry had both fled England in 1792 to avoid imprisonment, were convicted in absentia in December, and after immersing themselves in French revolutionary circles were imprisoned on suspicion of espionage during the Terror. Perry returned to England in March 1795 (after which he would resume publishing his suppressed journal *The Argus*, including work by Mary Robinson), and landed back in an English jail after spending 401 days in French prisons.[22] *The Oracle* moralized Perry's homecoming as a humiliation, complete with (invented) remorse:

> The *Jacobinical* system of France seduced him from his native country, and, in the miseries of the Revolution, he reveled for some time until he became obnoxious, *suspected* as an Englishman of being a friend of religion and Royalty.
>
> It was then that he felt the scourge which his own folly had invited. He was thrown into prison, and experienced all the horrors which massacres and perpetual dread and alarm occasioned. It was now high time to cast a longing eye to his native land...he arrived in London twelve days ago, inviting the abode of Newgate as an *asylum*, rather than dwell in the land of *discordant* and *merciless freedom*...

The conduct of this violent person, and his present situation [in jail], may serve as an useful lesson to all discontented or speculative persons in this country. (26 March 1795)

Foolishly 'in search of an happier clime' in France (*ibid.*), Perry serves as prototype for every antiJacobin villain, from Hamilton's Vallaton to West's Fitzosborn. Literally seduced by such traitors to their native land, Female Philosophers thus combine sexual and national treachery, a Gallicization that, as we saw, is also manifested as a corporeal deformation akin to that of Hottentots and 'Republican Belles'.

The grotesque results of Bridgetina's adherence to Godwinian practices, physical and philosophical, combined with her pursuit of Rousseauvian, revolutionary and 'primitive' passions, and her simultaneous advocacy of Wollstonecraftian feminism, illustrate the confounded mess that the 'Modern Philosophy' was in conservative eyes. And yet by embodying the heterogeneous nature of Modern Philosophy in the physically grotesque Bridgetina, Hamilton ironically makes it possible for readers to separate out the strands of this philosophy. Debates such as the one over the *Rights of Woman*, while always concluded by the assent to benevolent patriarchal authority, nevertheless distinguish *Memoirs of Modern Philosophers* as a counterrevolutionary novel willing to examine, even for rhetorical effect, the claims of radical and feminist philosophy in revolution-era Britain. Deeply engaged with political debates over the dangers of popular print culture, novel and romance, Hamilton distinguishes herself from More and West in the greater emphasis she places on discriminating, active reading. Like Hays and other feminists, argues Katherine Binhammer, Hamilton constructs 'the active female reader by shifting attention from *what* a woman reads to *how* she reads' ('Persistence' 5, orig. emphasis). Hamilton's conflicted critical reception, reflecting reviewers' discomfort with her advocacy of women's education and her forthright discussion of revolutionary politics, likewise set her apart from her more militant counterparts, even while she enjoyed the praise of other conservative writers like Maria Edgeworth, who noted approvingly that '[s]he does not aim at making women expert in the wordy war; nor does she teach them to astonish the unlearned by their acquaintance with the various vocabulary of metaphysical system-makers'.[23]

West and More were more pessimistic regarding the effects of print culture than Hamilton, even though both were popular and prolific writers. Only orthodox religion offered an antidote to the temptations of intellect for West and More, so that even in their advocacy of women's increased education, they remained deeply suspicious of intellectual pursuits. Intellectual pride was Eve's undoing, and since Satanic Jacobins, like the first Jacobin Satan, cannot be defeated in rational debate, they must be rejected outright on religious grounds. Determined to 'convince the younger part of my readers of the necessity of shutting their ears to the syren song' of philosophy, West directs readers to the 'rock of religion' (*Tale* 2: 149, 239).

Knowledge versus Duty was the opposition governing the counterrevolution-ary writings of More, West and Hamilton. Hamilton resolves British women's (and Eve's) choice between the two by subordinating one to the other: *'the knowledge of their duty'*, stresses Harriet's father, and Harriet assents (*Memoirs* 344, orig. emphasis). More similarly insisted, quoting Adam in *Paradise Lost*, that 'the most appropriate branch of female knowledge [...is] "household good"'(*Coelebs* 1: 2). Secular Knowledge divorced from Christian Duty smacks of Satanic scepticism. 'I cannot conceive of a greater compliment than to be compared to the Devil', enthuses Hamilton's philosopher Mr Glib: 'You do not know in what high estimation his character is held by modern philosophers' (357). Hamilton even offers a Christian alternative to this Satanic Mod-ern Philosophy: the Ancient Philosophy, and its first philosopher, Jesus Christ:

> He was the first philosopher who placed the female character in a respectable point of view. Women, we learn from the gospels, frequently composed a great part of his audience: but to them no particular precepts were addressed, no sexual virtues recommended. (103)

Like Macaulay, Hays and Wollstonecraft, who denied the existence of 'sexual' (sex-specific) virtues, Hamilton offers a vision of equality in God that resembles that of her rational Dissenting contemporaries. Yet in sanctioning divinely ordained distinctions, Hamilton is much closer to writers like More and West, who like Hamilton rejected the rationalist feminist insistence that Duty be subjected to the critique of Knowledge. West's contrast between the 'Saviour of the World' and 'the citizen of the world, who affects to despise the distinctions which the Lord of Life has sanctioned' similarly posited her conservative version of Christianity as the sole arbiter of worldly, especially international, politics (*Letters* 2: 478–9). These counterrevolutionary writers were the *avant-garde* of the '"feminisation" of religion...widely observed across Europe in the nineteenth century' (Rendall 73), who, as Polwhele had promised in 1798, would be rewarded with a 'vast...influence o'er the social ties' (32).

Loyal subjects and good Christians

Amelia Opie offered an even more ambivalent examination of the Female Philosopher in *Adeline Mowbray*. In the 1790s, Opie had been part of the same radical Dissenting circle as Godwin and Wollstonecraft, but her marriage to the society painter John Opie in 1798 and her conversion to Quakerism in 1824 signalled departures from her earlier support of radical politics. *Adeline Mowbray* is loosely based on Godwin and Wollstonecraft's courtship and is generally read as a repudiation of radical principles, if not a betrayal of her former friends, given the tragic conclusion of their marriage. In Opie's novel, the Modern Philosopher Glenmurray and the heroine Adeline live together outside of marriage with predictably tragic results, including Adeline's deathbed recantation. Yet instead of a traditional antiJacobin diatribe against such a fall into vice, Opie offers a complex critique of the 'hypocritical society which shuns the lovers', a society that as Roxanne Eberle has argued, appears 'incapable of understanding the true nature of intellectual thought', and in which marriage is characterized by 'bigamy, deceit', and inequality (135). The fallen but virtuous Female Philosopher Adeline is thus destroyed not by the contradictions of reason and passion thought natural to women, but by a society that moves violently against those who threaten its privileged illusions, chiefly marriage.

Unusually, Opie's Female Philosopher had read the radical philosophical canon as a male reader would, applying Rousseau, Montesquieu and Voltaire's claims of universal reason and rights to women:

> Adeline had…read Rousseau's *Social Contract*, but not his *Julie*; Montesquieu's *Esprit de Lois*, but not his *Lettres Persanes*; and had glowed with republican ardour over the scenes of Voltaire's *Brutus*, but had never had her mind polluted by the pages of his romances. (57)

A major departure from the sexualized Female Philosophers of most counter-revolutionary writers, *Adeline Mowbray* grants Wollstonecraft's philosophical struggle a rare dignity and seriousness despite the narrative's denouement. Adeline's practical application of new philosophy's 'forbidden doctrines' is a fatal mistake, and in her deathbed recantation she repudiates her intellectual rebellion against marriage as potentially destructive 'of the whole fabric of civilized society' (42, 244). Yet ultimately, argues Eberle provocatively, '*Adeline Mowbray* is not a condemnation of Wollstonecraft but rather a call for more texts like *The Vindication of the Rights of Woman* and the *Wrongs of Woman; or, Maria*' (128). But the 1798 *Wrongs of Woman* and the *Memoirs* had linked the philosophical claims of the *Rights of Woman* with the taint of licentiousness that Adeline cannot escape. It thus seems impossible that in 1805 Opie would advocate such a return to a feminism historically beyond reach; that is, that of the 'unfallen', undisgraced 1792 Wollstonecraft. In 1803, the anonymous *Defence of the Character and Conduct of the Late Mary Wollstonecraft Godwin*, probably the boldest defence of the feminist in the Romantic period, concluded much the same as did *Adeline Mowbray* regarding society's hostility to the enlightened 'system' of the Female Philosopher: 'Her's is certainly founded in Nature and Reason, and so far is consistent with Truth; it is therefore well adapted for the conscientious Moralist and Philosopher: but it is inapplicable to persons of gross appetites and vulgar apprehensions; that is, to the great mass of mankind.'[24] Adeline is thus the tragic example of a Wollstonecraftian Female Philosopher in a post-revolutionary world, where advocating radical feminist principles, or radical republicanism, courts certain disaster.

Opie's alternative to idealized marriage (the response to the Female Philosopher's challenge in Hamilton, Opie and More) is the all-female, interracial household of Rosevalley, including the fugitive slave (now devoted servant) Savanna, the novel's boldest speaker in defence of women. Anne Mellor reads Opie's Rosevalley as a female utopia that rejects 'the masculinized political realm altogether as irredeemably brutal, corrupt, and self-destructive' (*Mothers*: 105). And yet this same female world 'entirely cut off from the masculine "public sphere"', warns Eberle, 'threatens to become the claustrophobic space of the "domestic sphere" later in the century' (146). Uniting 'moral motherhood and sentimental abolitionism', *Adeline Mowbray*'s Rosevalley replaces paternalism with a 'civilized and honorable form of life-long servitude', that, according to Carol Howard, nostalgically reconstructs a female 'society of docile laborers and benevolent land-owners' (364–5). The ambiguities of Savanna's rebellion, on the one hand, and her selfless devotion to Adeline on the other (and the ease with which Opie disappears Savanna's family so that Savanna can serve Adeline's), leaves in the wake of the Female Philosopher's failed system the familiar notion of philanthropic gentry (and what Spivak termed 'colonialist benevolence' (161)) popularized by conservative writers like More, Hamilton and Sarah Scott (in *Millennium Hall*).[25]

The retreat from public politics and practical philosophy in *Adeline Mowbray* mirrors what conservatives throughout the 1790s advocated as the proper course for women to follow: individual acts of charity and not general utility, according to Hamilton; Christian self-improvement and not political reform, according to More.[26] The narrator of *Dorothea; or, A Ray of the New Light*, had identified Wollstonecraft's 1798 *Memoirs* as the watershed after which the public roles available to women have been inevitably curtailed given Wollstonecraft's fate (1: 130). Thus the redeemed 'fair democrat' (1: 35) in *Dorothea* concedes

> without reluctance, to abdicate the rights of equality…whilst she confines the energy of her mind within the gentle bonds of domestic cares and pleasures, and employs her active spirit, not in awakening discontent and rebellion amongst her poorer neighbors, but in ameliorating their situation. (2: 237)

No longer 'sons and daughters of liberty', but 'loyal subjects, and good Christians' (*Dorothea* 2: 240) are the only roles available according to counterrevolutionary women writers.

Excluded from these categories are political writers who do not primarily claim authority from this stance of 'loyal subjects' and 'good Christians': cosmopolitan, Francophilic or otherwise antinationalist writers who, like Barbauld, promote 'active citizens' and not subjects; 'daughters of liberty' like (the prerepentant) Adeline Mowbray and Mary Robinson (whose pseudonyms included 'A Daughter of Liberty'), who traced their arguments to radical French political traditions, not organized religion; 'philosophers' like Wollstonecraft who sought to 'make women rational creatures, and free citizens' (*Rights of Woman* 178). Despite More's success in the public sphere, she never advocated that others, especially women or plebeians in general, should take up the pen and follow her example of dictating virtuous behaviour (indeed, she insisted that her Sunday Schools taught the poor to read, not to write). In fact, More proved a harsh patron to the plebeian poet Anne Yearsley when Yearsley began exerting her financial and editorial independence from the genteel More, who maintained rigid notions of how the working classes ought to behave.

In submitting all political claims to religious duty and doctrine, More, Hamilton, West and even Opie foreclosed women's unprecedented access to secular political and philosophical discourse, whether militantly in More's case, satirically in Hamilton's, or more ambivalently in Opie's. More than mere rhetoric, this repeated humbling of Female Philosophy's claims before those of loyal subjects and good Christians gave the deathblow to an early humanist and rationalist feminist tradition that had flourished in the 1790s. Drawn from the rational Dissenting Christian tradition and often adamant about the claims of passion alongside reason, these Female Philosophers nevertheless placed rational critique (even of reason's dominion) at the centre of their liberatory visions. They were secular and humanistic, because while they generally claimed that universal equality ultimately derived from a divine source (and that sexual oppression violated God's will), they addressed equality in a humanistic, political and earthly sphere, without requiring that their readers share their religious convictions or nationalist sentiments, and without internalizing politics via the rhetoric of personal sin and salvation. Laws and government were human-made, not God-made, argued Barbauld in *Civic Sermons*, and should be reformed, here and now. Even her passionate defence of the centrality of public worship to civic life was framed in humanistic terms: 'It is of service to the cause of freedom therefore . . . that there is one place where the invidious distinctions of wealth and titles are not admitted; where all are equal . . . Every time Social Worship is celebrated, it includes a virtual declaration of the rights of man.'[27]

In contrast, More's hostility to political reform was in part grounded in her belief that the poor would receive heavenly recompense for earthly inequalities: 'I read my Bible, go to church, and look forward to a treasure in Heaven', says the pious blacksmith in *Village Politics*; 'Ay, but the French have got it in *this* world', complains the deluded mason, who will be converted to loyal subject and good Christian (361, orig. emphasis). As loyal subject and good Christian became synonymous (a conflation anathema to rational Dissenters, who continued to struggle for more inclusive notions of religion), so did women's writings need to be confined to this increasingly narrow continuum. In her novel set in revolutionary France, *Julia, and the Illuminated*

Baron (1800), the American writer Sarah Wood justified her political intervention (in a European matter, no less) on religious grounds, a familiar move in counterrevolutionary women's writings: 'I am apprehensive from the perusal of the title page, that JULIA may, by some, be considered, a political work; as I have ever hated female politicians, I think it absolutely necessary to declare it is not' (vii). Entirely

> unacquainted with politics, I should have viewed a revolution of the greatest part of Europe as it respected them, with unconcern and indifference...But when we see the greatest part of the world, throwing off the shackles of religion, and becoming by profession, as well as by precept, infidels; it is impossible not to consider it as a revolution from piety and from morality; and leaving politics intirely [*sic*] out of sight, we shudder at the present view. (vii–viii)

There is nothing remarkable in women writing publicly and politically from positions of religious authority, as this is one of the oldest Western traditions of women's public speech and writing (as well as being the oldest tradition prohibiting women's speech and writing). But as a reaction to 1790s Female Philosophers who had carved out a new role from different philosophical (humanist, rationalist, Francophilic) traditions and at great personal risk, these retreats into Christian loyalism, enforced by repressive laws and accompanied by contempt for 'female politicians' who entered into this same debate from different perspectives, resulted in the negation of hard-won liberties that would be unavailable again for many decades.

The forays of Female Philosophers into French Enlightenment philosophy marked an important advance in women's access to and involvement in continental political debates. The counterrevolutionary backlash that engulfed them, along with male radicals and reformers, increasingly demanded that British subjects prove their loyalty, in part by cultivating a xenophobia, and more specifically, a Francophobia. Masterminded by such formidable literary innovators as Hannah More, and enforced by the series of repressive laws curtailing freedom of speech, publication, foreign correspondence, association and *habeas corpus*, the conservative backlash in the 1790s 'word war' succeeded in making terms like 'liberty' and 'patriot' suspect. As Charlotte Smith complained in *The Emigrants* (1793), 'the very name of Liberty has not only lost the charm it used to have in British ears, but many, who have written, or spoken, in its defence, have been stigmatized as promoters of Anarchy, and enemies to the prosperity of their country' (*Poems* 134).

More's didactic pamphlets directed at the disgruntled plebeian population, distributed by the government by the tens of thousands, were central to this successful stigmatization of the Francophilic language of reform, as this counterrevolutionary catechism from *Village Politics* illustrates:

Tom. What is it to be *an enlightened people?*

Jack. To put out the light of the gospel, confound right and wrong, and grope about in pitch darkness.

Tom. What is *philosophy*, that Tim Standish talks so much about?

Jack. To believe that there's neither God, nor devil, nor heaven, nor hell: to dig up a wicked old fellow's rotten bones, whose books, Sir John says, have been the ruin of thousands; and to set his figure up in a church and worship him.

Tom. And what is a *patriot* according to the new school?

Jack. A man who loves every other country better then his own, and France best of all.

(363–4, orig. emphasis)

'Philosophy', 'an enlightened people', 'patriot': what in other eras or circumstances British patriots could have boasted of, counterrevolutionary writers made synonymous with atheism, Satanism, licentiousness and finally treason. It is with this striking contrast in mind that we should consider Female Philosophers' impressive persistence in carving out such politicized public roles in the face of increasingly xenophobic pressures to remain loyal subjects and good Christians.

Internationalism

The feminism of radical women entering into the 1790s 'word war' was internationalist in outlook and origin. In part this was because these 'Female Philosophers', 'female politicians' and 'unsexed females' generally supported and shared links with both the abolition and antiwar movements. These social movements also accommodated politically conservative and traditional positions on issues of gender, class and religion, hence the clashes within such groups whenever we isolate one particular issue (for example, women's education in More and Wollstonecraft, or the rights of 'poor people' to influence government in Barbauld and More). In focusing on the French Revolution's impact on British women's political writing, I have tried to demonstrate how the Revolution and revolutionary wars continued to expand the horizons of British women writers' imaginations and influence. Internationalism and universalism were present in abolition and Christian Dissent broadly conceived, yet so were nationalism and xenophobia. It was ultimately the Tory Clapham sect of Wilberforce and More that successfully pushed abolition through parliament, and who as Nigel Leask notes, 'were anxious to distance their campaign from discredited radical dissent' and religious rivals like the Unitarians who were characteristically universalist (447).

It is thus particularly important to discriminate between the varieties of Christianity through which some women claimed authority to speak in the revolutionary crisis. The nationalist providentialism of Grant, West and

More (and of the prophetess Joanna Southcott), bears little resemblance to the universalism of Hays' and Barbauld's Unitarianism (which itself often takes a back seat to their civic identities). More's and Hamilton's brands of Anglican evangelicalism and Episcopalian Presbyterianism, respectively, are preoccupied with sin and personal salvation, and share little with Wollstonecraft's and Barbauld's association of divinity with passion.[28] These varied approaches to Christianity translated into radically different political positions, perhaps most divisively so on the issue of the war against France.

The abolition movement was similarly divided by its relationship to the war and to the discourse of natural rights on which many pro-revolutionary abolitionists relied. Rare were the occasions when the Jacobin Republic in particular could be recommended as an example for British emulation by politically moderate Britons. Watkin Tench, a British naval officer imprisoned in France during the Terror, published an account of his experiences that is unusually fair-minded about French politics and the questionable claims of British patriotism. Candid about England's hypocrisy regarding slavery, Tench took the unusual further step in granting the government of Robespierre (an abolition supporter) due credit in this regard. The Jacobin Republic had abolished slavery in its colonies on 4 February 1794, and all former male slaves were granted French citizenship (free black men had been enfranchised in 1792). In the National Convention, Danton used France's abolition of slavery to accuse England of gaining its commercial wealth from slavery; while Tench disagreed, he recognized the irresolvable contradiction in Britain's engagement in a war on the grounds of defending 'British liberty', while it continued slavery and the slave trade in its colonies, unlike republican France. 'If the opulence of England be founded on the basis of African slavery', he wrote, 'if the productions of the tropics can be dispensed to us only by the blood and tears of the negro, I do not hesitate to exclaim – "Perish our commerce; let our humanity live!" ' (108). In extending male suffrage and citizenship across racial and religious lines, the example of France presented Britain with a stark contrast, particularly for those supporting abolition of the slave trade but opposed to democratization at home.

Throughout the 1780s, the British Society for the Abolition of the Slave Trade had pursued an intensifying campaign for abolishing the slave trade through petitions and boycotts, and as Helen Thomas argues, this campaign was successful because of 'its *internationalist* agenda and . . . its links with the increasingly popular tenets of radical dissenting Protestantism' (35, orig. emphasis). As David Brion Davis has documented, 'Les Amis des Noirs' in Paris and the British Society for the Abolition of the Slave Trade both looked to the 'antislavery international' established earlier by the Quakers' transatlantic commercial links (see Davis 213–54). Yet the internationalism driving white abolitionism also coexisted with a self-serving nationalist motivation that offered a 'patriotic image of Britain as a freedom-loving people' and sought to contain commercialism in ways consistent with conservative Anglican and Tory interests, such as those of More's Clapham Sect (Hudson 560). White abolitionism shifted into new forms of colonial domination at the turn of the nineteenth century (through the Clapham Sect's missionary activities and forced 'repatriation' schemes, as in Sierra Leone), because its internationalism was inseparable from larger strategies of imperial and commercial expansion. After all, while European cosmopolitanism became associated with radical egalitarianism in the 1790s, the cosmopolitan tradition nevertheless remained compatible with commercial and even imperial expansion, a continuation of elite Enlightenment cosmopolitanism. What is significant to note is how the war with France seemed simultaneously to curtail the international dimensions of British culture (through legislation and public pressure), even as it intensified them, discursively through popular debates on the European and global dimensions of the crisis, and literally through Britain's widening colonial struggle with France and alliances with other monarchies.

Abolition was to suffer from the very internationalism that had been its strength in the 1780s, for the perceived links between British abolition and French claims for universal rights finally scuppered the 1792 parliamentary drive. Watkin Tench, in his contrast of the Jacobin Republic's abolition of slavery and Britain's ongoing profits from it, is a rare example of a patriotic British observer willing even to consider the Jacobin Republic's potential lessons for the British nation. Helen Maria Williams was even bolder in her insistence that Francophobic British nationalism cannot deny its connections with the slave trade:

> Ah, let us, till the slave-trade no longer stains the British name, be more gentle in our censures of other nations! I know not how that partial morality can be justified, which measures right and wrong by geographical divisions; and, while it pours forth the bitterest of declamation against the human crimes in France, sanctions them in Africa. (*Letters* 2: 4:176–7)

All liberatory movements, abolition included, that could be associated with the French cause were suspect after 1793. Napoleon's later opposition to abolition helped make the cause acceptable to Parliament, part of British abolition's successful strategic shift away from the revolutionary implications of internationalism and towards the imperialist benefits of nationalism.

Female Philosophers and Modern Philosophers were the most visible examples of British radicals who deliberately associated themselves with a revolutionary cosmopolitanism in the face of an ever-growing xenophobic loyalism. National and 'geographic divisions' were increasingly strictly patrolled, not only literally, in the Alien Act, trade embargoes and criminalization of international correspondence that the British government legislated in the 1790s, but in literature, theatre and culture at large. Committed feminist cosmopolitans like Hays, Wollstonecraft and Williams went against great public pressure, codified in criminal laws, in critiquing British nationalism from consistently Francophilic perspectives. While the secular and civic public roles created by these Female Philosophers, like 1790s abolitionism, faced strong opposition because of their unabashed internationalism, as I discuss in the Epilogue, Female Philosophers' Francophilic internationalism established an unappreciated feminist legacy that continues into the twenty-first century.

2
Mary Robinson and Radical Politics: The French Connection

> In proportion as women are acquainted with the languages they will become citizens of the world. The laws, customs and inhabitants of different nations will be their kindred in the propinquity of nature.
>
> Mary Robinson, *A Letter to the Women*
> *of England on the Injustice of Mental Subordination* (1799)

A Female Philosopher who continued to praise Wollstonecraft in print after the publication of the latter's scandalous *Memoirs*, Mary Robinson remains a chameleon figure in modern accounts of Romanticism, radicalism and feminism. Robinson's numerous pseudonyms and generic versatility contribute to the current critical emphasis on her performative literary personas; she cultivated a 'Romantic theatricality' and aesthetic of sensibility that as Judith Pascoe, Stuart Curran, Jerome McGann and others have persuasively argued, invites us to reconsider William Wordsworth's Romanticism of authenticity as an alternative to Robinson's powerful precedent.[1] Robinson published widely: newspaper poetry in the Della Cruscan circle, popular Gothic romances, an ambitious sonnet series in *Sappho and Phaon* (1796), poems of social and existential crisis in *Literary Tales* (1800). Robinson's political reputation is as diffuse as her literary identities are numerous: having campaigned for Fox in the Westminster election of 1784, she also defended Marie Antoinette in *Monody to the Memory of the Late Queen of France* (1793), and faced conservative ire in such 'Jacobin' novels as *Walsingham* (1797) and *The Natural Daughter* (1799). The author of poems in favour of abolition, Robinson also had a lengthy relationship with Banastre Tarleton, a prominent Whig supporter of the Liverpool slave trade, for whom she may have written antiabolition speeches. A friend of Edmund Burke who studied at Hannah More's academy, Robinson publicized these elite connections even while she cultivated the friendships of notorious radicals like Wollstonecraft, Godwin and Robert Merry.

Robinson's political affinities, and the familiar contours of her body of work, situate her comfortably as a liberal Whig, broadly in support of the early stages of the Revolution, but, beyond her sexual politics, not a radical writer. Yet if we consider 1790s reform along the eclectic, fragmented outlines described by Mark Philp (not as a coherent 'movement'), and if we investigate further into Robinson's involvements in print culture, we can also see how she moved closer to supporting popular reform throughout the 1790s. It is easy to imagine the prerevolutionary Robinson enjoying the 'latitudinarian culture of the political elite' in which Burke and Paine, for example, could collegially discuss the merits of American independence (Philp, 'English Republicanism', 250). But once the Revolution controversy began, outlines Mark Philp, 'those seeking reform and a greater parity of representation were represented as irresponsible revolutionists and were rhetorically tainted with French republicanism in its most virulent form' (250). Yet Robinson continually associated herself with this Gallicized radicalism, an ideologically and rhetorically diverse tradition that, like that of Modern Philosophy, was 'wholly imprecise' except as a hostile formulation in the counterrevolutionary writings of loyalists (257).

Robinson's connections to Whig politicians like Fox and Sheridan are well-known, in part because Robinson wanted them so in order to increase her social standing through her sexual alliances with these powerful men. Yet the resulting further supposition – that she was not engaged with more radical aspects of 1790s reform – can create a critical blindness, or at the least a disregard, for evidence to the contrary. Part of this disregard stems from the general neglect of her novels and non-fiction prose, and the as yet unmined wealth of her unattributed newspaper publications. The issue here goes beyond Robinson and our estimation of her works and politics. I am interested in Robinson as a test case of how much, and what kind of work still needs to be done before we can propose master narratives to encompass women's writing in this period.

Robinson's consistent praise of French politics, culture, literature and gender relations ran against the grain of Britain's increasing nationalism. This Francophilia provides both an overlooked consistency (like her theatrical self-fashioning) in her literary endeavours, and a catalyst for her radicalization. Initiated by her positive experiences in *ancien régime* France, Robinson's ongoing exploration of French intellectual and political traditions in her prose and poetry became a key component of her literary aspirations, particularly as they relate to women. Robinson's praise of France's salon culture and its feminized aristocracy is central to such texts as *A Monody to the Memory of the Late Queen of France* (1793) and the radical feminist *Letter to the Women of England on the Injustice of Mental Subordination* (1799). Yet her Francophilia does not represent a nostalgic return to an earlier aristocratic cosmopolitanism in the face of a progressive, bourgeois British nationalism. In pamphlets such as the *Impartial Reflections on the Late Queen of France* (1791) and *A Letter to the Women of England*, novels like *Angelina* (1796), *Walsingham* (1797), *The Widow* (1794) and *The Natural Daughter* (1799), and poems like *Ainsi va le monde* (1790), Robinson deliberately challenges the increasingly nationalist tenor of British politics by offering a radical and feminist critique of class and gender privilege: a revolutionary cosmopolitanism that she shared with her fellow Female Philosophers. More so than Wollstonecraft and even Hays, Robinson deserves reconsideration as a so-called 'Anglo-American' feminist whose Francophilia facilitated her continual efforts to bridge the division between difference and equality that preoccupied nineteenth and twentieth-century feminism.

Boldly advocating the Rights of Woman, like Wollstonecraft and Smith, Robinson also had much to say on the sexual (and national) constraints implicit in the Rights of Man controversy. Women's involvement in 1790s radical politics continues to interest scholars trying to account for the gendered dimensions of the Rights of Man. Because of the exclusionary nature of the Rights of Man, it remains difficult to find significant traces of British women's involvement with organizations such as the corresponding societies and other publicly identifiable radical groups.[2] Regarding this gender impasse in working-class radicalism, Anna Clark has argued in *The Struggle for the Breeches* that

> Since its inception, plebeian radicalism had encompassed two divergent traditions, Painite egalitarianism and civic humanism, which had very different implications for gender politics. Paine's notion of inherent human rights broke free from the conventions of political thought, and...opened up the possibility of female citizenship. Instead of following this path, plebeian radicals combined the fraternal solidarity of their old artisan culture with the masculine rhetoric of civic humanism to demand radical male citizenship. (157)

Clark's incisive examination of the divergent paths within plebeian radicalism is useful to keep in mind when considering the dilemma of middle and upper-class women like Robinson, Wollstonecraft, and Smith, broadly sympathetic towards a republican tradition that, in both its plebeian and bourgeois formations, increasingly excluded them in theory and practice. Rejecting the notion of a nostalgic golden age of the patriarchal 'free-born Briton', these educated feminists instead looked forward and across the channel for these liberties, reinventing the citizen of the world ideal in the process.

'The citizen of the world is the only true philosopher', says Robinson's eponymous hero in *Walsingham*: 'he examines without prejudice; he judges from experience' (2: 199). Significantly, Robinson's 'citizen of the world' is available to women also, for as her female protagonist advised in her novel of the French Revolution, *Hubert de Sevrac*, 'To become a perfect citizen of the world, every minute particle of creation should be deemed worthy of investigation' (1: 296). A Scottish Protestant married to a French Catholic aristocrat, the émigrée Emily de Sevrac resembles the binational heroines in

Charlotte Smith's fiction, and readily accepts the Revolution's unveiling of the misery that made possible her family's privilege, 'a transient scene of delusive pleasure' (2: 211). As a citizen of the world pursuing 'universal knowledge' (1: 192) through transnational connections and travel, Emily embodies the fusion of internationalism, rationalism and sensibility that Robinson hoped would minimize the distinctions of rank and sex, her most consistent political targets.

While these feminists struggled to gain access to what Mary Hays termed the 'right to reason' (*Letters* 84–5), Anna Clark has shown how male radicals in the 1790s struggled to forge a political and class identity in significant degree through their masculinity: for example, through displays of homophobia, libertinism or sexual respectability. The appeal of Paine's 'rights of man', however, was through universal reason, not through men's God-given role as fathers and husbands, that is as patriarchs. While a long feminist tradition has dismissed universal reason as a 'false universal'[3] that implicitly excluded nonreasoning beings like women and non-Europeans, as we saw in Chapter 1, Enlightenment rationalism appealed strongly to Female Philosophers. 'In the abstract', argues Clark, 'Paine's notion of citizenship could apply to women because it was not essentially dependent on the association of masculinity with the power of the head of household' (145). Painite reason was one means to enfranchisement for both radicalism and feminism, but equally significant was the impact of the French Enlightenment, itself historically intertwined with earlier British thinkers like Locke, Newton and Bacon. Though they widely rejected the counterrevolutionary epithet of 'Jacobin', the English 'Jacobins' with whom Robinson was associated (personally as well as in the press), despite their varied evocations of nationalist liberty, were engaged in an 'implicitly international' project that she shared (Philp, 'Fragmented Ideology', 69).

The free-born Briton ideal found in the writings of radicals like Price and Priestley used the myth of the Norman Yoke in ways generally not available to women, by projecting into the Anglo-Saxon past a democratic golden age of consensual, constitutional government. As Stephen Behrendt argues, for women 'there could be little solace in the Radical yearning for a return to the Anglo-Saxon ideal that had no more place for them than the contemporary socio-political structure seemed to have' (85). The consensus among late eighteenth-century historians, particularly of the Scottish and French enlightenment, held that 'the brutalized condition of "savage" women marked the distance that had to be traveled in the achievement of a desirable civil society' (Rendall, 'Tacitus Engendered', 63). While a minority projected into the past a 'Gothic feminism' native to northern Europe, as Jane Rendall has argued, '[i]t was to be the modernizing and "Anglo-British" [not Germanic or Norman] version of the nation's history which dominated by the end of the eighteenth century' (66). This then was the quandary faced by women writers like Robinson, Smith, and Wollstonecraft, whose politics and feminism grew increasingly more radical throughout their careers, even as radicalism grew increasingly masculinist and nationalist. Robinson's response (while remaining committed to the progressive effects of commerce and enlightenment) was to create a mythic golden age in which women *were* pre-eminent – the French salon culture of the *ancien régime* – as a feminist alternative to the Norman Yoke argument.

Robinson was unique among Romantic-era feminists in the way she attempted to fuse discredited aspects of *ancien régime* courtly culture (the salon and the empire of beauty) with bourgeois and Enlightenment models of women's equality through reason. The latter aspect of her political aesthetic she shared with her friends Wollstonecraft and Godwin, but unlike them she remained committed to recuperating the refinement and splendour associated with elite women's idealized role in polite culture, especially in France. Also drawing together 'feminine' and 'masculine' discourses and experiences, Robinson's contemporary Mary Hays had insisted on the dialectic between passion and reason in her literary dialogue with Wollstonecraft and Godwin, *The Memoirs of Emma Courtney*. Robinson similarly drew on radical, ostensibly 'masculine', discourses of reason and universal equality, while insisting on women's deserved 'pre-eminence' within what she described as the 'Aristocracy of Genius'. I have discussed the contradictions within Robinson's Aristocracy of Genius in *Fatal Women of Romanticism*; I introduce this paradox here as a feminist example of the 'fragmented ideology of reform' traced by Mark Philp. Philp discounts oversimplified notions of 'a sufficiently discrete entity, "the reform movement"', because of the contested connections between the French and British contexts throughout the 1790s. 'Much of the argument and rhetoric of the 1790s', Philp argues, 'revolves around the presence or absence of a link between principles and practice in France', and the absence or presence of a link between French and British reform ('Fragmented' 59). Robinson's under-appreciated radicalism, her celebrated radical feminism, and her consistent Francophilia (*ancien régime* and revolutionary), ideally situate her in order to interrogate this 'fragmented ideology of reform' along not only national and class lines, as in Philp, but also according to gender.

Because of its unique aspects, Robinson's prolific career challenges our assumptions of how to place women writers along the political spectrum of the 1790s. Reading Robinson's neglected prose, her occasional poetry and hitherto unattributed anonymous texts, this chapter aims to illuminate an unfamiliar Robinson by shifting our focus to her considerable engagement with radical print culture. The specifics of Robinson's publishing history can bring out new readings of the texts in question, even increasingly well-known novels like *Walsingham*. Robinson's involvement in newspaper and periodical publishing is well-known, yet the extent of her unsigned and pseudonymous works in these media remains unclear, though it is thought to be extensive. Beginning with an examination of occasional poems

Robinson published in the mid-1790s, I will then focus on the national crisis of 1797, through which I make a case for new pseudonyms that I suggest Robinson used to write politically charged contributions to newspapers, even more incisive than those by her persona 'Tabitha Bramble'. Most of the poetry discussed in this chapter remained uncollected in the posthumous *Poetical Works* edited by her daughter, and is as yet unexamined by modern scholars. Within this new understanding of Robinson's involvement in radical print culture, I then resituate her 1790s novels in relation to the popular press, where Robinson reprinted excerpts and poems from her novels.

In the final section, I follow a Francophilic thread through her poetry, novels, and essays, in order to better situate her writings in the tradition of 1790s republicanism and its resistance to British nationalism. French culture appealed to Robinson in its dual (some would say mutually exclusive) late eighteenth-century aspects: both in the *ancien régime* connotations of aristocracy and femininity, and in its republican association with rational philosophy and political egalitarianism. Both of these aspects of French culture were vilified in 1790s Britain, often simultaneously. Robinson attempted to combine these opposed aspects of French culture into an idealized, cosmo-politan and politically radical alternative to British culture. It is via this Francophilia, moreover, that Robinson's distinctly feminist critique of British radicalism and its often gendered notions of rights and liberties emerges most clearly. This then is Robinson's unique value for our understandings of British radical culture and its relationship to the French Revolution, in addition to her work's sexual politics and theatrical self-fashioning. Just as theatricality remained a mutable constant throughout her literary development, so did Francophilia, itself of course associated with *ancien régime* artifice and spectacle, but increasingly in the 1790s, with that other dangerous import, revolutionary cosmopolitanism.

Robinson's occasional poems

Judith Pascoe's edition of Robinson's *Selected Poems* and Caroline Franklin's facsimile reprint of Robinson's posthumous *Poetical Works* published by her daughter in 1806, have proved immensely helpful to scholars reassessing Robinson's significance as a Romantic poet. Yet in Robinson's case it is particu-larly significant to return to the original published versions of the poetry. The three-volume *Poetical Works* revises many of the poems from the earlier versions, strips prefatory and other prose materials accompanying the poems, and omits many of Robinson's politically controversial poems altogether. Robinson's daughter published the *Works* as a memorial to her mother's poetical powers and reputation, in the process purging from the collection the controversial elements of her mother's career. 'The title "Works", is associated with canon formation', argues Neil Fraistat in *The Poem and the Book*, 'and implies that the poet is sufficiently important to have established a public

canon' (26). In a letter to publishers, Robinson's daughter described the proposed *Poetical Works* as containing 'every poem written by Mrs. Robinson
from the year 1784 to the year 1800'[4]: that is, as the authorized canon of her
mother's body of work. Because we are currently re-establishing Robinson's
'public canon', it is important to remember that the full extent of Robinson's
uncollected newspaper and periodical writings, and in particular of her
political writings, remains unaccounted for.

The birthday odes of 'A Daughter of Liberty'

Robinson's 'Ode for the 18th of January, 1794' illustrates the complex, multi-
valent political registers in which she wrote. First published in *The Oracle*,
the poem uses the Queen's Birthday (18 January) as an occasion to examine
the striking divisions between the rich and the poor:

> For FANCY might, per chance, descry
>   The woe which PLEASURE's TRIBE ne'er saw!
> The bleeding breast! the phrenzied eye!
>   That chill the soul with dreadful awe!
> FANCY might paint th' embattled plain!
> The shrieking wife! the breathless swain!
> The blazing cot! the houseless child,
> Driv'n on misfortune's rugged wild! [5]

Robinson returned to the occasion of the Queen's Birthday the following
year in her poem 'St James's Street, on the Eighteenth of January 1795',
later known as 'The Birth-Day'. Written during the worst winter in living
memory, the political register seems even sharper than the previous year's,
in part due to Robinson's characteristic use of pointed oppositions embedded
in quatrains:

> HERE, amidst jewels, feathers, flow'rs,
>   The senseless Duchess sits demure;
> Heedless, of all the anguish'd hours,
>   The Sons of *modest worth* endure!
> All silver'd and embroider'd o'er,
>   She knows not, and she feels not pain;
> The Beggar, freezing at her door
>   She views, with insolent disdain! (*Morning Post*, 21 Jan. 1795)

As in the poems 'The Wintry Day' and 'January, 1795', Robinson's highly
effective use of energetic quatrains to embody social division makes expert
use of a popular form for political ends. These two poems on Queen Charlotte's
birthday, in 1794 and 1795, denounce the growing divide between rich

and poor, and the effects of war on the impoverished population; as such they are not distinctly radical, but liberal in their opposition to an oblivious aristocracy.

In an important re-evaluation of Robinson's nineteenth-century legacy, Stuart Curran has recently argued that '"The Birth-Day" is without precedent in English poetry...for its radical metonymic construction' ('Mary Robinson', 13). In a sensitive reading of 'The Birth-Day''s poetics, Curran reveals how the atomizing effects of Robinson's serial juxtapositions of luxury and suffering accumulate in a 'lyric of pure surface', whose 'political power comes not from statement but from effect, not from substance but from figuration' (13, 12). Yet by the time this revised 1795 poem had become known as 'The Birth-Day' (in her posthumous *Poetical Works* of 1806), Robinson had toned down the conscious cruelty of the aristocracy, and thus, arguably, had distanced the poem from the specific circumstances of its composition, as reflected in its original title which anchored the poem in both space and time: 'St. James's Street. On the Eighteenth of January, 1795'.[6] Building on Curran's perceptive reading of the surface significance of Robinson's revised poem on the Queen's birthday, I want to inquire further into the immediate impetus for Robinson's occasional January poems and their political significance. In addition to their figural and metrical effects, Robinson's occasional poems derive much of their political power through the specifics of their publishing contexts.

The Queen's birthday is only the surface occasion of 'Ode for the 18th of January, 1794', the first of Robinson's poems on the subject. When we place Robinson in the familiar territory of aristocratic excess, the 'Ode for the 18th' reads like a straightforward anti-luxury critique that eighteenth-century writers of all political stripes wrote. When we place the poem within its immediate political context of January 1794, not only does a new poem emerge, but a new Robinson, one writing in support of radical reformers. The immediate occasion for the 'Ode for the 18th', I suggest, is actually the sedition trials of the British Convention reformers, Skirving and Margarot (convicted in the first and second weeks in January, respectively). This poem belongs to a series of little-known radical writings Robinson wrote between 1794 and 1795, the most shocking being her letter to Lord Advocate Robert Dundas protesting his decision to uphold the sentences of transportation for the Scottish reformers convicted of sedition in 1793 and 1794.

The prefatory note accompanying 'Ode for the 18th' in the *Oracle* tells us the poem 'is the verse of a Daughter of Liberty', and the poem moves between an almost frantic desperation at unnamed recent events, and a likewise desperate appeal to the Queen for mercy and pity (*Oracle*, 18 Jan. 1794). The pomp and circumstance accompanying public celebrations of the Queen's birthday are overwhelmed in this poem by the 'temporary death' brought on by Winter's 'threat'ning storms malignant': well might Robinson's readers, she acknowledges, choose to ignore the bloodshed and injustices of the recent past in order to enjoy the 'gaudy sight' of 'present joys', that is the royal birthday celebrations:

> No more Reflection, sorrowing Maid;
>   O'er Reason cast thy awful veil!
> Where Mirth, in careless garb array'd,
>   And Smiles, and thoughtless Jest prevail!
> For should'st thou trace, with pensive mien,
> The fatal, agonizing scene!
> Where legions wade through human gore!
> And DEATH shoots swift from shore to shore!
> The splendid glare of revelry would fade,
> And all its phantoms sink in Sorrow's whelming shade!
> (*Oracle*, 18 Jan. 1794)

Robinson's poem turns our attention instead to the bloody battlefield that 'Pleasure's Tribe', the elite, disregards—where the 'shrieking wife' confronts 'the blazing cot', and 'legions wade through human gore!'. In Robinson's skilful hands the occasion of the Queen's birthday becomes an opportunity to comment on the barbarity of the government's war against France.

Robinson's poems on the Queen's Birthday were not alone in using such events to comment on public political sentiment. On 20 January, 1795 the *Morning Post*, which had just published her second poem on the Queen's Birthday, 'St. James's Street. On the Eighteenth of January, 1795', reported on the festivities in St. James Palace for the Queen's birthday:

> Never was there seen so gloomy a Birth-Day in this country as that of yesterday. Care and despondency seem to sit on every brow; the affected smiles of Ministers shewed that disappointment and [desperation] resided in their hearts; and instead of being a day of joyous gratulations, a settled melancholy and dread apprehension for the safety of the Nation, pervaded the Assembly, and made them inwardly condemn the measures of those wretched men in whom they had reposed their confidence, and who, if they are suffered to remain in power, must bring certain and eternal destruction on the Kingdom.

As the war continued throughout the 1790s and domestic economic crises deepened, the royal birthday celebrations became controversial displays of pomp and luxury in hard times. By the time Robinson's poem was republished as 'St. James Street. The Birth-Day' in the 1798 *Morning Post*, the paper commented that same day on the inappropriateness of such festivities:

> the appearance of yesterday will convince the ROYAL FAMILY how fruitless it is to attempt to draw forth grandeur and gaiety at a season

when poverty and dejection prevail. The Court was not so well attended yesterday as on ordinary drawing-room days. (19 Jan. 1798)

'Newspapers assessed the degree of support for government policy by measuring participation in royal rituals' like the birthday celebrations, writes Marilyn Morris, and '[f]rom 1795 to 1798, the number of guests at royal birthday galas dropped off, and the opposition papers had their day' (143–4). Robinson's occasional verse on such royal rituals belong to this larger political struggle over the war abroad and at home. They begin to appear in 1794 because that year was particularly significant for Robinson's radicalization, as it was for the English reformers as a whole who were galvanized by the shocking convictions of the reformers in Edinburgh.

The 'female patriot' and the British Convention

Robinson's 1794 writings are embedded in, and engage with, a political crisis precipitated by the state trials of radical reformers in Scotland in 1793 and early 1794. Thomas Muir, founder of the Friends of the People in Edinburgh, along with Thomas Palmer, had been convicted of sedition in the autumn of 1793 and sentenced to transportation to Botany Bay.[7] William Skirving and Maurice Margarot, key participants in 'The British Convention of the Delegates of the People, associated to obtain Universal Suffrage and Annual Parliaments', had been convicted of sedition in January 1794 and also sentenced to transportation. Lord Braxfield presided over all the Scottish sedition trials, and the consensus then, as now, was that the convictions represent 'one of the most shameful pages of Scottish judicial history' (Goodwin 306). While in scholarship on Romantic-period literature the 1793 and 1794 trials have been overshadowed by the subsequent treason trials of Thomas Hardy and Horne Tooke, the unprecedented conviction and transportation of the British Conventionists preoccupied the media, and the thinking of those sympathetic to reform, in the early months of 1794.

Skirving's and Margarot's convictions (7 and 14 January, respectively) set in motion a series of political responses in the popular press, in light of which Robinson's writings of this month should be reread (see Appendix 1 for a timeline). An anonymous poem 'To Messrs. Muir and Palmer' printed in the January 14, 1794 *Morning Post* hails the earlier convicted reformers as 'Friends of the slighted People – ye whose wrongs/ From wounded Freedom many a tear shall draw'. Muir and Palmer had advocated parliamentary reform through constitutional means, and their convictions in September 1793 had inspired the redoubled efforts of Scottish reformers, and the foundation of the more radical British Convention that October and November. There is no specific evidence to associate this poem with Robinson, but the fusion of sensibility and radical politics is characteristic of her poetry on such political figures as Robert Merry (in *Ainsi va le Monde*), and representative of the political register that the literature of sensibility (Merry's and Robinson's) evoked in the 1790s.

Following these convictions, the Society for Constitutional Information (SCI) held a general meeting at the Crown & Anchor Tavern and issued a series of resolutions denouncing the convictions. The day after this SCI address, Robinson published 'Ode on the 18th of January' in the *Oracle*, which also printed detailed accounts of Skirving and Margarot's trials on 14 and 18 January. It is in this unfolding set of events that we ought to read 'Ode on the 18th of January'. The ode is printed between an account of the Queen's Birthday on one side, and the news column on the other side, including notices of Muir's transportation preparations and Margarot's trial (a condensed account of which appears on the last page). Introduced as the 'verse of a Daughter of Liberty', 'Ode for the 18th of January' addresses two distinct occasions, a testament to Robinson's uncanny ability to write in distinct registers simultaneously. The poem uses a storm from the North (perhaps North Britain, that is Scotland) to allegorize poverty and repression in wartime England: 'Chill'd by the black tempestuous North, the poor of England ask "Ah! when will SPRING return?/ Do all like us distress endure? –/ So cold! So wretched! and so poor?"' The poem moves through such distressing scenes of poverty, to the indifference of the elite, to an invocation of Hope and Pity. In a fashion similar to Shelley's masterpiece 'Ode to the West Wind', which reflected on the Peterloo massacre of 1819 more subtly than his polemical 'Masque of Anarchy' of that same year, Robinson employs seasonal metaphors to address a political crisis whose outcome is by no means assured, as in Shelley's ambiguous conclusion ('If winter comes, can spring be far behind?').

Robinson uses this dual occasion (of Queen's Birthday and sedition trials) to political advantage, hinting subtly that perhaps the Queen's recommendation of the royal mercy would be a virtuous and appropriately feminine use of her influence. The poem suggests that despite the elite's obliviousness to suffering, the queen's acute sensibility may move her to mercy:

> Yet, if amidst the gaudy sight,
> A sparkling tear of liquid light,
> Caught by a sigh from PITY's breast,
> Should fall, to gem the regal crest!
> Oh! let it shine, with heaven's approving blaze,
> An attribute sublime, to mock inferior rays! (*Oracle*, 18 Jan. 1794)

The accompanying prose account of the 'Queen's Birth-Day' similarly approves of Queen Charlotte's 'mercy' and 'pardon' by carefully distinguishing these virtues from Marie Antoinette's 'deplored' 'interference in POLITICAL CONCERNS':

> The unhappy Antoinette, we are persuaded, might have been alive and honoured by her subjects at this moment, if, with the true feminine policy of the BRITISH QUEEN, she had kept herself aloof from all political

intrigue, and firmly refused to intermit herself between the SOVEREIGN and his PEOPLE, – except for the gentle purpose of *mercy* and *pardon* to the WRETCHED. (*Oracle*, 18 Jan. 1794, orig. emphasis)

This 'true feminine policy' of mercy and pardon referred to in Robinson's poem and in the prose account may be merely an abstraction evoked in the light of a generalized distress, or it may be a carefully worded appeal for royal pardon of the convicted reformers. The 14-year transportation sentences issued in Scotland by Judge Braxfield were virtually death sentences, and sent shock waves not only through the popular reform groups but through the Whig opposition and English population in general. Lord Stanhope, Sheridan and others had all made motions in Parliament concerning the convictions of Muir and Palmer (Wharam 67).[8] In these parliamentary debates, the Prime Minister supported the Scottish verdicts, and 'when Secretary Dundas wrote to Lord Braxfield to tell him that the sentences which had been imposed were the subject of complaints in England, he wrote back with his advice that the royal mercy should not be extended to the convicts' (Wharam 67). This final possibility of lessening the harsh sentences for the Scottish reformers may have been Robinson's immediate occasion for her 'Ode on the 18th of January' and its praise of royal mercy. What is remarkable about Robinson's political and rhetorical range is the multiple levels on which she works, even in a single poem like the 'Ode'.

She addressed this 1794 reform crisis even more dramatically in a hitherto unidentified personal appeal to Robert Dundas written on January 23, possibly marking the debut of her 'Tabitha Bramble' pseudonym (see Appendix 2). As 'Tabitha Bramble', Robinson fired off an angry letter to the Lord Advocate of Scotland, Robert Dundas, who had upheld the sentences of transportation for the Edinburgh reformers. 'On the one hand', Robinson writes, 'we have the Reformers contending for certain principles, & certain renovations which every body allows to be founded in Justice. On the other, Government prosecuting in a rigorous manner such honest endeavours.'[9] Robinson then rejects the state's argument that such reform efforts in a time of war constitute sedition: 'the trite argument of this being an improper time for Reform will be found wanting in the Balance of Posterity'. The prosecutor's summation at Margarot's trial, widely reported in published accounts, had insisted instead that

I submit to you whether a man that wishes well to his country, would come forward and insist upon a reform, Parliamentary or not Parliamentary, at such a crisis; which would create discontent in the minds of the people, when every good subject would promote unanimity among the lieges to meet the common enemy. (*Trial of Maurice Margarot* 172)

Such 'discontent among the people' according to Judge Braxfield, 'may naturally in the end have a tendency to promote violence against the state', which 'will very naturally end in rebellion' (171). John Barrell has demonstrated how according to Braxfield's reasoning, 'any discussion whatsoever, or any grievance whatsoever' could be construed as sedition, regardless if those expressing grievances intended to promote rebellion or not (*Imagining* 164).

Robinson discounted Braxfield's alarmist reasoning by appealing both to historical precedent, via the Glorious Revolution, and to Posterity, via the promise of the French Revolution. During the Glorious Revolution, 'The Nation was roused to fury, it took ample justice on the authors of their wrongs', she warns. Robinson then cites a recent precedent of governmental tyranny and the retaliation it inspired six short months ago:

> The sanguinary harsh measures employed against the Reformers, are with some degree of Propriety, attributed to you. Mr. Muirs, & now Mr. Skirvings & Margarots cruel treatment have added to your Lordships unpopularity: a few more will render you perfectly odious. It will then be reckoned honourable to deprive Society of such a *Pest*. Some Male, or rather more likely some Female hand, will direct the Dagger that will do such an important Service; and Britain shall not want a Female Patriot emulous of the fame of *M. Cordet* [*sic*].

Here the fate of the convicted reformers requires a 'Female Patriot': no longer the 'true feminine policy' of royal mercy as in the Ode, but the 'honourable' example of a republican female assassin, Charlotte Corday. Leaving aside the rhetoric of British feminine propriety versus French feminine meddling, Robinson responds to domestic political tyranny by invoking French republican liberty, that is Braxfield's 'common enemy'. This Corday allusion also sets Robinson apart from conservative British uses of Corday's assassination of the Jacobin journalist Marat to signify divine retribution against French atheism and republicanism.[10] It is a remarkable political address by any standards, and demonstrates why our understanding of Robinson's political range requires revision.

By defending the Conventionists' 'principles and...renovations' (universal male suffrage and annual parliaments) as 'founded in Justice', Robinson situates herself at the radical end of the Foxite Whig spectrum, closer to the reformers in question. The Foxite Whigs had defended Muir and Palmer before Parliament, and were similarly outraged at the Conventionists' convictions, but they did not share the parliamentary reform goals of the radical societies.[11] Robinson expresses outrage like her Whig friends, but also defends the Convention's goals, and even amplifies Margarot's (unfounded) boast during the Convention that the reformers enjoyed the support of a majority of the people (see Barrell, *Imagining* 153). 'Your Lordship is perhaps ignorant of the Extent to which the principles of Reform have diffused themselves', she writes to Dundas: 'When I say that two thirds of the Country are so inclined, I am positive I do not exceed the number'.

Robinson's letter also makes visible the significant extent to which this radicalism was both masculinized and often nationalistic. Her 23 January letter to Dundas echoes the SCI's 17 January address on the same subject, with subtle differences. The SCI, with Horne Tooke presiding, made a number of resolutions at their meeting, including:

> Resolved, That we call to mind, with the deepest satisfaction, the merited fate of the infamous Jeffreys, once lord chief justice of England, who at the era of the glorious revolution, for the many iniquitous sentences which he had passed, was torn to pieces by a brave and injured people.
> Resolved, that those who imitate his example, deserve his fate.[12]

Judge Jeffreys had overseen the execution of over 300 men and the transportation of hundreds more in Monmouth's rebellion; he died in the Tower after attempting to escape to France following James II's flight. Jeffreys had also tried Algernon Sidney for the Rye House Plot, Sidney and John Hampden appearing throughout 1790s reform literature as martyrs for a long-standing British tradition of liberty. The SCI's precedent for retribution against Dundas is thus a staunchly nationalist and masculine one, citing these examples of the Protestant heroes of the Glorious Revolution, in opposition to the Francophilic Catholic tyranny represented by James II and Jeffreys.

While Robinson also evoked such patriot-heroes (her dual protagonists in *Walsingham*, for example, are associated with Sidney and Hampden),[13] she remains conscious of the gendered exclusions on which such nostalgic formulations of English liberty are based. Like the SCI, Robinson cites the Glorious Revolution as moral precedent, but she chooses as her instrument of retribution not the (implicitly masculinized) Protestant English people, but Charlotte Corday, a French republican woman. Robinson's letter to Dundas is dated a week after the SCI's resolution at the Crown and Anchor; the direct echoes of this address in her letter suggest that she may have heard or read an account of the SCI resolutions. Her provocatively direct means of addressing Dundas in a letter, and the French republican 'female Patriot' that she invoked as her figure of justice, represents a feminist and Francophilic alternative to the SCI's response to the crisis. Corday embodied Justice in the 'Female Hand', and through her Robinson imagined avenging her 'Country's wrongs'. As I have argued elsewhere, pro-revolutionary writers like the young Robert Southey hailed Corday's politicized violence as a source of inspiration for further acts of rebellion.[14] Thus the immediate French context that Robinson evokes in her conclusion could represent exactly the sort of rebellious collusion with the 'common enemy' against domestic order that Braxfield branded as sedition in Margarot's trial. Such a 'Female Patriot' was unthinkable both to the French Jacobins (who had executed Corday in 1793) and British conservatives, and perhaps even the British radicals in question.

On the same day that Robinson wrote her letter defending the convicted reformers Muir, Skirving, and Margarot (23 January), Godwin wrote to Joseph

Gerrald (who would soon be convicted and transported along with Skirving and Margarot) advising him on legal strategies. Gerrald's best bet, wrote Godwin, was to rely on the ancient Bill of Rights, 'the fundamental article of that constitution which Englishmen have been taught to admire'.[15] The ancient rights of Englishmen were a crucial part of the Convention's strategy, as John Barrell has shown: the Convention drew 'together the three main strands of the movement for universal manhood suffrage by providing them with a common object: Paine's universalist discourse of rights, the Anglo-Saxonist tradition of the 'free-born Englishman', and the less antiquarian nationalism of those who looked back to the Convention Parliament as the originating moment of the English constitution' (*Imagining* 148). Yet British radicalism's nostalgia for the pre-Norman 'free-born Briton' and for the liberties granted under the 'original' constitution, as Stephen Behrendt acknowledges, 'had no more place for [women] than the contemporary socio-political structure seems to have' (85). Hampden and Sidney (whose posthumous writings on the Anglo-Saxon constitution were influential in the 1790s) were heroes in that constitutional tradition, and Judge Jeffreys the arch villain. Robinson attempts to rewrite this familiar radical narrative with a distinctly modern and feminist version of the female citizen. Robinson's support of the British Convention's founders through her Welsh persona of Tabitha Bramble, while evoking the example of the French republican assassin Corday, is a striking instance of her radical politics, at once feminist and cosmopolitan.

Robinson's letter is probably her (and in fact any Romantic woman writer's) most daring political intervention known to us. Robinson signed the letter 'Tabitha Bramble' perhaps in order to protect herself via such a satirical pseudonym (that of a ridiculous spinster known for her malapropisms in Smollett's *Humphrey Clinker*). As we shall see, Robinson began publishing poetry as Tabitha Bramble in response to the crisis of 1797; this letter thus may mark the debut of this persona, at once protecting her anonymity in 1794, and establishing the controversial course of one of her most politically charged pseudonyms. Robinson's occasional poetry (the two royal birthday poems discussed thus far) were far more nuanced than this bold letter (or the later Bramble poems), their politics deflected through a complex series of rhetorical sleights of hand that can easily disappear altogether if we lose sight of the specific circumstances in which they were published. When considered together, Robinson's January 1794 appeals in support of radical reformers – the ode and the Dundas letter – bring gender to the fore: either in hinting at the royal mercy in a poem praising the queen's benevolence, or in threatening a hanging judge with the prospect of feminized, revolutionary violence.

The Laureate Odes

A second set of occasional poetry that Robinson wrote throughout the 1790s are her Odes on the New Year, which like the royal birthday poems use an established form to critique the world they are supposed to celebrate. The

New Year odes provide further evidence of Robinson's sharp-edged political poetry, and of her unmasked ambition to claim the role of poet laureate from counterrevolutionary rivals. Marlon Ross notes how the established form of the 'occasional poem was normally written by great men for great men: by poets laureate for royal personages, by the patronized for their patrons, by grateful gentlemen for military officers on the success of a battle' ('Woman Writer' 95). Romantic women poets, on the other hand, 'felt more at ease with the sentimental version of the form', for example, marking the private occasion of the death of a loved one, with Barbauld's *Eighteen Hundred and Eleven* being a controversial exception (96). Like *Eighteen Hundred and Eleven*, Robinson's Laureate Odes presume to speak to an entire nation about international events, claiming not a prophetic authority as in Barbauld's case, but a wholly secular one.

Henry James Pye was the poet laureate from 1790 to 1813, appointed by Pitt as a reward for his dogged support in Parliament. The steady stream of verse propaganda he produced made Pye the object of every genuine poet's ire (for example, in numerous works by Peter Pindar and in Byron's *Vision of Judgment*). Commissioned by the state, the laureate's annual odes would be set to music by the court composer and performed in the State Drawing Rooms (Gray 210). Pye's annual odes in particular were despised, and 'helped to give the deathblow to the annual ode. Never again was a Poet Laureate compelled to write regularly a birthday ode in honour of His Majesty' (Gray 204). In 'Ode for the New Year, 1794', Pye employs the familiar seasonal metaphors of wintry death to justify war and its promised rewards: 'mid the elemental strife/ Brood the rich germs of vernal life' (*Oracle*, 2 Jan. 1794). His ode for the New Year is essentially an ode to the new war against France:

> Say shall BRITANNIA's generous sons embrace
> In fold of amity the harpy race
> Or aid the sword that cowardly fury rears,
> Red with the widow's blood, wet with the orphan's tears?
> (*Oracle*, 2 Jan. 1794)

The *Morning Post* replied a week later with its parody of the ode, by 'Master Goose Pye, Eldest Son' of the poet laureate, whose schoolboy verse concludes instead that 'This seems a war of furious foreign Kings,/ Pretending friendship unto God Almighty' (9 Jan. 1794).

Robinson's 'Ode for the New Year', also published 9 January 1794 in the *Post*, shifts the focus from Pye's martial and seasonal metaphors of blood and regeneration, to an entirely different allegorical plane. Hope, Nature, Pity, Peace and other feminine principles look down onto an entire continent, in fact an entire planet, engulfed in war: 'This whirling ORB's disastrous space'. Despite Robinson's use of allegorical figures, the poem moves relentlessly through scenes of more upon more suffering, 'Heart-piercing cries of

Pain, and deep'ning GROANS of WOE!' Leaving behind the patriotic platitudes found in war propaganda like Pye's Ode, Robinson presents a frantic and entirely feminine response to war, in which exiled principles like Hope and Peace struggle to 'FORM a GLORIOUS BOWER o'er FREEDOM's BLEST DOMAIN!' As in other antiwar poetry of this decade, as Behrendt, Favret and Mellor have argued, the rhetorical stance is deliberately feminine, so that the domestic bower is the true home of freedom, in opposition to a significantly masculinized 'FURY' who urges 'MAN with MAN, like TYGERS fierce', to indulge in the 'rage of ARMS'.

Robinson's alternatives to the laureate odes carefully redirect Pye's bellicose cliches into consciously feminized visions of war's futility, an argument 'very much a part of the Radical agenda' (Behrendt 91). Her 'Ode on the 18th of January, 1794', which as I have argued used the queen's birthday to draw attention to the fate of the Scottish 'martyrs', was followed by numerous other such annual odes, for example 'St. James Street, on the 18th of January, 1795', which was then revised and reprinted until it reached its posthumous version as 'The Birth-Day'. She continued the practice as 'Tabitha Bramble' as well, demolishing Pye's 'Ode for the New Year, 1798' in her preemptive 'Ode Fourth. For New Years Day', published before Pye's poem. Churning out his repetitive loyal odes for his annual £200, the laureate is but a prostituted hack – 'the *glow-worm* of the Court, A thing that shrinks from true Promethean rays!'[16]

Robinson's annual odes are consistently preoccupied with the themes of war and liberty, using important occasions to raise her radical agenda. These annual odes culminated in 'The Birth-Day of Liberty', published 7 April 1798 in the *Morning Post*, and later included in her unfinished blank-verse epic *The Progress of Liberty*. 'The Birth-Day of Liberty' marks Robinson's ongoing evolution in her annual odes, for here it is the 'lusty form' of Liberty whose birth Robinson celebrates in a republican vision of creation, in which Liberty, not god (or monarch), rules the earth and its laws:

> For thou,
> Like the vast Orb [the sun], wert destin'd to illume
> The mist-encircled world, to warm the soul,
> To call the pow'rs of teeming Reason forth,
> And ratify the laws by Nature made! (*Morning Post*, 7 April 1798)

The following instalments that would make up the blank verse unfinished epic are deliberately Miltonic, rivalling *Paradise Lost's* account of creation with Robinson's own original vision of Liberty's preeminent role in history, an aspiring epic vision developed from her earlier occasional verse.

Pye continued publishing his odes throughout the 1790s, with the French consistently standing in for demonized aggressors: a 'harpy race' in 1794, they are 'Fell demons, urg'd by hell's behest' in the 1796 annual ode, and in the invasion scare of 1797 the French are 'the ruthless foe,/ Deep trench'd with blood, yet thirsting still for more,/ Deaf to the shrieks of agonizing woe'.[17] Pye's depiction of the French as a monstrous race apart is representative of the increasingly paranoid atmosphere of war-time Britain, especially in 1796 and 1797 when the domestic economic crisis and the invasion scares converged into what may have been the decade's nadir.

Robinson and radical print culture

Robinson's ability to span a continuum of political registers, from that of Foxite Whig to radical satirist and feminist, merits comparison with Robert Merry's similar movement 'beyond the circles of Whig gentlemen towards the Dissenters and radicals' of the SCI (Mee 111). Merry's relationship to Robinson has typically been considered in light of their 1780s correspondence in newspaper poetry of sensibility, via their respective pseudonyms Della Crusca and Laura Matilda. Radicalized by the Revolution like Robinson, Merry too claimed the role of laureate in his *Laurel of Liberty* (1790), in which he directed British readers to 'turn to France and see/ Four Million Men in arms, for Liberty!' (ll. 419–20). Robinson's *Ainsi va Le Monde* (1790), a celebration of the French Revolution inspired by Merry's poem, was revised in the 1806 edition of her *Poetical Works*, stripped of Merry's notorious name both in the dedication and in the poem. 'Mixing eroticism with political radicalism', notes Jon Mee, 'it was this extended exchange' between Merry and Robinson in 1790, 'rather than the high period of Della Cruscanism proper, which brought forward the angry Tory satire of Gifford's *The Baviad* in 1791' (112).[18]

Merry moved to Paris in 1792, presented his *Laurel of Liberty* to the Convention, immersed himself in radical politics, and became the President of the British Club by December 1792, presiding over meetings which called for the coming Convention of England, Scotland and Ireland (Alger, 'British Colony', 675). Eulogized in the *Monthly Magazine* as a poet to whom 'the genius of liberty instantaneously communicated all its enthusiasm',[19] Merry earned the name '"Liberty" Merry' through his French activities and publications, like his *Reflexions [sic] Politique sur La Nouvelle Constitution* (1792), which argued for direct democracy and an end to genius' neglect: 'le philosophe éclairé, l'homme des lettres philanthrope languissoient dans l'indigence ou dans l'obscurité' (19).[20] Returning to England in 1793 and finding his mail opened and his movements watched by the government, Merry stayed one step ahead of the police before immigrating to the United States in 1796 (Clayden 283–5; Adams, 'Robert Merry', 30–3). Having become friends with Godwin in 1793, it was Merry who introduced Godwin to Robinson in 1796, the origins of that extraordinary correspondence in which Robinson addressed Godwin as 'my dear philosopher'.[21]

Merry's association with Robinson remains a missed opportunity for seeing the extent to which she was involved with Francophilic radical circles and print culture, beyond Johnson's London circle which scholars of Romantic radicalism tend to see as the centre and circumference of their inquiries. Like '"Liberty" Merry', the 'Daughter of Liberty' Robinson transformed herself into a radical satirist, joining the eroticized 'materialist tradition of sensibility' that Jerome McGann has restored (80), to the even more dangerous materialist traditions of French revolutionary politics. Possessing 'as unalterable a revolutionary spirit as that of Shelley' (Clifford 24), Merry drew together those aristocratic, radical and eroticized sensibilities that the later poet also shares with Robinson. All three poets' subsequent reputations proved difficult to recuperate in the nineteenth-century reception of sensibility, just as their radicalism has proved difficult to restore given twentieth-century criticism's often narrow understandings of class (and sexual) politics.

The crisis of 1797

Robinson's work from 1796 to 1798 shows her increasingly radical engagement with current political crises, domestic and foreign. Occasional poems written in this interval under hitherto unidentified pseudonyms, as well as wholly neglected novels like *Angelina* (1796) and understudied ones like those set during the Revolution, offer compelling new evidence of Robinson's increasing involvement with French revolutionary politics. The year 1797 marked a low point in British political repression, with naval mutinies in April and May reflecting growing dissatisfaction over the economic and human costs of war with France. The failure of Lord Grey's parliamentary reform bill, and the aggressive dispersal of the London Corresponding Society mass demonstration at St. Pancras that summer, saw the growing disarray of both Whigs and the reform societies by the end of the year.

Reviving her radicalized pseudonym Tabitha Bramble, Robinson published a numbered series of political Odes and popular songs beginning on 8 December 1797 that address this crisis. 'A Simple Tale (Addressed to the Most Expert of Jugglers)' in the 13 December 1797 *Morning Post* is a satirical allegory depicting Pitt's unpopular taxation policies as a conjuring trick by a Juggler, who robs naïve locals and then threatens his victims with the legal 'conjuration' of Pitt's reign of terror:

> The rustics murmur'd; some, ('tis said),
> Swore they wou'd break the Juggler's head –
> While he, by *conjurations* strong,
> Threaten'd to hang, transport, imprison
> Each growling knave, whose daring REASON
> Against his magic Highness wagg'd the tongue!

Robinson's Pitt satires resemble Merry's 1794 'Signor Pittachio' satire, published in radical papers like the *Courier* and *Telegraph* and circulated as a broadside, in which the unpopular minister dazzles the public with policies as insubstantial as a lantern show.[22]

In another ode in Robinson's series, titled 'A New Song' and published in the *Morning Post* on 19 February 1798, Tabitha Bramble names Pitt as chiefly responsible for this climate of repression in which 'VIRTUE and HONOUR are WATCH'd and BETRAY'd!':

> While, with taxes on taxes, the fathomless Pitt,
> Still palsies our virtue, and bids us submit;
> Tho' we starve and go naked, we dare not complain,
> For the devil that drives hold's the T[reasur]y's *rein!*

It is no surprise that these poems were omitted from the posthumous *Poetical Works*. Pitt had begun a six-part essay series in the *Anti-Jacobin* in November 1797, attempting to justify his deeply unpopular taxes, intended to finance Britain's spiralling war costs. Robinson's 1797 odes and songs are politically savvy attacks on these and other government policies, published at a time when expressing contempt for the King or his ministers was a punishable offence. None of these poems are reprinted in the 1806 posthumous edition by her daughter, who asserted that the Tabitha Bramble poems were 'lighter compositions considered by the author as unworthy of a place in her collected poems' (Robinson, *Memoirs* 2: 148). In fact, we already know that Robinson used 'Tabitha Bramble' not for 'lighter compositions', but for her sharpest social barbs, especially feminist ones deflating both the sexual double standard and the affectations of femininity. Lisa Vargo's reading of the six Bramble poems incorporated in the *Lyrical Tales*, moreover, illustrates how Tabitha Bramble's 'raucus bluntness' makes possible Robinson's 'liberatory unmasking of the hypocrisy of sentiment' central to Wordsworth's project in the *Lyrical Ballads* (49, 43). Contemporary newspapers reveal the extent to which this feminist antisentimentalism was immersed in radical politics, often commenting on current government policies on taxation, public debt, political repression, and war. Once we read the Tabitha Bramble Odes of 1797–98, the 1794 letter to Dundas no longer seems an anomaly, but part of Robinson's ongoing radicalization, readily visible in her uncollected periodical and newspaper publications.

Restoring Robinson's poems to their radical occasional roots also reveals new pseudonyms under which she wrote. One example of this is her pseudonym 'Humanitas', which has not previously been identified. As 'Humanitas', Robinson published 'Verses on the Nineteenth of December 1797' in the *Morning Post*, a poem which, like the Birth-Day poems and *Ainsi va le Monde*, appears in the 1806 *Poetical Works* with its title stripped of specifics: 'Written on a Day of Public Rejoicing'. More than a general protest against public spectacles in the face of widespread want, this poem addresses the crisis of 1797. December 19 was the date of the royal procession to St. Paul's, another display of pomp and luxury that failed utterly to appreciate the degree of public dissatisfaction, as Robinson's poem makes clear.

> WHILE shouts and acclamations rend the skies,
> From the deep Ocean, bleeding cold, and wan,
> See groaning SPECTRES in a body rise!,
> To mourn the mis'ries of ambitious Man! (*Morning Post*, 19 Dec. 1797)

The spectres that Robinson raises to haunt this royal spectacle are those of the sailors and soldiers who have died in the war, destroying families in the process: 'The many suff'rers who in anguish pine – The SOLDIER's, SAILOR's kindred – left behind!' 'Suspend the shout of triumph!' urges Humanitas in light of the growing casualties. A different (explicitly male) 'Humanitas' had published *War a System of Madness and Irreligion* the previous year, concluding that Paine was premature in declaring an Age of Reason, 'when a barbarous, inhuman and irrational system universally prevails'.[23] Robinson would have agreed with this, perhaps taking on this pseudonym in order to connect her antiwar poem to this larger tradition. Humanitas (George Miller) had also appended to his philosophical argument Elizabeth Moody's poem 'Anna's Complaint; or, The Miseries of War', which is the feminized complement to his angry polemic:

> Thou, cruel WAR, what hast thou done!
> Thro' thee the mother mourns her son;
> The orphan joins the widow's cries;
> And, torn from love—the lover dies. (Moody: 63)

As the ungendered 'Humanitas' Robinson joins to this female distress over the domestic costs of war a politically specific target (the king and his ministers) and date (the royal procession). Moreover, Humanitas's 'Verses' appeared in the *Morning Post* next to an account of Pitt hanged in effigy the previous day. The specifically antiministerial context and content, as well as the pseudonym, distinguishes Robinson's poem from other women's antiwar poems, which like Moody's often focus on the effects of violence on the domestic sphere. Robinson seems uniquely able to span such distinctions of genre and gender, a skill requiring us to investigate further the surprising extent of her ventures in the radical press.

Robinson's novels and the radical press

Perhaps the most telling example of Robinson's elided radicalism is found throughout her numerous novels, which have been discussed largely in terms of their sexual politics. Robinson's novels and essays are even more forthright in their political claims than much of the poetry, yet beyond the critique of sexual privilege found in *Walsingham*, *The Natural Daughter*, and *Letter to the*

Women of England on the Injustice of Mental Subordination, little has been said of her prose. Of her émigré novel *Hubert de Sevrac*, so at odds with the counterrevolutionary thrust of most émigré writings, *The European Review* complained that 'What we least approve of in this work is an evident partiality towards French Philosophy, and something too much of the cant of French Democracy' (v.31 (1797): 35). *Walsingham* in particular had infuriated the ministerial papers when its hero proclaimed that 'had not such men and Rousseau and Voltaire existed, the earth had still been shackled by tyranny and superstition' (3:264). And even the *Analytical Review* despaired of the political picture painted by *The Widow, or Picture of Modern Times* (1794): 'If the following be a true representation of the manner in which the great often sport with the happiness of their inferiors, we shall be obliged to admit a worse idea of high life than we have hitherto entertained' (v.18 (1794): 453). The best-known representation of how the great sport with the happiness of their inferiors – *Caleb Williams* – was also published in 1794, and the time has come to return Robinson's novels to the radical tradition that Godwin represents. 'You say you were *born* to rule your vassals!' says Robinson's hero to an aristocrat in *The Widow*; 'their humble origin, places them in a position to *obey*; but that is the effect of chance, not *right*' (187, orig. emphasis).

Like *Caleb Williams*, Robinson's later novels are preoccupied with the problem of arbitrary power, particularly in *Angelina* (1796). In *Angelina*, Robinson uses a nightmarish Gothic narrative of pursuit, madness and imprisonment to expose the network of power making possible both Britain's empire abroad and tyranny at home. The arbitrary authority exposed in *Angelina* is gendered (as in Wollstonecraft's subsequent *Wrongs of Woman*), and also contextualized within the contemporary climate of political persecution and the contested slave trade. The heroine's father, a wealthy merchant who is both physically abusive and determined to condemn his daughter to 'legal prostitution', pursues his daughter relentlessly, and overtly links her desired 'independence' to larger claims for independence:

> independence is the stalking-horse for all sorts of absurdities. I should like to know what would become of my plantations if such doctrines are encouraged...Haven't I made a fortune by slavery? and I warrant independence had nothing to do with the business. (3: 102)

Drawing on the long-standing eighteenth-century feminist comparison between colonial and marital slavery, Robinson embeds this feminist critique within a Gothic novel drawing on both Radcliffe and Godwin. Echoing *Caleb Williams* (1794), Robinson's heroine rails against 'the dangers of authority when placed in the hands of minions, who, instead of being the protectors of the people, become the scourges of mankind' (3: 28). She holds out hope, however, 'that the resistance of firm and patriotic spirits, may, at all times, repel the encroachments of arbitrary power, and rescue the human race from the shackles of oppression' (3: 28–9). The political critique on behalf of 'the people' in *Caleb Williams* is here consciously broadened to include women, marking a useful transition between Godwin's novel and Wollstonecraft's *Wrongs of Woman*.

Independence remains the central focus of *Angelina*, as Wollstonecraft noted approvingly in her review of the novel (*Works* 7: 461), and the embattled heroine writes many poems celebrating this theme. One such poem was reprinted in the radical periodical *The Argus*, published by the republican Sampson Perry while imprisoned in Newgate for libel against the House of Commons. Robinson made regular practice of reprinting poems from her novels in newspapers like the reformist *Morning Post*, but this is the first solid piece of evidence linking her to a radical publication like the *Argus*. Originally a newspaper co-owned and co-edited by Perry and Jonathan King (another associate of Robinson's), the *Argus* grew increasingly more radical in 1792 as it publicly supported the LCS and Paine (see Werkmeister 339–77). Threatened with imminent imprisonment for publishing the *Argus*, Perry fled to France in 1792 like Paine and Merry. After convicting and outlawing Perry in absentia, the government shut down the *Argus*, and in its premises set up the ministerial *True Briton*. In Paris, Perry joined the British Club of republican expatriates, and remained a figure of great interest for the French revolutionary government, who saw the *Argus* as the most sympathetic English paper and hoped to influence it (the British government believed that the *Argus* received French funding, which French archival sources do not rule out).[24] Writing in *La Chronique du Mois* in 1793, Perry announced that he would continue to publish the *Argus* in France, writing that the paper, devoted to 'European Freedom...has only been transplanted from the region of tyranny, injustice, and oppression to the happy soil of liberty and equality' ((Jan. 1793) 80).[25] The *Moniteur* also announced that the French *Argus* would be published jointly by Perry and Merry (3 Jan. 1793). By 1795 Perry had returned to England, continued to correspond secretly with expatriate republicans like John Hurford Stone in Paris,[26] and resumed the unrepentantly radical *Argus*, including Robinson's poem from *Angelina* and others by Merry. As we saw in Chapter 1, Perry's return and reimprisonment furnished loyalists with the archetypal antiJacobin narrative of the Gallicized radical who repents of his revolutionary folly. Robinson's literary connection to Perry, probably via their mutual friend Merry, suggests her very different reading of Perry's political endeavours.

Robinson's untitled poem celebrates 'fair INDEPENDENCE' and boldly renounces 'worldly power': 'I ask not wordly pow'r to rule/The drooping child of misery's school:/ To tyrannize o'er him, whom fate/ Has destined to a lowly state' (*Argus* (30 Jan. 1796) 300). Described as the work of a 'fair author', Robinson's *Angelina* poem is the only female authored work in the *Argus* that is identified as such. This is not surprising given that Perry's prospectus for the *Argus* sets out a staunchly masculine standard:

With respect to Poetry – as these are not the piping days of Peace, no admittance can be given to *Love Sonnets* or *Elegies on the Deaths of Blackbirds and Linnets*, But for those grand...Compositions which have distinguished of late a few of our countrymen, under the names of Odes to Liberty...These,...the emanations of a strong male poetic genius, will always be received with gratitude. (*Argus* 2)

That her heroine's lyric in praise of 'fair independence' appears in a suppressed republican journal as the work of a 'fair author' beautifully illustrates Robinson's feminist interrogation of British radicalism's reliance on gendered notions of independence and citizenship. The novel's title, *Angelina*, suggests a sentimental novel riddled with love sonnets, yet what the reader discovers is a feminist meditation on arbitrary power, one in dialogue with Godwin and written by a close friend who addressed him as 'my dear philosopher' in their correspondence, and confessed that 'There have been periods when I have almost idolized you'.[27] As the author of many Odes to Liberty, Robinson is uniquely qualified for this distinction of sole feminist contributor to this otherwise staunchly masculine paper.

The *Argus* 'Independence' poem and another from *Angelina* existed in manuscript in 1794,[28] the year of Robinson's letter defending the British Convention, and the year when Godwin, also closely following the treason trials, published *Caleb Williams*. In addition to reprinting the poems in order to sell more novels,[29] Robinson amplified the politics of her novels by embedding the novels in distinct political debates via the daily papers, such as freedom of the press in *Walsingham*'s case (as we shall see), and republican liberty, in *Angelina*'s. Both novels and their extracted materials, but particularly *Angelina*'s link to the suppressed *Argus*, significantly expand the political range in which Robinson wrote, and do so not merely through their content, but also through their publishing contexts.

A second anonymous *Argus* poem published in 1796, 'Existing Circumstances. An Impromptu', has all the hallmarks of a Robinson occasional poem, thematically and stylistically:

> NEWLY improved treason laws,
> Empty stomachs, and lock'd jaws;
> Bread each revolving week assiz'd,
> SPIES and EMPERORS subsidiz'd;
> The rich and poor are all complaining,
> Taxes the last shilling draining;
> Folly pension'd, knaves rewarded,
> Merit always disregarded.
> War, the harvest of contractors,
> Money brokers, bank directors;
> But to their country ceaseless pain,

> For millions squander'd, thousands slain.
> Haggard wants the land distressing,
> Commerce sinking, debt increasing.
> Fair truth and justice fled away,
> And *MUM* the order of the day. (*Argus* 227)

Pitt's 'reign of terror', in which silence was the order of the day, is linked to the entire economic and social fabric of Britain's bleak domestic situation. Here it is 'fair truth', instead of 'fair independence', that is the victim, along with 'merit disregarded', a Robinsonian constant. I believe this poem to be Robinson's, though unlike the *Argus* poem on Independence, I have been unable to connect it to a signed source. It bears an unmistakable resemblance to Robinson's 'January, 1795', the final stanza of which reads:

> Honest men, who can't get place;
> Knaves, who shew unblushing faces;
> Ruin hasten'd, Peace retarded!
> Candour spurn'd, and Art rewarded! (*Selected Poems* 358)

Published in the *Morning Post*, 'January, 1795' illustrates the furthest political reach of Robinson's signed poems. Incorporated into the 1806 *Poetical Works* like the six Tabitha Bramble poems (of 39) that concerned themselves with feminine and aristocratic excess, the *Morning Post*'s 'January, 1795' is the more liberal incarnation of the *Argus*'s radical 'Existing Circumstances'. The latter is far more politically explicit and localized: it goes beyond the earlier poem's scathing revelations of the wealthy's complicity with war and poverty and of genius' privations, and like the 1797 series of Tabitha Bramble odes that focused on Pitt's policies, it concentrates on specific economic policies (taxes, debt, contracting, profiteering) and legal restrictions (treason, libel). If 'Existing Circumstances' was not written by Robinson, it nevertheless demonstrates how closely her metrical and stylistic trademarks integrated into radical print culture.

Other pseudonymous poetic series in the *Argus* (by 'Nettle') and *Morning Post* (by 'Poeta Inter Minores') share these characteristic overlaps with Robinson's known poetic oeuvre. In these cases, as with the politically specific Tabitha Bramble poems excised from the posthumous *Poetical Works*, they address specific issues and crises, not more abstract, generalized excesses of war or wealth. 'Nettle' wrote a series of 'Extempore' poems in the 1796 *Argus*, which resemble Robinson's signed extempore poems:[30]

> Should Englishmen grow rather warm
> For parliamentary reform;
> The consequences they soon may feel;
> For Britain has A NEW BASTILE [*sic*].

> Should ENGLISHMEN, in short, run mad,
> In seeing times so very bad;
> Should they expose the state's decay,
> There's Bedlam, or there's Bot'ny Bay. (*Argus* 444)

If Nettle is Robinson, the pseudonym may have reappeared in Robinson's signed poem 'The Nettle and the Daisy', published in the *Morning Post* (22 Jan. 1800). The poem contrasts the pampered beauty of the Daisy with the 'Insulted, vex'd' Nettle, armed by misery with the sting of vengeance. It is both natural and just, the Nettle insists, that 'FATE gives the pow'rful *sting*, to meet OPPRESSION's hand'. Throughout her career Robinson increasingly turned from the showy beauty of poetry to its sting, urged by 'repeated wrongs, and proud disdain'. Poeta Inter Minores is another good candidate for Robinson's political verse, publishing dozens of short satirical poems in the *Morning Post* in 1797, often extempore or occasional like the Tabitha Bramble poems of that year also published in the *Post*. 'An Impromptu. In Praise of Female Literature' celebrates women's learning via Vossius's *De Philologia*, as Robinson's *Letter to the Women of England* would do in 1799 (*Morning Post*, 21 Nov. 1797). More typically, Poeta Inter Minores enjoys the full range of Tabitha Bramble's satirical barbs: deflating the self-importance of the leisured classes as easily as the policies of Pitt: 'That P[itt] is a war-loving man,/ We woefully feel and discern' ('The Minister', *Morning Post*, 26 Oct. 1797).[31]

Poeta Inter Minores and Nettle share with Humanitas and Tabitha Bramble's uncollected verse a penchant for political directness that was dangerous, even prosecutable, in post-1795 (post-Treason Trials and Gagging Acts) Britain. All four of these pseudonyms wrote in poetic genres especially suited to addressing immediate events as only the daily press could: extempores, impromptus, occasional odes. Robinson's celebrated improvisational skills in poems like 'The Haunted Beach' thus should be considered in their political, as well as performative, dimensions. We know that many of Robinson's most politically direct poems were omitted from the posthumous edition, and that she also published anonymously. Her connection to the *Morning Post* and now with the *Argus* is established; these additional series in these papers thus deserve further investigation. Whether or not they are Robinson's, these additional pseudonyms are important for understanding how closely enmeshed her poetry was within the diverse political matrix of newspapers and periodicals at this period when, as Jon Klancher has shown, their audiences, rhetorical range and political registers were growing increasingly distinct.

Freedom of the press

Robinson's increasingly radical interventions in a wide range of periodicals and newspapers throughout the 1790s, and her strategic use of pseudonyms, illustrate not only a theatricalized self-presentation but a canny knack for self-preservation in the face of growing restrictions on the press. Unjust restrictions on the press become thematic constants throughout her novels after the sedition trials of 1794, the watershed year for Robinson's radicalization. Robinson's *Natural Daughter, The False Friend* and especially *Walsingham* have begun to attract critical attention, though generally this focuses on the feminist sexual politics of the novels, not on their significant engagement with radical and print politics.[32] *The Natural Daughter* (1799) in particular is deeply involved in print culture debates surrounding the French Revolution. Through her autobiographical heroine, a writer, Robinson illustrates a cross section of different kinds of periodicals read by her female characters, distinguishing their content, audience, and the corruptions they are prey to. In *The False Friend* (1799), Robinson dramatizes how the treason laws and climate of paranoia were abused for repressive ends. The heroine is detained before a Lord Justice, charged by a scheming landlady with possessing a packet of treasonous papers: 'the packet is a most suspicious packet: it looks and it smells like treason', says the landlady, 'and it is the duty of every loyal subject to be careful, and to examine all writings that pass through their hands; and to give information where they find such symptoms of guilt' (3: 297). Robinson reveals the Justice to be a criminal libertine and the landlady a French spy, consistent with her vision of counterrevolutionary measures as covert repression.

Robinson invited such politicized readings of her novels both by addressing contemporary controversies, and by excerpting provocative passages from *Walsingham* (1797) in the *Morning Post* in order to reach a more diverse audience, beyond those able to afford her novels. *Walsingham's* complex plot centres on a disinherited orphan Walsingham Ainsworth, whose female cousin Sidney inherits the family estates instead of him because s/he crossdresses as a man. Demystifying sexual and class privilege in one gesture, *Walsingham* was rightly identified by the *Anti-Jacobin* as a dangerously philosophical novel, and its inclusion in Gillray's 'The New Morality' (1798) cartoon accurately placed this novel in the camp of fellow radicals like Godwin, Tooke, and Wollstonecraft. One excerpt from *Walsingham*, published in the *Morning Post* as 'On the Diurnal Prints', reveals how the specifics of textual production, not just of textual content, are a key feature of both the free press and its repression. 'What right have the *canaille* to know the transactions of the upper world?' asks an aristocrat; Walsingham replies:

That right which is the scourge of overbearing licentiousness, which raises the bulwark of freedom above the chaos of folly and deception, and illumines the low hovel of honest industry, equally with the loftiest abode of pride and dissipation. Heaven forbid that the time should ever approach when the source of public information, which has so long been the pride of Englishmen, shall be closed and annihilated![33]

Walsingham praises the daily papers in particular as 'the bulwark of freedom', to which the aristocrat replies that '[t]he daily papers are too cheap', and 'their price should be raised above the pockets of the vulgar' (3: 253). Robinson's aristocrat echoes government prosecutors in treason trials of popular publishers like Daniel Eaton, accused of targeting the *Rights of Man* part II 'to the lowest orders of the people'.[34] Pitt's Stamp Tax was designed precisely to elevate the price 'above the pockets of the vulgar', as the *Morning Post* reminded its readers each day for years by listing both its original price (3 pence) and its doubled price due to 'Mr. Pitt's Tax'.[35] By including such a debate in both an expensive novel and a newspaper, Robinson skilfully highlights the class issue central to radical debates on the free press.[36]

The power of 'men of letters' (in *Walsingham* 3: 260) and women of letters (in *Letter to the Women of England* and *The Natural Daughter*) is visible in the lengths government will go to criminalize them, as she wrote in her essay on the 'Present State of the...Metropolis of England' (1800):

> Works of extensive thought and philosophical research have been watched with more malevolence than justice. Political restrictions have been enforced, to warp the public taste; and the gigantic wings of Reason have, at times, been paralyzed by their augmenting severity.

Yet 'even our prisons have been illumined by the brilliancy of talents', continues Robinson in a probable allusion to the 'microcosm of enlightened republican civility' in Newgate prison, where radical writers like Perry continued to publish (McCalman 98). The consequences of such repression of the free press can be deadly, as the repentant aristocratic hero of *Hubert de Sevrac* finally realized: 'Had the tongues of my countrymen been at liberty, their swords had been unstained with blood!' (2: 208–9). As in other radical accounts, Pitt's 'reign of terror' on the press is implicitly connected to the Reign of Terror in France, which *Hubert de Sevrac* chronicles.

'Present State of the...Metropolis' presents Robinson's countervision to Pitt's reign of terror on the press: London as a global republic of letters, where a full range of print media circulates freely, as do the international and commercial influences uniquely available in this world capital.[37] Robinson's manifesto of metropolitan culture was published in the *Monthly Magazine* by Richard Phillips, a radical advocate of animal and prisoner rights who had already served three years for seditious libel. The *Monthly Magazine* was known for its 'cosmopolitan, "continental" frame of mind', covering foreign literature in detail as well as controversial political debates (Carnall 161). In keeping with the *Monthly*'s cosmopolitanism, Robinson catalogues how the metropolis has benefited from French and German influence on British literature, theatre, architecture, art, language and fashion. Specifically, she praises '[t]he great number of emigrants who have become our inmates since the French revolution, [and] have contributed to this wide circulation of knowledge', adding that 'some of the best translations from the German have been the productions of female pens'. Robinson then praises the radical Dissenter Anne Plumptre, whose popular translations of Kotzebue were precisely what Wordsworth warned against a few months later when he complained about an influx of 'sickly and stupid German tragedies' in the Preface to the 1800 *Lyrical Ballads*.[38] Wordsworth's anxiety over the unpredictable effects of print media on the public taste, exacerbated by the 'rapid communication of intelligence' in the mass media, stands in significant contrast to Robinson's commitment to the democratic effects of a free press. Robinson shares this conviction with radical reformers who, according to Kevin Gilmartin, 'were convinced that the press necessarily promoted liberty and reform' (24). Whether in the internationalism of her ambitious occasional odes (and radical connections), or in the cosmopolitanism of her visions of metropolitan print culture, Robinson enjoyed unrivalled access to an international political and poetic stage.

Conclusion: Robinson's feminist Francophilia

> In proportion as women are acquainted with the languages they will become citizens of the world.
> Mary Robinson, *Letter to the Women of England* (1799)

Robinson's concept of the Citizen of the World derived from her lifelong Francophilia, which evolved from a Whig model of an aristocratic cosmopolite, to a republican model drawing on enlightenment universalism. Robinson's revolutionary cosmopolitanism grew in part from her early introduction to the intellectual refinements and social liberties of courtly life, and attempted an intriguing intersection of the ideals of both radical 'correspondence' and aristocratic 'conversation'. As the lover of men like the future Prince Regent and Fox, Robinson in her youth moved in the most elite circles. The combination of her middle-class origins, aristocratic aspirations, intellectual ambition, and increasing political radicalism placed Robinson in a unique position, enabling her to consider new models for literature's social and political roles. She never wholly abandoned the aristocratic cosmopolitan ideal, and instead continued to revise and expand it to correspond to her liberal and later radical politics. Robinson's aristocratic aesthetic stands in marked contrast to Wollstonecraft's middle class aesthetic,[39] with its suspicion of effeminacy and artifice; she also goes much farther than her friend in embracing the sensuality associated with French femininity, an important example of so-called 'Anglo-American' feminism's French connections, as I discuss in the Epilogue.

Robinson's links to Gallicized republicans like Merry and Perry are the most obvious traces of this radicalized French connection, yet they are found throughout her writings, even in Robinson's support for the British

Convention. A crucial aspect of the government's case against the Conventionists had been that the British Convention, rather than advocating constitutional reform as it claimed, was attempting to implement a French republic in Britain: 'In its daily business and proceedings the convention had seen fit to adopt French revolutionary forms of address and procedures', such as addressing each other as Citizens and dating their official 'proceedings "the First Year of the British Convention"' (Goodwin 302). Robinson's letter to Dundas, evoking Charlotte Corday and not the Protestant English people as her avenger, consciously oversteps the line between pursuing (British) constitutional reform and invoking republican (French) revolution, something only popular radical groups like the LCS and the British Convention dared to do.

A Francophilic thread remained central to Robinson's radicalization from royal mistress to satirical scourge of Pitt and radical feminist. The prerevolutionary Robinson, mistress to the Prince, was a committed Whig, poetically and politically; she consistently championed commerce, refinement, and the arts as leading to cultural progress. This aristocratic ideal, visible in her stage career and performative aesthetic, was at home in the *ancien régime*. Yet like Olympe de Gouges (author of the *Declaration of the Rights of Woman and of Female Citizen* (1791)) – a radical feminist, actress, and monarchist admirer of Marie Antoinette – Robinson also embraced the Rights of Man for feminist ends. France symbolized for Robinson not just a lost golden age of aristocratic privilege, but, as I have argued in *Fatal Women of Romanticism*, a utopian 'aristocracy of genius' uneasily situated within a 'republic of letters'. Robinson located this utopian promise in women's centrality to French salon and court culture, making possible their role in the Enlightenment and hence in the Revolution, as she saw it.

Robinson's trip to France in 1783, immediately following her rejection by the Prince of Wales, was an illuminating experience for the ambitious actress. In the courtly splendor of Versailles, Robinson seemed to find the proverbial paradise of women, where feminine display, wit, and sensuality prevailed. The social prominence of French actresses in particular, and the access their visibility gave them to the highest ranks of society, bore little resemblance to the status of actresses in England (see Berlanstein). French women's access to print culture was severely curtailed during the *ancien régime*, especially by comparison to British women, yet Robinson's *ancien régime* experience (while identified as an actress and courtesan, not a professional author) permanently associated in her mind elite *salonnières* with the public influence she would later seek for women writers.

Her essay on the 'Present State of . . . the Metropolis' locates in this foreign and feminine source of *ancien régime* femininity the radical Enlightenment that she saw as the prelude to democratic progress:

> In France, even in the days of despotism, genius was deemed the ornament of the courts; and men as well as women were honoured with the most

brilliant distinctions. Versailles had its female constellations; and, though the brilliant sallies of wit predominated in the scale of popularity, the genuine splendour of literature was looked up to, and worshipped with unbounded adoration.

As she elaborated in her *Letter to the Women of England*, it was in the salons of aristocratic women that the radical Enlightenment was nurtured:

The younger branches of male nobility in France, were given to the care of female preceptors; and the rising generations of women, by habit, were considered as the rational associates of man. Both reason and society benefited by the change...the republic of letters had more ornaments of genius and imagination...The influence they [women] obtained contributed greatly towards that urbanity of manners which marked the reign of Louis the Sixteenth. The tyrants of France, at the toilettes of enlightened WOMEN, were taught to shudder at the horrors of the Bastille: which was never more crowded with victims, than when bigotry and priestcraft were in their most exulting zenith. (61–2)

Robinson's idealization of the 'female constellations' of the French salon's oral culture complements her consistent emphasis on British women's role in print culture, which she wanted to institutionalize in a 'UNIVERSITY FOR WOMEN' and an 'ORDER OF LITERARY MERIT' (*Letter* 92, 93), endeavours she hoped to stimulate with her list of eighteenth-century women writers appended to the *Letter*. Drawing together *ancien régime* notions of the oral culture of privileged femininity, with an increasingly radicalized devotion to the free press, Robinson towards the end of her life worked towards a unique, conflicted and unpopularly cosmopolitan ideal of art's relation to the social.

Dena Goodman, Joan Landes, and others have offered competing explanations of the significance of women's salons for the Revolution, with Goodman countering Landes' argument that the *philosophes* (and therefore the Jacobin republicans) were widely opposed to women's influence, by examining how many *philosophes* benefited from women's critical roles as mediators and nurturers of philosophical debate. Considered together, the diverse work of Landes, Goodman, Gutwirth and Hunt (in *The Family Romance of the French Revolution*) sustains a consensus that republican France excluded women from public politics, while as Landes and Goodman each document, elite women had enjoyed political and social influence through institutions like the salon, the court, and the theatre. In a major departure from earlier accounts of revolutionary misogyny, Carla Hesse has argued in *The Other Enlightenment* that French women's greatly increased access to print after 1789 'opened up the unprecedented opportunity for women to participate in public political discourse and debate, and indeed to debate the appropriate place for women within a democratic polity' (55). Basing her argument on a close examination of the quantity and nature of French women's publications from 1789 to 1800 (not on male representations of women), Hesse concludes that the demise of women's oral culture in the *ancien régime* (for both *précieuses* and *poissardes*) was replaced by a flourishing print culture in which women enjoyed new-found public influence and access (through, for example, the abolition of guild restrictions in1791, and the National Convention's subsidization of women's publications).[40]

Robinson's transformation from *ancien régime* actress and courtesan to revolutionary-era professional writer, and a radicalized feminist one at that, mirrors French women's changing access to public culture. In *Letter to the Women of England*, she addresses English women's public influence in terms of a shift from oral to print culture, contextualizing this shift in her present moment's political and sexual restrictions on women's speech (and on their access to hear political speech):[41]

> The embargo upon words, the enforcement of tacit submission, has been productive of consequences highly honourable to the women of the present age. Since the sex have been condemned for exercising the powers of speech, they have successfully taken up the pen... The press will be the monuments from which the genius of British women will rise to immortal celebrity. (90–1)

A master of the intricacies of print politics, Robinson recognized that her historical moment presented women with unprecedented opportunities in the republic of letters, even as it foreclosed other opportunities, such as the ability to address 'public councils' directly (*Letter* 91).

Robinson's concept of the republic of letters and her outspoken support for the free press coexisted with her insistence that this republic include both men and women. Robinson's dual emphasis on what modern scholars have tended to gender as distinct 'spheres' (print culture versus oral culture, public sphere versus private sphere) lends support to recent challenges to Jürgen Habermas's theory of the public sphere as a masculine, rationalist, bourgeois phenomenon. The reintroduction of religious discourse, women writers, plebeian writers, and even seventeenth-century writers into the distinctively rationalist, property-owning, masculine and eighteenth-century concept of the public sphere theorized by Habermas, reflects women's unprecedented involvement in the 1790s 'word war'.[42] Robinson's unique ability to cross these formerly distinct 'spheres' attests to her ongoing value as exemplar and innovator of Romantic modernity.

Robinson valued in the *ancien régime* both feminized salon culture and the radical 'Philosophism' of the Enlightenment (for which latter offence, Polwhele complained, her novels 'merit the severest censure' (17)). Britain lacked both of these liberating traditions, and from Robinson's cosmopolitan, feminist vantage point, one solution for British women of genius was to leave British provincialism behind, and head for the continent:

> Lady Hamilton, and Helen Maria Williams, are existing proofs, that an English woman, like a prophet, is never valued in her own country. In Britain they were neglected, and scarcely *known*; on the continent, they have been nearly IDOLIZED! (*Letter* 65, orig. emphasis).

By 1794 Robinson too had determined to 'quit England forever', dreaming of moving to Smollett's villa near Pisa that her brother had bought, 'one of the many *temptations* to quit England'.[43] A reader (and translator) of French and Italian, like Williams and Smith, Robinson looked to the continent for cultural and political liberation: 'In proportion as women are acquainted with the languages they will become citizens of the world', she affirmed (*Letter* 91).

The textual and Francophilic specifics of Robinson's restored radicalism that I have traced enlarge not only our understanding of women writers and revolutionary politics, but, I hope, contribute to ongoing inquiries into the relationship of the romantic novel to poetry, of popular print culture to canonical Romanticism, of gender to genre. Whether in poetry, novel, or essay Mary Robinson consistently expanded her circle of intellectual interest to include continental Europe, especially France, and her political circle to include both Whig politicians and self-exiled radicals. Shortly before her death in 1800, Robinson celebrated metropolitan public culture (in the 'Metropolis' essay), in all its multilingual and multicultural confusion. What a marked contrast to the 1800 Wordsworth, who as John Lucas has argued in *England and Englishness*, moved increasingly towards nativist abstractions of the English 'people' as he moved 'from city to country' (6). Unlike her contemporaries Wordsworth, Southey, and Coleridge, Robinson grew progressively more radical throughout the 1790s. And like Charlotte Smith and Helen Maria Williams, who also had connections to French radical circles and advocated continental emigration, Robinson came to see herself as a citizen of the world.

Appendix 1: January 1794 timeline

January 1794

2	Pye, 'Ode for the New Year, 1794', *Oracle*.
6–7	Skirving tried and convicted of sedition.
7	Robinson, 'Ode for the New Year', *Morning Post*.
9	Robinson ['Supreme Enchanting Power!'], *Morning Post*; 'Anistrophic Ode for the New Year 1794, by Master Goose Pye', *Morning Post*.
13–14	Margarot tried and convicted of sedition.
14	*Oracle* publishes accounts of Skirving's and Margarot's trials.
14	'To Messrs. MUIR and PALMER' (unsigned poem), *Morning Post*.
17	Society for Constitutional Information holds general meeting at Crown & Anchor Tavern and makes series of resolutions denouncing sedition trials.
18	Robinson ('Daughter of Liberty'), 'Ode on the 18th of January' in *Oracle*; *Oracle* publishes accounts of Skirving's and Margarot's trials; Queen's birthday.
20	London Corresponding Society holds general meeting at Globe Tavern, Fleet Street, where 1000 attended and approved the 'Address... to the People of Great Britain'.
23	Robinson (Tabitha Bramble), letter to Dundas defending Skirving and Margarot.
28	Robinson, 'Lines Written on Monday, January 27, 1794' (later inserted in *Angelina*).

Appendix 2: Letter from 'Tabitha Bramble' to Robert Dundas*

Right. Hon. Robert Dundas
Lord Advocate for Scotland.
My Lord,

It is impossible for any Person to behold with an Indifferent Eye, the transactions which are now carrying on in this Country. On the one hand, we have the Reformers contending for certain principles, & certain renovations which every body allows to be founded in Justice. On the other, Government prosecuting in a rigorous manner such honest endeavours. – You have the honour, or rather the misfortune from your situation, to be the chief agent in such prosecutions. But reflect, my Lord, that the trite argument

---

* This letter, dated 23 January 1794, is held at the Public Record Office (HO/102/10 f.121). Written along the margin in another hand is: '(in Lord Advocate's of the 27th Jan[y]. 1794.)' (original parentheses). There is no postmark. I have compared the handwriting of Tabitha Bramble in this letter to signed letters by Mary Robinson, and believe it to be hers.

of this being an improper time for Reform will be found wanting in the Balance of Posterity. I remember, & your Lor[dshi]p knows well, that the Reformers previous to the Glorious Revolution, were more few, more despicable, more oppressed than any Reformers now a Days. The wanton cruelty, the perversion of Justice, the unheard of Oppression employed towards these Men, soon however attached to their cause the feeling & the moderate. The Nation was roused to fury, it took ample justice on the authors of their wrongs. Thank God we have not at this day the same causes of Complaint: But they are sufficiently strong to excite the murmurs of the people. Your Lordship is perhaps ignorant of the Extent to which the principles of Reform have diffused themselves. When I say that two thirds of the Country are so inclined, I am positive I do not exceed the number. Do not imagine that because certain Corporations are ever ready to re-echo the self dictated applauses of Magistrates, & to thank them for exertions, which in better times would have brought them to the Gallows or because a Jury can be found that will <u>vote</u> as your Lordship pleases, that therefore you enjoy the confidence of the People: Very far from it. Corporations in every country are the least numerous & the most servile of the Community. They have certain interests which are most closely connected with the Ruling Party. But even among these Monopolists such are the charms of Truth, there are many Friends of Liberty. Your Lordship is daily losing in the esteem of the Rabble. The sanguinary & harsh measures employed against the Reformers, are with some degree of Propriety, attributed to you. M^r. Muirs, & now M^r. Skirvings & Margarots cruel treatment have added to your Lordships unpopularity: a few more will render you perfectly odious. It will then be reckoned honourable to deprive Society of such a <u>Pest</u>. Some Male, or rather more likely some Female hand, will direct the Dagger that will do such an important Service; and Britain shall not want a Female Patriot emulous of the fame of <u>M. Cordet</u>, in

 Your Lor[ship]^s. humble Servt.

  Tabitha Bramble

Jan. 23^d 94.

3
Virtue and Terror: Robespierre, Williams and the Corruption of Revolutionary Ideals

> It was under [Robespierre's] domination that I was imprisoned, nearly lost my head and saw many of my friends and relations of both sexes go to the scaffold. If I am so lacking in rancour against his memory, it is because it seems to me that all the horrors perpetrated by those who preceded him, surrounded him, betrayed him, and destroyed him, have been piled upon his name... In men's memories, the defeated always have a bad place. At least I am willing to allow M. de Robespierre the fine name of Incorruptible.
>
> Aimée de Coigny, Duchesse de Fleury,
> French royalist and British spy

Romanticism's 'sympathy with power'

Marie Antoinette and renowned republicans like Charlotte Corday and Madame Roland have been the focus of much attention by feminist scholars of the French Revolution; in literary studies, these public female figures have proved significant for women writers' conflicted responses to the revolutionary crisis and women's changing roles within it.[1] Studies of canonical male Romantics, meanwhile, have emphasized these poets' responses to male figures like Maximilien Robespierre, Napoleon and Jean-Jacques Rousseau. Rather than revisit this familiar ground, I wish in this chapter to examine the significance of Robespierre for women writers. In privileging gender (unconsciously in the case of canonical studies) by considering influence solely along gendered lines, and resistance largely across gendered lines, we miss out on the dynamic political interplay between the increasingly unstable gender boundaries of the revolutionary era (see Hunt, 'Unstable Boundaries'). Robespierre's pivotal role in the Reign of Terror inspired a remarkable series of writings by women, which reveal both a predictable resistance to Jacobin sexual politics, and the limits of this middle-class feminism itself.

Robespierre's symbolic function in canonical British Romanticism is best known to modern readers through Samuel Coleridge and Robert Southey's tragedy *The Fall of Robespierre* (1794) and William Wordsworth's *The Prelude*. William Jewett summarizes that for these 'poets...the temptation of "sympathy with power" can be seen as generating ambivalence more than celebration or lamentation'.[2] This ambivalence towards Robespierre's radical republican experiment is voiced most clearly by Wordsworth's confession in *The Prelude*: 'I felt a kind of sympathy with power' (X. 416). Wordsworth's ambivalent aspiration towards 'the virtue of one paramount mind' embodied in Robespierre reveals, argues Greg Dart, the *Prelude*'s 'radical purpose, emerging clearly out of the tradition of confession fostered by Rousseau and Robespierre' (180). In both Book X of *The Prelude* and *The Fall of Robespierre*, male poetic identity and power remain the focus of modern scholarly inquiry, yet in a curiously ungendered way. The gendering of Wordsworth and Coleridge's fascination with Robespierre is significant, particularly in light of Robespierre's self-constructed role as icon of virtuous, Rousseauvian masculinity.

In Coleridge and Southey's *Fall of Robespierre*, Robespierre's disgust for effeminacy is readily visible in his denunciation of the Jacobins who conspired against him:

> And shall I dread the soft luxurious Tallien?
> Th'Adonis Tallien? banquet-hunting Tallien?
> Him, whose heart flutters at the dice-box? Him,
> Who ever on the harlots' downy pillow
> Resigns his head impure to feverish slumbers! (7)

Priding himself on his 'steel-strong Rectitude of soul' (9), Robespierre belittles conspirators like Barère for their lack of masculine rigor: 'like a frighted child behind its mother,/ Hidest thy pale face in the skirts of – *Mercy!*' (12).[3] Central to Coleridge and Southey's ambivalent fascination with Robespierre's oratorical power is their acknowledgement of its misogyny. Robespierre's misogyny is highlighted through a direct contrast with the play's sole female voice, Adelaide (Tallien's wife), who laments

> The peaceful virtues
> And every blandishment of private life,
> The father's cares, the mother's fond endearment,
> All sacrificed to liberty's wild riot. (13)

Adelaide concludes with a plaintive song: 'Tell me, on what ground,/ May domestic peace be found?' Coleridge and Southey deliberately oppose this idealized voice of feminine 'domestic peace' to Robespierre's 'stern morality' and 'cool ferocity' (15, 36). They do this in order to denounce the violation of domesticity and private virtue exemplified by the Terror, yet inadvertently they reveal the shared misogynist roots of both Robespierre's stern morality and Rousseau's idealized 'domestic peace'. Adelaide's 'blandishments of private life' were idealized not only by Coleridge (actively engaged in the pantisocracy scheme at this time) but by Robespierre himself and the Jacobins, who had famously outlawed all women from participating in public politics following the 1793 executions of such dangerous examples as Marie Antoinette, Madame Roland, and Olympe de Gouges.

The Fall of Robespierre concludes with another tyrant's rise in Robespierre's place – Barère – and he likewise remembers the fallen Girondin regime as Robespierre would, as one corrupted and led by women:

> Roland preach'd
> Of mercy – the uxorious dotard Roland,
> The woman-govern'd Roland durst aspire
> To govern France; and Petion talk'd of virtue,
> And Vergniaud's eloquence, like the honeyed tongue
> Of some soft Syren wooed us to destruction. (36)

Coleridge in his Dedication of the play stated that his goal was 'to imitate the empassioned and highly figurative language of the French Orators' (3). Central to this Romantic male poet's meditation on oratorical power is the gendered aspect of that power, which, as Coleridge makes abundantly clear, is misogynist in the Jacobins' case. Thus, in Jacobin eyes (above, Barère's), Roland was notoriously ruled by his more intelligent and ambitious wife; their ally Pétion, mayor of Paris and friend to British republicans, was also married to a prominent *salonnière*; Vergniaud, the Girondin most renowned for his eloquence, was distrusted even by his ally Madame Roland for his predilection for sensual pleasures, and thus here he appears as a feminized Syren. The prominent role played by women in Girondin circles, whether as objects of sexual desire or as intellectual subjects, emerges in the play as a key point of dispute between warring factions. Moreover, Coleridge and Southey's tragedy dramatizes how the transfer of power from one tyranny to another, from the Robespierrists to the Thermidoreans, remains fatally at odds with the 'peaceful virtues' embodied by Adelaide, the sole female presence in this revolutionary landscape where any affinity for femininity is attacked as weakness and corruption.

The Fall of Robespierre allows us to glimpse the complex gender politics central to Jacobin notions of virtue and power, specifically surrounding Robespierre, and it is important to take notice of this dimension of male poets' 'sympathy with power'. Even more important are the deeper contradictions of gender surrounding the figure of Robespierre during the 1790s, which *The Fall of Robespierre* only begins to reveal in its portrait of Robespierre as misogynist. Perhaps the greatest contradiction regarding Robespierre and women is that, despite the misogyny he inherited (and amplified) from Rousseau, women admired and were fascinated by him. Male observers (and

Romantic poets) shared in this fascination with the 'Incorruptible' Robespierre and his mystical rhetoric of Rousseauvian virtue, but his effect on women was frequently commented upon by contemporaries, particularly his critics. As the self-styled embodiment of Rousseauvian masculine virtue, Robespierre appropriated women's (and men's) passionate admiration for the author of the *Confessions* and *La Nouvelle Héloïse* and based both his public persona and private life on Rousseau's example.

Women's responses to Robespierre in this regard have not yet been explored in our accounts of Romanticism and revolution. In this chapter I examine the significance of Robespierre, as both historical and symbolical figure, in the works of Helen Maria Williams, Mary Robinson, Fanny Burney and others. In Williams's multi-volume *Letters from France*, Robinson's novel *The Natural Daughter*, and Burney's novel *The Wanderer*, Robespierre appears as the avatar of Terror itself. What is at stake here is not Robespierre's role in literary history (as a new version of the Gothic villain, or the villain of early historical novels), but his role as the embodiment of certain revolutionary ideologies, and women writers' critiques of revolutionary politics through such symbolic figures. One might assume that as the embodiment of the Terror, Robespierre appeared only as the 'sanguinary monster' of counter-revolutionary and Girondin caricatures. While this inhuman ferocity is readily visible in the Robespierre of Robinson, Burney, and especially Williams (as in the *Fall of Robespierre*), Robespierre and the Reign of Terror he presided over are also fundamentally concerned with virtue. At the height of the terror in 1794, Robespierre famously linked virtue and terror as the twin attributes of revolutionary government; his evocative formulation of 'terror [as]...an emanation of virtue' inspired women writers' responses to revolutionary politics and their sexualization. Robespierre, because of his unique role as the self-styled disciple of Rousseau and the embodiment of *le peuple*, is a key figure in the gendered imaginary landscape of revolution in women's Romantic writings. In these decidedly feminist yet also ambivalent accounts, his rise and fall marks the dead end of one tradition of Virtue, originating in the writings of Rousseau.

Helen Maria Williams and the sex of terror

Published from 1790 to 1796, Helen Maria Williams's *Letters from France* were among the most influential British accounts of the French Revolution, written by Williams while she lived in Paris almost continuously from 1790 onwards. An influential *salonnière*, Girondin supporter, and feminist, Williams in her eight volumes of *Letters from France* incorporated a 'heterogeneous medley of voices, and a formal disorientation' that transformed the revolution into a collective experience centred on the distinctly feminine and politically liberating potential of sensibility (Favret, *Romantic* 94). As Mary Favret has argued, for Williams the 'revolution is represented by and as the woman's sensitive heart' (*Romantic* 64). Most modern critics engaged in the important task of restoring Williams to her rightful place at the centre of British revolutionary debates share this vision, elaborated most fully by Gary Kelly in *Women, Writing and Revolution* (and promulgated by Williams herself, as is widely acknowledged), that her *Letters* present the moderate revolution (of 1789) as feminine and liberating, and the Jacobin revolution (of 1793) as masculinist and oppressive. Preemptively deflecting charges of inappropriate meddling in the unfeminine affairs of politics, Williams famously enthused that 'my political creed is entirely an affair of the heart' (1:1:66), and suffused her *Letters* with the language and landscape of romance, casting herself as heroine. 'Williams takes this role to its extreme', notes Favret, 'when she casts herself...in the collective and diffuse role of "the people"', and in particular in her portrayal of Liberty in a revolutionary theatrical production in 1790 (*Romantic* 64). Scholars such as Chris Jones, Vivien Jones, Gary Kelly, Elizabeth Bohls, and Deborah Kennedy have demonstrated the significant extent to which Williams's representation of revolution is deliberately feminized through its focus on the Revolution's female victims and heroines, and its reliance on the feminized aesthetics of romance, the familiar letter, and travel writing.

Building on this important body of work on Williams's feminine revolutionary sensibility, I want to focus on the later volumes of the *Letters from France* (1795–1796), in order to examine closely Robespierre's role in Williams's revolutionary romance. If Liberty is her romantic heroine, argues Vivien Jones, then 'Williams's Gothic villain is the levelling "monster" Robespierre' ('Femininity', 303).[4] Yet readings of the later *Letters* do not explore further Robespierre's significance for Williams's project, even though the last four volumes are largely preoccupied with Robespierre's rise and fall, with volume three of the second series taking its title from his name: *Letters Containing a Sketch of the Scenes Which Passed in Various Departments of France During the Tyranny of Robespierre* (1795). It was common for his opponents to refer to the Reign of Terror (September 1793 to July 1794) as the 'Tyranny of Robespierre' or 'Reign of Robespierre' (as in Burney's case in *The Wanderer*), equating the man with the excesses of the Jacobin republic. Williams's fascinating portrait of Robespierre, however, provides a highly subjective account of the revolutionary leader, without which her own self-fashioning as 'Liberty' or 'the people' cannot be understood properly.

Central to understanding Williams' political and aesthetic goals in the *Letters from France* is Robespierre's own self-constructed role as the Revolution itself, and *le peuple* incarnate.[5] Williams's unrelenting attack of Robespierre throughout the *Letters* thus represents not just her partisan revenge in the name of her ousted Girondin friends, but her own rhetorical struggle with Robespierre over the terms of his ascendancy. Revolutionary discourse was highly charged from the start, with warring factions struggling to define and redefine such constructs as Liberty, Equality, Virtue and the People.[6] In Britain this 'crisis in representation', as Steven Blakemore's book of that title demonstrates, demanded that writers continuously 'reimagine and rewrite' (Blakemore 14) the Revolution, through competing histories, and as Nicola Watson has documented, through rewriting *La Nouvelle Héloïse* in particular. Like all writers entering into this discursive fray, Williams struggles to redeem terms like 'sensibility' and to claim 'liberty' and 'virtue' exclusively for her political allies. In the later volumes of *Letters*, moreover, Williams specifically and methodically attempts to undermine the Robespierrist claim on political virtue and liberty, tacitly countering Robespierre's claims to embody *le peuple* with her own claims to embody Liberty.

Much of Williams's rhetorical and aesthetic strategy in the *Letters* she owes in fact to Robespierre, both by negative example and, more surprisingly, by a perceivable ambivalence towards the man himself. As Wordsworth and Coleridge entertained a difficult 'sympathy with power' regarding Robespierre, so Williams intermittently and reluctantly acknowledges the virtues of Robespierre's idealized goals in the Rousseauvian republic of virtue. What I hope will emerge in this reading of the *Letters* is thus not Williams's familiar vilification of Robespierre as monster, nor her feminist championing of moderate 'Liberty', but rather her uneasy rivalry with Robespierre for the role of true representative of the French Revolution.

The Incorruptible

Williams's decision to focus so much of her attention in the later *Letters* on Robespierre, and to portray him as embodying the worst excesses of the Terror, is consistent both with his own self-representations as the spirit of the Revolution, and with Thermidorean and Girondin rhetoric in which he became the scapegoat for the crimes of others and the radicalism of the *sans culottes*. It remains difficult to gain even a moderately objective understanding of Robespierre's revolutionary career because of the unprecedented degree of demonization his image underwent after the coup of 9 Thermidor (27 July 1794), in which he and his closest allies (St. Just, Couthon, Le Bas and the younger Robespierre, his brother) were overthrown by a rival Jacobin faction led by Collot d'Herbois, Billaud-Varenne, Tallien and others. The influential work of conservative French historians like François Furet and Patrice Gueniffey have portrayed Robespierre as consistently and inevitably a terrorist, an embodiment of the logical conclusion of the ideals of 1789.[7] Yet as William Doyle and Colin Haydon have recently suggested in their essay collection, *Robespierre*, this unsatisfyingly static reading grows out of over two hundred years of consistent vilification of Robespierre, making more nuanced analyses of his significance difficult to find. As Doyle and Haydon argue, Robespierre remains a fascinating enigma for historians:

How far did *he* make a difference? Was his oratory largely retrospective justification of events that tidal factors, or other people, had initiated? How far was he the plaything of social forces that he could not comprehend, let alone control? Was his justification of the Terror whilst in power always implicit in the espousal of the Manichean discourse of the early Revolution, in which the politics of the righteous could not tolerate dissent? (7)

In her consideration of similar questions, the stalwart republican Williams contributed to the early (French) antiJacobin (and British counterrevolutionary) tradition of reading Robespierre as the inhuman initiator and embodiment of the Terror, a monstrous usurper of the true course of Revolution theorized by moderate intellectuals in 1789.

Yet the historical Robespierre differs utterly from the 'sanguinary demon' of her *Letters*. An orphaned scholarship student and provincial defence lawyer, Robespierre gained his influence in the revolutionary government as an impassioned orator in the Jacobin club and Paris Commune, that is, not through direct legislative office but through popular influence. Robespierre was president of the National Convention only from 22 August to 5 September 1793, and again from 4 to 18 June 1794 (during the Festival of the Supreme Being), and yet he has become inextricably linked to the institutionalization of Terror. Robespierre 'took no part in the revolutionary tumult of September and October' 1793 and 'was oddly silent in the weeks when terror was made the order of the day' (Jordan 23). His appointment to the Committee for Public Safety on July 27, 1793 coincides nicely with that Committee's gain of unconditional powers that autumn, but as historian David Jordan argues, '[w]e may presume Robespierre supported this accumulation of power in the hands of the Committee, but there is no evidence he worked for these measures ... Robespierre's fingerprints are not visible on the legislation initiating the Terror, nor on many of its more shrill acts', like the law of Suspects (17 September) (23–4). Robespierre did take a personal role in the prosecution and execution of the Girondins in October, however, and it was this above all else that for Williams transformed him into the embodiment of Terror.

Robespierre was renowned for his oratory, and in the autumn of 1793 and spring of 1794 he gave a number of important speeches before the National Convention, refining his highly abstract doctrine of Terror. It is this vision of Terror that Williams struggles to undermine and rewrite, all the while reflecting in her language. Grown increasingly paranoid of internal and external plots following the fall of the Girondins, Robespierre in November 1793 denounced the enemies of the Revolution as corruptors of Liberty: 'l'auguste liberté étoit travestie en un vile prostituée' ('august liberty has been travestied into a vile prostitute' (qtd. in Jordan, 27)). Again and again Robespierre warned of the plots to seduce and destroy Liberty: 'In the shadows crime conspires the destruction of liberty'. 'Robespierre's world, during the final year of his life', writes David Jordan, 'was a fearful and a fatal place, inhabited by the enemy without and within' (27). This is the world Williams also inhabits in *Letters from France*, a landscape drawn not only in the language of aesthetics as Elizabeth Bohls has illustrated, but also according to Williams's increasing obsession with the overthrow of 'the reign of Robespierre'.

Robespierre attempted to counteract the vortex of conspiracy and counter-conspiracy that he saw surrounding Liberty through the radical ideology of Terror, as spelled out in his speech of 17 Pluviôse (4 February 1794). 'The government of the revolution', he said, 'is the despotism of liberty against tyranny'.[8] Robespierre arrived at this notion of the 'despotism of liberty' by linking terror with Rousseauvian virtue:

> Now, what is the fundamental principle of popular or democratic government...? It is virtue. I speak of the public virtue which worked so many wonders in Greece and Rome and which ought to produce even more astonishing things in republican France – that virtue which is nothing other than the love of the nation and its laws...
>
> If the mainspring of popular government in peacetime is virtue, amid revolutions it is at the same time [both] virtue and *terror*: virtue, without which terror is fatal; terror, without which virtue is impotent. Terror is nothing but prompt, severe, inflexible justice; it is therefore an emanation of virtue.[9]

'Unlike the conflation of morality and politics', writes Marisa Linton, 'the linking of virtue and terror appears to have been without precedent', and in fact violated a key axiom of Montesquieu's *L'Esprit des Lois* that virtue and terror are politically opposed (50). Robespierre's original vision of virtue and terror has been described in diametrically opposite ways: as the logical outcome of the Rousseauvian utopianism of 1789, so that as Furet has said 'the Revolution speaks through him in its most tragic and purest discourse'; and conversely, as a 'belated attempt by the Montagnards to justify and explain – even to themselves – a process which was already happening', that is, the intensification of the Terror.[10] Williams was immersed in the events of the Terror, imprisoned on the orders of the Committee of Public Safety (October to November 1793), and still mourning the deaths of her Girondin friends while writing her *Letters*. Her perspective on Robespierre's doctrine of Terror thus understandably diverges from these more detached interpretations of the Terror as either a logical consequence of Rousseauvian republicanism or the unfortunate response to revolutionary crises. Fellow radicals like Wordsworth, for example, could look back even late into the 1790s and still cautiously attribute the Reign of Terror to the war with England and other monarchial powers (see Maniquis). But more was at stake for Williams than perhaps for any other British observer of the French Revolution, Wordsworth included, because of her unprecedented degree of involvement in revolutionary politics through successive regimes.

Her attempt to replace Robespierre as the embodiment of the Revolution and *le peuple* targets Robespierre's ideological innovations as well as his public persona, deliberately rewriting each. Robespierre is thus much more than the villain of her version of the Revolution as Gothic romance. As Wollstonecraft would do with Burke and Rousseau in her *Vindication of the Rights of Men* and *Vindication of the Rights of Woman*, respectively, Williams attempts to wrestle key terms like Liberty and Virtue out of the hostile hands of her adversary (here, Robespierre), and back into those of her ideological allies, in her case the educated and bourgeois Girondins. Liberty is particularly significant in Williams's *Letters*, as all modern critics have noted in discussing Williams's triumphant role as Liberty in the 1790 private theatricals described in the first volume of her *Letters*.

Robespierre's rhetoric portrayed Liberty as armed, at once the victim of factions and the avenging agent of Terror: only 'in attacking [factions] head-on', he wrote, 'in plunging the dagger of liberty into their hearts, can we rescue liberty from all the scoundrels who want to destroy it' (qtd. in Jordan, 28). Like Virtue, Liberty without terror is impotent. Both victim and avenger, Robespierre's Liberty is dangerously similar to the groups of working-class women who came to hear him speak, and, despite his emerging contempt for publicly active women, supported the rise of the Montagnards and the overthrow of the Girondins. Recounting the overthrow of the Girondins in May 1793, Williams depicts Robespierre as surrounded by debased female admirers:

> But Robespierre with his commune, his Jacobins, and his body guard of revolutionary women, who were in the van of the attack, and stood in the passages of the convention armed with poniards, which they pointed at the bosoms of the such of the deputies as attempted to leave the hall, had gone too far to recede. (2:1:73)

Williams blamed Robespierre himself for perverting Liberty: 'her cause [has] ... fallen into the hands of monsters ignorant of her charms, by whom she has been transformed into a Fury' (2:2:212). Robespierre's sexuality, or lack thereof, was consistently an object of speculation among his enemies. Williams's account of Robespierre surrounded by a body-guard of women implies he is unnatural and emasculated, unable to appreciate Liberty's charms as any heterosexual man of feeling would.

Robespierre's severe asceticism was frequently commented upon by observers, praised by his supporters as a sign of his single-minded devotion to public virtue, and denounced by his enemies as a sign of his inhuman coldness and cruelty. Robespierre's ostensibly sexless quality as the Incorruptible coexisted with the undeniable enthusiasm he exhibited and generated during his impassioned speeches, drawing large female crowds and even love letters. The Girondins belittled him for his female admirers, likening him to a priest with his superstitious female followers:

> He has all the characteristics, not of a religious leader, but of the leader of a sect...he obtains women and the feeble-minded as his followers; he gravely receives their adoration and their homage...he is a priest.[11]

In Girondin attacks on Robespierre like this one (probably by the feminist Condorcet) and like Williams's, Robespierre's appeal is thus de-eroticized and misogynist at the same time. Like the Girondin Charlotte Corday and other publicly active revolutionary women, Robespierre found that his politics of virtue were reduced to an indicator of sexuality (as either excessive or insufficient) according to the perceiver's political agenda.

Written in 1824–5, the monarchist historian Adolphe Thiers's retrospective view of Robespierre is also representative in its contempt for Robespierre's female admirers, and demonstrates the persistence of his feminine associations:

> Covetous of flattery and respect...He was surrounded by a kind of court, composed by a few men, but chiefly of a great number of women, who paid him the most refined attentions. Constantly resorting to his residence, they manifested the most unceasing solicitude for his welfare; they were continually praising amongst themselves his virtue, his eloquence, his genius; they called him a divine creature, and quite exalted above our human nature. A superannuated marchioness was the principal of this proud and bloodthirsty pontiff. Nothing is so certain a demonstration of the public infatuation as the gross admiration of the women. It is they also, who, by their active attentions, their language, and their restless affectation, make it appear ridiculous.[12]

The phenomenon of Robespierre's large female audience, whether infatuated visitors as in this account, or armed working-class Jacobins as in Williams's, consistently appears in such antiJacobin accounts as a means of proving him 'ridiculous' and unnatural.

The source of this female interest in Robespierre, as Williams would have understood, was his highly successful appropriation of the role of Rousseau's chief disciple, a living incarnation of the Legislator Rousseau imagined in his *Social Contract*, and the idealistic martyr of the *Confessions*, Robespierre's two favorite books. We know from Greg Dart's *Rousseau, Robespierre and English Romanticism* that the extent to which Robespierre's embodiment of Rousseauvian principles influenced the male Romantics has been underappreciated. To the growing body of work on Rousseau's influence on women Romantics we should likewise introduce the significance of Robespierre, who historians consistently describe as 'enthralled by Rousseau' (Jordan 30). Robespierre's three key political principles were derived from Rousseau, in particular the *Social Contract* and the *Confessions*: first, 'the virtuous self: that is, the man (or woman) who stands alone, sustained only by private conscience'; second, that 'vitrue was most likely to be found amongst ordinary people'; third, 'the theory of the "general will", ... made famous in the *Social Contract*, [which] meant something more than an amalgam of the will of every person in the body politic: it was a right-thinking will' (Linton 40–1). In his hagiographic *Dédicace aux mânes de Jean-Jacques Rousseau*, Robespierre dedicated himself to Rousseau's teachings: 'I want to follow your venerable path...I shall be happy if, in the perilous course that an unprecedented revolution just opened up before us, I remain constantly faithful to the inspiration that I have drawn from your writings!' (qtd. in Blum, *Rousseau* 157). During the brief period of his ascendancy from 1793 to 1794, Robespierre attempted to put into practice Rousseau's highly theoretical notion of the Republic of Virtue, complete with the exclusion of all women, including his militant female supporters, from public life (according to the emerging doctrine of 'republican motherhood'). Conservative historians like Furet and Simon Schama read the Terror as the logical outcome of the Rousseauvian enthusiasm of 1789 in part for this reason. For this reason also Williams in her last four volumes of the *Letters from France* struggles against Robespierre's interpretation and appropriation of Rousseau, putting herself forward as rival disciple. Williams's friends the Rolands had claimed this role for themselves before they were ousted by Robespierre's allies. Brissot in particular, the most well-known of the deputies from the Gironde (also known as Brissotins), was their foremost Rousseavian disciple; for years Williams planned to produce an English edition of Brissot's memoirs, which she had compared to Rousseau's *Confessions* (*Letters* 2:3:60). 'The corpus of Rousseau's work formed the arsenal from which revolutionaries at all points of the political spectrum drew their arms', Carol Blum reminds us, and 'by far the most ardent and adept of Jean-Jacques' disciples formed the nucleus of the Jacobin organization during...the Jacobin Republic' ('Representing', 124).

Modern accounts rightly credit Williams with popularizing an enthusiastic revolutionary discourse, both feminine and sentimental. Wollstonecraft's review of the first volume of *Letters from France* (1790) in the *Analytical Review* echoes, with a hint of irony, Williams's own self-representation as 'truly feminine', displaying 'such an air of sincerity' (*Works* 7: 323). Yet sublime enthusiasm and sincerity were also Robespierre's chief virtues according to his admirers and his own self-representation, drawn from Rousseau's confessional style. His renowned power as an orator came not from eloquence or dramatic flair, as in the cases of his rivals Vergniaud and Danton, but from the sense of conviction and intensity that he conveyed through his eyes and voice. 'His voice is strained', wrote one German observer, inspiring awe and compelling an absolute silence…it is his eyes that are the most lively part of him; they search the faces of his hearers and appear almost to read the opinion of each one of them in the expression of his countenance. It is certainly this optical power that is the cause of the spell that he casts over many of his audiences. (in Rudé, ed., *Robespierre* 84)

Williams's friend John Moore grudgingly conceded that despite opinions to the contrary, Robespierre was an 'enthusiast', not a 'hypocrite'.[13] Robespierre's unflinching devotion to an absolute transparency of emotion derived entirely from Rousseau, as even enemies like his Thermidorean rival Dubois de Crancé admitted:

this man, who was steeped in Rousseau's moral teaching, had the strength to emulate his master; he shared the austerity of his principles, his manner of life, his unsociability, unwillingness to compromise, proud simplicity, and even the moroseness of his disposition; and although he lacked Rousseau's talents, Robespierre was no ordinary mortal.[14]

Modelling the Jacobin Republic's policies on the teachings of Rousseau, Robespierre tried to bring to life a utopian Republic of Virtue, complete with the state religion of the Supreme Being, the radical separation of the sexes, the state education of children, and the rule of the general will. This 'despotism of liberty' was far from the Rousseauvian ideal of sensibility that educated literary women like Williams, Roland and Staël admired in their competing readings of texts like *Emile*, *Confessions*, and especially *La Nouvelle Héloïse* (instead of the *Social Contract*). Williams's *Letters* challenge Robespierre's reading of Rousseau, offering herself, as Madame Roland did even more overtly in her *Memoirs*, as an alternative disciple of the citizen of Geneva. Williams's rivalry with Robespierre makes visible the gulf often found between women's and men's equally impassioned responses to Rousseau: for often radically different reasons, and typically through different texts, women and men found in Rousseau a wealth of contradictory possibilities for virtue.

Several times in her *Letters*, Robinson evokes the flight from the city and into the virtuous countryside that Rousseau repeatedly pursued in his *Confessions*. The vertiginous structure, if it may be called a structure, of the latter four volumes of the *Letters from France*, is often puzzled over by modern scholars.[15] Williams cannot bring herself definitively to end the Terror, and Robespierre's life, but instead returns repeatedly to scenes of suffering virtue, after celebrating, from her present vantage point, the destruction of Robespierre's tyranny. Two of these temporary respites from the unfolding violence in Paris are figured as pastoral retreats into Rousseauvian rural solitude. Williams returns to this gesture of flight, I suggest, not merely as psychological and aesthetic escape into 'nature', but as a strategic return to *her* Rousseau. Williams wants to return with her reader to the gentle morality of the savoyard vicar, to the domestic tranquillity of Julie's Clarens, and away from Robespierre's Rousseau – the stern Legislator of the Republic of Virtue. Williams returns to Rousseau in order to separate him from Robespierre, and thus to separate what Robespierre has fused – Terror and Virtue – thereby finally ending the Terror.

The day before the overthrow of her Girondin friends (31 May 1793), Williams recounts a trip to Rousseau's home at Montmorency on the outskirts of Paris:

> we had wandered until evening, amidst that enchanting scenery which Rousseau once inhabited, and which he so luxuriously described. Alas! while the charms of nature had soothed our imaginations, and made us forget awhile the scenes of moral deformity exhibited in the polluted city we had left; while everything around us breathed delight, and the landscape was a hymn to the Almighty; the assassins were at their bloody work, and plotting the murder of our friends. (2:1:165)

We need to look beyond the ubiquitous discourse of nature/deformity, country/city, virtue/vice to glimpse the significance of Williams's rhetorical move here. In returning to the philosophical source of the Revolution – Rousseau's retreat at Montmorency, the scene of his greatest productivity – on the eve of the Girondins' overthrow, Williams implies that Rousseau is betrayed along with the Girondins. The emotive words she uses – luxuriously, enchanting, soothed – are in deliberate contrast to Robespierre's renowned asceticism, subtly reminding her readers of the aspects of Rousseau that she values and Robespierre betrays. Like Rousseau the victim of conspiracy and treachery, Williams repeats his gesture of retreat to Montmorency.

In popular accounts, Robespierre was rumoured to make this same symbolic pilgrimage shortly before his downfall, when he mysteriously disappeared from public view a month before his final speech to the Convention on 8 Thermidor. While Robespierre's most reliable biographer notes that 'strong local tradition . . . credits him with having spent some part of the summer of 1794 at Rousseau's Hermitage at Montmorency', the more fantastic rumour that Robespierre went to Montmorency to join 'in mystical communion with Jean-Jacques' on the eve of 6 Thermidor is highly unlikely (Thompson, *Robespierre* 2: 219). Williams would probably have been familiar with these popular rumours of Robespierre's pilgrimage(s) when publishing her *Letters* one year later. It is clear that both Williams and Robespierre were well versed in the political significance of such symbolic gestures of affinity with Rousseau, especially on the eve of crisis.

The struggle between the Girondins and Jacobins, culminating in the overthrow of the former by the latter in the summer of 1793, is the event by which Williams organizes and judges the unfolding chaos of revolution. Her interpretation of this struggle 'is built upon her sense of class difference', confirms Doborah Kennedy (*Helen Maria Williams*, 112). She is 'sympathetic to the disadvantaged until they take politics into their own hands', notes Elizabeth Bohls, thus remaining in the end an 'ambivalent revolutionary' (138). As the perceived leader of the *sans culottes* and the radical Paris commune, Robespierre spoke through and for (as he saw it) *le peuple*; Williams and her bourgeois Girondin allies, in contrast, feared the working classes of Paris and their increasingly radical demands for economic equality. Madame Roland's biographer Gita May pinpoints her subject's miscalculation in this regard, a miscalculation that Williams shared in following the Rolands uncritically: 'It was Mme. Roland's fatal mistake to believe that the Jacobins represented only the ragged mobs of Paris while the Girondists were the spokesmen of the whole people of France' (230). Madame Roland in her *Memoirs* thus attributed the break between Robespierre and her allies in the autumn of 1792 to personal rivalry, an interpretation favoured by many after-wards (like Williams) who preferred to demonize Robespierre. 'Consistently', writes Gita May,

> emphasis is placed upon personal, rather than ideological, motives in her comments on the Brissot-Robespierre rift...[O]f the dubious wisdom of declaring war against the whole of Europe...not a word is said. Rather Robespierre's campaign against Brissot and his ministry is interpreted solely in the light of petty jealousy and private rivalry. (214)

And such is the case with Williams's *Letters from France*, which does not concede the wisdom of Robespierre's antiwar stance (even with the benefit of hindsight, when his prediction that the war would benefit the royalists, by engulfing the young republic in a struggle against a coalition of monarchies, proved correct). Neither do we see the abolitionist Robespierre (banning slavery in all French colonies in February 1794), nor the Robespierre who earlier had stood against capital punishment and legislative corruption. Instead, Robespierre in the *Letters* is a demonic, supernatural force of evil, a vision designed to outlive and replace the historical man himself and thus to avenge the executions of Williams's friends.

As much as Williams tries to separate the idealized Girondins ('a radiant constellation in the zone of freedom') from the demonized Montagnards ('sanguinary and ambitious men who passed along the revolutionary horizon like baneful meteors') these groups are interconnected and jointly complicit (2:2:78). Robespierre frequently attended Madame Roland's salon before the split of 1792, and it was she who named him the 'Incorruptible'; her husband was known as the 'Virtuous Roland', an alternate emanation of Jean-Jacques. Williams is particularly scathing towards Barère, an early Brissotin who joined the Committee of Public Safety; similarly, she does not acknowledge how men like Louvet (a proscribed Girondin) were also members of the

Jacobin club. Modern scholars of Williams tend to follow her lead in separating the 'moderate' Girondins from the 'extreme' Jacobins, like so many proverbial sheep and goats. Yet Carol Blum affirms that the ambitious Girondins themselves introduced the manichean tone of moral suspicion that was later associated with the Jacobins: 'Much of the early rhetorical shift toward a bloody moral polarization of political life must be attributed to the Gironde' (*Rousseau* 169). Mme. Roland in particular, according to Gita May, was 'one of the first to advocate methods of intimidation and repression against all suspicious elements' (164). Thus, beyond attending to Williams's bourgeois class politics and feminism, we need to locate her *Letters* within this labyrinthine revolutionary discourse derived from Rousseau, and consider the ideological role Robespierre played in her political thinking.

Released from prison in the winter of 1793, Williams returned again to Rousseau, and in a sense *as* Rousseau, in her own reverie as a solitary walker, contemplating the alienation of Paris from the 'natural' goodness of the countryside:

> It was in these walks that the soul, which the scenes of Paris petrified with terror, melted at the view of the soothing landscape, and that the eye was lifted up to heaven with tears of resignation mingled with hope. I have no words to paint the strong feeling of reluctance with which I always returned from our walks to Paris, that den of carnage, that slaughter-house of man. How I envied the peasant his lonely hut! for I had now almost lost the idea of social happiness. My disturbed imagination divided the communities of men but into two classes, the oppressor and the oppressed. (2:2:4)

The close of this remarkable passage could as easily have come from Rousseau's *Confessions* as from Williams's *Letters*. Williams makes the same essential link (for entirely opposite purposes) between Rousseau and Terror that Robespierre made: for Williams, the Terror represents the corruption of Rousseau's ideals, and for Robespierre, their materialization. Rousseau's rejection of Parisian corruption and self-characterization as a solitary, virtuous martyr beset by enemies is characteristic of his radical externalization of evil. As Jean Starobinski has argued,

> the Terror seems...to be, on the political level, homologous with that which unfolds on the mental level in the autobiographical writings of Rousseau. To safeguard the conviction of his own radical innocence, Jean-Jacques must reject the evil to the outside, to impute it to a universal plot formed by his enemies.[16]

Williams and Robespierre inhabit and shape this same 'culture of fear' (Jordan 28), and their dualistic, Rousseauvian denunciations of the evil Other are, finally, interchangeable. Williams's vision of the 'oppressors and the oppressed' mirrors Robespierre's ('There can be only two groups in the Convention ... the good and the wicked, the patriots and the counter-revolutionary hypocrites'),[17] and both echo Rousseau. Williams in her *Letters*, like Robespierre in his speeches, attempts to reverse the polarity of oppressor and oppressed, Jacobin and Girondin, part of the larger Rousseauvian struggle between the Gironde and the Jacobins. '[F]or both groups', concludes Blum, Rousseau's concept of virtue 'furnished a model for attributing absolute evil to opposing parties, for refusing to envisage compromise with any persons with whom the group was not identified, and for viewing death as the rational alternative to failure of virtue' (*Rousseau* 139). In setting up her allies as the absolute antithesis of the 'sanguinary' Jacobins, Williams both perpetuates this dangerous dualism of absolute evil and good, and also implicitly vies with Robespierre for the role of Rousseau's true heir.

Williams's account of the Festival of the Supreme Being yields the most striking example of this struggle to supplant Robespierre, and at the same time a significant instance of the 'sympathy with power' experienced by male Romantics. Modern scholarship has focused on Williams's account of the Festival as the apex of her antiJacobin critique, in which she 'presents the festival itself as a total contrast to the Fédération which had thrilled her in 1790'; in Jacques-Louis David's highly orchestrated ceremony, writes Chris Jones, '[s]pontaneity has now given away to obedience, nature to art' ('Helen Maria Williams' 14). While this aspect of Williams's account is often commented upon, a curious subtext in this section of the *Letters* remains neglected. Throughout these latter four volumes of the *Letters*, Williams invokes Robespierre directly only as monstrous villain, and indirectly, as I have shown above, through her subtle attempts to reclaim Rousseau from Robespierre while using their shared rhetoric. She does not excerpt Robespierre's numerous speeches, but maintains strict control of Robespierre's representation, showing him only as monster and never as persuasive orator or enthusiast. But in her account of the Festival of the Supreme Being, she excerpts Robespierre's famous speech instituting the Cult of the Supreme Being as the state religion, the sole such excerpt in the *Letters*. Robespierre's speech on the Cult of the Supreme Being (7 May 1794) put into practice Rousseau's plan for a state religion, and David's festival of June 8 'was the literal enactment of Rousseau's prescription' (Blum, *Rousseau* 249).

'While Robespierre behind the scenes was issuing daily mandates for murder', begins Williams, 'we see him on the stage the herald of mercy and peace' (2:3:142). Like Williams, Robespierre had been appalled by the atheistic Festival of Reason (Nov. 1793), and like a good Rousseauvian placed the doctrine of immortality central to his notion of morality:

Will man be inspired with more pure and elevated sentiments by the idea of annihilation, than by that of immortality? Will it produce more respect for his fellow creatures, and for himself? more attachment to his country? stronger resistance to tyranny? (Robespierre, qtd. in *Letters* 2:3:143)

Opposing both 'ultraradical' atheists and counterrevolutionary priests, Robespierre celebrated instead a Rousseauvian religion of sensibility, as Williams's excerpt continued:

> Let us institute the festival of glory; not of that glory which ravages and enslaves the world, but that which enlightens, comforts and gives it freedom; of that which, next to their country, is the chief object of worship to generous minds. Let us institute another festival more affecting still; the festival of misfortune. Wealth and power are the idols of slaves; let *us* honour misfortune; misfortune, which humanity cannot chase from the earth, but which it can soften and cheer. (Robespierre, in *Letters* 2:3:145–6)

Using the language of the heart, Robespierre's speech on the Supreme Being marked a key step in his self-elevation, like Rousseau before him, to the role of Messiah. As another English observer acknowledged in dismay, Robespierre 'is compared, not by an individual but by a body of people, to the Messiah, "annoncé par l'Etre Supreme, pour reformer toute chose [*sic*]"' (Tench 117–18). Robespierre's Supreme Being speech drew both adulation (for example, from the prophetess Catherine Theot, who proclaimed him the second coming), and increased resistance amongst his enemies in the Convention. His death followed a few months later, after which, as the English observer continued, 'he is said to manifest himself "comme Dieu, par les merveilles"' (Tench 118).

In this heated atmosphere of idolatry and vilification, Williams herself reveals a muted admiration for Robespierre's sublime discourse: 'Though we were not deceived as to the habitual character of Robespierre, we imagined that the overthrow of all the rival factions might have softened in some measure his obdurate heart' (2:3:145). Williams cannot concede that Robespierre is genuinely moved to sublime enthusiasm like she is, and yet in this moment, while resorting to the cool detachment of the editorial 'we', she catches herself before she too is seduced by the Incorruptible. This extended excerpt and her editorial comment is the closest Williams comes to acknowledging that perhaps Robespierre, like Williams and her Girondin allies, speaks in the sincere voice of the Rousseauvian enthusiast and lover of liberty. Williams's excerpt of Robespierre's speech, and the brief glimpse of his 'softened' heart, suggested but immediately denied, is the closest she comes to acknowledging Robespierre as a human, potentially virtuous, political rival. Significantly, this pivotal episode of the *Letters* is not included in the abridged edition often cited in modern studies, *Memoirs of the Reign of Robespierre* (1929).[18]

At stake in her assessment of Robespierre is the legacy of Rousseau and the true course of the Revolution, and also, closer to home, Williams's own role in the Revolution. The final volume of Williams's *Letters* chronicles the aftermath of Thermidor, including the trial of Fouquier-Tinville, the chief prosecutor during the Terror. She attended his trial and was dismayed at the inability of the prosecutor to move his audience to outrage as an enthusiastic orator would:

> the effect was somewhat lost from the incapacity of the speaker, who in a low and monotonous accent read his paper with all the tame professional indifference of an attorney... I could not but lament that this part of the process, so replete with every subject that could inspire an orator, had not fallen into better hands. I figured to myself Erskine pleading such a cause, and into transports of madness he would have thrown his audience! – how he would alternately have harrowed up our souls, and fixed us in sullen despair! –... how he would have painted the appeal of innocence, the magnanimity of patriotism, the indignation of virtue. (2:4:46–7)

On one level this self-reflexive moment 'describes not what some imaginary orator *might do*, but what Williams *has done* in her seven volumes of *Letters*', so that, as Deborah Kennedy has argued, '[t]he entire passage sketches the ideal spokesperson for the Republic... none other than [Williams] herself' ('Spectacle', 109, 110). Yet the stated subject of her later *Letters* is not Thomas Erskine, the renowned defender in the British treason trials, but Maximilien Robespierre, whose danger lay in precisely his ability to throw his audiences, especially women, into the 'transports of madness' for which Williams is eager.

Williams's meditation continues in a crescendo of revolutionary fervour eerily reminiscent of the moralistic enthusiasm associated with Robespierre's speeches:

> how he would have dwelt on the violation of law, on the perversion of justice! – how he would have contrasted the sanguinary monsters with their victims – and at length, with the enthusiastic fervor of his sublime eloquence, how he would have humbled our bursting indignation into reverence of the unsearchable decrees of Heaven, and persuaded us that the permission of so much evil is yet consistent with the plan of general good. (2:4:48)

'He' can only be Robespierre, whose revolutionary ideology of enthusiasm and justice is summed up above, complete with a justification for the 'despotism of liberty', that is, the Terror that is ultimately 'consistent with the plan of general good'. After four volumes of recounting in graphic detail the mass executions, irrationality, and disregard for human rights that characterized the Terror, Williams herself is swept up in the call for violence. In wishing for a sublime orator who could summon the madness and wrath of the crowd (herself included), she obliquely invokes Robespierre, in the same language as he himself spoke as and for *le peuple*. This self-reflexive moment unintentionally acknowledges her participation in this very human (as opposed to demonic) culture of fear which she had hitherto projected solely onto Robespierre.

Williams concludes her account of the Jacobins' prosecution with a further insight:

> While that desire of retribution, which is natural to the human mind, was satisfied in contemplating the great criminals dragged to punishment by the strong arm of national justice, sensations of softer pleasure were excited by observing the delightful transition which these momentous scenes produced in the situation of private individuals. (2:4:52)

Briefly acknowledging her desire for retributive justice (the public executions of over 50 members of the commune), Williams quickly moves on to 'sensations of softer pleasure' in a characteristic shift away from the unpleasant realities of 'national justice'. Clearly there is pleasure in watching Fouquier-Tinville and other enemies responsible for the deaths of her friends, being prosecuted and executed, yet this pleasure is difficult to reconcile with Williams's idealized vision of Girondin revolution.

Such published accounts of the Thermidorean trials circulated widely in Paris in 1794 and 1795, generating a tremendous public backlash against the Jacobins, making 'the *right to vengeance legitimate*' (Baczko 148). Most importantly, they 'accelerated the move from the question: *How to dismantle the Terror?* to the problem: *How to terminate the Revolution?*' (Baczko 148). In the revolutionary discourse of the Jacobin Republic, Robespierre came to embody the Revolution itself. His death was used by fellow republicans like Williams to begin to make sense of the overwhelming chaos that had been the Terror; even more painfully perhaps, Robespierre's death required republicans to take stock of the Revolution itself. Williams's obsessive return to the fall of Robespierre throughout her final volumes mirrors her return to this question regarding Robespierre's role as the Revolution. 'It was impossible that this state of extreme violence could be permanent', Williams writes (2:3:151–2), and Elizabeth Bohls concludes: 'She is right, of course, it ends with the fall of Robespierre. Her final volumes circle restlessly around this key occurence with a refusal of linear narrative that conveys a deep sense of discontinuity' (136). The discontinuity, I suggest, is produced by the disastrous consequences of Robespierre's successful embodiment of the Revolution.

Williams cannot end the Terror in these later volumes, cannot bring herself to fix the end of the Terror in the death of the 'terrorists', because their chief ideologue has so completely bound himself up with the fate of the Revolution that the end of Robespierre may indeed spell the end of the Revolution. The violence of the Revolution does not end with Robespierre's death, as Williams herself experiences in the vindictive pleasure found in the Thermidorean trials. Williams's *Letters* (and modern accounts of them) emphasize her association with the softer pleasures found in the private, feminine domain that is threatened by a hypermasculine Terror. Yet in the interstices of this unabashedly Girondin mythology we see a far more complex account of revolutionary politics, in which Williams and Robespierre share a common discourse, a common hero, and occasionally even common motives: love of virtue, pleasure in retribution, and a desire to embody the Revolution.

The romance of Robespierre

Beyond his central role in Williams's revolutionary chronicles, Robespierre also emerged as the quintessential villain in romances and novels.[19] Williams had famously characterized France as the 'region of romance' (2:2:178) and in her *Letters from France*, written to an imaginary English correspondent, tried 'to construct a political romance: if obtrusive barriers could be overcome, France and England could understand each other and be united' (Favret, *Romantic* 75). Mary Robinson's novel set in England and France during the Terror, *The Natural Daughter*, imagined the nightmarish potential of such a national romance between France and England, through an antisentimental sexual union of Robespierre and an English antiheroine. As we shall see, Robinson followed Williams in casting Robespierre as a modern, politicized avatar of the classic libertine villain, whose political ambition and 'bloodthirstiness' is sexualized into a libidinal pursuit of Virtue.

In contrast to such posthumous visions of Robespierre as libertine monster, while he lived the actual Robespierre often inspired entirely different reactions from women: desire and devotion. Like his hero Rousseau, and despite the misogyny that was central to both their political and sexual ideals, Robespierre received the adulation and amorous correspondence worthy of Saint-Preux. One *citoyenne* (the sister of Mirabeau) wrote to Robespierre offering to help instruct children in the *Catéchisme de la Nature*, and pledged her devotion to him personally:

Mon cher Robespierre, non, je ne te quiterrai jamais; ne crains pas cela; j'aurai des vertus en suivant tes conseils et tes exemples; et, loin de toi peut-être, un autre air que le sol que tu habites me perdrait. Non; ferme et invariable, tu es un aigle qui plane dans les cieux, ton esprit, ton coeur est séduisant, l'amour du bien est ton cri d'armes.[20]

Rousseau's seductive virtue is even more so in Robespierre's Republic of Virtue, where women struggled to participate in this collective project to make Jean-Jacques's ideals a reality. Robespierre's 'seductive heart' was never more so than after his famed speech on the Supreme Being, to which as we saw, even Williams responded emotionally. One young widow from Nantes wrote to Robespierre several weeks after his Supreme Being speech, offering him her virtuous devotion:

Mon cher Robespierre,

Depuis le commencement de la révolution je suis amoureuse de toi, mais j'étais enchaînée et j'ai su vincre ma passion. Aujourd'hui que je suis libre, parce que j'ai perdu mon mari à la guerre de la Vendée, je veux, en face de l'Etre suprême, t'en faire la déclaration.

Je me flatte, mon cher Robespierre, que tu seras sensible à l'aveu que je te fais. Il en coute à une femme de faire un tel aveu, mais le papier soufre tout et on rougi moins de loin qu'en face l'un de l'autre. Tu es ma divinité suprême et je n'en connais d'autre sur la terre que toi: je te regarde comme un ange tutellaire et je ne veux vivre que sou [sic] tes lois; elles sont si douces que je fais le serment, si tu es aussi libre que moi de m'unir avec toi pour la vie.[21]

A modern day Julie who at first sublimated her passion for her Saint-Preux because she was married, the young widow is irresistibly drawn to what many admirers of Robespierre would have recognized – his self-styled resemblance to Rousseau as misunderstood enthusiast and martyr.

Robespierre's devoted female following embodied the crisis of gender that lay at the heart of the Revolution's sentimental politics and their aestheticization. Feminists like Williams and Robinson foregrounded gender in their revolutionary critiques, yet in their monologically malevolent depictions of Robespierre, they simultaneously (and impossibly) tried to negate the heroic and desirable qualities of virtually all villains in this tradition. Ambrosio in Lewis's *The Monk* (1796) inspired similar displays of female devotion, particularly at the novel's beginning when we witness the barely sublimated sexual response his sermon inspires in the crowds of women who come to hear and see him. Lewis's novel unmasks this public display of virtue as repressed vice, culminating in some of the Gothic's most notorious displays of crowd violence and graphic physical suffering, and earning the novel pride of place as one of Sade's favourites. Yet Ambrosio remains a sympathetic, conflicted character, and it is precisely his ambivalent status as antihero (and Saint-Preux's over-determined status as Romantic hero) that Williams and Robinson are eager to avoid in their representations of Robespierre. In Radcliffe's *The Mysteries of Udolpho* (1794), Montoni represents the opposite extreme to Ambrosio – absolute lack of sensibility – and yet Emily 'never beholds Montoni without marking the sublimity of his maleness, "the fire and keenness of his eye, its proud exultation, its bold fierceness, its sullen watchfulness"' (Johnson 104). Montoni's utter lack of feeling (the inverse of Ambrosio's excess), writes Claudia Johnson, inspires Emily with desire for a presentimental 'lost masculinity', a 'fearful attraction to the very qualities that make Montoni so forthrightly misogynist' (104). These Gothic villains and antiheroes inhabit the same culture of fear and partake of the same sentimental politics, as do historical agents like Robespierre, Robinson and Williams. The latter two's feminist responses to Robespierre thus attempt to avoid the dangerous attractions his sexualization opened up, while nevertheless connecting his 'tyranny' to misogyny.

Posthumous accounts of Robespierre like Robinson's and Williams's are notoriously unsympathetic, especially when contrasted with his above-quoted amorous correspondence. Another English observer in 1795, the captured officer Watkin Tench, distrusted this tendency to demonize Robespierre:

> many of the relations, which, on authority seeming good, I every day hear and read of his towering ambition and capricious cruelty, are too extravagant to be credited...I am sensible that truth will often be sacrificed to passion...To screen themselves from odium, all the subordinate tyrants fix upon him, and attribute to his orders, the innumerable butcheries and acts of oppression which they have perpetrated. (116–17)

In particular, Tench notes that the two most notorious episodes of the Terror were attributable to Carrier and Collot d'Herbois, not Robespierre, and that many more citizens must have been complicit:

> The 'noyades, fuzilades, and republican marriages' of Carrier at Nantes; joined to the exploits of Collot d'Herbois at Lyons... almost tempt one to believe, that a majority of the nation were at one time accomplices in its crimes and miseries. (120)

The mass drownings (*noyades*), mass shootings (*fuzillades/mitraillades*), and execution of men and women who had been stripped and bound together ('republican marriages'), are described in graphic detail in volume three of Williams's 1795 *Letters*. Tench cites these episodes as evidence that Robespierre has been made the scapegoat for the crimes of others, and more disturbingly, for the complicity of many. The imprisoned royalist spy Madame de Fleury similarly resisted this tendency to scapegoat Robespierre, as this chapter's epigraph shows. Other contemporaries agree with Tench, and with modern historians, that Robespierre and his Committee of Public Safety did not order the massacres at Nantes, but in fact tried to rein them in in their campaign to oust the 'ultra-revolutionaries' in March 1794; in the spring of 1794 Robespierre and his allies also tried to centralize the Terror in

Paris, arresting the members of the revolutionary committee of Nantes for the mass drownings (12 June).[22]

Nevertheless, Robespierre became synonymous with the Terror, and in women's fiction this association took some fascinating turns. In Mary Robinson's *The Natural Daughter* (1799), Helen Craik's *Adelaide de Narbonne with Memoirs of Charlotte de Cordet* (1800) and Fanny Burney's *The Wanderer* (1814), Robespierre emerges as a sexualized avatar of violent ambition, in effect the embodiment of men's Reign of Terror on women. These feminist critiques of French and British gender politics do more than use the name of Robespierre to conjure up the ultimate allegorical libertine villain. In their representations of Robespierre as Terror we glimpse an early and unidentified strand of the historical novel, in which two specific historical crises – Robespierre's crafting of the ideology of Terror, and the gender crisis of the revolutionary decade – are fused in sensationalized feminist narratives. What intrigues and appalls these writers is Robespierre's perversion of Terror as an emanation of Virtue. Drawing heavily on Williams's *Letters from France*, Robinson and Craik share a desire to sever Robespierre and the Terror from the virtuous legacy of 1789. They do this in order to support their far more limited (than Robepierre's) claims for economic and political reform, but also for protofeminist ends that reveal at once an understanding of Robespierre's (ironic) representativeness as male authority, and surprisingly, their ambivalent fascination with Robespierre as Rousseau's disciple.

Representing Robespierre

Romantic writers encountered epistemological and ideological difficulties when representing Robespierre that remain significant for understanding his Romantic reception. Robespierre himself projected a sense of disembodied asceticism and sublime idealism 'that would transcend all representation and escape all misrepresentation', part of his mystique which observers either idolized or vilified.[23] Williams chose to depict him as monstrous, cannibalistic and above all demonic, transforming his otherworldliness into a virtually supernatural, distinctly inhuman, malignity. Robinson, on the other hand, chose to dramatize the unnatural union of Virtue and Terror that he embodied, in the process critiquing not only British conservative political and sexual values, but also the underlying misogyny that they shared with Rousseau. Yet as in Burney's *The Wanderer* and Craik's *Adelaide de Narbonne*, Robinson's *Natural Daughter* resists representing Robespierre directly, instead evoking him as a demonic presence just out of sight, a perpetual threat to female safety and chastity. Their shared resistance to representing Robespierre attempts to deny Robespierre the Satanic grandeur he possessed in Coleridge and Southey's *The Fall of Robespierre*, where he was described as 'rising awful 'mid impending ruins;/ In splendour gloomy as the midnight meteor,/ That fearless thwarts the elemental war'. Williams's *Letters* do compare the Terror to Milton's hell, though she is careful to avoid endowing Robespierre with the heroic attributes of Milton's fallen angel, insisting always on his undifferentiated 'malignity'.[24] Robespierre's Satanic attributes did emerge in Gothic villains like Ambrosio and Montoni, whose ambiguous appeal as antiheroes is precisely what feminists like Williams and Robinson tried to occlude by strategically limiting Robespierre's appearances.

Physical representations of Robespierre share a number of conventions still with us today, such as his green spectacles, paleness, and immaculate silk coats. '[T]he range of meanings with which Robespierre's physical image is [typically] invested suggests that he is used to "figure" a particular ideological program' (Rigney 116). Comparing early historians' representations, Ann Rigney shows, for example, how Robespierre's pallor is consistently noted, but depending on the historians' political persuasion, it signifies either his visionary purity or cold-blooded cruelty. His fastidiousness, likewise, exemplified by his carefully powdered hair and elegant silk clothing, signifies either a hypocritical vanity, or an aesthetic purity that extends to his politics. Williams, in a rare description of Robespierre the man, reads these physical details as signs of his hypocrisy:

> It is remarkable enough, that at this period Robespierre always appeared not only dressed with neatness, but with some degree of elegance, and, while he called himself the leader of the sans-culottes, never adopted the costume of his band. His hideous countenance, far from being involved in a black wig, was decorated with hair carefully arranged, and nicely powdered; while he endeavoured to hide those emotions of his inhuman soul which his eyes might sometimes have betrayed, beneath a large pair of green spectacles, though he had no defect in his sight. (2:1:194–5)

Williams emphasizes the gulf between his true self and the false image projected – for her purposes, Robespierre *is* representation, a deliberate reversal of his celebrated 'politics of authenticity' (Jordan 30).

For Williams, central to Robespierre's inauthenticity is his refusal to honour feminine beauty, part of the wholescale Jacobin rejection of the *ancien régime* conventions of beauty and chivalry. Writing in prison, Williams recounts being visited by friends forced to abandon their bourgeois appearance for fear of reprisals:

> The dress of our visitors was indeed not a little grotesque, the period being now arrived when the visible signs of patriotism were dirty linen, pantaloons, uncombed hair, red caps, or black wigs. (2:1:193–4)

'Every man who had the boldness to appear in a clean shirt', she continues, was labelled a 'scented fop' of the *ancien régime* (a *muscadin*). Robespierre, in Williams's eyes, hypocritically monopolized forms of adornment at once aristocratic and feminine, and denied these to those 'naturally' entitled to them (particularly women), violating both class and gender conventions and thus detaching his politics from any authenticity. Robespierre's effeminacy, far from an instance of the positive 'feminizing' of Revolution that Gary Kelly has traced in Williams's *Letters*, leads easily to his cruelty, as Williams wrote earlier regarding the 'lightness of the French character': 'Effeminacy and cruelty are oftentimes not remote from each other' (1:3:150). The silk-clad and immaculate Robespierre thus functions as much more than the figurehead of the 'masculine' Revolution, or the hypermasculine villain in a Gothic pursuit of Williams's Liberty. Surrounded by women admirers and 'bodyguards', Robespierre appeared 'ridiculous', unnatural and effeminate, as we saw earlier in Williams's, Thiers's and Girondin accounts. In Robespierre we see the final, disastrous conclusion of the crisis of gender Johnson has deftly charted in *Equivocal Beings*. Robespierre joins the twin strands of sensibility's dangerous experiment – he represents at once Burke's dreaded 'ascendancy of monstrously coldhearted men' and Wollstonecraft's 'feminized, sentimental men' (Johnson 7).

Mary Robinson takes Williams's fundamental distrust of Robespierre's sexual and political authenticity further, casting Robespierre in a pivotal (yet nearly invisible) role in her controversial novel *The Natural Daughter*. Robinson's novel undermines British class and gender hierarchies in a brilliant reversal of sentimental conventions. Following the divergent paths of two complementary sisters, Martha and Julia, Robinson's narrative uncovers the sexual and economic predation and hypocrisy at the heart of polite British society, much as Burney would do more ambivalently in *The Wanderer*. The heroine Martha defends Wollstonecraftian notions of feminist and political reform, and is labelled a whore and liar by a hypocritical British high society, including her husband. Her sister Julia, meanwhile, affects a feminine sensibility drawn straight from Rousseau, wincing at any sign of cruelty to animals yet failing to act charitably towards the poor. Appearance and reality, sense and sensibility, nature and culture are all oppositions governing the unfolding plot, in which Julia rises to the height of power through her machinations, while Martha's authentic virtue is repeatedly punished. The novel's conclusion rewards Martha with love and marriage (with an apparent rake revealed as virtuous), while Julia dies in Paris during the Terror, after the startling revelation that she had become the mistress of Robespierre.

Educated by a French governess in a 'splendid mansion' and possessing a 'temper [that] seemed soft even to the excess of sensibility', Julia is one in a long line of Rousseauvian heroines in British Romantic fiction (93, 127). Her unique value lies in the ideological lengths Robinson is willing to go in her interrogation of sensibility's political significance, in revolutionary politics and British polite society. Julia's path of seduction as the 'model of feminine excellence' (93) leads to the logical apex of her Rousseauvian career – as the mistress of Robespierre. Robinson thus dramatically illustrates Rousseauvian Virtue taken to its Robespierrist limit, in the institutionalized form of the Terror. In so doing, Robinson reveals at once the hypocrisy and unworkability of sentimental ideals, both in the Rousseauvian tradition authorizing the Revolution and the Burkean tradition of chivalry impelling counterrevolution. Rousseau's ideal is hypocritical because, contrary to Rousseau's and Robespierre's reliance on a politics of authenticity and transparency, Julia gains influence through her seductive performance as virtuous heroine. Robinson illustrates how Rousseau's sexual double standard renders his ideal (and the actual Republic of Virtue) hopelessly corrupt. Rousseauvian virtue remains an unworkable abstraction in *The Natural Daughter*, both as embodied in Julia and as literalized in Robinson's descriptions of revolutionary Paris as excessively carnal, materialistic, and luxurious, the inverse of Robespierrist sublime asceticism:

> On our arrival at Paris, we found everything wild and licentious. Order and subordination were trampled beneath the footsteps of anarchy: the streets were filled with terrifying *spectacles*; and the people seemed nearly frantic with the plenitude of dominion; while the excess of horror was strongly and strikingly contrasted by the vaunted displays of boundless sensuality. (163)

Here Robinson shares in the antirevolutionary rhetoric of British conservatives who consistently derided French revolutionary principles as hypocritical theories that masked licentious desires and indulgence. Yet it is significant that she places a sexualized Robespierre at the source of this corruption, and at his side 'the soft, seducing fiend' Julia (281). After a series of trials the heroine Martha finds herself imprisoned in Paris in July 1794, and discovers her sister Julia transformed into a 'barbarous' and 'unrelenting judge' (289), less the mistress of Robespierre than his female emanation. Robinson's narrative matches the bewildering speed of 9 Thermidor, as Robespierre is suddenly led to the guillotine, 'pale, ghastly, lacerated, trembling' (290).

   This sole glimpse of Robespierre deliberately reduces him to a physical body, broken and shaking, in deliberate contrast to Robespierre's self-representation as sublime incarnation of *le peuple*. Robinson shows us the weakness of mere flesh, not only in its sexual demands (masked as virtue) but in its very fragility. When the historical Robespierre was captured, he shot himself in the jaw in a thwarted suicide attempt, making his final hours of captivity (and public display) excruciating and humiliating. Williams's *Letters* had exploited this final humiliation for political effect, suggesting that he was too cowardly to commit suicide and was in fact shot by a gendarme (a popular theory at the time).[25] Both Williams and Robinson conclude the abstract 'reign of Robespierre' by consciously reducing it to the final dismal hours of a broken and terrified body. In denying Robespierre the heroic stoicism of Mme. Roland and Corday, Williams and Robinson exact a final revenge on behalf of Robespierre's victims. Yet, in these brief glimpses of Robespierre's physical demise, both authors also literalize the shocking disparity between Robespierre's 'tyranny' and his corporeal vulnerability, ironically opening up the more disturbing insight that he was the convenient scapegoat for the accumulated crimes of many.

Robinson, following Williams, the Thermidoreans, and British conservatives, casts Robespierre as absolute tyrant, wallowing in sexual and luxurious excess reminiscent of an oriental despot. Martha discovers Julia's corpse after her suicide in Robespierre's looted apartments, and Robinson tells us much about Robespierre by showing us the ruined grandeur left in his wake:

> She found the gates all open; the populace had plundered the apart-ments; she entered the saloon, beyond the anti-chamber; the floor was deluged with blood! murder had been permitted to blur the face of noon-day, and the abode of guilty luxury now presented the mere wreck of desolation...
>
> As soon as the first spell of horror had subsided, she rushed through the apartments wild and astonished; the hangings which were of velvet were torn from the walls and trampled by the multitude; the costly plates of looking-glass were shattered in every direction;...the splendid lustres torn from their suspending chains, and strewed about in glittering fragments. She entered the chamber of the exterminated monster: the bed on which he had slumbered, but not reposed; the pillow on which he had, for many preceding months, pressed his guilt-fevered brain, now supported the head of the lifeless, self-murdered Julia. (290)

Robinson's nightmarish account of Thermidor echoes Williams's famous metaphor in *Letters from France*: 'Upon the fall of Robespierre, the terrible spell which bound the land of France was broken' (2:3:190). Martha unmasks the revolutionary enchantress and enchanter, revealing the 'unbounded sensuality' beneath the virtuous facade, now a shattered hall of mirrors. Robinson's melodramatic account of Thermidor 'recalls nothing so much as the October 1789 assault upon Versailles' argues Sharon Setzer; her 'portrait of Robespierre reads much like an exercise in narrative revenge as it reverses the Jacobin charges against the Queen' in a powerful 'gender reversal' ('Romancing' 544). Setzer's perceptive account of Robinson's revenge on the Queen's executioners illuminates Robinson's personal and feminist interests. Yet as with Williams, Robinson's specific engagement with Robespierre's politics (beyond sexual politics) demands examination – in Robinson's case, her literalization of the union of Virtue and Terror in the union of Julia and Robespierre.

Robinson's sexualization of Robespierre's doctrine of Terror (17 Pluviôse) reveals the misogyny at the heart of Jacobin and Rousseauvian Republic of Virtue from a feminist standpoint, and simultaneously acknowledges women's problematic fascination with this tradition in theory and practice. While Robespierre attracted many female admirers, unlike rivals like Danton and Vergniaud he also maintained a scrupulously virtuous and ostensibly asexual private life. From 1792 he lived as a lodger with an artisan family, the Duplays, in a veritable fantasy of domestic tranquillity and modest comfort straight out of Rousseau (or the early Radcliffe). Mme. Roland, an early admirer of Robespierre (the feeling was not mutual), famously dubbed him the Incorruptible, and his enemies of all ranks and nationalities generally accepted this appellation as accurate. 'I do not think he could have been bought at any period of the Revolution', wrote an English visitor in 1794, for 'he is beyond the reach of gold'.[26] Williams's friend John Moore also conceded that Robespierre 'is allowed, even by those who detest many parts of his character, to be incorruptible by money'.[27] It is significant, then, that Robinson chose to sexualize Robespierre's corruption, deliberately resisting his self-representation and relying on popular rumours that beneath Robespierre's public virtue seethed private vice. While sexualization of politics is not unique to the revolutionary period, Robespierre's sexualization in women's writings elevates his rise and fall, like that of Marie Antoinette, to the level of a historical crisis in gender relations.

Rumours that Robespierre kept mistresses and indulged in orgies were rife in the final months of his life. One of the most famous victims of such sexualization of politics, Wollstonecraft wrote to Imlay in August 1794 to ask if it were true that 'Robespierre really maintained a *number* of mistresses' (*Collected Letters* 261; orig. emphasis). That was the rumour in the Convention, she noted, but nevertheless she would not accept that anything but vanity could corrupt Robespierre: 'Should it prove so, I suspect that they rather flattered his vanity than his senses' (ibid). Pamphlets accusing Robespierre of maintaining mansions and concubines throughout France circulated in the Thermidorean climate of paranoia, and Robinson exploits these in her feminist critique of misogyny in *The Natural Daughter*. Unlike Coleridge and Southey, who show Robespierre vilifying the Girondins' supposed effeminacy while maintaining his own masculine 'steel-strong rectitude of soul', Robinson undermines his self-presentation to reveal its misogynist origins in Rousseau. Robinson's vision of Robespierre's ruined mansion as the scene of despotic oriental excess echoes contemporary accounts by his Jacobin rivals. According to one Thermidorean journal, for example, it was in a royal mansion at Issy that Robespierre supposedly

> hatched the plots that would destroy liberty; it is there that, with...many other accomplices, the ruin of the people was prepared, among the most uproarious orgies. It was the Trianon of the successor of the Capets; it is here that, after meals for which the whole neighbourhood was requisitioned, the tyrant rolled on the grass pretending to be shaken by convulsive

movements; in the presence of the court which surrounded him, he pretended to be Illuminated, in the manner of Mahomet, so as to impress
fools and ingratiate himself with knaves.[28]

One tyranny succeeds another, with the new actors appropriating the palaces
and excesses of those they have supplanted. Robespierre's career was cut
short by a conspiracy from within the Jacobin club, which circulated rumours
that he intended to abolish the republic and become an absolute tyrant, a
conspiracy echoed in the writings of Girondin opponents like Williams as
well. Barras, a Montagnard who had helped to overthrow Robespierre,
helped spread this rumour that Robespierre and his allies 'abandoned themselves to every excess' like 'sultans' and 'satyrs', and aspired to the absolute
power of royalty (qtd. in Baczko 13).

Robespierre's supposed ambition to absolute rule culminated in the rumour
that he had planned to marry (or had succeeded in marrying) the imprisoned
daughter of Louis XVI, Mme. Royale. In the fictitious *Political Testament of
Maximil. Robertspierre* [sic] published in London in 1796, Robespierre con-
fesses that 'from the death of Louis the XVIth I aimed at the throne he knew
not how to occupy' (4).[29] 'I now possess the sovereign power, but not the
name', he continues, and either 'the throne or the scaffold must soon be my
lot' (5, 7). His fellow Montagnards have offered 'to marry me into the Capet
family' (7) to help him reach the throne, but even this fictitious Robespierre
is suspicious of such offers, 'produced only by fear of their own safety' (7).
Nevertheless, in the chaotic hours between Robespierre's arrest, release and
capture on 9 Thermidor and his execution the following day, a rumour circulated through the *sections* of Paris that Robespierre was a royalist aspiring to
tyranny, and that he planned to marry Mme. Royale to assure his role as
sovereign. Bronislaw Baczko has traced this rumour and concludes that 'it did
not come "from below", from a disoriented crowd...It was launched from
"above,"' by the Committees of Public Safety and General Security, to rally
the sections and the military, to channel their emotions, and overcome their
hesitations' (16). Both Montagnard conspirators and British conservatives
stood to gain from branding Robespierre a tyrant. Barras, the Montagnard
who had helped spread the rumours of Robespierre's orgies which Robinson's
novel reflects, later confessed that these rumours were cynically designed to
deceive the public: 'The people could not be persuaded that Robespierre was
a tyrant, other than by associating him with ideas of former royalty'.[30]
Robespierre's characterization as a tyrant with royal ambitions in both
Williams and Robinson is thus not primarily a feminist response, an allegory
of the absolute power of patriarch, husband, or father.

In the high-stake ideological struggles of 1793 and 1794, 'Robespierre the
tyrant' became a myth endowed with a bewildering series of contradictory
significances. British feminists used the myth to allegorize institutionalized
misogyny (men's Reign of Terror on women). French Jacobins used the

myth in their factional power struggles. For British radicals, the myth served as an oblique vision of England's own domestic tyranny, as well as of the masculine agency of the male Romantic poet (for Coleridge, Southey and Wordsworth). Counterrevolutionaries (French and British) used the myth as evidence for the heartlessness of French revolutionary principles and their inevitable descent into violence. Robespierre's rise to power and his role in the Terror could also be read, then and now, as the tragic enactment of Rousseauvian virtue on the corrupting stage of revolutionary politics. The latter vision was the Incorruptible's, shared by his women admirers (and later, politically sympathetic Marxist historians), in direct contrast to feminists like Williams and Robinson, who were particularly suspicious of his appeal to women and the working classes. Their illumination of the misogyny central to Robespierre's 'corruption' of Rousseau's ideal should not be isolated from the demonstrably counterrevolutionary, chivalric, and occasionally misogynist inflections of their own visions. It is thus not Robespierre's personal corruptibility that is at stake in their narratives, but that of the Rousseauvian ideal he embodied – Virtue – mired in a discursive and political crisis that rendered any such political or gender ideals virtually impossible to distinguish.

Republican marriage

One significant commitment shared by all of the women writers considered in this chapter – Williams, Robinson, Craik, and Burney – is their overtly feminist demystification of marriage as oppressive to women. All four writers transgressed either the conventions or laws of marriage in their controversial private lives;[31] more importantly, all four politicized such transgression in their writings. Robinson, writing overtly in the 'school of Wollstonecraft', was the most vocal and daring in this respect, as was Craik, a great admirer of Robinson. Craik began *Adelaide de Narbonne* with bracing clarity: 'Adelaide de Narbonne had the supreme felicity of finding herself a widow almost from the hour she became a bride' (1:1). Following eighteenth-century feminist practice, Robinson and Craik consistently liken marriage to slavery, and like Burney in *The Wanderer*, graphically illustrate the economic, emotional, and physical privations women endure as a result of their dependence. Given these writers' conscious identification of marriage (alongside inheritance and property laws) as an institution in urgent need of reform, it is curious that they do not celebrate the French Revolution's liberalization of divorce, marriage and inheritance laws.

On the contrary, like loyalist denunciations of the Revolution as a premise for sexual licence (found in the works of Burke, More, West, Hawkins and numerous others), their nightmarish visions of 'republican marriage' deny the benefits to women of such liberalization, and seem instead to see only an intensification of men's dominion by other means.

In Burke's *Letters on a Regicide Peace* (1796), French marriage reform has a cascading effect: 'With the Jacobins in France, vague intercourse is without reproach; marriage is reduced to the vilest concubinage; children are encouraged to cut the throats of their parents', culminating, literally and graphically, in 'cannibalism' (*Works* 6:153). Sade's *Philosophy in the Boudoir* (1795) envisioned this same extreme version of liberalized republican sexuality as a pornotopia: 'All men therefore have equal rights of enjoyment in all women'.[32] The Sadean visions of Robespierre offered by these women writers in fact prove incorrect (as Burkean loyalists also insisted) Godwin's optimistic prediction that '[t]he abolition of the present system of marriage appears to involve no evils', certainly not those of 'brutal lust and depravity' (*Enquiry* 763).

It was Robespierre's accumulated monstrous associations that women writers used to eclipse the potential feminist value of France's new divorce and inheritance laws, seeing in these reforms a similar potential for radical libertinage as did Sade, and as antiJacobin novelists had seen in Godwin's philosophical rejection of marriage. Having already ended primogeniture, in August and September 1792, the Legislative Assembly had declared adults 'no longer subject to paternal authority' and established divorce, giving 'mothers equal rights with fathers in control over the children' (Hunt, *Family Romance* 41–2). As a civil contract, marriage was now dissoluble by either party. In September of the following year, the National Convention went even further and 'granted illegitimate children equal rights of inheritance': 'Society and the state', writes Lynn Hunt, 'were now asserting the superiority of their claims over the family' (66). More radical yet, in December 2003 'the Convention voted to establish state-run primary schools, and a week later it made attendance obligatory in principle', with Robespierre's approval: 'The country has the right to raise its children', he declared; 'it should not entrust this to the pride of families or to the prejudices of particular individuals' (67).

While many of these reforms would be reversed, especially with the Napoleonic Code of 1804, they remain important milestones in family and women's rights (in fact, it was only in 1975 that divorce became as easy to obtain for French women as it had been in 1792 (Hunt, 'Unstable Boundaries', 45)). So why didn't outspoken feminists like Robinson and Williams (or for that matter Smith)[33] praise such laws in their writings, when these laws resembled the reforms they desired in Britain? Because in replacing the authority of fathers with that of the state, the republican reforms simultaneously eliminated maternal authority, both literally and symbolically. Divorce and the equalization of custody and inheritance rights were part of British feminists' agenda, but robbing families (and thus mothers) of their authority over children was unacceptable. Yet this had been Rousseau's vision of public education (theorized in his essays and ironically mirrored in his own abandonment of his children), and thus Robespierre's also.

In instituting this element of Rousseau's ideal of the virtuous society, Robespierre enacted a version of Rousseauvian virtue anathema to feminists like Williams and Wollstonecraft, who admired elements of Rousseau's sensibility and social contract, respectively, that were favourable to women, and like many French women contemporaries 'identified strongly with Rousseau's persona of persecuted virtue' (Trouille 5). Julie had served as 'the ideal mother-educator' as well as the idealized romantic beloved, a powerful combination for Rousseau's female readers, especially in contrast to the negative representations of women's influence in essays like *Social Contract, Discourse on Inequality*, and *Letter to d'Alembert* (Trouille 28, 20). For these progressive English writers, Robespierre came to represent not only the corruption of their revolutionary ideals, but more specifically, the misogynist corruption of Rousseauvian virtue beyond feminist redemption.

Burney evoked Robespierre repeatedly in *The Wanderer* as a constant threat to the heroine Juliet's life, manifested through his agent's forced marriage to Juliet. As in Robinson's *Natural Daughter*, 'republican marriage' becomes the means for men's legal control of women, and for Jacobin usurpation of political dominion over the Revolution. Robinson's novel recounted the near-death experience of Mrs Sedgley during the Terror, where she faced a revolutionary version of the ultimatum faced by all Radcliffean heroines: either forced marriage or 'live burial' in a convent. Radcliffe's Gothic narratives liberate her heroines from this sexual barbarism and usher them into the new bourgeois order of companionate marriage with a man of sentiment. Robinson's Mrs Sedgley faces this same impossible choice while imprisoned during the Terror: '*ou Marat, ou la guillotin!*' [sic] (*Natural Daughter*, 167). To escape this traditional Gothic impasse, she is instead disastrously 'married *à la Revolution*' to an English traveller who 'promised to secure my emancipation' (ibid 166). This Englishman seems the epitome of virtuous manhood (as he would have been, were this Radcliffe's novel), yet in Robinson's masterful antisentimentalism, he turns out to be a cruel hypocrite, the English counterpart of the misogyny represented by Marat and Robespierre.

In *The Wanderer*, readers learn how the heroine Juliet's troubles began when she was blackmailed into marriage ('in a civil ceremony, dreadful, dreadful!' (715)) by an agent of Robespierre seeking her wealth. Similarly, in *Adelaide de Narbonne*, the eponymous heroine is the victim of a forced revolutionary marriage to a Jacobin ally of Marat, who desires to possess her ancestral wealth. Economic and sexual control are fused in marriage, whether *ancien régime* or revolutionary. These writers use the civil ceremony of revolutionary marriage to strip conventional marriage of its aura of legitimacy and sanctity, instead revealing the naked power grab it entails. Thus, republican agents of Robespierre and Marat may as well be agents of an absolutist ruler like Montoni or Manfred: as far as these women's accounts are concerned, they remain part of the same false sentimental economy, selling the 'promise of emancipation' in exchange for women's subjection. It is as though the legal reforms briefly offered up in the Jacobin Revolution cannot yet revise the prevailing sentimental forms of resistance to marriage – these writers are not ready to abandon the ideal of companionate marriage to sentimental men (it concludes all their novels). They cannot abandon this ideal because the civil ceremony of republican marriage (and likewise divorce) demystifies the union even as it increases women's liberty, and that is a price they are unwilling to pay. The civil constitution of the clergy (12 Feb. 1790) similarly faced opposition from English supporters of the Revolution, who typically came from Dissenting backgrounds and found the materialism associated with French radical traditions alien and undesirable. But the desacralization of marriage threatened to rob these feminist critiques of the language and narratives they had up till now used to resist it – those of sentimental romance.

Wollstonecraft and Robinson (and their caricature in *The Wanderer*, Elinor) also critiqued marriage through the opposing discourse of antisentimental rationalism, but while this Enlightenment tool could be used to uncover the oppression marriage entailed, it seemed to offer nothing in its place. Elinor, Burney's vision of a Wollstonecraftian feminist, reaches this literal dead end at the conclusion of *The Wanderer*; she is persuaded not to commit suicide by the sentimental hero, who counters her materialism with his faith in the immortality of the soul as the seat of love and virtue. Anne Grant responded similarly to Wollstonecraft in 1794, warning that her rationalist critique 'shewed [sic] us all the miseries of our condition' but 'robbed us of the only sure remedy for the evils of life, the sure hope of a blessed immortality'.[34] Yet Wollstonecraft and her fellow Female Philosophers were neither atheists nor materialists, and indeed Grant reveals the actual ideal threatened by Wollstonecraft's philosophy: women's 'superiority'. For Grant, women are 'more gentle, benevolent and virtuous' than men, but only because they live 'secure and protected in the shade'; Wollstonecraft's philosophy is 'every way dangerous' because it desacralizes women in the process of revealing this security as an illusion. 'A Representation of the Horrid Barbarities Practised upon the Nuns' (Illustration 1) graphically visualized the horrors opened up when women are literally desacralized. Desacralization leads to disorder, madness, and destruction, as Robespierre also believed, toppling atheists like Hebert and institutionalizing the cult of the Supreme Being to contain the dangerously unpredictable influence of materialism.

Ironically, it was Robespierre who appears as the agent of this desacralization of marriage in women's narratives. In fact, what Robinson and Williams fear the most is the desacralization of women (and mothers) and the culture of sentiment that valued them. Robespierre becomes in their imagination, as Sade was in real life, the destroyer of the sacredness of women. His accumulated misogynist associations, along with the overwhelmingly

negative British perceptions of the Jacobin Republic in general, were compelling enough to override the otherwise significant feminist appeal of
republican legal reforms in marriage. But one final revolutionary episode
concretized Robespierre's status as the demonic scourge of feminine virtue,
and ironically it was not his own doing. Perhaps the most notoriously
bloodthirsty of the Jacobins was Jean Baptiste Carrier, who shocked Jacobin
and British alike with the mass drownings (*noyades*) he ordered at Nantes.
Williams describes these episodes in graphic detail, in particular the 'republican marriages':

> Some of these victims were destined to die a thousand deaths; innocent
> young women were unclothed in the presence of the monsters; and, to
> add a deeper horror to this infernal act of cruelty, were tied to young
> men, and both were cut down with sabers, or thrown into the river; and
> this kind of murder was called a republican marriage. (2:3:42–3)

The inverse of long-sought liberalization, 'republican marriage' acquired a
wholly nightmarish association as the lowest point in women's revolutionary history. 'The fury of these implacable monsters seemed directed
with particular violence against that sex', writes Williams, 'whose weakness
man was destined by nature to support' (2:1:214). 'Republican marriage'
became the ultimate example of men's sadistic abuse of women, and
Robespierre the infernal bridegroom. Robespierre had actually recalled
Carrier and other regional proconsuls in February 1794 when the Committee
of Public Safety heard of the mass killings in Nantes and Lyons. Robespierre's
name, however, became inseparable from such shocking excesses as
'republican marriages', and in the historical romances of Robinson, Craik
and Burney these incidents loom large as the nadir of women's oppression.

In these women's writings, 'republican marriages' were the logical conclusion
of French misogyny, not feminist reform. British opponents of the Revolution
would agree with this; they found much to object to in the Francophilic
writings of Robinson, Williams and Burney, and yet they had common
concerns regarding the dangers of the French desacralization of marriage.
That it was the French who crossed this line came as no surprise to loyalist
defenders of British 'domestic virtue, femininely frail', like Lucy Aikin; after
all, she wrote in *Epistles on Women*, everyone knew that the French were
'A spurious rabble and adulterous race,/ Steept in corruption, destined to be
base'. Whether *ancien régime* gallants or 'adulterous' materialists, the French
lack the sentimental appreciation of feminine virtue that Burke, More and
Aikin proudly located in British companionate marriage.

Laetitia Matilda Hawkins lamented the French divorce laws at greater
length in her anti-Williams, nationalist diatribe, *Letters on the Female
Mind ... With Particular Reference to the Dangerous Opinions Contained in the
Writings of Miss H. M. Williams* (1793):

In France, notwithstanding all their boasted freedom and equality, women have suffered an irreparable, and a most barbarous degradation in the dissolution of the marriage union at pleasure. A few of the licentious may at first be pleased with this freak of liberty; but nine tenths of the Gallic ladies will soon be weary of it: they will perceive that they are disgraced: pride will restrain some, fear others, from owning that their adored system of anarchy could be in any point erroneous: they will look with a malignant eye on the respectable English wife. (2: 199)

These envious French women will then seek to infect English wives with the spurious claims of liberty: 'One art which they will certainly use, is that of exciting us, by their example, to take part in politics, in whatever can render us unamiable and ferocious' (2: 200). Thus, according to a ubiquitous Burkean logic, the ultimate effect of these infectious French reforms will be that the Revolution's 'modern philosophy' will dissolve all 'social ties subsisting in human nature – the parental, the filial, the fraternal affections, love, friendship, gratitude, are all obsolete or vulgar prejudices' (Hawkins 2:202). And yet Williams and her fellow feminists, reviled by Hawkins for writing publicly on French revolutionary politics, similarly characterized the Jacobin Republic as severing the sacred ties of family, marriage, and romance during the Terror, most spectacularly in the murderous 'republican marriages' that parodied liberalized sexual relations.

The 'republican marriage' of Virtue and Terror, like that of Julia and Robespierre in Robinson's *Natural Daughter*, in fact marked the intensification of *ancien régime* marriage (British and French) as domestic slavery and disguised libertinism, the perversion of the companionate marriage ideal and of a just society as a whole. Forced marriage was the axis around which all progressive women's narratives, Gothic and sentimental, revolved; in the 'reign of the terrific Robespierre' this feminist trope reached its most extreme evocation and found its most notorious villain, despite the beneficial legal changes made possible by the Jacobin republic. In Craik's *Adelaide de Narbonne*, the liberalization of marriage laws is twisted into an even greater weapon against women: here it is Robespierre's ally Marat who passes legislation 'compelling women of rank, birth or riches, to engage in marriage with persons of the lowest origins' (3: 266). Women in these revolutionary narratives return again and again to the same impossible choices – marriage or convent, Marat or the guillotine – a feminist acknowledgement of misogyny's continuity across regimes, but also a sentimental resistance to the lost promise of companionate marriage, and women's privileged role therein.

The legal reform that did catch women's imaginations as a sign of the Revolution's empowerment of women was the abolition of monastic vows. In the novels of Smith, Robinson and Craik set during the revolutionary decade (as in prorevolutionary works by men), French women immured in convents against their wills become synecdoches for women's general oppression in marriage as well as *ancien régime* oppression as a whole, reflecting the realization of Wollstonecraft's heroine in the *Wrongs of Woman*, that 'marriage had bastilled me for life'. British writers had long figured Catholic barbarism as a pointed contrast to the Protestant English ideal of companionate marriage, most successfully in Radcliffe's Gothic romances. The liberation of women from French convents is much easier to celebrate than is divorce; given that there are no convents in Britain, such liberation could serve as a deflected critique of oppressive British marriage, and simultaneously an occasion for self-serving nationalism. The liberalization of divorce laws, on the other hand, without precedent in the sentimental economy (or nationalist self-image) of Britain, is far more dangerous. It is Wollstonecraft, of course, who dares to do this in her unfinished *Wrongs of Woman*, whose heroine, imprisoned in a madhouse by her husband, speaks boldly on behalf of making divorce available to British women. The disgusted judge declares her insane for advocating such 'French principles'. Popular antiJacobin fiction in the 1790s had successfully conflated 'French principles' with libertinism, the spurious emancipation of 'women from the domination of religion, gentleness, and modesty', as one conservative novelist archly suggested (*Dorothea* 1:1–2). By 1797, when Wollstonecraft wrote *Wrongs of Woman*, French divorce laws had already become more restricted, but Wollstonecraft had lived in Paris during the Terror and become infamous for her own apparent 'republican marriage' to Imlay. Williams likewise took advantage of France's liberalized laws, living with John Hurford Stone after his Parisian divorce from his English wife in 1794, and yet she did not praise such reforms in her writings (except for the abolition of the *lettre de cachet*).

The Natural Daughter, Adelaide de Narbonne, Letters from France and *The Wanderer* are innovative hybrid narratives that incorporate both sentimental and Gothic traditions, and in their engagement with contemporary revolutionary politics help establish that important new genre, the historical novel. Robespierre looms large in these troubled narratives, even if just off stage, as the historical and symbolic agent of the desacralization of women, wives, and mothers. Williams found Robespierre's competing persona as *le peuple* particularly vexing, and made this the object of her formidable critique; yet as I have argued, Williams's motivation was grounded significantly in her political loyalties to the ousted Girondins, not to an abstract devotion to the 'feminization' of Revolution. Likewise, it is important to read her fellow British feminists within this larger political struggle, too often underestimated in literary and feminist scholarship that tends to privilege gender as a category apart from the internecine struggles within French party politics. As the embodiment of the Jacobin Republic (not of the Revolution, as he wished), Robespierre in these troubled feminist visions reveals at once the boldness of revolutionary British feminism, and its limitations.

Conclusion: Williams and revolutionary regimes: new directions

> Commercial schemes, like others, are sometimes visionary; here, however, there is solid ground.
> John Hurford Stone in Paris, letter to William Stone, spring 1794

We know of the significance of Williams' cosmopolitan Parisian salon, which attracted political and literary figures from across Europe; along with her revolutionary chronicles published in London and Paris, the salon remains central to modern literary assessments of Williams as a figure of genteel, moderate, and feminized Girondin republicanism, struggling to avoid arrest (unsuccessfully) and execution (successfully) at the hands of different regimes. Williams's self-characterization as primarily a sentimentalist in her republicanism ('my political creed is entirely an affair of the heart' (*Letters* 1:1:66)), and her absolute distinction between 'moderate' Girondins and 'extreme' Jacobins, are often reflected virtually unaltered in modern literary scholarship (a notable exception is Elizabeth Bohls, who examines the class politics of Williams's landscape aesthetics). Yet Williams's immersion in revolutionary politics, when investigated more closely, tells a different story than that of the persecuted, feminine Williams victimized by the masculine forces of Robespierrist extremism. It is important to examine this more ideological aspect of Williams's revolutionary career not so as to impugn her liberal credentials, but rather to better appreciate the courage with which she plunged into the revolutionary fray. I will sketch briefly three examples of Williams's involvement, covert and overt, in revolutionary intrigue that I suggest raise her profile as a controversial revolutionary actor, beyond her existing status as Girondin *salonnière* and liberal chronicler.

The first two examples are drawn from Williams's mysterious flight to Switzerland in 1794. Williams's published account of that trip, *A Tour in Switzerland* (1798), and the *Letters from France*, suggest that she and her friends had to flee Robespierre himself, because the April 1794 decree requiring all foreigners to leave Paris made remaining in France dangerous. This xenophobic measure, like the October 1793 arrest order of all English in Paris, was anathema to self-identified citizens of the world like Williams and her British Club circle, and serves as further evidence of Robespierre's personal paranoia in her writings. Chris Jones and Deborah Kennedy have helpfully contextualized this flight, and especially the *Tour in Switzerland*, in light of Williams's ongoing sentimental and political evolution, although the exact cause of the flight, and Williams's activities while in Switzerland, remains a mystery.

But archival evidence suggests that Williams's flight was partly if not largely due to (and certainly made possible by) her and Stone's political and commercial affairs. As we know, Williams's lover, the radical Dissenter and president of the British Club, John Hurford Stone was married to an English woman, Rachel Coope, when he and Williams began their romance.[35] Stone is assumed to have divorced his wife in 1794, but until now this was unconfirmed, and the unusual circumstances surrounding this divorce unknown. Stone divorced his wife on 6 June 1794 in Paris.[36] At that same time in England, John Stone's brother William was charged with sedition for his correspondence with his brother in Paris, in which John allegedly advised William on French plans to invade England and overthrow the monarchy (William was acquitted by proving that he and his brother had actually advised against invasion). This correspondence had probably come to light in part through Sampson Perry (editor of the suppressed *Argus*), to whom Stone entrusted letters but subsequently broke off relations. Stone's 1794 political intrigues are labyrinthine and only partly covered in Woodward's important *Une Amie de la Révolution*, still the main source for biographical information on Williams. Though the Committee of Public Safety issued its decree in April 1794, and Williams received her *ordre de passe* a week later, Stone and Williams left for Switzerland July 1 or 2, one week after Stone's divorce was registered with the Paris authorities. Stone and Williams were issued with passports because according to Stone he was charged by the Committee of Public Safety with the task of gathering intelligence on English politics and obtaining English newspapers in Hamburg.[37] These hitherto unconfirmed covert activities on behalf of the Jacobin government, which Williams does not mention in her writings, were precisely the sort of activities that the British government alleged William Stone conspired with.

Stone and Williams were deeply involved with revolutionary politics, not only during the Girondin republic (and not only through publications and salons), but during the Jacobin republic, the Directory, Consulate, and Empire. As honorary and later naturalized French citizens,[38] Stone and Williams bravely threw their lots in with the shifting tides of French revolutionary politics, well beyond the polite Girondin circles that Williams eulogized in her *Letters from France*. Their survival through successive regimes is a testament to their complete and courageous embroilment in party politics and commercial ventures, not to any detachment as persecuted outsiders or sentimental witnesses. While Williams liked to portray the flight to Switzerland in particular as a terrifying instance of a Rousseauvian persecution, their flight was made possible by Stone's canny involvement with the Jacobins (and radicals in Britain), and by his ambitious commercial dealings in which Williams also played a key part. Moreover, while in Switzerland, Stone and Williams had an even more disturbing brush with persecution, this time at the hands of the English. Stone's friend Nicolas Madgett, an Irish Jacobin member of the British Club serving as the official Translator for the Committee of Public Safety, alerted the Committee on 1 October 1794 that Rachel Coope, Stone's former wife, was in Switzerland and en route to England so that she could betray Stone, his brother, and

William Jackson during the latter two's looming treason trials.[39] Madgett denounced Rachel Coope to the Committee, urging them to arrest her in Hamburg before she could reach Britain and incriminate the men with her accumulated knowledge of their secret plans, including Jackson's secret mission to Ireland, which she had gained from reading John Hurford Stone's correspondence.[40]

Even in this climate of increasing xenophobia (in France as in Britain), the Committee could see the value of helping a useful self-declared French citizen like Stone, and recommended that the republic's agents in Copenhagen and Hamburg detain Coope before she could leave.[41] Unlike Williams and Stone, Coope was travelling on a forged passport, the Committee determined. Lacking the Jacobin connections of her former husband and his new lover, Rachel Coope attempted a desperate flight that seems to resemble Williams's version of the story more so than does Williams's own Swiss voyage. Coope's fate is uncertain, though she does not appear as a witness in the published accounts of William Stone's trial, and so perhaps she never made it back to Britain. Madgett denounced Coope at the request of Stone, still in Switzerland, and also relayed a request that the latter's passport be extended so that he could continue to manage the situation there. Williams's possible involvement in this unfortunate affair illustrates the impossibility of maintaining a virtuous purity from such compromises and mutual betrayals in times of crisis like the Terror, despite the absolute distinctions between 'oppressors' and 'oppressed' that she sought to maintain in her writings.

It is true that as foreigners, Williams and Stone were particularly vulnerable during the Terror. While in Switzerland on official business, with a passport issued by the Committee of Public Safety, Stone found it difficult to convince the French consul in that country that he should be accorded the full rights of a French citizen while resisting the persecutions of his fellow traveller Jackson, an MP: 'I feel some indignation that a French citizen should, especially at the present moment, feel the weight of his ministerial English authority', he wrote.[42] Recent research, however, has challenged the assumption that revolutionary cosmopolitanism was abandoned in practice for the nationalistic rights of Frenchmen that undeniably dominated in rhetoric. Michael Rapport, in *Nationality and Citizenship in Revolutionary France: The Treatment of Foreigners 1789–1799*, examined both the rhetoric towards, and the actual treatment of, foreigners, and argues that

> The persistence of foreigners in French society, and the protection of those who were useful and who posed no apparent threat, suggests that, even in the most xenophobic days of the Terror, the Revolution never created a closed society which excluded along lines of nationality... The Revolution, therefore, left cracks in the edifice of the national order. In fact, if not in theory, these cracks permitted the limited existence of a cosmopolitan practice of citizenship. (339, 344)

Williams and Stone slipped through these cracks because of their work with the revolutionary government, and because of their profitable commercial ventures. The latter occupied a great deal of Williams's energy while in Paris, but makes little appearance in her writings.

Jacqueline LeBlanc has examined the significance of commercial sensibility in Williams's writing, arguing that '*Letters* demonstrates an intriguing and radical correspondence between revolutionary politics and a culture of commercial sensibility' (26). Williams's affinity for commercial refinement is not merely rhetorical, but a consequence of Williams's and Stone's extensive commercial ventures in France. As David Erdman writes, 'Stone was...a complete believer in the Revolution as an opener of the wealth of nations to an enterprising entrepreneur' (237). In this respect Stone and Williams fit the mainstream of British radical republicanism (of Paine and Thelwall, for example), which '"democratized" commerce as a means of reconciling trade and republicanism' (Claeys 290). A coal merchant in England, in France Stone owned a porcelain factory and traded in cotton, wine, and silk (Stern 311). In 1793 Stone established a long-lived printing press with which Williams was also deeply involved, and by 1806 came to own. Also in 1806, this 'English Press' became the official printers for the government's tax and excise papers, signalling Williams's and Stone's increasingly high profile associations with the French government (Stern 344).

Among the many titles printed or published by the 'English Press' at Paris were works by Thomas Jefferson, Joel Barlow, both parts of Paine's *Age of Reason*, a new translation of Volney's *Ruins* (1802), as well as French translations of Williams's volumes.[43] Stone aggressively pursued English and continental connections to establish his press as 'the emporium of literature' and wrote to his brother in November 1793 that '[i]t depends on some measure on you, whether what I have begun shall fall or be the first establishment of the sort in Europe' (Howell, *State Trials* 1215, 1210). Crucial to this commercial success, as well as to Stone's commission to the Committee of Public Safety, was his ability to procure English newspapers, prints, and books via Hamburg. 'There is only one English bookseller' at Hamburg, Stone told his brother in spring 1794, 'and he scarcely does anything'; 'It would be very advisable to have duplicate copies of the more important reports, and decrees lodged at Havre, to come here by neutral vessels for the purpose of being translated' (Howell, *State Trials* 1263). Moreover, he and Williams also were launching a 'most magnificent' national magazine in January 1794, for which 'Miss H. M. Williams will be the conductor in chief', he explained to his brother; 'we have the capability of doing any thing', and 'are tolerably rich', he enthused (1218).[44] Stone in particular wanted travel accounts to translate into French, as 'travels never fail of one and two editions. This connexion [*sic*] is a very important one, and falls into our general plan', for which the Press had already 'twenty or thirty different articles' in their catalogue (1223).

The flight to Switzerland in the summer of 1794 coincided with Stone's increasingly ambitious printing and banking schemes that spring, as detailed in letters to his brother in London. Shipments of books and papers between the Stones traversed the channel regularly, and it seems that the 1794 flight from the Terror was thus as much Stone's political errand for the Committee of Public Safety as urgent business venture for Stone and Williams. Williams must have had a share in these printing, publishing and bookselling ventures, because by 1806 she owned the English Press. In that year, Williams and Stone filed an *Acte de Union*, establishing that, for her remarkable investment of 40,000 livres, Williams was the proprietor of the business and equipment, while Stone ran the operations.[45] A New York bookseller selling English Press publications noted in his 1806 *Catalogue* that their titles 'are all printed under the care of Helen Maria Williams, and are remarkably correct' (qtd. Stern 345). By now the English Press had also begun the immense job of printing the tax records (using 58 presses), and by 1811 the massive multi-volume works of Alexander von Humboldt (20 presses), which soon bankrupted the press due to the expense (Stern 346–9). Before this ambitious venture failed, however, we can see in the English Press's catalogue the influence of Williams's knowledge, literary and commercial, of the transnational literary marketplace: from sentimental novels (*The Vicar of Wakefield, The Man of Feeling, Evelina*) to the Gothic (*The Monk, Poetry of the Monk, Mysteries of Udolpho, Children of the Abbey*) to numerous travel narratives, to that herald of the free market, *The Wealth of Nations*.[46] Williams excelled in these aesthetic traditions, especially in travel writings and translations, the English Press's professed specialities.

Williams and Stone's profitable ventures in printing, publishing and translating, as well as Stone's role in printing numerous official publications under the Empire (Stern 347), add an important dimension to Williams's success (and indeed survival) as revolutionary chronicler. Escaping the Terror through a complicated set of commercial and political connections involving the Jacobin government, Stone and Williams also escaped arrest under Napoleon despite his repression of the press. Although Williams's papers were confiscated in the well-known incident in which her 'Ode to Peace' (1802) offended Napoleon by failing to praise him, Stone was not arrested the following year when, after the end of the Peace of Amiens, British men were ordered to be detained. 'For some reason', writes Deborah Kennedy, 'Stone was not subject to this rule, probably because of his significant property and business interests in Paris' (*Helen Maria Williams* 180). These commercial interests involved Williams intimately, and were centred on their profitable understanding of transnational (and especially transatlantic) literary exchange. Despite the xenophobia of successive French regimes in times of crisis, citizens of the world like Stone and Williams thrived because, as Rapport has documented, they were among the foreigners who made themselves indispensable to French commerce and government. After her ill-fated

1803 edition of the forged *Correspondence of Lewis the Sixteenth* (published by the English Press), Williams did not publish her own work until 1815, a testament to Napoleon's restrictions on the press, 'one of many writers forced into silence during his reign' according to Kennedy (ibid 183). Yet I suggest that silence does not accurately describe Williams's publishing activities during the Napoleonic era, as she was busy with the English Press, and working hard on her own translations of Humboldt for them.

Despite the severe restrictions of women's rights under the Napoleonic Code of 1804, and Napoleon's persecution of intellectual women like de Staël, Carla Hesse suggests that there also exists substantial evidence of Napoleon's patronage of women's writings (50–1). An early example of this was Mme Fortunée Briquet's *Dictionnaire historique, littéraire et bibliographique des françaises et des étrangères naturalisées en France* (1804), which was dedicated to Napoleon with his permission, and included a glowing account of Williams. 'Envain dira-t-on qu'une femme ne doit point se mèler de politique', writes Briquet: 'quand la cause est belle, qu'importe le sexe de ceux qui la défendent' (544). It is worth considering why a politicized, foreign and intellectual woman like Williams continued to enjoy a high standing in Napoleonic France, while others like Staël were exiled. Hesse offers a controversial revisionary account of women writers' status in revolutionary France:

> Not even at the moments of greatest public anxiety about the public influence of women (especially during the Terror and under Napoleon), is there evidence of systematic discrimination against writers on the basis of sex. It was content not gender that mattered. It was *what* they wrote and published, rather than *who* wrote and published, that mattered. (52)

Briquet in 1804 suggested something similar, perhaps, when she noted that 'On est étonné que Mademoiselle Williams ait survécu au 9 thermidor an 2: car elle fut du parti de la Gironde' (544). Party politics, not gender, sealed the fates of public women like Olympe de Gouges (monarchist critic of the Convention), Mme. Roland (Girondin critic of the Jacobins), and Mme. de Staël (constitutional monarchist critic of Napoleon) according to Hesse (48).

I have suggested that it was party politics, commercial enterprise and class interests that together were responsible for Williams's antipathy to Robespierre and her flight to Switzerland, and also that these involvements helped her and Stone survive, and even flourish. While I think Hesse underestimates the force of each revolutionary regime's rhetorical hostility towards public women explicitly on the grounds of gender (and oversimplifies a distinction between 'content' and 'gender'), Hesse does offer an important corrective to the current feminist consensus in which gender often eclipses every other category. Williams's complex involvements with French political and print culture need to be examined apart from the accounts she offered in her publications, which too often are reflected directly in modern assessments.

Even when the issue at stake was primarily one of women's sexual oppression – marriage and divorce in the Jacobin Republic – Williams, like Robinson, Craik and Burney, approached the issue from multiple perspectives, the 'rights of woman' (or more accurately the rights of mothers), encompassing one set of considerations, alongside those of class and ideological interest. As I have argued, 'Robespierre the tyrant' in all of their writings served many purposes, among which a feminist understanding of a Jacobin 'reign of terror on women' was but one. Rousseau, Robespierre and Napoleon served as protagonists, or more often villains, around which British writers could organize revolutionary narratives to explain the chaos of unfolding events. It is a serious omission when prevailing accounts of male Romantic writers' self-fashioning via these seminal figures entirely neglect the significance of gender, so apparent to contemporaries. Similarly, accounts of these women's writings on the Revolution should not eclipse the relationship of sexual politics to the wider fields of political and print culture in which gender played a crucial part.

4
Citizens of the World: The Émigrés in the British Imagination

> I at last made up my mind; and seeing myself deserted by my fellow citizens I decided to renounce my ungrateful country, in which I had never lived, from which I had never received goods or services, and by which ... I found myself so disgracefully treated.
>
> Jean-Jacques Rousseau, *Confessions*

> Thrown by misfortune from the bosom of my country, I early learned to be a Citizen of the World. – In what obscure corner of it ... shall *I* ever find a quiet asylum?
>
> Charlotte Smith, *Marchmont* (1796)

Emigration and travel were abiding preoccupations in Charlotte Smith's writings. They were also personal passions that were rarely indulged by the author, who needed to write ceaselessly to support her nine children. Smith's devotion to her beloved Sussex countryside in the *Elegiac Sonnets* and *Beachy Head* have (re)established her as a major Romantic poet with a rare talent for evoking the sublimity found in the particular, the minute, and the local. Inseparable from this devotion to the local are Smith's cosmopolitan longings, most visible in her novels and their evocation of the citizen of the world ideal. Although this identity, as in the above epigraph from *Marchmont*, is typically claimed by her heroes, Smith's well-known autobiographical interventions into her works should be expanded to include, in addition to her self-portraits in female victims of unjust institutions, her male citizens of the world.

The revolutionary dimensions of the citizen of the world ideal are particularly significant for Smith because of the underestimated extent to which she was engaged with French revolutionary politics in the early 1790s. The mixed reception of *Desmond* (1792), Smith's radical novel defending the progress of the French revolution thus far, signalled the decline of her fiction's critical popularity in a reactionary Britain, but left her republican sympathies undiminished. Significantly dated 20 June 1792, the date of the Tuilleries invasion in which a humiliated Louis XVI was forced to wear the revolutionary bonnet, Smith's Preface to *Desmond* locates her knowledge of French politics in her own direct experience, bypassing Laetitia Hawkins's earlier admonition that 'every female politician is a hearsay politician'. Smith writes that her account of revolutionary politics is 'drawn from conversations to which I have been a witness, in England, and France, during the last twelve months' (*Desmond* 45). Like Williams, Smith claims authority as an eye-witness, and a participant in those increasingly circumscribed activities, international correspondence and conversation.

Although modern critics have largely dismissed Smith's assertion of a French voyage in 1791, archival evidence suggests this was a distinct possibility. French government records detailing arrivals of elite foreigners name one Englishwoman, Mme Smyth, who arrived in Paris in the week of 10–17 September 1791.[1] Known details of Smith's life at this time allow for the possibility of this Parisian voyage (see fn.1). Her sister Catherine Dorset's disapproving admission that in 1791 Smith 'formed acquaintances with some of the most violent advocates of the French Revolution' should therefore not be limited to her acquaintances in England, and neither should the *Critical Review*'s comment, in its review of *Desmond*, that Smith 'is connected with the reformers, and the revolutionists'.[2] Given that no one has offered a compelling account of why such a trip would have been impossible, I suggest that the preponderance of evidence supports Smith's claim that she did visit revolutionary Paris.

Smith would not have been without connections in Paris, because like Robinson she was part of a network of Francophilic radicals including Joel Barlow, Helen Williams, William Godwin and Mary Wollstonecraft. The American republican Joel Barlow and his wife Ruth were in England in July 1791, and by the following summer had returned to France on covert political business (Woodress 118, 125). While in England, Barlow met with Britons sympathetic to the revolution, who moved in the same circles as Smith (Wollstonecraft, Godwin, Priestley, Price, Warner, and Hayley), no doubt sharing the benefit of his experiences in Paris. After Barlow's return to Paris, the radical 'Friends of the Rights of Man associated at Paris', known as the British Club, acknowledged Smith alongside Williams in their 18 November 1792 meeting in which they celebrated the republic's recent military victory over the Austrians with numerous toasts, including: '[to] the Women of Great Britain, particularly those who have distinguished themselves by their writings in favor of the French revolution, Mrs [Charlotte] Smith and Miss H. M. Williams'.[3] Before this toast, Smith had been corresponding with Barlow, a British Club member soon to receive honorary French citizenship and to join the National Convention. In November 1792, Smith wrote to Barlow of her admiration for his *Advice to the Privileged Orders*, presented by Paine to the National Convention on 7 November, and his *Letter to the National Convention* (advocating the liberalization of naturalization laws).

Barlow must have seemed to Smith the living embodiment of the Citizen of the World ideal, starting out as a poet among the 'Connecticut wits', travelling to France for a combination of commercial and idealistic reasons (which become significant for Smith's final novel), and immersing himself in revolutionary politics. Barlow espoused a revolutionary cosmopolitanism with which Smith's 1790s writings are preoccupied: 'The Principles of this revolution are those of universal peace', he wrote in 1792, 'because it takes away every motive for national hostility, and teaches the people of all countries to regard each other as friends and fellow-citizens of the world' (*Political Writings*, 219). A few weeks after the British Club toasted Smith, she wrote again to 'Citoyen' Barlow, denouncing 'les formules de l'ancien esclavage' and asking for assistance on her plan to visit Paris (again?) in the following March or April, a plan 'on which my *rebellious* heart is set' (*Collected Letters* 51, orig. emphasis).[4]

As a citizen of the world, Barlow enjoyed a freedom that Smith could only dream of. Her letters of the early 1790s reveal a growing dissatisfaction with England, and a desire to emigrate. In January 1794 she is again restless and seeking a permanent move: 'I dont love England to tell you the truth, & have always meditated flying away from it if my fetters or any part of them should fall off' (*Collected Letters*, 96). Writing to Joseph Cooper Walker, Smith inquired about the logistics and costs of immigrating with her children to Switzerland, as the Terror was then in full swing (ibid). Emigration was hotly debated in the 1790s, as it implied (in Smith's case overtly) a radical rejection of British national superiority, often for the chimerical attractions of a new world. As we saw earlier, counterrevolutionary novels like Hamilton's *Memoirs of Modern Philosophers* and Walker's *The Vagabond* often featured emigration schemes to a wilderness as the apex of revolutionary folly.

Particularly embarrassing for British conservatives were cases of Britons immigrating to revolutionary France. Tom Paine, Robert Merry, Sampson Perry, John Hurford Stone, Helen Maria Williams and a host of other Britons associated with the British Club all moved to France in order to avoid government prosecution for revolutionary activities (Paine and Perry) and/or because of a powerful affinity for the possibilities introduced by the Revolution (Stone, Merry, and Williams). Paine, Merry, Perry, Stone, Williams and many other expatriate friends also faced criminal imprisonment under revolutionary regimes; the French archives are full of police reports and plaintive statements of British Club members who fell victim (though usually not fatally) to the paranoia induced by the real presence of British spies in Paris. Propagandistic accounts of such 'English Jacobin' emigrants as Paine and Perry reaching the logical conclusion of their modern philosophy in French prisons, had provided counterrevolutionary novels with a central plot device, as we saw in the first chapter.

French emigrants fleeing revolutionary France likewise provided much propaganda value for British conservatives. The French émigré phenomenon remains curiously neglected in accounts of British responses to the Revolution, despite its significant impact on British literature and politics. This chapter attempts to provide a framework within which to consider this influence: first, through a range of writings on the émigrés, largely counterrevolutionary; and second, through the novels of Charlotte Smith, wherein emigration becomes the literalization of her cosmopolitan ideal, not a counterrevolutionary lesson about the superiority of the British nation. As with Williams's response to the Revolution and to Robespierre as its avatar, at the heart of Smith's vision of cosmopolitan emigration lies her ambivalent response to Rousseau.

Displacement and the just society

> Upon what point of the habitable world, then, immense as it may be, shall we find a retreat?
>
> August Lafontaine, *Clara Duplessis and Clairant:*
> *the History of a Family of French Emigrants* (1797)

The literature inspired by the French émigrés throughout the 1790s, like the literature of travel to which it is related, consistently sought to (re)locate the just society. Scattered across Europe and the new world, but having a disproportionate impact on British politics and culture, the French émigrés required that the British address a range of questions regarding native liberty, justice, and national character. While conservatives in the tradition of Burke used the émigré theme to idealize Britain as a refuge from French atheism and anarchy, the true home of liberty and justice, progressive writers used the émigrés to critique everything from homegrown British xenophobia, to Britain's injustices against its own subjects, to Britain's role in fomenting war and thus contributing to the Terror.

Beyond questions of foreign and domestic politics, which the émigrés in Britain uniquely combined, these exiles also necessitated a reevaluation of the conventions of sensibility, especially as inherited from Rousseau. The plight of the émigrés exacerbated a crisis already in progress: that of sensibility's role in a virtuous society, as we saw in Williams's complex responses to Robespierre as Rousseauvian Legislator. As objects of sympathy and subjects searching for diverse visions of community, the émigrés inspired narratives questioning the viability and location of virtue itself, in the process reconsidering Rousseau's legacy for the cultural imagination. Nicola Watson has examined in detail how 'revolutionary politics were understood crucially in terms of sentimental fiction – and in particular the plot of a single novel, *La Nouvelle Héloïse*' (4). Along with the *Confessions* (particularly significant for Williams and Robespierre, as we saw) and *Emile*, Rousseau's *La Nouvelle Héloïse* provided an aesthetic and political landscape in which British writers imagined their visions and countervisions of desired social and sexual relations. Rousseau's ideal rural community of Clarens, centred on Julie and her capacity for virtuous affection, became in the Romantic imagination a paradise regained. Like Williams' *Letters from France*, Wollstonecraft's *Wrongs of Woman* and Shelley's *Frankenstein* pursue this Rousseauvian ideal society to its feminist, radical limits, even while critiquing its underlying misogyny (most incisively via Darnford, Wollstonecraft's version of Saint-Preux/Rousseau). The émigrés' geographic and political displacement invites a further critical move, historicizing the impossibility of Rousseau's ideal by committing the émigrés to a futile quest for it across a nearly unrecognizable Europe. The serial émigré Rousseau himself popularized this pervasive 'historical pessimism',[5] of course, from his quests for such ephemeral retreats as Les Charmettes and the Island of Saint Pierre memorialized (and fictionalized) in the *Confessions*, to the tragic conclusions of *Emile* and *La Nouvelle Héloïse*. The émigré crisis brought this pervasive Rousseauvian sense of a lost ideal, typically read in terms of psychological or poetic identity in canonical Romanticism, abruptly into historical focus. Whether standing for an *ancien régime* paternalism (in counterrevolutionary writings), the early political ideals of the Revolution (in Williams and Staël, for example), the fantasy of a private retreat from revolutionary politics (as some argue for Mary Shelley), or a cosmopolitan ideal of a new kind of society (as in Smith and Robinson), this virtuous imagined community always proves elusive.

A German novel translated into English in 1797, August Lafontaine's *Clara Duplessis and Clairant: the History of a Family of French Emigrants*, illustrates beautifully the new questions the revolutionary crisis forced Romanticism to confront regarding its ideals. Like most novels engaged with revolutionary politics, *Clara and Clairant* is preoccupied with how Rousseau's writings create expectations (either false or virtuous ones, depending on one's political perspective) that are then put into practice in revolutionary contexts. The love of Clara and Clairant, like that of Julie and Saint-Preux, crosses class barriers and is forbidden by Clara's aristocratic father; the Revolution overthrows such 'distinctions of rank', and here the novel takes an unexpected turn. Rather than celebrating the Revolution as sentimental (as in Williams's tale of the Du Fossés in *Letters from France*), or vilifying it as the unnatural consequence of dangerous philosophy, this émigré tale illustrates how the revolutionary European landscape renders Rousseau's ideals futile.

Clara is a Rousseauvian idealist, dreaming of how she would live with Clairant, a farmer's son, 'in a thatched cottage, disguised as a peasant and forgotten by the world' (1: 92). With the outbreak of revolution, Clairant rejoices that 'Now, Clara, we can be married publicly under the protection of the nation'; they try to elope, but instead of following the sentimental plot that Clairant hopes for – civil marriage that rejects class distinctions and paternal authority – Clara's father, the Viscount Duplessis, takes his family to Germany. Once Clara begins her life as an émigré, the Rousseauvian plot, whether counterrevolutionary or republican, is uprooted along with her. From Luxembourg, to Metz, Treves, Coblentz and Embs, Clara and her family move within an expatriate world of aristocratic families. Wealthy émigrés often recreated the rituals of rank wherever they went (usually amongst continental aristocratic circles) for as long as resources allowed, and even 'seemed to amplify the "cascade of disdain" that marked old-regime social relations' (Doyle, Introduction xix). '[W]e have also balls, concerts, assemblies', writes Clara to Clairant (2: 11), slipping further from her Rousseauvian idealism as her distance from France grows. Remaining in France, Clairant, meanwhile, becomes a more patriotic republican, eventually joining the revolutionary army. The growing physical distance between them illustrates their political and historical differences as well, as France moves forward into uncharted political waters, while the émigrés retreat further, literally, into the old world.

The lovers' correspondence registers the pressure of revolutionary events, and of geographical distance, on their romance in such a way as to reveal the impracticality of Rousseauvian ideals within an increasingly bewildering continental context. The King and Queen's flight to Varennes in June 1791 occasions a flurry of letters between the lovers that reveals how their geographic distance reflects a growing political difference. Writing from Coblentz, 'the Paris of the emigrants' (2: 67), Clara is appalled by the treatment of the absconding royals, reflecting her father's counterrevolutionary politics. 'Well', replies Clairant, 'your father's politics are again in the wrong... How can you believe the impartiality of French emigrants?' (2: 95). Their class difference has become literalized as a geographic, soon to be a national, difference, increasingly difficult to surmount. Once the emigrants are banished on pain of death, the rupture is final, writes Clairant:

> France itself, the only country in the world which appeared to protect our union, the only country in which to love me could be a virtue in you, the only country in which Nature has broken its chains, and in which persecuted love could find an asylum; – well, this France itself is thirsty of your blood!
> This haven is closed against us on pain of your life. Upon what point of the habitable world, then, immense as it may be, shall we find a retreat? (2: 146)

This last sentence becomes the question all émigrés ask, one particularly resonant with feminist British women writers, who connected powerfully with this sense of displacement. France as an asylum of virtue and 'persecuted love', instituting Rousseauvian ideals in its unprecedented liberalization of inheritance, marriage and divorce laws (1790–3), is now inaccessible to the émigrés.

As the war engulfs more of the continent, the Rousseauvian ideal at the heart of this sentimental novel reaches its breaking point, becoming incompatible with the new political realities of Europe. 'Alas', despairs Clairant, 'why am I born in a time when even the happiness of possessing you, if I should obtain it, would still leave me with the regret of not being able to embrace you, but on the smoking wreck of my country?' (3: 145). No secluded valley, no hermitage, exists for these Rousseauvian lovers: 'these valleys of which you speak with so much enthusiasm', writes Clairant to Clara, 'are they not known to the inhabitants of the neighborhood? Paths, even roads, border on them; all the environs are filled with emigrants' (2: 268). If discovered in France, Clara would be put to death, and likewise the republican Clairant if discovered in a warring country. In fact they briefly reunite for an idyll in a remote German cottage, only to be discovered by her father whose *ancien régime* powers are undiminished outside of France. Clairant is arrested, Clara dies, and the novel ends with the narrator, a German officer, explaining how he came to meet Clairant and tell his story through the interspersed letters that we have read.

The narrator explains Clairant's crisis in terms of the classic sentimental struggle between love and duty: 'Clara and his country established a violent struggle in his heart: it was two affections become irreconcileable [*sic*]' (2: 209). But this conflict is the product of a new political reality, brought into being by an unprecedented revolution and new political group – the émigrés – who 'were unable to live with the France the revolution had made' (Doyle, Introduction xv). These were not exiles, as William Doyle clarifies:

> Political exile is as old as history, but the émigré was a creation of the French Revolution. Unlike the British Jacobite exiles, who offered a recent parallel, those who left France during the Revolution were not simply motivated by loyalty to a deposed dynasty. Almost a third of those who left France went before the fall of the monarchy. Nor were they 'constructively' expelled for one overwhelming reason, like the Huguenots, who had outnumbered them a century previously. The Emigration began as a voluntary exodus, and until late in 1791 official policy was to urge the exiles to return. (Introduction xv)

The official policy changed once émigrés (like Clara's father and brother) attempted to involve foreign monarchies in overthrowing the Legislative Assembly and reinstating absolutist monarchy. The royal family's disastrous flight to Varennes in June 1791 was intended to join the Comte d'Artois' émigré coalition in Coblentz, and instead 'fatally undermined the prospect for a constitutional monarchy' (Doyle, Introduction xxi). This minority of recalcitrant political émigrés helped radicalize the new government's increasing paranoia and restrictions against emigration, which combined with the imminence of war, culminated in the series of laws on emigration passed April to October 1792, ultimately declaring émigrés banished 'à perpétuité' (Greer 30). Clairant's increasingly desperate pleas to Clara to return to France echo the official appeals made to the émigrés before the confiscation of their lands and banishment became official. The lovers' separation and tragic end illustrate sentimentally the political reality of émigré-era France, namely that '[b]y the end of 1790 there were already two Frances: that of the Revolution, within the frontiers, and that of the counterrevolution, at Brussels, and Coblenz and Turin' (Greer 23). Possessing first-hand knowledge of this unfolding rupture, Williams perceptively connected the plight of the émigrés to their counterrevolutionary ambitions:

> Cruel indeed has been the fate of the French emigrants in every circumstance, and in every situation in which they have been placed! It is their lot to feel, that by kindling the flames of war throughout Europe, that by directing the hostile sword of foreign potentates against their country, they are the remote cause of every wound with which that country has bled, and of every crime with which it has been polluted. (*Letters* 2:4:169)

In a November 1792 letter to Barlow, Smith similarly spoke of the émigrés in measured tones: 'They should suffer the loss of a very great part of their property; & all their power – But they should still be consider[e]d as Men & Frenchmen' (*Collected Letters* 49). What a far cry from the overwhelmingly counterrevolutionary portrayals (French and British) of the émigrés during the 1790s, which like the sentimental accounts of the 'martyred' royal family, flooded popular culture as the war effort intensified. Smith's and Williams's acknowledgement of the émigrés' complicity was rare in a Britain polarized by fears of domestic rebellion. Émigré-authored plays like *The Emigrant in London*, by 'An Emigrant' (London, 1795), children's books like Mme de Genlis's *The Young Exiles* (London, 1799) and the *Journal of a French Emigrant, fourteen years old* (London, 1795), and patriotic British works like Maria Julia Young's *Adelaide and Antonine: or The Emigrants* (1793) and Mrs Pilkington's *The Noble Emigrants* (1801), popularized a sentimental vision of the émigrés as virtuous aristocratic families fleeing from monstrous anarchists.

Numerically and ideologically, England was perhaps the European country most affected by the influx of émigrés that began in July 1789 with the ostentatious departure of the royal princes, increased with the clerical emigration of 1790 and the military emigration of 1791, and intensified in the autumn of 1792 once the republic was declared. Of the more than 130,000 people estimated to have emigrated (until the émigré lists were closed in 1799), amounting to half a percent of the French population (Greer 20), on average approximately 12,500 emigres per year reached Britain, with an many as 20–25,000 at the highpoint in late 1792.[6] 'It can be argued', writes the most recent historian of the émigré phenomenon, 'that the most significant contribution the émigrés made to the Counter-Revolution was the image they presented to the British government and public at a crucial point in the crisis', that is, once the republic was established (Carpenter, *Refugees* 35). Embraced by conservatives in the 1790s and inspiring novels by Dickens and Conan Doyle, as well as the popular *Scarlet Pimpernel*, the émigrés, writes Kirsty Carpenter, embody 'the enduring fascination of the British for the Counter-Revolution and particularly for their part in it' (*Refugees* 152).

The émigrés' counterrevolutionary significance is also crucial for understanding the revolutionary uses that they also served, as in Williams's astute political assessment quoted above. The émigrés must bear some responsibility for their role in antagonizing the Assembly and fomenting war, just like, Williams continues, Britain must accept its responsibility in its own, geographically distant, reign of terror, the profitable slave trade:

> Ah, let us, till the slave-trade no longer stains the British name, be more gentle in our censures of other nations! I know not how that partial morality can be justified, which measures right and wrong by geographical divisions; and, while it pours forth the bitterest of declamation against the human crimes in France, sanctions them in Africa. (*Letters* 2:4:176–7)

Williams opens up the debate beyond the confines of racial and 'geographical divisions' – not just the aristocratic émigrés, but the global victims of European ambitions must be acknowledged in the revolutionary debates. Williams's inclusive humanitarian gesture is representative of the internationalism the émigrés inspired in prorevolutionary writers like Mary Robinson and especially Charlotte Smith. Writing in overt (and unpopular) opposition to the tide of British nationalism in general, and the patriotic propaganda generated by the émigrés specifically, antinationalist writers like Robinson and Smith used the figure of the émigré to highlight transnational injustices, in France as in Britain.

Smith in particular developed a uniquely cosmopolitan feminism that looked farther across national and continental boundaries as the revolutionary wars continued, in search of an elusive community that could live up to Rousseauvian ideals while overcoming their contradictions. While *Clara and Clairant* had stayed within the confines of Rousseau's sensibility, dramatizing its demise under the pressure of revolutionary events, Smith, like so many of her contemporaries who were drawn to Rousseau's compelling vision of virtue, is both more ambivalent towards the revolutionary ideals popularly associated with Rousseau, and more critical of their shortcomings. Expanding her scope to consider the global plight of economic and political refugees, French émigrés, and British society across the isles and from different classes and both genders, Smith in her revolutionary 1790s novels develops a notion of the Citizen of the World that is surprisingly mobile and self-critical, even if finally not universally inclusive.

The asylum of the unfortunate

> Oh England, how truly doth thou deserve the double title of parent and asylum of the unfortunate.
>
> *The Emigrant in London: A Drama in Five Acts* (1794)

> I know not if any country has less to boast of as to their genuine liberality and enlargement of mind than England.
>
> Charlotte Smith, *Marchmont* (1796)

In nationalist hands, the émigrés afforded opportunities for extending Britain's ideological superiority and national pride through an ecumenical Christian charity. The Wilmot Committee was set up in September 1792 'to relieve the sufferings of the French Clergy', collected more than £12,000 in its first two months, and by 1794 had taken over the government's work of distributing relief to all émigrés.[7] Hannah More was closely involved with this charitable foundation, though she declined Charles Burney's offer to assume publicly the role of *'their Chair-woman or female Mr Wilmot'*.[8] She did however, write a pamphlet whose profits she donated to the relief fund (*Considerations on Religion and Public Education*, 1794). Yet as Angela Keane has shown, More's main concern in the pamphlet was to prevent the spread of secular education to Britain, enlisting the 'Ladies etc. of Great Britain' to help maintain Christianity's ascendancy in an era when, as she confided to Walpole, 'blasphemy and atheism have been allowed to become familiar to the minds of our common people'.[9] Echoing Burke, More wrote that 'it is not so much the force of French bayonets, as the contamination of French principles, that ought to excite our apprehensions' (*Considerations* 22). In her private correspondence regarding the émigrés, she revealed an undiminished Francophobia that was inseparable from her nationalist Christianity: 'I am not disappointed in the character I always [feared?] of that cruel people; and their whole conduct illustrates a favourite position of mine that arts and sciences, wit and learning, do little towards taming and civilizing that savage – the human heart without religion'.[10] Throughout the émigré crisis, More's ecumenical spirit coexisted with an absolute faith in British national superiority.

As with white abolition efforts, the charitable movement to help the émigrés was ultimately as concerned with benefiting British society, as it was with the object of sympathy. The refractory French clergy (*réfractaires*), those who had refused to take the oath of loyalty to the Civil Constitution of the Clergy declared in 1790, were ordered banished or forcefully deported on August 26, 1792. 'Since approximately 30% of the secular clergy refused to swear the oath', Donald Greer calculates, 'the decree of August 26 banished about 30,000' clergy world-wide, as many as 10,000 of those to Britain (28, 94). While a minority (25%)[11] of the total emigrants, the refractory clergy were proportionately higher in Britain, as were the aristocracy, making them highly visible and sympathetic subjects for charitable propaganda efforts such as More's. Following this influx of clergy in the autumn of 1792, pamphlets like More's *Considerations* and Fanny Burney's *Brief Reflexions* [sic] *Relative to the Emigrant French Clergy* (1793) were published to aid the emigrant clergy. Burney also singled out 'the Ladies of Great Britain' as particularly important in the relief effort, yet unlike More she took a cosmopolitan approach to 'domestic peace': 'all Europe is involved by the circumstances which occasioned' the émigrés' 'misfortunes' (*Brief Reflexions* 8). Women's charitable efforts to support the war against France, as Linda Colley demonstrated in *Britons*, similarly enlarged the so-called feminine domestic sphere, illustrating that domestic peace cannot be isolated from foreign war. But More's Francophobic approach to this feminine intervention in international politics greatly outsold Burney's more cosmopolitan alternative, a sign of things to come.

The plight of the émigrés also served as object lesson in children's literature like Lucy Peacock's *The Little Emigrant* (1799) and Mary Pilkington's *New Tales of the Castle; or, The Noble Emigrants* (1801), wherein reversals of fortune inculcate Christian virtues like forbearance, humility, and industry. In contrast to Peacock's relative liberalism, Pilkington's novel engages with contemporary antirevolutionary politics in quite specific terms, having the aristocratic children bemoan the unknown fate of the royal family:

> 'Let us get away from that *terrifying Assembly*, or we shall be all sent to prison with the King'.
> 'The dear unfortunate king! And the lovely condescending queen!' sighed out the sympathetic little Julian; 'but oh mama! where is the dauphin?' (*New Tales* 6)

Julian is remarkably politicized for a 12 year old, and through him Pilkington dramatizes the organic family's revolutionary crisis as predicted by Burke. The inset tales referred to in the novel's title all address this Burkean concern with the sanctity of property and patriarchy, amounting to a juvenile literature that complements the antiJacobin novels directed at adults. The most influential such children's book, Mme de Genlis's *Les petits émigrés* (1798), was translated into English as *The Young Exiles* in 1799, and went through numerous editions (the villain, named Godwin, connects the counter-revolutionary French exiles with their British allies through this shared enemy). These popular didactic works, like the pamphlets and propaganda aimed at adults, were designed both to increase sympathy for the émigrés and to further the counterrevolutionary war effort by channelling British nationalism, ingeniously, along class and ecumenical lines, while underplaying national difference.

In addition to these pamphlets and didactic works, poems like Charlotte Smith's *The Emigrants* and Maria Julia Young's *Adelaide and Antonine* were also published partly in order to shape public consciousness on the émigrés. Young's *Adelaide and Antonine: or The Emigrants* (1793) exhibits the poetic equivalent of More's Christian nationalism, embracing the defeated French aristocracy into the unshakably patriarchal family of Britain. Besieged by Jacobins seeking to rape and pillage, Adelaide and her aristocratic family escape to England, described with Hannah Moreish rhetoric as a land of plenty:

> There – Liberty's expanding tree
>   Its lofty head majestic rears –
> There – ROOTED in its NATIVE soil,
>   A vernal bloom for ever wears!
>
> Luxuriant plenty round it smiles,
>   There – Ceres plants her golden store;
> Full crops reward the reaper's toil,
>   Who – BLEST WITH PLENTY ASK NO MORE.
>
> Pure health and peace adorn his cot,
> He ENVIES not the RICH and GREAT;
> Enjoys th[e] TRUEST RIGHTS OF MAN,
>   CONT[E]NTMENT in his HUMBLE STATE. (13)

It is the very rootedness of British liberty, its nativist stasis that ensures that 'the lov'd monarch reigns secure' (13). When Barbauld threatened this self-satisfied vision of British stasis in her prophecy of a defeated empire in *Eighteen Hundred and Eleven*, Anne Grant responded with her patriotic *Eighteen Hundred and Thirteen*, in which her triumphant survey of British imperial history includes this familiar vision of the émigrés sheltered beneath 'the British throne untouch'd and sacred':

> Here Safety, each ungentle sound represt,
> Sat, dove-like, brooding on her downy nest.
>   Beneath the shelter of her guardian wings,
>   She gather'd exiled princes, peers, and kings ... (59)

Radical writers like Smith would break with this politically conservative nativism, revealing the impossibility, not merely the hypocrisy, of its claim that liberty is 'ROOTED in its NATIVE soil'. The plight of the émigrés reveals, in Smith's works, the insufficiency of any notion of liberty rooted in nations, an important break with both conservative and radical traditions of native British liberty, and with the novel as 'the symbolic form of the nation-state' (Moretti 45).

In Young's poetic account of the émigrés' British assimilation in Britain, there are no linguistic, cultural, or national distinctions to overcome, a calculated optimism in the face of growing public anxiety regarding this influx of

French manners and religion. Not even this longstanding Catholic/Protestant division is a barrier to the emigrants' assimilation into a Christian Britain:

> There – true religion's temple stands,
> At VARIOUS altars MILLIONS bend;
> O'er all – her heav'nly radiance beams,
> O'er ALL – her fost'ring arms extend. (Young 14)

Christianity, like the British empire which it upholds, will subsume all religious and national differences through its universalizing ambition – we are 'all the creatures of one Creator', affirmed the decidedly antinationalist Burney (*Brief Reflexions* 12). Yet to nationalists like More, Young, and Grant, the defeat of French absolutism and French Catholicism confirmed the superiority of British Protestantism, confident that it could benevolently absorb its defeated enemies as the grateful subjects of one king.

Although published the same year, Young's emigrants poem and Smith's *The Emigrants* approach nationalist politics in diametrically opposed ways. Young's *Adelaide and Antonine* denies the historic significance of the end of the French monarchy by substituting in its place the British monarchy. For Young, the crisis in France is not a revolution, but a monarchy overrun, unaccountably, by anarchy, and effectively forced to relocate overseas. Presumably, such a crisis could happen anywhere, anytime. In Smith's *Emigrants*, in contrast, the revolutionary crisis is the direct result of a series of deteriorating conditions in France, conditions dangerously similar to those in Britain. The 'regal crimes' of French absolutism, Smith warns, are similar to the 'legal crimes' of Britain, which institutionalize a hierarchy of privilege and power desperately in need of reform. Smith seamlessly joins together the plight of the emigrant aristocracy and clergy to such 'internal exiles' as the British poor and the poet herself, through these parallel exclusions 'encoding her critique of British class prejudice, nationalism, and militarism', according to Kari Lokke (87). Thus, like Wollstonecraft and Godwin, Smith always locates individual suffering within a larger political matrix, so that, for example, while she pities the clergy and aristocrats, she also connects their plight to their own complicity in *ancien régime* oppression: they are 'Men, whose ill acquir'd wealth/ Was wrung from plunder'd myriads, by the means/ Too often legaliz'd by power abus'd' (*Poems* 145; see also 141, 143).

Smith's poem shares with its counterrevolutionary counterparts a particular concern for female suffering and female sympathy. Written with deliberately Miltonic echoes of *Paradise Lost*, as I have argued elsewhere, Smith pays particular attention to the plight of women exiles in a postlapsarian England.[12] This signature insistence on the connections between the private and public, female and male, foreign and domestic spheres repeatedly returns to images of suffering femininity. While 'emigration was overwhelmingly masculine', with only 15% of classified émigrés being women (Greer 91), the symbolic value and social impact of émigrées was undoubtedly higher. Smith's focus on four members of the French clergy and on four mother-child pairs in *The Emigrants* (the author included) illustrates the disproportionate symbolic impact of these two vulnerable groups.

For Smith, Britain is not Austen's 'home land' of liberty and plenty, but a mirror of *ancien régime* corruption. The seemingly endless series of émigré wanderers along the Sussex coast, like the wandering poet herself, find no refuge from the ills of British 'legal crimes', that is institutionalized poverty, alienation, and exploitation. France and Britain are more alike than different, a controversial position that Smith literalized in her remarkable poem, *Beachy Head* (1807). A diachronic and crossdisciplinary meditation on the significance of place – Beachy Head, the closest point in England to France – Smith's poem reveals the inescapable connections between the two warring countries.[13] According to geographical evidence, Smith writes, France and England were once joined together, millions of years before England developed its insular nationalism. Separated by a 'vast concussion', the recent historical equivalent of which would be the Revolution, the two countries remain resistant to their shared history and political fate. In *Beachy Head*, Smith's resistance to nationalism goes beyond this desire to reverse her contemporaries' Francophobia, connected, as in the *Emigrants* and the later novels, to her pacifism. The Sussex landscape records a legacy of failed invasions: artifacts and tombs left behind by Romans, Danes, and French, alike unable to maintain their dominion over the English countryside. The victor here is not an eternal England, but nature, the only entity in Smith's poetic world that can withstand historical shifts through endurance and evolution, not conquest.

Much has been written on Smith's complex politics and poetics of nature, particularly as they relate to her innovative use of botany and her distinctly un-Wordsworthian, feminist approach to the sublime and the beautiful. What I would like to consider briefly here via the poetry is the supposed opposition that Smith sets up between politics and nature in her 1790s novels. In *The Emigrants*, the beleaguered narrator, faced with a stream of suffering émigrés, repeatedly tries to find comfort in pastoral retreat:

> How often, when my weary soul recoils,
> From proud oppression and from legal crimes...
> How often do I half abjure Society,
> And sigh for some lone Cottage, deep embower'd
> In the green woods... (*Poems* 136)

'There do I wish to hide me', says the autobiographical narrator in a Rousseauvian botanical retreat: 'well content/ If on the short grass, strewn with fairy flowers,/ I might repose thus shelter'd' (*Poems* 137). Yet what is characteristic about this pastoral escape is Smith's final refusal: 'Tranquil seclusion I have vainly sought', she says, unable to abandon 'affliction's countless tribes' (*Poems* 137). What would become the hallmark Wordsworthian retreat into the English countryside, and the basis of canonical readings of Romanticism's quietist retreat from revolutionary politics, is repeatedly foreclosed in Smith's poetry, just as her novels will deny the nationalist vision of England as asylum. England's 'NATIVE soil' of liberty provides a geological record of human oppression, and is thus in Smith's poetry not the 'asylum of the unfortunate', but an ever-changing landscape of temporary conquests and even more ephemeral shelters, providing only temporary solace to those residing in human time, that is in history.

The émigrés in England did however provide progressive writers with a unique opportunity to test nationalist claims of English liberality. Mary Robinson's émigré novel, *Hubert de Sevrac* (1796), provides an excellent example of how the émigré retreat to England could provide a radical critique of British society, not another instance of the 'enduring fascination for the Counter-Revolution' (Carpenter, *Refugees*, 152). Following the sentimental revolutionary crisis of all émigré novels, the aristocratic, binational (Scottish-French) émigré family of Hubert and Emily de Sevrac begin their quest for a virtuous refuge in the autumn of 1792, and as in *Clara and Clairant*, find temporary refuge in a Rousseauvian cross-class idyll (here, in Italy):

> It was in this romantic elysium that the family of de Sevrac first tasted happiness; all the glare of splendid life presented nothing so gratifying to the senses, or so soothing to the mind! It was here, that the emptiness of rank was forgotten, and the duplicity of courts remembered only with abhorrence. (1: 272)

Embroiled in Gothic plots of murder, rape, madness and greed, Robinson's émigrés endure a fortunate fall that as in Smith's novels, transforms them into 'citizens of the world', more sympathetic, egalitarian and feminist than their *ancien régime* counterparts. '[T]o become a perfect citizen of the world', says Emily de Sevrac, the émigrée mother, 'every minute particle of creation should be deemed worthy of investigation' (1: 296). As in Williams and Smith, the expulsion of the émigrés and the spiralling violence of the revolution are inseparable (here and in all of Robinson's later novels) from the *ancien régime* disparities of wealth that created such resentment. Sabina de Sevrac, the romantic heroine and daughter of the eponymous Hubert, condemns her family's complicity with this *ancien régime* oppression: 'The axe of vengeance succeeds the tortures of the dungeon!... Time was, when the few were happy, and the million wretched!' (2: 149–50). Not all émigrés become such enlightened citizens of the world, and Robinson contrasts

Hubert with the unrepentant émigré de Briancourt, a stereotypical libertine émigré persisting in *ancien régime* excesses.

Robinson narrates the enlightened émigrés' transformation into citizens of the world, or 'convert[s] of liberty' (3: 316), rejecting aristocratic and sexual privilege in one gesture, the elimination of *lettres de cachet* as 'an evil of the greatest magnitude' (3: 293). From Rousseau, to Robespierre and Sade, to Williams and Smith, the *lettre de cachet* was a synecdoche for *ancien régime* tyranny, which aristocrats like Hubert and de Briancourt had previously relied on, but which Hubert finally renounces: 'the dark volume [of history] would prove to the enlightened universe, that religion had been made a plea for the most inhuman sacrifices; avarice, the source of legal prostitution; and pride, the barrier between the virtuous and exalted' (3: 294). Robinson relocates her multinational émigrés (French-Scottish and French-English couples) in a utopian community somewhere in England. Yet Robinson's England is Wollstonecraft and Godwin's, plagued with religious intolerance, a growing gulf between rich and poor, and 'legal prostitution' (echoing Wollstonecraft's term for marriage in *Rights of Woman*). Indeed, in *The Widow* (1794), as in Smith's later fiction, a disillusioned Robinson suggests America as a better alternative to the continental wars than is England.

As in other contemporary novels ending in cosmopolitan retreats to England (for example, Smith's *Desmond*, *Marchmont*, *The Wanderings of Warwick*, Burney's *The Wanderer*, and Helen Craik's *Adelaide de Narbonne* and *Julia de St. Pierre*) Robinson's *Hubert de Sevrac* has a deliberately transnational focus on the privileges of class and gender that make English 'native liberty' as precarious and corrupt as that of the *ancien régime*. Concluding with an unmistakable prophecy that 'the hour of retribution is inevitable' and 'energy and philosophy will triumph' (3: 318), Robinson's émigré novel presents a radically different lesson than that imagined by nationalists. Her émigrés, like Smith's, arrive in England not as loyal subjects and good Christians, but as enlightened citizens of the world importing 'energy' and 'philosophy'.

Like Robinson, Smith became increasingly pessimistic about the likelihood of political reform in the 'NATIVE soil' of Britain. In Smith's revolutionary novels, she looks across national boundaries for alternative, multinational imagined communities. As they move from country to country, her protagonists find in nature comfort, shelter and inspiration that is distinct from the afflictions of culture, yet Smith's idealized nature is never an alternative to or escape from political conflict. Because, as *Beachy Head* illustrates, nature is inseparable from human history, as England is from the continent, British insular distinctness is no refuge from the European crisis. The self-satisfied piety with which the émigrés are embraced in counterrevolutionary writings is unthinkable in the harsh realities of Smith's novels, as her emigrants encounter suspicion, persecution, and penury in Britain. Robinson's war-time Britain in *Angelina* (1796) is similarly a dystopia full of suspicious locals and bereaved peasants, all of them 'materially affected by political events' (1: 32). Despite the bleakness of Smith's European canvas, she develops an early and feminist cosmopolitanism that connects British radical reform to the related projects of abolition and women's rights, a radical inclusiveness that as we shall see had telling limits when it comes to race, akin to male radicals' limitations on the rights of women.

Beyond naturalization and nationalization: Charlotte Smith's cosmopolitan novels

> When society shall be placed on the right footing, the citizens of any one state will consider those of any other state as their brothers and fellow citizens of the world.
>
> Joel Barlow, *A Letter to the National Convention* (1792)

In her final novel, *The Young Philosopher* (1798), Smith articulates a cosmopolitan feminist alternative to British nationalism, looking towards a postcolonial future in an idealized American republic as the solution to Europe's corruption. Smith's cosmopolitanism, so at odds with the nativism of contemporaries like Wordsworth and More, has four elements, all of them controversial in 1790s Britain: (1) a rejection of 'national character' in general; (2) a rejection of British, or even English, distinctness, whether in terms of genealogy, geography, politics, or virtue; (3) a refusal to be bound by the conventions or prejudices specific to place; (4) an appreciation, even idealization, of the transnational, whether in persons, literature, politics or place.[14] In short, Smith's novels respond to revolutionary crisis (philosophical, political, sexual) by forging a new imaginative possibility available to European men as well as women – the citizen of the world.

A critique of national character is prevalent throughout Smith's fiction, an outgrowth of the earlier eighteenth-century travel narratives and novels that explored the quirks of character found across the British Isles and abroad. In *Desmond* (1792), her first and most radical revolutionary novel, the eponymous English hero is a republican and self-confessed 'citizen of the *world*' (89), yet nevertheless distinguishes between the 'national character' (111) of the two women he desires, his French mistress Josephine, and the English Geraldine, whom he marries. Desmond's insistence on 'national character', given his desire for an English wife and French mistress, has been interpreted by Alison Conway and others as evidence of a nationalist logic underlying Smith's narrative. Yet as Eleanor Ty has also noted, *Desmond's* two 'national' heroines are doubles of each other (*Unsex'd* 140–2), allowing Smith to contemplate the consequences of desire pursued versus desire sublimated, as if splitting Rousseau's Julie into two distinct women. Ultimately, this notion of feminine 'national character' is central to Desmond's sense of patriarchal (in his case, republican) possession: despite his republican resistance to the *ancien régime* sexual tyranny of fathers and husbands, he ends the novel with a male fantasy: 'Geraldine will bear *my* name – will be the directress of *my* family – will be my friend – my mistress – my wife!' (414). As Anne Mellor concludes, 'Charlotte Smith forces us to recognize that both the chivalric code and the new ideal of republican citizenship (or fraternity) openly advocated by Desmond entail the same erasure of female political autonomy' (*Mothers* 119). *Fraternité* thus cuts across national and class lines, but *sororité* does not, at least not for Desmond and his vestigial, sexualized notions of national character. Yet the overall tone of *Desmond* is deliberately cosmopolitan, concluding with the planned retirement of an Anglo-French 'circle of friends' in the English countryside (414). With each successive revolution-era novel, Smith would widen this 'circle of friends', developing it into her cosmopolitan ideal, moving it farther from Britain in an attempt to abandon such local 'prejudices' as Desmond's sexualized 'national character'.

The *Old Manor House* (1793), its sequel the *Wanderings of Warwick* (1794), and *The Banished Man* (1794) move the action to the colonies, during the American war of independence, the intensifying slavery debates in West Indies, and the counterrevolutionary war engulfing 1793 Europe. In these novels Smith's critique of national character is more fully developed than in *Desmond*, and emerges when her world-travelling characters encounter (as they always do) exceptions to national stereotypes. Commenting on his own intense jealousy compared to his Portuguese friend's lack thereof, the English protagonist in *The Wanderings of Warwick* realizes that 'In this respect we seemed to have changed characters; and the jealousy which is, in the national character of the Portuguese, a feature so predominant, was transferred to the Englishman' (145). In *The Banished Man*, the English Ellesmere encounters a German innkeeper who refuses to help some Polish republican exiles: 'warm as he was in his zeal for the suffering party', Ellesmere did not 'exclaim against the inhumanity of his German hostess, and conclude that therefore all German hostesses were inhuman; but he reflected on a much more evident truth – how nearly *the people* of all countries are alike' (2: 43, orig. emphasis). Ellesmere and Carlowitz are politically opposed, yet the former's kindness to the latter inspires the Polish republican: 'The friendly interest which men of another country, and of other principles, took in his fate...had almost an instantaneous effect on the depressed spirits of Carlowitz' (2: 48). *The Banished Man* ends with a larger and more continental 'circle of friends' than did *Desmond*: the novel's international couples (Polish-English, French-English) will join a set of English economic exiles and French émigrés in Italy.[15]

While *Desmond*'s 'circle of friends' had retired to the English countryside in 1792, 1793 brought with it war, the Aliens Act, and the marriage of Smith's favorite daughter to an émigré aristocrat, developments which made Smith look further afield for a refuge. *The Banished Man*'s chief protagonist, the royalist émigré d'Alonville, allows Smith to detail the hostile reception many émigrés actually faced in a Francophobic Britain. Far from the conservative vision of Britain as the hospitable asylum embracing émigrés who shared its devotion to monarchy and a broadly defined Christianity, Smith's post-Aliens Act Britain is peopled with xenophobes of all classes. Upon arriving in England, her émigré is 'abused' by a 'mob' of 'lower class people' (2: 84), but also 'hissed and insulted in the streets of London' even though 'there was hardly an opulent, or even easily-circumstanced family in the houses that formed those streets, but what had contributed to relieve the necessities of the French, who had been thrown destitute on their shore' (2: 89). Mary Robinson's *Angelina* (1796) and *The False Friend* (1799) present similar visions of a post-Aliens Act and post-Treason laws British 'home land', suspecting any and all to be Jacobin spies or treasonous radicals.

Charitable campaigns on behalf of the émigrés did not stem the tide of Francophobia that many of these same nationalist campaigners, that is More and Young, had perpetuated, as Smith's émigré d'Allonville discovers upon his arrival in England:

> He saw numbers of his countrymen thrown from every comfort of life, on the bounty of a nation, which, by an effort of generosity, conquered, or at least concealed, their ancient enmity, to lend them assistance. Yet while the English with one hand rescued, with the other they seemed disposed to draw the sword against a whole people, of which the mass appeared to be sullied with crimes unknown before in the history of mankind. To the common people of England, who have little means of distinguishing, all foreigners were formerly considered as Frenchmen. They now heard of the atrocities committed by the French as a nation, and having still less the power of discrimination, involved every one of that nation in universal condemnation; adding to their long rooted national hatred, the detestation raised by these horrors. (2: 87–8)

Smith's access to émigré experience through her son-in-law is partly responsible for the increasing hostility to nationalism that we find in her novels, which decreased in popularity throughout the 1790s in part for this reason, I suggest. Burney, herself married to an émigré, likewise encountered much hostility towards her novel of the sufferings of an émigrée in British high society, *The Wanderer, or Female Difficulties* (1814). While the popular *Evelina* had contained caricatures of 'French character', after meeting her émigré husband, Burney lost her self-confessed 'impertinent and very John Bullish' prejudices, and became effectively exiled with her husband to France in 1802 (*Diary* 6: 16). Upon her return, Burney would discover that in post-Waterloo Britain, critics were even more intolerant of antinationalist critiques than in the 1790s, especially when antinationalism was coupled, as in Burney's writing (and Smith's), with a focus on 'female difficulties'.

British hostility to foreigners in general and the French in particular forces d'Allonville to leave for the continent, yet his experience of serial exile, mirrored by other characters , particularly female, throughout Smith's novels, makes possible a new condition, that of the citizen of the world:

> adversity, which has made me an exile, banished me from my country, robbed me of my friends and my fortune, and thrown me in some measure destitute on the world, has taught me ... to conquer prejudice, and to feel for the sufferings of others ... If my calamities have deprived me of my natural friends, they have been the means of creating for me others, who in the unruffled bosom of prosperity, I should never have found. (*Banished* 4: 340)

D'Allonville's letter closes Smith's 1794 novel, and echoes the author's own sentiments in this tumultuous year, when she inquired into the possibility of immigration to Switzerland. In seeking such a Rousseauvian refuge, one might say that Smith retreats from the realities of war into nature: Lorraine Fletcher argues that 'Her disillusion with the Revolution leads her increasingly to celebrate a Rousseauesque green world outside the politics of left and right, and in this sense she anticipates Wordsworth. Charlotte Denzil regrets the loss of her garden more than anything else about her past affluence' (221). Yet Smith's focus on maternal suffering has led to readings identifying Smith solely with overtly autobiographical characters such as the struggling writer Mrs Denzil. D'Allonville's account of serial banishment, reversal in fortune, impoverishment, sentimental education, and transnational connections also holds true for Smith (and Rousseau), although with nine children and an estranged husband she could not emigrate with a chosen lover like d'Allonville and Rousseau could. Like her sexually vulnerable heroines in these same revolution-era novels, Smith struggles against a wholesale legal and economic oppression unique to women, yet like her more worldly male heroes she also voices ideals of cosmopolitan communities beyond Britain's, indeed beyond national, borders.

Smith, like Robespierre and Williams in that same calamitous year of 1794, sought Rousseau's mythical landscape for political as well as personal reasons – not to escape politics in nature, but to return to the revolutionary ideals that they and virtually all their contemporaries imagined to originate, in their multifarious forms, in Rousseau's writings. Like the emigrants in *The Banished Man* and *Clara and Clairant*, the exiles of Smith's final novel, *The Young Philosopher*, seek to (re)create the promise of a Rousseauvian virtuous society. By 1798, the reach of Smith's circle of friends had expanded from this European utopia to the new world, where her sympathetic, multinational and multigenerational characters plan to relocate at the novel's conclusion. '*The Young Philosopher* offers the most complete fantasy of spatial and historical relocation', writes Angela Keane, 'of a new and equal community, of republican romance' (*Women* 106). As Keane, Mellor, and others have argued, Smith's republican romance is haunted by the 'pervasively patriarchal logic of revolutionary thought' (Keane, *Women* 88), the sexual contract in which such utopian freeholds are grounded. As equally important as her consciously gendered critique, I will suggest, are Smith's more reluctant attempts to come to grips with the colonial and commercial implications of her revolutionary ideals.

More than any of her previous novels, *The Young Philosopher* is concerned with the irreversible changes in Europe's political and physical landscapes, changes that make a just society impossible. What emerges from this bleak vision of Smith's present is an internationalist, Europhilic perspective – no longer are the protagonists English subjects who make alliances across national boundaries, but they are already deracinated binationals, whose lack of national identity, while making them vulnerable in a nationalistic state such as Britain, is also their best chance for liberation. While revolution awakened Smith's protagonists to their status as citizens of the world in previous novels, in *The Young Philosopher* her protagonists, female and male, are effectively born 'citizens of the world' through their complex international pedigrees and incessant wanderings. The Young Philosopher of the title is George Delmont, a Rousseauvian philosopher and gentleman farmer; yet as Elizabeth Kraft points out, the true protagonists are the beleaguered mother and daughter, Laura and Medora Glenmorris, whom Delmont befriends (xxiv). Medora, a 'child of nature' and Sophie-like 'counterpart' of Delmont, was, appropriately enough, born in Switzerland and raised in America. Medora's mother tongue is French – the language of Europe's cosmopolitan aristocrats relocated to the sphere of domestic virtue. She also speaks Italian, taught by her multilingual and re-naturalized father, Glenmorris, who has 'metamorphose[d] from a Scottish chieftain to an American farmer' (2: 152). Laura Glenmorris, Medora's mother, is the Italian-born child of a Dutch banker and an English would-be aristocrat. Acknowledging her debt to Wollstonecraft, and voicing a similar critique of the 'wrongs of woman' found in Wollstonecraft's 1798 novel, Smith catalogues the wrongs of woman in Britain in national as well as sexual terms through her use of mother and daughter protagonists.

Smith's novel goes beyond the critique of British nationalism and prejudice in *The Emigrants, Desmond* and *The Banished Man*, to reconfigure the condition of political exile as the true basis for virtuous life. In parallel tales of virtue in distress, Laura and Medora recount a series of close escapes from would-be rapists, fortune hunters and tyrannical parental figures. In doing so, these heroines illustrate women's institutionalized oppression in Wollstonecraftian fashion, but simultaneously suggest that women's disenfranchisement as national subjects can elevate them to citizens of the world. Laura tells of her Gothic pursuit by Highland relatives driven by greed and lust, while Medora will recount her similar ordeal in London. Drawing 'parallels between the cultural practices of the more "primitive" and superstitious clans and those of the more "civilized" and advanced society of London', writes Eleanor Ty, Smith demonstrates 'that there is essentially no difference in the two cultures' treatment of women' (*Unsex'd* 150). The 'wrongs of woman' are thus a transnational problem, both within Great Britain, and also across Europe and the Atlantic, linked as they are to empire and slavery, according to eighteenth-century feminists.

Smith's novels offer not only a radical critique of sexual and class privilege, as other critics have shown, but also establish a significant distinction between national subjects and citizens of the world. When Laura was imprisoned in a Highland castle by relatives seeking to prevent her unborn child's inheritance, she retained her wits by resisting their use of superstition to frighten her:

> The cry of an English bogie or sprite was heard, intimating the death of a person of that nation – but that was rather a miscalculation on the part of those who directed this machinery, for I was not only not a native of England, having been born at Florence, but I had never been naturalized. (2: 112)

According to the eighteenth-century anthropological logic by which time becomes spatialized, Laura has moved into the world of medieval Scotland and all its primitive passions. Yet as an Italian-born, Dutch-English woman who has travelled the continent, her post-revolutionary rootlessness (not her 'modernity') makes her immune to the superstitions of the place-bound and time-bound Highlanders. She is thus un-naturalized – neither nationalized as a subject, nor naturalized as if a native of that place, or of that time. In insisting on Laura's displacement, *The Young Philosopher*, like all of Smith's revolutionary novels, is a historical novel, demonstrating how 'one developmental stage collapses to make room for the next, and cultures are transformed under the pressures of historical events' (Trumpener 697). Smith's resistance to equating the national with the natural invites comparison to Lady Morgan's (Sidney Owenson's) union of the two in *The Wild Irish Girl* (1806), wherein Glorvina embodies an Irishness that is 'both *natural* and *national*' and thus resistant to colonization (120).

While Smith did take interest in the 'Celtic Fringe' in novels like *Celestina* and *The Young Philosopher*, she was not primarily concerned with problems of colonial reconciliation and national origins as were Morgan and Edgeworth. Rather, being reluctantly settled, but not at home in, her 'native' land, Smith imagines alternatives to such nationalization and naturalization. The 'transcendental homelessness' that Georg Lukács associated with the novel's modernity in *Theory of the Novel* (1920), is in Smith's case a specifically postrevolutionary historical phenomenon, setting her citizens adrift from the sentimental constants of previous fiction. In the above quote from *The Young Philosopher*, Laura's rootlessness makes possible her escape from a situation in which this very same vulnerability, as virtue in distress, originally placed her. Lest Laura's liberty seem like merely the accident of birth and fortune (that is, of place), in providing her with a cosmopolitan continental upbringing, Smith links her protagonists' rootlessness to the political reality of Britain's growing commercial and colonizing influence in the world. Laura is alone because her husband's friends 'were men who had either been carried to different parts of the world by the extraordinary changes which had happened within the last ten years in Europe, or had retired to the estates at a great distance from London' (215–6). Her husband, meanwhile, is abducted by an international band of privateers, a transnational 'heterotopia *par excellence*' according to Foucault (28), and one particularly resonant during the revolutionary wars.

Thus, Smith's 1790s novels mark a significant exception to the 'preWaverley' conceptualization of 'nationalism [as] a self-evident legacy, the result of unbroken continuity', that Katie Trumpener has persuasively outlined in *Bardic Nationalism* (697). According to Trumpener, precursors of the national tale like Smith's *Desmond* and Radcliffe's *Castles of Athlin and Dunbayne* (1789) rely on a localized national character and thus 'provide the national tale with its central plot device: the spatialization of political choices, presented as a journey of discovery through the British peripheries' (693). In Edgeworth and Morgan's national tales this spatialization will be dramatized via heterosexual romance, using an 'allegorical presentation of the contrast, attraction, and union between disparate cultural worlds' (ibid: 697). In Smith's cosmopolitan novels, in contrast, the national is uprooted from its natural location, with multinational protagonists wandering across landscapes similarly robbed of national stability.

Laura's ordeal begins when she is separated from her husband, who has been abducted by privateers. 'The men who plundered our house', recounts Glenmorris, 'were the crew of an American privateer, or rather of a large vessel fitted out at Morlaix [France], under American colours, but commanded by an English outlaw, and manned by English, American, Scotch, Irish, Portuguese and even three or four Genoese sailors; they were literally a party of buccaniers [*sic*], holding themselves accountable to no government, and ready to use their arms against all' (2: 146). In this volatile revolutionary landscape, Smith's ideal cosmopolitan communities are shadowed by such vicious versions of cosmopolitan cooperation as this multinational band of brigands. The privateers take Glenmorris to yet another version of cosmopolitan community – America, where those fighting against British rule find in the British Glenmorris an ally: 'they forgot that I was born a Briton, and a North Briton too, and belonging to those whose legions were then carrying fire and sword through their country, and they embraced me as a brother' (2: 148).

The privateers and patriots share with Laura and Medora an outlaw status that Smith, like Wollstonecraft, evoked repeatedly to illustrate women's disenfranchisement. For Smith this outlaw status places women literally outside national boundaries, not merely outside the law of the land as in Wollstonecraft. In fact, one could argue that the primary division in *The Young Philosopher* and Smith's other 1790s novels, is not between male and female, vicious and virtuous, poor and wealthy, but between those who are bound to place (and thus to time) and those who are not, as they see it. Once one attempts, or even imagines, uprooting from place, all these other oppositions also begin to fluctuate, hence émigré fiction's utopian dreams of 'anational' regeneration sustained in the nightmare of war-time emigration.

The brutal Laird of Kilbrodie voices the traditional (Burkean) *ancien régime* vision of this precarious anational status as one of lawlessness. Kilbrodie lusts after Laura and her fortune, and tries to convince her that her abducted husband is dead: 'those who had been seized by privateers, and who were not therefore considered as being in the slightest degree protected by the laws of nation, had been given to the natives of the country, to be tormented by every hideous invention of cruelty' (2: 115). Yet this is precisely Laura's own status in Britain, a woman not 'in the slightest degree protected by the laws of nation', and at the mercy of the 'natives of the country' like the Laird, who recognizes only the *droit de seigneur*. As her resolve also revealed, Laura's 'unnaturalized', foreign status also means that she is also not subject to the superstitions of nation or 'nature' – she uses reason to overcome the frailty and superstition thought 'natural' to Englishwomen of that time and place.

Laura's daughter Medora is similarly adrift from male protection, and she survives such displacement through her foundational education in Rousseauvian virtue. Resembling alternatively Emile's submissive Sophie and Saint-Preux's accomplished Julie, Medora is the female 'counterpart' (354) to the Young Philosopher Delmont, a 'child of nature' onto whom Delmont projects his fantasies of the promise of a just society realizable only in the new world. Born in Switzerland and raised as a 'Caledonian American', Medora embodies America as cosmopolitan haven for disparate people, the new world equivalent of the ideal Swiss society. Enlightenment continentals had long idealized Switzerland (Smith's own choice for emigration) as a cosmopolitan democracy (erroneously), the cradle of radical politics (via Rousseau), educational theory (via Pestalozzi), and science (via Lavater): 'limitrophe de l'Allemagne, de l'Italie et de la France, la Suisse est aussi un bon exemple de pluralisme en matière de langues, de religions, de politique et de culture' (Plongeron 119). Here Smith posits the final destination of Rousseauvian virtue in the 1790s – out of the corruptions of Europe and into the new world. This familiar vision of America as a regenerative virgin land coincides in Smith, as it did historically, with a revolutionary ideal of the citizen of the world, one whose utopian travels are made possible, ironically, by tracing the routes of colonial exploitation and what was rapidly becoming a global war.

The questions asked in *Clara and Clairant* in 1797 are posed with increasing urgency as a protracted war expands even farther as the decade continues – 'Upon what point of the habitable world, then, immense as it may be, shall we find a retreat?' (2: 146). The more immense the world becomes in Smith's 1790s novels, the more inhospitable it becomes for her wanderers, as war moves across the continent and to the West Indies, North and South America, and Africa in a colonial scramble to enlarge competing empires. The British government's war against the French 'formed part of a larger punitive project to strip France of all its peripheral territories, be they in Europe or the wider world', and succeeded in acquiring seventeen colonies during the French wars despite many setbacks (Mori 175, 180). For the republican Glenmorris, the recently independent America is the only retreat left in this global theatre of war, for only there can one realize the European dream of a 'citizen of the world'. Regarding his plan to take Medora and Delmont to America, Glenmorris says:

> it is not to the fastidious fine man of the day that I give my child; it is to a citizen of the world; to one divested not only of local prejudice, but I hope of all prejudices; to him, who can live wherever his fellow men can live; to him who can enjoy the spectacle of a new continent rising into a great state by its cultivators – *fair cities, substantial villages, extensive fields, an immense country filled with decent houses, good roads, orchards, meadows, bridges; where an hundred years ago all was wild, woody and uncultivated.* (129, orig. emphasis; quoting Crèvecoeur 66)

This retreat is not a national one, as America promises the elimination of European national distinctions, or rather their evaporation in its sheer immensity. Thus Barlow's 1790s writings consistently cast America as the foil to European nationalism, promising that '[t]he Americans cannot be said as yet to have formed a national character' (*Political Writings* 142).

Glenmorris quotes Crèvecoeur's 'What is an American?' rhapsody from his immensely popular *Letters from an American Farmer* (1782), which more than any other eighteenth-century account of America established the romantic ideals of the frontier through which it would continue to be known. For Crèvecoeur, America was the 'asylum' sought by all of Smith's protagonists:

> In this great American asylum, the poor of Europe have by some means met together, and in consequence of various causes; to what purpose should they ask one another what countrymen they are? Alas, two thirds of them had no country. Can a wretch who wanders about, who works and starves, whose life is a continual scene of sore affliction or pinching penury – can that man call England or any other kingdom his country? (Crèvecoeur 68)

In Crèvecoeur's 'promiscuous breed' of northern European outcasts – 'a mixture of English, Scotch, Irish, French, Dutch, Germans, and Swedes' (68) – we see the cast of characters of Smith's 1790s novels (though Smith also includes eastern and southern Europeans). Like Smith, Crèvecoeur 'could point out to you a family whose grandfather was an Englishman, whose wife was Dutch, whose son married a French woman, and whose present four sons have now four wives of different nations' (70). This utopian, cosmopolitan vision of the new world was developed by earlier French writers like Rousseau and Raynal, echoed by English rationalists like Godwin and Paine, and pursued by would-be revolutionary emigrants, largely the Girondins favoured by Smith, Williams, and Wollstonecraft – Brissot de Warville, Bancal d'Isaarts, and even the Rolands. All either travelled or hoped to travel, in some cases permanently to immigrate to, the new world in the early revolutionary period. Smith, however (like Wollstonecraft, and unlike Mme Roland), was highly critical of the patriarchal origins of the Rousseauvian ideal underpinning the Enlightenment's 'new world'. Her critique of the republican ideal is visible in the way British patriarchy reflects that of France, suggesting the inability of republican ideals to transcend the gender hierarchy (the sexual contract) authorizing their discourse of rights and liberty. Smith's transnational and radical feminism will not, however, make the further leap beyond European racial lines, as we shall see.

Desmond's final *couverture* of the long-suffering English wife and mother under the name of the male republican protagonist, made the masculinist origins of the citizen of the world impossible to ignore. In choosing an English wife and French mistress, this citizen of the world resembles closely the man of the world, two figures Smith explicitly distinguishes in *The Young Philosopher*: there, the hero, a 'citizen of the world' (169), marries the Swiss-born Caledonian-American, while his John Bullish, libertine brother, a 'man of the world' (251), desires her as his exotic mistress, and marries an English woman for her fortune. By desexualizing *'citizen* of the world' in this key distinction from *'man* of the world', Smith creates a potential space for an ungendered citizenship. Yet in *The Young Philosopher*, Smith connects the rights of man and wrongs of woman even more closely than in *Desmond*, leaving us in greater doubt as to the utopian goals of her cosmopolitan circle of friends, since they exchange European forms of patriarchy (primitive and modern, that is Highland and English) for a new world figured as Rousseauvian regeneration of 'ancient' patriarchy. In giving his daughter to Delmont, the old philosopher hands off to the young philosopher, their status as citizens of the world in fact made possible by the sexual contract that predates such Rousseauvian social contracts: 'it is not to the fastidious fine man of the day that I give my child; it is to a citizen of the world'. Here, as in *Desmond* and *The Banished Man*, Smith makes it clear that such republican masculine liberty is partly a nostalgia for (Biblical) patriarchal rule, a nostalgia shared by fellow feminists like Percy Shelley and antifeminists like

Rousseau. Medora feels most at home in the patriarchal America that she calls home – 'I had been used to the hospitality of America, where the stranger, of whatever nation or persuasion, is received with the simplicity of patriarchal kindness' (327). Smith has little to say about this patriarchal ideal as such, although as Elizabeth Kraft argues, she undermines this myth of enlightened male protection (as Wollstonecraft and Robinson did in *Wrongs of Woman* and *The False Friend*,[16] respectively) by revealing her vulnerable heroines left unprotected by 'men who are…somewhere else when trouble occurs' (Introduction, xxv). Smith leaves us to imagine that an independent Caledonian-American heroine of such pluck, despite her self-conscious emulation of English sentimental heroines like Pamela, has acquired her love of liberty in the multicultural American republic she calls home.

As Delmont's counterpart 'child of nature', Medora serves as the Rousseauvian complement to the 'citizen of the world', making visible the exclusively masculine nature of that citizen (and of philosophy) in earlier eighteenth-century traditions, even while distinguishing the *citizen* from the *man* of the world. In focusing her narrative largely on the physical resilience and presence of mind of Medora and Laura as they escape through a nightmarish series of incarcerations, Smith, like Wollstonecraft, insists that this Rousseauvian masculinist ideal of the patriarchal citizen of the world confront the real costs of patriarchy for women. Staël would do this most systematically in *Delphine* (1802) and *Corinne* (1806), according to Lori Jo Marso, by contrasting Rousseau's 'manly citizen' with the superior example of her heroines as 'loving citizens' (103). While Smith does not offer such distinct female alternatives to Rousseau's virtuous citizens, she remains a significant innovator of the 'cosmopolitan heroine' that Staël and the post-*Wild Irish Girl* Owenson would later popularize, distinct from their contemporaries' 'national heroines'.[17]

Smith's cosmopolitan heroines are bewildered by a Europe irreversibly changed by the displacements of people and borders resulting from the revolutionary wars. Even in London, Laura cannot find help because of 'her long residence out of England' and because her husband's friends 'were men who had either been carried to different parts of the world by the extraordinary changes which had happened within the last ten years in Europe, or had retired to the estates at a great distance from London' (215–6). The rupture initiated by the revolutionary wars forever altered the sentimental landscape in novels like *Clara and Clairant*, *The Banished Man*, *Marchmont*, and *The Young Philosopher*, fissuring Europe in ways inconceivable to pre-revolutionary sentimental travellers (like Sterne's, for example, who had travelled to France during the previous war). As the 'citizen of the world' hero of *Marchmont* laments while fleeing across a war-torn France in 1793, unable to escape into the idealized bowers he occasionally discovers, 'Alas! How changed, since his [Sterne's] animated pen depicted it, are all but the local charms of this country!' (*Marchmont* 4: 69). Smith's travellers wander in a landscape cut off from the sentimental aesthetics guiding their predecessors, whether in the British countryside or abroad. During her 1794 travels throughout the landscape of *La Nouvelle Héloïse* (visiting Clarens and Chillon), Williams similarly lamented that while 'All in nature is still romantic, wild, and graceful, as Rousseau painted it...the soothing charm associated with the moral feeling is in some sort dissolved' by the political 'sorrows that have the dull reality of existence' (*Tour* 2: 179–80).

The second explanation for Laura's helplessness – her friends' retreat to the 'local charms' of the English countryside, the utopian solution in pre-war *Desmond* – is thus also not an option for Smith's later protagonists, as it also ceased to be for Williams in her Swiss travels during the Terror. Smith's *Beachy Head* rejects on intellectual and social grounds such an escape into Rousseauvian nature, by gently upbraiding the reclusive Visionary, as much Wordsworth as the *Young Philosopher's* Armitage. In *Marchmont*, while the peripatetic hero finally regains his long-sought Eastwoodleigh estate, he has no intention of living there, instead accepting a house in Clapham Common for several months, an appropriately temporary retreat for a hero who despairs that 'it does not seem that European earth will permit me to exist on its surface!' (4: 39). *The Young Philosopher's* closing dialogue makes it clear why such refuge is foreclosed according to Smith's antinationalism. Delmont's mentor is the Godwinian writer Armitage, suspected of Jacobinism, though in reality a moderate constitutional monarchist who at the novel's conclusion urges Glenmorris to stay in 'his native land' (351). 'If I have those I love with me', Glenmorris counters, 'is not every part of the globe equally my country? And has not this, which you are pleased to call my native land, thrown me from her bosom when I might have served her? Did she leave me any choice between imprisonment and flight?' The plight of this citizen of the world is thus also woman's, via his wife and daughter's serial imprisonments and flights, making women the true citizens of the world. 'Can I love to live in such a country only because I drew my first breath in a remote corner of it?' asks Glenmorris (352). In contrast to the more radical Smith and Glenmorris, Armitage is ultimately 'among the moderates and quietists', a Wordsworthian nativist and idealist: 'you endure all things, you hope all things, you believe all things', says Glenmorris to his friend (352).

Armitage, while allied with Glenmorris and the citizens of the world, is place-bound, a staunch defender of benevolent monarchy who 'holds all the wild schemes of universal equality as utterly impracticable' (247). As a British subject, albeit a reformer, he does not take the final step with Smith's citizens of the world, beyond (they imagine) the confines of nation. '[W]e will once more cross the Atlantic', dreams Glenmorris, 'and I will try to teach [Delmont], that wherever a thinking man enjoys the most uninterrupted domestic felicity, and sees his species the most content, *that* is his country' (352). Voiced here in the language of masculinist primitivism, of Crèvecoeur and Rousseau, Smith's concept of the virtuous citizen of the world is nevertheless feminist at its core, via the Wollstonecraftian revision of 'domestic felicity' on which her novels insist. Brief glimpses of domestic felicity are always destroyed by economic and political violence, particularly against women, hence the progressively wider dispersal of the 'circle of friends' in each novel, to *The Young Philosopher*'s most abstract because most idealized vision of a truly 'new world'.

An American mirage

Smith's cosmopolitanism looked increasingly to the new world as the true home of the citizen of the world because she, like leading radicals Godwin and Paine, saw in the new world the fulfilment of Locke's and Rousseau's notions of political rights separate from property rights. In *Political Justice*, which Smith read the year before she published *The Young Philosopher*, Godwin had similarly idealized the colonies: 'Men who are freed from the injurious institutions of European government, and obliged to begin the world for themselves, are in the direct road to be virtuous' (680). Paine's *Rights of Man* had singled out America as the destiny of liberty. 'As America was the only spot in the political world, where the principles of universal reformation could begin', he reasoned, 'so also was it the best in the natural world . . . Its first settlers were emigrants from different nations, and of diversified professions of religion, retiring from governmental persecutions of the old world, and meeting in the new, not as enemies, but as brothers' (2: 181–2). 'Paine and Godwin', Nicholas Roe argues in *The Politics of Nature*, 'justified emigration as a return to an uncorrupted life that would necessarily produce a moral reformation' (49). Whether such emigration could reform sexual relations remains to be seen, according to Smith, who like most contemporary feminists was not interested in returning to a 'state of nature' (neither was Rousseau, we should remember).

Southey and Coleridge's Pantisocracy scheme of 1793–4, in which 12 couples were to retire to the banks of the Susquehanna, is part of this ubiquitous European dream of utopian emigration that Smith's 1790s novels share. Pantisocratic republicans like Dyer, Southey, and Coleridge shared with Smith's male emigrants, whether French, English, Scottish or Polish, a benevolent patriarchal vision of the virtuous society. The 'little society' of Pantisocracy, Coleridge wrote, 'was to have combined the innocence of the patriarchal age with the knowledge and genuine refinements of European Culture'.[18] Smith, like Wollstonecraft and Robinson, was never so innocent as to believe this of 'the patriarchal age'. These feminists' persistent foregrounding of the sexual oppression inseparable from class hierarchy casts doubt on Paineite, Godwinian and Rousseauvian radicalism even while indebted to these traditions.

The connections among the French émigrés, Smith's cosmopolitan 'circle of friends', Pantisocracy, and revolutionary utopianism (French and new world) form a dense network of personal and political contacts, commercial enterprises, and international philosophical debate. This transnational matrix locates Smith squarely in a Franco-Anglo-American network of republican sympathizers, beyond the metropolitan Johnson circle that has tended to overshadow the multifocal dimensions of radicalism and feminism in Britain. Like Robinson and her underappreciated links to the cosmopolites Robert Merry and Sampson Perry, and Wollstonecraft and Williams's celebrated immersion in continental and American radical circles while in France, Smith was intensely interested in the Revolution, and in Warner, Godwin, and especially Barlow, she had direct connections to Francophilic radicalism.

Joel Barlow had originally come to France in 1788 as the chief agent for a large-scale emigration scheme, a colonial enterprise that may have inspired Smith's utopian vision in *The Young Philosopher*. At the very least, the cosmopolitan scope and disastrous outcome of this colonial venture illustrate one possible destination of the 'citizen of the world' ideal and its inescapable contradictions. Barlow was hired as the exclusive agent of the Scioto Company of Ohio, and arrived in France with orders to sell two million acres of what was then the Northwest wilderness to French and Dutch investors. Barlow sold nothing for over a year, becoming instead immersed in radical politics in Paris and then England, which he visited in 1788 and again in 1791, meeting with figures like Wollstonecraft, Paine, Godwin, Price, Holcroft, Tooke, and Smith's patron William Hayley (Woodress 118). Only after the fall of the Bastille did Barlow, with the help of Scottish engineer William Playfair, begin selling land to émigrés, one million livres' worth by the end of 1789.[19] By May 1790, approximately six hundred French émigrés arrived in Alexandria, only to discover that the deeds Barlow had sold them were worthless. Nearly 500 of these émigrés finally reached 'Gallipolis' in the Ohio wilderness by October 1790, to find four log blockhouses with dirt floors to house them, and no actual rights to the land (see Illustration 4). Barlow, Playfair, and the American speculators were all complicit in this fiasco, although modern American accounts of Barlow like to portray him as the naïve dupe of his associates. By 1792, only 300 of the émigrés remained in Gallipolis, and half that by 1794, the rest having died or drifted away. In 1796 the republican philosopher Volney visited the fabled Gallipolis and was 'struck by its forlorn appearance; with the thin pale faces, sickly looks and anxious air of its inhabitants', and complained of the speculators' gross exaggerations of the ease and plenty the émigrés could expect.[20]

The largely Parisian population Barlow recruited for this utopian scheme seems representative of the French émigrés as a whole, particularly those in the nobility and luxury trades who left soon after the fall of the Bastille: aristocrats, officers, doctors, merchants, and artisans like goldsmiths and watchmakers, along with indentured servants. They enrolled a total of five gardeners and one farmer (Moreau-Zanelli 146–50). Utterly unsuited to the

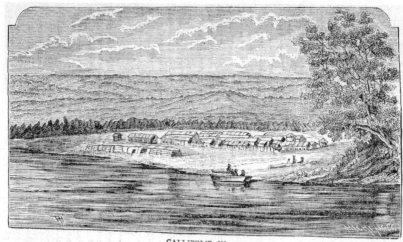

GALLIPOLIS IN 1791

Illustration 4 'Gallipolis in 1791', Anon. Reproduced from John Abbott, *The History of the State of Ohio* (Detroit: Northwestern, 1875). Courtesy of the University of California, Davis

hardships of wilderness life, Barlow's émigrés are in this respect representative of Smith's citizens of the world. Advertised in Brissot's *Patriote François* and in published prospectuses in 1790, Gallipolis was described in cosmopolitan terms sure to have attracted figures like Desmond, the Glenmorrises, and Smith herself: 'Ce n'est point une terre isolée', proclaimed the Compagnie du Scioto, boasting of an 'organisation multinationale' with buyers from Germany, England, Scotland, Ireland and Holland (qtd. in Moreau-Zanelli 103–4). As Barlow's friend and correspondent in the early 1790s, when he was deeply immersed in this land speculation bubble, Smith imbibed this popular vision of America as 'the asylum of freedom' and 'refuge of distressed Europeans', in Crèvecoeur's famous words (*American Farmer* 37).

Popular French travel writings like Crèvecoeur's *Letters from an American Farmer*, Brissot de Warville's *Travels in the United States of America* (1792), along with Anglo-American accounts like Thomas Cooper's *Some Information Respecting America*, Gilbert Imlay's *Topographical Description of the Western Territory* (1792), and Barlow's own romantic *Vision of Columbus* (1787), created an uncritical fantasy that was equal parts republican utopia and commercial get-rich-quick scheme. For example, the Dissenter Joseph Priestley, driven out of Britain like so many of Smith's protagonists, immigrated to the Susquehanna in 1794, becoming an inspiration for the Pantisocracy's 'little circle'. In fact, Charles Piggott's *Political Dictionary* (1795) defined emigrant as 'one who, like Dr Priestley or Thomas Cooper, is compelled to fly from prosecution, and explore liberty in a far distant land, probably America' (17). Yet Priestley's political emigration was inseparable from land speculation schemes like Barlow's Gallipolis, for as Wil Verhoeven has argued, 'Radical travellers like Imlay and Cooper did not travel to *see* things; they travelled to *sell* things: radical ideas, of course, but also, and perhaps more so, *land*' ('Land-Jobbing', 189). Priestley was Cooper's father-in-law, and with him intended to sell land in America, publishing a *Plan de Vente* in France (Eugenia 1074). Cooper, Priestley and Coleridge were known to each other; Brissot, Imlay, Crèvecoeur, and Barlow were also acquainted, as it seems Brissot was an early participant in the Gallipolis bubble.[21] In England, Godwin, Johnson and Wollstonecraft, and in France Wollstonecraft, Williams, Stone, Imlay and their Girondin friends all moved in the same cosmopolitan and commercial circles. Even Williams dreamed of emigrating with the Barlows to America in 1794, 'to form a menage' with them in that country (see Kurtz and Autrey 46).

As a friend of Godwin and Barlow, an admirer of Wollstonecraft and Crèvecoeur, Smith participated in this transatlantic exchange regarding America that was at once cultural and commercial. Her 'little circle of friends', like the famous *Cercle Social* of the Brissotins in Paris whose British connections have been documented by David Erdman, and like the Pantisocratic 'little society', emerged from the same European historical crisis. These utopias, because put into practice, are more accurately described as 'heterotopias', following Foucault's distinction in which heterotopias (for example real places like the colony and the brothel) are 'something like counter-sites, a kind of effectively enacted utopia in which the real sites, all the other real sites that can be found within the culture, are simultaneously represented, contested, and inverted' (24). Thus, such American heterotopias were inseparable from, indeed literally unrealizable without, the land speculation schemes of Imlay, Playfair, Barlow, Cooper, Priestley, Brissot and so many other citizens of the world, and the mechanisms of exploitation which they enlisted. These radical emigration schemes capitalized on the established eighteenth-century association of cosmopolitanism and commercial empire, while presenting themselves as co-existing within 'peaceful and mutually beneficial consumer communities' (O'Brien 19).

'You ask me what appear to be the most general inducements for people to quit England for America', wrote Cooper in *Some Information Respecting America* (qtd. in Eugenia, 1075). 'In my mind, the first and most principal feature is, *the total absence of anxiety respecting the future success of a family . . .* Poverty, such as in Great Britain, is almost unknown'. The Tory *British Critic* was sceptical of such radical claims, but also feared an exodus of naïve British subjects: 'When this book [*Some Information*] was first announced we were inclined to consider Messrs. Imlay and Cooper as rival auctioneers, or rather show-men, stationed for the allurement of incautious passengers . . .

To the thinking part of the nation, however, there will not appear in the publications very strong allurements to emigration' (*British Critic* 5 (1794) 26). Smith's narratives of national dislocation were shaped by this larger debate on emigration, which grew increasingly anxious in periods of economic stress.[22]

By December 1789 Barlow had reported having sold over one million livres' worth of land in Ohio, and once the first émigrés embarked for Gallipolis he believed he was on the road to fortune: '20,000 people will be on those lands in 18 months & our payments will be made in 12'.[23] Under more financial strain than Barlow, Coleridge and Southey combined, Charlotte Smith with her nine children and spendthrift, abusive husband would have had an utterly different evaluation of Cooper's inducement that in America one could experience '*the total absence of anxiety respecting the future success of a family*'. As modern feminist readers of Smith's 1790s novels attest, in her works the institution of family appears an illusion of protection at best and a nightmare of abuse at worst. Like her fellow 1790s feminists, Smith is a more fearless critic of family romance than her radical male contemporaries.

By 1798 of course, Gallipolis had failed, as had the progress of the French Revolution in Smith's eyes, though not its principles. Switzerland was also no longer a refuge after the French invasion of 1798. As sophisticated a reader of nationalism as of the Romantic pastoralism she so eloquently voiced in her poetry, Smith responded to this European failure to achieve her Revolutionary ideals by reversing the real/ideal dichotomy governing the distinction between the 'ideal' new world versus the 'real' old Europe. The cosmopolitan Laura, Medora, and Glenmorris have already crossed the Atlantic in both directions by the start of *The Young Philosopher*, which charts their troubled return to Britain to claim an ancestral inheritance. In Britain, Laura is incarcerated in a madhouse and loses her mind (in that order), Medora is nearly raped and nearly loses her mind, and Glenmorris lands in debtor's prison. Laura reflects that 'in coming to England she had sacrificed substantial happiness to the pursuit of a chimera, which, even if it could be attained, was not worth one year, nay, not one month, of the tranquil happiness and domestic comfort' they enjoyed in America (301). 'I do not love to be in a country where I am made to pay very dear for advantages which exist not but in idea', agrees Glenmorris (351). In Walker's *The Vagabond* (1799), the radicals' doomed emigration to Kentucky (inspired by Imlay's account) encounters exactly such difficulties and disillusionment, prompting a recantation of the 'chimerical' revolutionary ideals found in all counterrevolutionary narratives. In Smith's dizzyingly self-aware narrative crossings, not the earlier utopian schemes of Gallipolis or Pantisocracy (or of *The Vagabond*), but the harsh present-day realities of British class privilege are dangerous 'chimeras', something her marathon inheritance battles taught her first hand.

Unlike these previous failed utopias, Smith's are decidedly multinational and multilingual, in addition to being protofeminist, reflecting the author's international experience. Despite its cosmopolitan marketing, Gallipolis was all French and founded in hope that 'France shall find herself renovated in the Western World', as one of the émigrés wrote (qtd. in Hart, 193). Cooper's Susquehanna settlement and Coleridge's Pantisocracy were to be distinctly English and exclusively Anglophone.[24] Even Barlow's American epic, *The Vision of Columbus* (1787), the visionary drive of the Gallipolis scheme, prophesized a monolithic America become 'one great empire': 'At this blest period, when thy peaceful race/ Shall speak one language and one cause embrace' (2: 248). Such displaced nationalist visions of utopian empire are wholly at odds with the multilingual cosmopolitanism of Smith, Williams and Robinson, even while sharing a resilient Europhilia.

Conclusion: the limits of cosmopolitanism

I...have at times had a very great inclination...to pack up my children and my books, in which consist all my riches, and, like a female Prospero, set forth for some desart island – or any island but this dear England of ours.

Charlotte Smith, The Banished Man (1794)

The persistent nationalism, monolinguism and patriarchalism of Gallipolis and Pantisocracy, and the more cosmopolitan communities of Smith's citizens of the world, share a threshold status between emigrant refuges and nascent colonies. Not only through the commercial and colonial infrastructure, funding, and institutionalized knowledge that make such heterotopias possibilities, but also via their sexual, class and racial contradictions, émigrés and colonists share a burden of European corruption that no distance can leave behind. Smith's self-characterization as a 'female Prospero' via her autobiographical Mrs Denzil character in the above epigraph illustrates, albeit unconsciously, the inability of the European imagination to escape the concrete consequences of its liberatory fantasies. As Prospero discovered, there are no uninhabited island refuges.[25]

Like patriarchal romance's unspoken reliance on sexual oppression, colonial slavery haunts all of these utopian undertakings, Smith's included. The American freehold imagined in *The Young Philosopher* is unlikely to include slaves, but of course slavery and such yeoman farmer ideals coexisted in the United States, and specifically in Crèvecoeur's *American Farmer*, where he invoked the familiar distinction between the evils of southern plantation slavery and the benevolently paternalistic model of northern slavery.[26] In *The Wanderings of Warwick*, Smith's citizens of the world reach as far as Portugal, Jamaica, Central America and the United States, where the eponymous hero purchases for his wife 'a mulatto woman' (40). The plot, as in all of Smith's 1790s novels, is that of a fortunate fall, through which the protagonist sheds a series of ideological certainties and prejudices: 'Had I never passed through the severe trials of indigence', Warwick concludes, 'I might...have still been the dissipated Man of the World' (288). Among these lost certainties are those of the abolition debates, which Smith examines in a series of framed counterpoints.

At the heart of Smith's presentation is Warwick's contention, supported by the author's footnote, that upon first-hand observation '[t]he condition... of the negroes is certainly in some respects even preferable to that of the English poor' (62). This familiar anti-abolitionist argument, supplemented in Smith's note with a favourable reference to her acquaintance[27] Bryan Edwards's antiabolitionist *The History, Civil and Commercial, of the British Colonies in the West Indies* (1793), was famously inverted in Coleridge's 1795 'Lecture on the Slave Trade': 'I appeal to common sense whether to affirm that Slaves are as well off as our Peasantry, be not the same as to assert that our Peasantry are as bad off as Negro Slaves...?'[28] Yet that is also Smith's point, as Warwick catalogues the downward spiral of the landless labourer in Britain, from single ploughman to impoverished family man, then smuggler and soldier, before dying alone in the work-house (62–5). Warwick presents a range of slave experiences, as did Crèvecoeur, so that the paternalistic model is held up as modestly superior to the brutality of British hypocrisy towards peasants at home. While Warwick purchases a slave as though hiring a servant, he nevertheless affirms his opposition 'against every species of slavery', as it 'produces at once servility and ferocity' in slave and owner alike (66).

Through Warwick's ruminations regarding slavery, Smith enlarges her cosmopolitan inquiry to consider, but not resolve, the chief contradiction in the Enlightenment doctrine of universal human rights. Republics like France and America struggled with the contradictions between exclusionary practices and universalizing theories, in terms of how to define the human and the citizen. Even a proabolition, radical republican like John Hurford Stone was lured by the profit associated with colonial exploitation: in 1792 he sought to invest in the troubled Sierra Leone colony of 'repatriated' former slaves, in order to further 'the abolition of the slave trade, and the civilization of the inhabitants' (Howell, *State Trials* 1305). After all, civilization and profit progressed hand in hand: 'in proportion to the extent of the civilization may be the extent of the profits, regarding the affair in a view more near and interesting to our mercantile feelings' (*ibid*). As a downwardly-mobile member of the gentry with nine children to support, one whose long-sought family inheritance came from slave plantations, Smith did not need to entertain 'mercantile feelings', or dreams of civilization and profits, in order to pursue the level of wealth that only such colonial enterprises could bring. And yet Smith grew increasingly uneasy about the source of this wealth, to the extent that her fictional protagonists progressively resist the corruption intrinsic in inheritance (turning their backs on it in *Marchmont* and *The Young Philosopher*).

While she vilified slavery as an abstract evil in many works, Smith did not expand her notion of the Citizen of the World expressly to include slaves or former slaves (an example available to her in the black republicans of the 1791 St Domingue Revolution). Smith's correspondence regarding the 1800 sale of her family's largest estate, Gay's sugar cane plantation in Barbados, is strictly businesslike regarding the 171 slaves that made up over £11,000 of the estate's £20,000 value. She even haggled with the buyer regarding individual slaves, some of whom, she argues, had been 'worth nothing' due to old age, and whose deaths therefore were 'rather a relief than a disadvantage to the Estate' (*Collected Letters* 353). In contrast to the coldly capitalist register of this letter, also in July 1800 Smith wrote to Mary Hays employing the familiar eighteenth-century feminist rhetoric in which marriage is equated to slavery. Although separated from her abusive, wastrel husband, Smith writes, 'I am still in reality a slave & liable to have my bondage renew'd' (350). Lord Egremont's help in securing the Barbados inheritance, she continues, amounts to his buying her freedom: this 'Nobleman... saw the difficulties I was struggling with & did what only a Man of his property could do, & by one act of generousity [*sic*] set me free – My family have now a clear estate worth nearly twenty thousand pound in the West Indies, & this I am this year about to sell' (350). As with Jane Eyre and her inheritance, Smith's independence comes at the expense of West Indian slaves, something Smith seems unwilling to acknowledge, despite the irony in her letter to Hays.

Written while these negotiations were taking place, Smith's Jamaican romance, 'The Story of Henrietta' (1800), features a hero who, like Marchmont, Glenmorris, and Smith herself, pursues the restoration of a 'hereditary estate'. Once confronted with the horrors of slavery upon arriving in Jamaica, Denbigh 'so extremely dislike[s] the nature of the property' that he gladly sells it at a loss (2: 9), much as Smith did that same year. Following the marriage/slavery analogy as in Smith's letter to Hays, 'Henrietta' tracks two parallel rebellions: both Henrietta and the island's slaves (and free blacks) rebel against the tyranny of Henrietta's father, who 'has been used to purchase slaves, and feels no repugnance in selling his daughter to the most dreadful of all slavery' (2: 76–7). As in many of her feminist contemporaries' writings on slavery, Smith implies that white women's marital slavery is 'most dreadful' because of their conscious, as opposed to merely corporeal, suffering, something Smith clearly believed regarding her personal circumstances, which involved both emotional and physical abuse.[29] Yet Smith seems most concerned with exploring the moral ambiguities of rebellion and revolution, and as in *Warwick*, presents a range of perspectives on the peculiar institution.

'Henrietta' dramatizes Wollstonecraft's brief but telling comparison of slave rebellion (perhaps in San Domingo) to feminist rebellion in the *Rights of Woman*: 'Slaves and mobs have always indulged themselves in the same excesses, when once they broke loose from authority. – The bent bow recoils with violence, when the hand is suddenly relaxed that forcible held it' (83). Responding to Rousseau's warning in *Emile* that women 'are apt to indulge themselves excessively' in liberty (83), 'Wollstonecraft censures slaves' reactions', argues Moira Ferguson, but given her disdain for 'passivity and servitude... could be hinting that women should emulate the San Domingo insurgents and fight back' (28). If Wollstonecraft considers the disturbing possibility that 'what slaves can do, white women can do' (Ferguson 28), then perhaps Smith considers the reverse, likewise censuring violent rebellion, but through the extensive connections between these two forms of bondage, pushing herself to imagine the rights of the slaves she sold in order to secure her children's wealth.

While Henrietta does rebel, escaping from both her father's tyranny and that of the maroon rebels who capture her, this vision of white female rebellion, like Brontë's in *Jane Eyre*, does not escape the racial hierarchy governing its claims to liberty. The maroons, in contrast to the sympathetic Henrietta, are alternatively humanized, bestialized, sentimentalized, and libertinized through different characters' perspectives, reflecting the author's (and her culture's) ambivalence on the issue. The wives of the maroon leader, the 'General', are not the sentimentalized black female figures found in Opie and More, though they do defy their husband and help Henrietta escape, for the self-interested reason of jealousy. Neither is the General a revolutionary hero like the historical General Toussaint Louverture, though he does appear 'to be more humanized than the rest' (2: 305). Ultimately, the violence employed by these revolutionaries, as in the Terror, is for Smith an understandable but unforgivable result of the legacy of absolutist oppression, whether British or French. French revolutionaries were likened to rebelling slaves in both conservative and radical texts, beginning with Burke's disparaging comments that the revolutionaries resembled 'a gang of Maroon slaves suddenly broke loose from the house of bondage' (*Reflections* 41). Writing outside the traditions of racist Francophobia (Burke) *and* that of sentimental abolition (Opie and More), Smith also deliberately rejects the 'aesthetic glorification of slavery' (Bohls 57) found in overtly racist writings like Janet Schaw's West Indian travel journal, and the antiabolitionism of Anna Maria Falconbridge's *Two Voyages to Sierra Leone* (1794) (see Bohls; Coleman, *Maiden Voyages*). Instead, Smith focuses on the violence central to British wealth and power, whether located in new world Edens or within the English home, illustrating what Laura Brown has described as 'the necessary intimacy of structures of oppression and liberation in... eighteenth-century culture' (174).

The new world utopias of Gallipolis, Pantisocracy, and Crèvecoeur's Pine Hill all eventually foundered on these same irreconcilable contradictions of colonial displacement and slavery that Smith explored in her later writings. Barlow sold land still inhabited by native Americans; Pantisocracy imploded in part due to Coleridge and Southey's quarrel over the appropriateness of including servants and slaves; Crèvecoeur returned from Europe to his beloved Pine Hill to find the estate burned, his wife killed, and his children vanished after an Indian attack. Walker's *The Vagabond* combined these disasters in its ill-fated Kentucky scheme, a virtual catalogue of counter-revolutionary barbs against emigration. At once émigré refuges and commercial (sometimes slaveholding) colonies, these heterotopias illustrate the impossibility of evading the contradictions of radical Enlightenment, even in the admirably cosmopolitan and feminist formulations envisioned in Smith's fiction.

Clairant's question in 1797 was clearly a rhetorical one: 'Upon what point of the habitable world, then, immense as it may be, shall we find a retreat?' The implied answer – nowhere – bears at once the dual aspects of timeless utopia, and the historically acute sense that the 'habitable world' of the turbulent 1790s had revealed, uniquely and irrevocably, that the Enlightenment foundations of these revolutions were self-contradictory. Liberty, equality, fraternity, the rights of woman, and the 'citizen of the world' are the imperfect ideals of an imperfect people, imperfections most evident in their radical embodiment during the Jacobin republic. 'We have had a long moment for consideration of the many ways in which the Jacobins fell short of realizing the promises of a revolution of universal human rights', writes Lynn Hunt in an important reassessment of the Jacobin republic's 'misogyny' ('Male Virtue', 206). It is perhaps now time, Hunt concludes,

> to look at their strategies from the other end and consider how their principles of individualism, autonomy, and contractual rights forced them into positions about the rights of children and women that were unimaginable even to themselves before 1789, perhaps before 1793. (206)

As we saw in Chapter 3, the Jacobin Republic had provided French women and children with unprecedented liberalization in inheritance, property and divorce laws, the very laws that radical British feminists, Smith in particular, boldly advocated in their revolution-era writings. And yet the Jacobin Republic 'did not support full civil rights for women' (200), but in fact violently expelled women from public political activity. As I argued earlier, for feminist Girondin-sympathizers like Williams and Robinson, such wholescale female exclusion during the Terror effectively eclipsed any such liberalization the Jacobins introduced. Yet these British feminists shared with the Jacobins common goals, philosophical origins, and rhetoric that we cannot afford to ignore.

Like the limitations of Jacobin universal human rights, radical writers like Smith, Robinson, Wollstonecraft and Williams did not achieve a utopian universality in their diverse visions of virtuous communities. Smith's 'citizens of the world' never acknowledge the debt their cosmopolitan citizenship and privilege (like Smith's inheritance) owes to colonial slavery. Williams cannot or will not acknowledge the competing claims of working-class radicalism in her accounts of the Revolution, particularly in her dismissal of Robespierre and the Jacobins as demonic aggressors, not political actors vying with her allies for a different interpretation of Rousseauvian virtue. Wollstonecraft's contradictions in her formulations of the rights of men and rights of women are well known, both in terms of her class allegiance and enlightenment prejudices (oversimplified by some as 'racism' and 'misogyny'). Robinson is by far the most contradictory of these four, forming an early alliance with Tarleton, a chief spokesman for the slave trade, but later immersing herself in controversial aspects of radical reform.

Robinson, Smith, Wollstonecraft and Williams, for all their differences, had available to them a tradition of sensibility, above all via Rousseau, and an enlightenment inheritance open to utopian possibilities of universality but riddled with exceptions. Their diverse contributions to British culture in the 1790s and beyond are significant because of the unprecedented degree to which their writings opened up the discourse of radical rights (not merely of moral influence) to include women as a sex. The unremittingly hostile reception received by these four writers in the counterrevolutionary British cultural climate is evidence of the radical nature of their vision, perceived as a distinctly Gallicized danger to Britain's precarious stability. That they often only featured white middle-class women in their feminist correctives to gender-neutral and misogynist formulations (republican and counter-revolutionary, French and British) should not detract from the boldness of their visions. Religiously oriented writers like Opie, More, and Hamilton (in *Letters of a Hindoo Rajah*) were more direct in their critique of British imperialism and sometimes explicitly included women of colour in their visions of female-centred Christian domesticity, but they also strictly curtailed the public and political (as opposed to the moral and religious) dimensions of this purifying female influence.

One consistent feature of the radical discourse of the rights of woman at the turn of the nineteenth century was its secular (not atheistic) outlook, in opposition to the 'the "feminisation" of religion...widely observed across Europe in the nineteenth century',[30] of which counterrevolutionaries like More, Hamilton, West and Opie were the avant garde. Wollstonecraft and Williams were Dissenting Christians, and Smith and Robinson were nominally Anglicans, though none of them write with an explicitly Christian or religious agenda. Hamilton (Presbyterian/Episcopalian) West

(Anglican), More (Evangelical) and the later Opie (Quaker), in contrast, shared a deep distrust of secular notions of equality and put their faith instead in a universal Christian equality before God, despite the 'unalterable' material inequalities institutionalized in class and sexual hierarchies. For West, the choice was an absolute and mutually exclusive one, between allegiance to the 'Saviour of the World' or the 'citizen of the world' (*Letters* 2: 479).

Just as Jacobins in 1793 and 1794 offered limited and contradictory visions of 'universal human rights' within a secular framework, so radical women writers made possible new ways of re-imagining what had seemed previously to be timeless truths: the divine rights of kings and fathers, primogeniture, the superiority of Europeans, the submission of wives and children. These ideological givens collapsed in the revolutionary 1790s, revealed to be constructed by fallible and interested human beings, in likewise fallible and limited critiques. In order to understand the historical realities in which radical women writers forged such unprecedented visions of feminist potential, our readings of their 1790s writings should carefully distinguish the scope of their visions, their priorities, and their conditions of possibility, from our own. And we should remember that our own inquiries would not be possible without theirs, part of postmodernity's enduring debt to Enlightenment self-critique. Like the Jacobins who enacted radical legislation to benefit women and families, these women writers 'did not support full civil rights' (Hunt, 'Male Virtue' 200) for all those groups most academics would today consider fully enfranchised citizens. But we are, of course, as deeply conflicted today over what constitutes a 'person' and their 'rights' as those in the 1790s, although our disputes take different forms, regarding different issues.

Smith had compared the restoration of Marchmont's hereditary estate to the restoration of Versailles and the *ancien régime*, and had linked the restoration of Denbigh's estate to the perpetuation of Britain's slavery empire in 'Henrietta'. Via her cosmopolitan heroes, she firmly rejected both restorations, even while distancing herself from the revolutionary violence that toppled both regimes. Likening herself to a 'female Prospero' in search of a desert island, she also illustrated the impossibility of escaping the consequences of these European conflicts. Like Barbauld, Smith looked forward, across the channel, and eventually across the ocean, to a cosmopolitan American republic when European politics seemed to abandon utterly their liberatory potential. When we look a decade later to Waterloo, the restoration of European monarchies, and the Holy Alliance, the lasting value of this brief window of opportunity that cosmopolitan women writers of the 1790s took advantage of appears even more remarkable. Like those 'second-generation' Romantics, Byron and the Shelleys, Smith, had she lived long enough, would probably have been equally appalled at the post-Napoleonic consolidation of monarchial and national power. It was up to writers whose lives and publishing careers spanned this generational divide, like Lady Morgan, Fanny Burney, Anne Plumptre and Germaine de Staël, to carry this cosmopolitanism forward into increasingly hostile terrain.

Epilogue:
Napoleonic Challenges and Cosmopolitan Legacies

> Is there not something strange and rather revolting in speaking of the French, as most have done for these twenty years past, with the utmost abhorrence and contempt, – and pouring ourselves over their country the moment it is accessible, to mix in their parties and bring home their fashions?
>
> Anna Laetitia Barbauld, letter to Mrs Fletcher (1814)

The short-lived Peace of Amiens had reopened the continent to tourists from the British isles, and Napoleon's 1814 abdication once again promised to make France accessible to Britons eager 'to mix in their parties and bring home their fashions', as Barbauld complained of her compatriots' hypocrisy (*Works* 2: 142). Writers like Maria Edgeworth, Fanny Burney, Amelia Opie and Anne Plumptre had travelled to France during the 1802 Peace, experiences reflected in Edgeworth's two *Tales of Fashionable Life* set during the Revolution ('Madame de Fleury', 1809, and 'Emilie de Coulanges', 1812), Burney's *The Wanderer* (1814) and Opie's *The Warrior's Return* (1808).[1] Plumptre arrived in France with her friend Opie,[2] but unlike most tourists she stayed once the war recommenced, not as a self-exile like Burney, but as a devotee of revolutionary principles who hoped to emigrate permanently.

A radical Dissenter from Norwich, Plumptre is best-known for her 1801 novel, *Something New*, in which she offered an unprecedented (and unresolved) critique of the conventions of romance and beauty via her unattractive heroine. A fearless advocate of the 'female philosopher' in her earlier novel, *Antoinette Percival* (7),[3] Plumptre merits comparison with her counter-revolutionary contemporary Elizabeth Hamilton and her very different handling of the female philosopher and the ugly heroine in *Memoirs of Modern Philosophers*. Robinson had praised Plumptre's popular translations of Kotzebue's plays in her cosmopolitan essay on the 'Present State of the Metropolis of England', and Plumptre's unabashed Europhilia also characterized her most remarkable work, *A Narrative of a Three Years' Residence in France*

(1810). Plumptre's *Narrative* revived in 1810 a revolutionary Francophilia long out of favour, boldly defending both the Revolution and Napoleon as its hero. Numerous travel accounts of France, especially Paris, flooded the British press after the 1802 Peace, but Plumptre distinguishes her *Narrative* from these accounts by emphasizing her unusually lengthy residence, her travels throughout the whole of France, her proficiency in French, and her immersion in local customs. But it is the extended political argument that truly sets Plumptre's account apart from those of her contemporaries, whose antiNapoleonic and antirevolutionary biases Plumptre refutes point by point. Like Lady Morgan in her controversial *France* (1817), Plumptre maintains an unpopular allegiance to the French Revolution by celebrating Napoleon as its hero, and in the process deflates British national superiority (especially in its institutionalized 'national religion') in a manner reminiscent of their revolutionary cosmopolitan predecessors of the 1790s.

'[R]epresented as one of the most execrable monsters' (3: 270) in British portraits relying on rumours that he instigated massacres (at Jaffa), razed villages (at Binasco), and even poisoned his own plague-ridden troops, Napoleon in Plumptre's *Narrative* is instead the bearer of peace, liberty and religious tolerance to a grateful Europe. Most galling to British loyalists would have been Plumptre's repeated comparisons between the legitimacy of Napoleon's reign and that of the British monarchy: 'Bonaparte...reigns in France by the same title as the house of Hanover reigns in England, by the wish of the people' (3: 394). Similarly, the valour of Napoleon's military exploits is equivalent to those of British heroes: 'if a St Vincent or a Nelson be a *hero* for sending thousands to meet their fate at the bottom of the great deep, how can Bonaparte be a *murderer* when thousands fall by his sword in the field of battle?' (3: 356–7, orig. emphasis). Like her 1790s cosmopolitan predecessors, Plumptre will have none of the nationalism that increasingly relied on Francophobia. 'We have believed these things' about Napoleon as usurper and murderer, she concludes,

> because his talents have thwarted our views; because while we wished to reduce France to insignificance as a power, and annihilate any hope she might have of one day becoming our rival in commerce and manufactures, we have seen him raise her to a height of power far beyond what she ever before attained...and we have seen him endeavouring to consolidate that power...by giving the utmost encouragement to industry and the arts. (3: 318)

Implicitly countering her friend Helen Maria Williams's view of Napoleon as an enemy of the arts and of intellectuals, Plumptre praises his pursuit of cultural, as well as political, progress. Even the looting of Italy's art becomes in Plumptre's critique another occasion to expose British hypocrisy: 'While all England was eager to repair to France during the short interval of peace...anxious to see the rich treasures of art' that Napoleon's conquests had brought to Paris, the English 'have been incessantly labouring to represent those treasures as her shame and her reproach' (3: 351). No nation is above enjoying the spoils of war, for after all, 'France has only retaliated upon Italy her own spoilation of Greece' (3: 352). Britain has as much to answer for in the Indian massacres inspired by her imperial ambition – at Seringapatam, she notes – as Napoleonic France in her Near East exploits, 'yet we always reckon that among the *glorious achievements of British valour*' (3: 289, orig. emphasis).

Consistently elevating Napoleon to Europe's hero while deflating British superiority, Plumptre's *Narrative*, like Barbauld's *Eighteen Hundred and Eleven*, provides a blistering critique of Britain's self-image at a critical time in the war against France. France had enjoyed a string of victories in the Peninsular campaign, and the British army had withdrawn from Portugal by 1809, leading ultimately to the resignation of Foreign Minister Canning, Secretary at War Castlereagh, and Prime Minister Portland over the unsuccessful and unpopular war. The response of the Lake Poets to this crisis, as Simon Bainbridge has shown, was to boost the war effort through a 'remorseless dehumanization and demonization of Napoleon' in works like Coleridge's essays for the *Courier* (1809–10) and Wordsworth's *The Convention of Cintra* (1809) (128). Plumptre's 1810 *Narrative* is defiantly out of step with these canonical, conservative writers, and is instead an important but overlooked predecessor of those later unrepentant Bonapartists, Hazlitt and Byron.

In its review of another proFrench book published in 1810, the *Anti-Jacobin Review* was appalled at such sentiments '[a]t a period like the present...when the fate of Europe (this island alone forming an honourable and an important exception) hangs...on the nod of one individual'.[4] Referring to Napoleon as 'the Corsican' and 'the Usurper', in keeping with British practice, the *Anti-Jacobin's* vision of Napoleonic France enduring worse than *ancien régime* despotism is typical of British accounts:

> They overthrew the throne; they demolished the altars; they destroyed all distinctions of rank; and for what? To erect a low-born foreign usurper on the ruins of an ancient dynasty; to maintain a venal prelacy, and stipendiary priests...In a word, they have waded through seas of blood to reach a haven of slavery and wretchedness. (356)

Plumptre devotes her *Narrative* to reversing this ubiquitous British view of the '*iron* sceptre of...Bonaparte': 'under this *iron* sceptre', she writes, 'there are no feudal tenures, no corvées, no seigneurial rights, no game laws, no oppressive and overgrown hierarchy, no pains and penalties for religious opinions, no privileged orders' (3: 382, orig. emphasis). Plumptre's unspoken challenge is that Napoleonic France enjoys more liberties than Britain. Nationalism like the *Anti-Jacobin's* is thus in Plumptre's mind an impoverished and xenophobic form of true national spirit: 'our attachment to OLD ENGLAND is not so much a desire to see the country great, as to partake as largely as possible each one individually of what we consider as English comforts' (3: 322). 'We are rather a group of individuals', she concludes, while 'the French are much more of a nation' (3: 322). For Plumptre, it was the Revolution, and Napoleon's institutionalization of its promise, that could transform France into the kind of egalitarian and tolerant nation that Barbauld had hoped for in her 1790s polemics urging British reform.

Plumptre's *Narrative* was first and foremost a polemic in support of Napoleonic France, strategically designed to counteract the vast majority of British writings on the subject. Yet in a private letter written sometime during her 1802–05 French residence, Plumptre reveals her disappointments with the present state of France to a friend interested in emigrating with her family:

> I own I feel excessively disappointed in the state of France and regret that the sanguine friends of the French Revolution are in so great an error with respect to the effect it has produced in the country. I came hither with the idea of finding the education of the youth a principal object of the cares of the government. Alas no! – that most important object is lamentably neglected. I blame not in this the great man who is at the head of affairs. I admire more than ever what he has done for the tranquilizing [sic] men's minds and restoring peace and good order among all ranks, but the State of France was such when he was placed in his present post that many many years must elapse before he can establish all things upon the good footing that is to be wished.[5]

Plumptre probably wrote this at the start of her visit during the Peace of Amiens, as she was still then in Paris and the possibility of a British family immigrating to France was conceivable. The letter therefore probably reveals the initial shock of disappointment of someone who has long idealized a country from afar, while the published *Narrative* represents a view tempered by time (and the political exigencies of 1810).

Even in this candid letter, Plumptre remains an unwavering Bonapartist, but acknowledges the economic hardships of postrevolutionary France:

> the revolution has been a scene of outward splendor but of inward misery. France is crowned with military glory, the Fame of her arms is spread all over the globe, but among all ranks of people we hear nothing but curses on the revolution and the misery it has occasioned. The country has been impoverished by it, and the effect of that is, that the people are like hungry wolves and gain is become almost the sole object of every one's pursuit. This is not a pleasing picture but it is a true one, and you will scarcely think it exaggerated when you recollect the sentiments with which I entered France.

Plumptre had arrived during the Peace of Amiens with the hope of remaining permanently, she reveals later, but now 'How long I shall remain here must depend upon circumstances'. But even by 1810, five years after her return to England, she does not publish this 'true' picture, but a strategically 'pleasing' one (which, as she would have known, would please virtually no one in Britain). As she confessed to her friend,

> I give you my sincere opinion upon these things but I wish not to have that opinion generally cited but to remain between you and me. I do not wish to give the enemies of the general cause of liberty such a triumph as to know that the great struggle which has been maintained here in its defence has hitherto been productive only of misery.

Privately disappointed but publicly unrepentant, Plumptre published her *Narrative* in order to support this 'general cause of liberty', whose best hope, she insisted, was Napoleon. In 1810 Britain, there was no room for more nuanced or qualified accounts of Napoleonic France – every publication on the subject was inevitably a polemic, and Plumptre chose to aid 'the great struggle' for a 'rational system of freedom' by defiantly locating this potential land of liberty in France, not Britain.

It was Lady Morgan's *France* (1817) that drew the most critical fire for its proNapoleonic and Francophilic politics, even though *France* was not as radical or systematic in its critique of British nationalism as Plumptre's *Narrative*. Morgan's national tales like *The Wild Irish Girl* and *Woman, or, Ida of Athens* (1809) had won her immense popularity, as well as critical hostility in conservative British journals like the *Quarterly Review*; her foray into international politics therefore attracted a great deal of attention. *France* was based on Morgan's visit to Paris in 1816, and like Plumptre's *Narrative*, it deliberately countered the British consensus of France as impoverished, degraded and oppressed with a Francophilic celebration of the nation's revolutionary legacy. In keeping with her identification of national spirit with women in her novels, Morgan highlights the high standing of French women as a key indicator of how France has benefited from the Revolution. 'There is perhaps no country in the world, where the social position of woman is so delectable, as in France' (*France* (1817) 1: 162), she writes, referring both to the *ancien régime* 'empire of women', and to postrevolutionary republican motherhood. Morgan positions Rousseau's great love in the *Confessions*, Mme Houdetot, as a symbol of France's transformation from *ancien régime* to republic. Emphasizing Houdetot's consistent virtue throughout this historical shift from *ancien régime* adulterous aristocrat, to republican mother and grandmother, Morgan ingeniously rehistoricizes the two halves of *La Nouvelle Héloïse* to praise French women's virtue under both gendered regimes. Like Mary Robinson, the prorevolutionary Morgan remained committed to the theatricalized self-presentation and aristocratic aesthetics associated with the *ancien régime*, hence her similar celebration of France's 'delectable' appreciation of women, both as lovers and as mothers.

Like all the revolutionary cosmopolitans discussed thus far, Morgan consistently holds the *ancien régime* responsible for the darkest hours of the Revolution: 'Those who gave the revolution its sanguinary character were no miraculous progeny, no spontaneous product of the new order of things, but the home-bred children of despotism' (*France* (1817) 1: 90). Napoleon, meanwhile, is 'the greatest captain of the age', who carried through many of the Revolution's desirable religious and civil reforms, and 'though his light be extinguished, the track of his course will long brighten the political horizon of Europe' (1: 97, 108). The *Quarterly Review* could barely contain itself, writing a 26 page review exposing in detail the 'Jacobininsm – Falsehood – Licentiousness, and Impiety' of Lady Morgan's *France* (v.17 (1817): 264). She is a traitor to her class in celebrating the Revolutionary heritage and denouncing the Restoration, and verges on atheism in her proNapoleonic critique of church authority – charges which the *Quarterly* implicitly considers as aimed at British 'legitimate' government by an Irish nationalist. Educated at a French Huguenot school and having family connections to France, Morgan relied on a 'pattern of triangulation, inserting Ireland into the discussion of England and France', as Jeanne Moskal has argued, in order to undermine British dominion through such longstanding Irish-French allegiances ('Gender' 187).

Napoleon's defiance of ecclesiastical power, in France and elsewhere on the continent, was particularly significant for admirers like Morgan (a self-identified Irish Catholic) and Plumptre (a rational Dissenter), who had little love for Britain's 'national religion'. Both Morgan and Plumptre praised Napoleon for replacing *ancien régime* superstition and corruption, and Jacobin dechristianization, with an unparalleled (that is unBritish) religious tolerance, inclusive of Jews, Catholics and Protestants (*France* (1817): 49–53; *Narrative* 1: 122–39). Yet as Moskal has shown, Tory antiCatholics like the travel writer Mariana Starke could also, along with Edmund Burke, claim Napoleon as a 'Protestant hero' ('Napoleon' 184). The Napoleon of the first Italian campaign proved popular with a wide range of British observers, from radicals like Hazlitt to conservatives like Starke and Burke, who welcomed his defiance of papal authority. After Napoleon was named Consul for Life in 1802, vindications of Napoleon like Plumptre's and Morgan's were very rare, however.[6] In addition to remaining sympathetic to the post-1802 Napoleon, Morgan and Plumptre were intent on raising France's profile in British eyes, in part in order to critique British policies closer to home. The antinationalism central to their critiques, embedded in their prorevolutionary Francophilia, connects them both to more politically conservative writers like Burney, and to revolutionary precursors like Smith and Robinson.

Entire books were devoted to denouncing Morgan's unrepentantly prorevolutionary account of France. William Playfair's two-volume *France*

As It Is, Not Lady Morgan's France (1819) revived the loyalist attacks on 1790s revolutionary writers like Smith and Robinson by accusing the author of intending 'to excite a desire of imitation, and create a discontent in Britain, where people formerly considered themselves more free and happy than in France' (1819, 1: 9). Playfair had been Joel Barlow's partner in the Gallipolis scheme in the early years of the Revolution, but by 1795 had turned sharply against the Revolution, and devoted his career to attacking those who, like Morgan, persisted in advocating 'the treble power of liberty, anarchy, and despotism' (Playfair 1: xlviii). In France, Defauconpret's *Observations sur l'ouvrage intitulé La France, par Lady Morgan* (1817) similarly made it clear that Morgan's prorevolutionary account was unacceptable under the Restoration, and indeed the French authorities issued an injunction banning Morgan from re-entering the country (Campbell 150).

While not as radical as Plumptre in her support of Napoleon and his revolutionary legacy, the Irish Morgan had dared to resituate Britain as one player among many in a cosmopolitan European framework, wherein Napoleonic France represented the height of cultural and civic achievements. In the Preface to the third edition of *France* (1818), Morgan responded to her negative reviews, complaining that she 'has been represented as antinational; she wished only to give a more social, a more *European* turn, to the habitual feelings of her countrymen' (1: xv, orig. emphasis). This cosmopolitan '*European* turn' was also the project of her post-*Wild Irish Girl* novels, as Deidre Lynch has argued: probably as a result of *Corinne's* influential 'fantasy of trans-nation', Morgan's 'national types' of heroine like Glorvina in *The Wild Irish Girl* increasingly 'are outnumbered by hybrid heroines' like the binational heroines of *Ida of Athens* and *Florence Macarthy* (1818) (Lynch 63, 70).

Morgan aspired to the intellectual and cultural authority of her era's most illustrious cosmopolite, Germaine de Staël, whose genius she described as '[f]ostered amidst philosophical inquiries, and political and social fermentation...its scope vast, its efforts vigorous' (*France* (1817) 2: 231). Playfair in turn dismissed *France* as 'a wretched imitation of works written by Madame de Stael and the Countess of Genlis' (1: 10). The influence of Staël's *On Literature* (1800) and *The Influence of the Passions on the Happiness of Individuals and Nations* (1796) is visible in *France*, yet the two authors parted ways when it came to Napoleon. Napoleon had seen 'to it that *On Literature* and *Delphine* were violently criticized in the press' (Balayé 18), and had *On Germany* (1810) pulped and Staël exiled. Staël's championing of national distinctiveness in *On Germany* and *Corinne* (1807) had challenged Napoleon's ambition of continental domination, in the latter text by crowning the female genius Corinne, a deliberate affront to the emperor who had banished her (see Kadish 119). These well-known features of Staël's personalized conflict with Napoleon were in Staël's opinion attributable to Napoleon's 'hatred of all independent beings,' especially 'exceptional women' like herself who were not fit to be judged by '[t]he common people', sentiments similar to those of Williams and Mme Roland regarding Robespierre.[7]

Staël's support of the principles of 1789 and her contempt for the Bourbon Restoration were equally unacceptable in Britain by the time Morgan praised her in *France*. Staël was no radical: her liberalism ranged from constitutional monarchism to a moderate republicanism as envisioned by the Legislative Assembly, while consistently advocating that persons of distinction, not the common people, were best fit to rule. In *Considerations on the...French Revolution* (1818), she had criticized even the moderately republican Girondins, who 'must have been bitterly sorry for the means they had used to overthrow the throne', given that the Jacobins then used these same means against them (*Extraordinary Woman*, 367). Williams objected to Staël's critique of the Girondins in her *Souvenirs de la Révolution française* (1827), yet significantly both writers shared an intensely personalized approach to the revolutionary politics with which they had first hand experience. In their similar attacks on Napoleon (and Robespierre, in Williams's case) as their personal persecutor, Staël and Williams provide an alternative to canonical Romanticism's abstractions of Napoleon and Robespierre as avatars of masculine poetic power or political agency. Staël and Williams also stand in marked contrast to Plumptre and Morgan, whose very different (and briefer) experiences in Napoleonic and Restoration France allowed them to maintain a radical Francophilia increasingly unpopular in Britain, while also denying Napoleon's persecution of women and intellectuals,[8] central to Staël's and Williams's perspectives.

This impressive range of women's accounts of Napoleonic and revolutionary France consistently addressed how this revolutionary inheritance was gendered, a quality shared with the more outspoken advocates of the 'rights of woman' in the 1790s. The monarchist Fanny Burney, self-exiled to France with her émigré husband from 1802 to 1812, returned to Britain to publish *The Wanderer* in 1814 and discovered how unpopular this earlier feminism had become, especially when coupled with a critique of nationalism. Appalled by *The Wanderer*'s Preface, in which Burney claimed to have enjoyed 'ten unbroken years' of tranquillity in Napoleonic France, John Wilson Croker snapped that 'she ought not, as an Englishwoman, as a writer, to have debased herself to the little annotatory flatteries of the scourge of the human race' (*Quarterly Review* (1814): 130). *The Wanderer*'s female philosopher, the Wollstonecraftian Elinor, is particularly unwelcome in 1814: 'The revolutionary spirit, which displays itself in the sentiments and actions of Miss Elinor Joddrel, is, fortunately for a bleeding world, now no longer in existence', wrote the *British Critic*'s reviewer (n.s. 1 (1814): 385).

Yet even British Romanticism's most celebrated avatar of this revolutionary spirit – William Hazlitt – dismissed Burney's *The Wanderer, or Female Difficulties*. Hazlitt's review reveals his resistance to incorporating his feminist contemporaries' gendered critique of revolutionary politics into his own understanding. Burney is 'a very woman', whose devastating portrait of how the British class hierarchy is gendered is lost upon Hazlitt: 'The difficulties in which she involves her heroines are indeed "Female Difficulties"; – they are difficulties created out of nothing' (*Edinburgh Review* 24 (1815): 337). Burney's female difficulties conflate the abuses of Jacobin France and war-time Britain, a transnational and implicitly feminist gesture unacceptable to both archconservative nationalists like Croker, and Francophilic male radicals like Hazlitt. *The Wanderer*'s hostile reception, like that of Morgan's *France*, illustrates at once the male critical consensus, radical and counterrevolutionary, that women writers have no business in revolutionary politics, and the stubborn determination of women writers to maintain their revolutionary cosmopolitanism.

Williams and Morgan were the most persistent in this regard, the latter publishing in 1821 her even more controversial *Italy*. 'This woman is utterly *incorrigible*', complained an exasperated Croker in the *Quarterly*, where once again he enumerated Morgan's 'series of offences against good morals, good politics, good sense, and good taste' (v. 25 (1821): 529, orig. emphasis). In a letter to Moore, Byron praised Morgan's *Italy* as 'fearless and excellent', and yet despite his praise of Morgan and debt to Staël's cosmopolitanism,[9] Byron did not take the further step of incorporating their gendered critiques of national and revolutionary politics into his own perspective (like Hazlitt, and unlike Shelley). '[F]ew of our female readers can remember the *egalité* [*sic*] mania, which once infested the bosoms of their sex', noted the *British Critic*'s review of *The Wanderer* (n.s. 1 (1814): 385). This is more wishful thinking than anything, for certainly Burney, Plumptre and Morgan carried elements of this 1790s feminism into the new century in their writings on the French Revolution.[10] The *Anti-Jacobin Review* continued to make this connection for its readers: in its review of *Corinne*, it reminded readers that Corinne, 'like Mrs Wolstonecroft, offered to live with Lord Nelvil during her life without marriage' (32 (1809): 459). The *Anti-Jacobin* thus linked extra-marital passion to extra-national passion, and declared both to be equally unnatural: 'Madame de Stael has attempted to unite Italian and French voluptuousness with English virtue; but it will not do; to every real observer of human nature it is evidently a physical impossibility' (*ibid.*: 456). Plumptre had also alluded to this 1790s feminism by praising Wollstonecraft's *Historical and Moral View ... of the French Revolution* (as well as Smith's first revolution-era novel, *Celestina*, 1791, and Barbauld's 'Corsica'), but such overtly positive associations with 1790s feminist cosmopolitanism were rare (*Narrative* 1: 217, 2: 284, 3: 399).

As an outspoken rational Dissenter and defender of the 'female philosopher', Plumptre is a rare example of a 1790s feminist who continued to champion revolutionary cosmopolitanism into the early nineteenth century. Her undiminished Francophilia, like Morgan's, attests to the transnational legacy of modern Western feminism, both in expanding the French revolutionary 'rights of man' to include women, and in controversially urging British readers to emulate France as the land of liberty. Plumptre, like Wollstonecraft, had located in France a desirable 'rational system of liberty', and to this rationalist facet of revolutionary feminism Robinson and Morgan added a concurrent fascination with the 'delectable' privileges enjoyed by elite Frenchwomen under the *ancien régime*. These dual aspects of French political and polite culture, which I discussed in the early chapters, were central to the development of modern Western feminism, although this tradition has ironically been characterized more narrowly as 'Anglo-American feminism' in twentieth-century accounts. The Francophilic challenges to British nationalism that Plumptre and Morgan boldly put forward during the Napoleonic wars are in fact part of a neglected legacy of revolutionary cosmopolitanism first embraced by 1790s feminist writers, with repercussions that continue into twenty-first-century feminist and philosophical debates.

In the 1790s, Female Philosophers had addressed an international political crisis with unprecedented boldness, visibility, and long-lasting effects, laying the groundwork for so-called 'Anglo-American feminism'. Wollstonecraft has emerged as the central figure in this tradition, as her *Vindication of the Rights of Woman* is generally considered the 'founding text of Anglo-American feminism', to quote Cora Kaplan (34). Yet Wollstonecraft's evolving cosmopolitanism, evident in her later writings on France and Scandinavia, has remained curiously occluded in twentieth-century accounts of her feminism, which typically focus on the *Rights of Woman*.[11] Thus, while Wollstonecraft has remained central to modern feminist theory and philosophy, the Francophilic origins of her radical politics have often been distorted by twentieth-century feminism, with unfortunate results.

'Anglo-American feminism' was constructed as a hostile formulation in the 1980s (like 'female philosopher' in the 1790s), so that Wollstonecraft's revival in the 1970s and 1980s, like her 1790s heyday, is inseparable from a crisis within feminism. Anglo-American feminism was constructed in opposition to 'French feminism' by Toril Moi in her influential *Sexual/Textual Politics* (1985) and this national distinction has remained a staple of feminist theory, despite ongoing challenges. Moi's 'dialectical project', writes Susan Stanford Friedman, established 'Anglo-American Feminist Criticism' (Part I) as the thesis, 'French Feminist Theory (Part II) as the antithesis, and Kristeva . . . as the implied synthesis that moves beyond the inadequacies of the prior position' (247). This 'dialectical reductionism' (Friedman 248) has contributed to an entrenched misreading of Wollstonecraft that has only recently been challenged. As the origin of Anglo-American feminism, Wollstonecraft supplies the tradition's supposed rejection of sexuality and corporeality, and limits its critique to middle-class, liberal, rationalist, individualistic, and implicitly white concerns (typically claiming equality with men in these respects). 'French feminism', meanwhile (and unbeknownst to the

French themselves) is imagined to be more radical, to embrace sexuality, femininity and corporeality (often advocating an essential female difference), and is epitomized by the work of Irigaray, Cixous, and Kristeva (never mind that the latter two consistently resist describing themselves as 'feminist').[12]

The hybrid 'Anglo-American feminism', like its dialectical opposite 'French feminism', is useful in retroactively understanding so-called second-wave feminism's struggle to classify and cohere its heterogeneous elements into a liberatory dialectic, though many now argue that 'the term "Anglo-American feminism" has outlasted its usefulness' (Nussbaum, '(White)' 263). But modern radical, collectivist, and/or 'Third World' feminisms were not the first to undermine Anglo-American feminism's apparent coherence. A persistent misreading of Wollstonecraft (and stubborn focus on this sole figure) has made possible this reductive Anglo-American feminist model in the first place, obscuring her (and her fellow travellers') sophisticated positions on class, race, nation and, especially, sexuality and the body, just as the diverse traditions within 'Anglo-American feminism' are obscured by this reductive hybrid term. As we saw in Chapter 1, in the 1790s the 'empress of female philosophers' presented a dangerous mix of corporeal, sexual, philosophical, rational, foreign and collective political temptations to fellow women. Wollstonecraft's arguments for universal equality were so far on the lunatic fringe, conservatives feared, that they could even lead to advocacy on behalf of children's rights and animal rights. But, above all, Wollstonecraft's radical feminism was perceived as hopelessly French and thus foreign to native British self-control and moderation. In other words, in the 1790s, Wollstonecraft represented the inverse of 'Anglo-American feminism': an unrecognizably radical, sexually positive, passionate and collectivist (via general reform) figure, bringing 'Gallic mania' to British women.

Consistently portrayed as a disciple of Rousseau and (more improbably) materialist *philosophes*, the founder of Anglo-American feminism forged her 'liberal, middle-class and white' feminism in the heat of French revolutionary debates on abolition, the rights of woman and the rights of man – the origins of modern Western concepts of universal human rights. While Wollstonecraft supported abolition, she also relied on the commonplace eighteenth-century comparison of white women's sexual slavery in marriage to colonial slavery. Virtually all white women writers of her era made some version of this comparison, within different rhetorical traditions and often with different ends in mind. Hannah More, for example, advocated 'sentimental abolition' from a combination of nationalist, racist, Christian, humanitarian and missionizing interests that, when combined, played an important role in the abolition of the slave trade. Author of the oft-cited *Slavery, A Poem* (1788), More also published *The White Slave Trade* (1792), in which the 'arbitrary, universal tyrant', Fashion, appears more inhumane towards women of leisure than any West Indian slave owner, not even allowing his 'slaves' the Sabbath (*Poems* 392). A 'grotesque jeu d'esprit' according to Deirdre Coleman ('Conspicuous' 354), the hyperbolic comparison central to More's *White Slave Trade* nevertheless remains a recognizable (albeit extreme) one in white women's approach to abolition, from eighteenth-century feminists to Jane Austen and Charlotte Brontë.

As Moira Ferguson observed, Wollstonecraft made over 80 references to slavery, both colonial and harem-based, in *Rights of Woman* (Ferguson, 9). In drawing such comparisons and distinctions between middle-class white women's figurative slavery and the literal enslavement of women in the colonies (and in the harem, as imagined by eighteenth-century Britons), Wollstonecraft brought rationalist arguments against slavery into the centre of modern feminist debate, more subtly than did More in *The White Slave Trade* that same year. 'By theorizing about women's rights using old attributions of harem-based slavery in conjunction with denotations of colonial slavery', argues Ferguson, 'Wollstonecraft was a political pioneer, fundamentally altering the definition of rights and paving the way for a much wider cultural dialogue' (33). Wollstonecraft did not provide or imagine the perspective of women of colour in her critiques (unlike sentimental abolitionists like More and Opie, who wrote in the voices of black female slaves in order to evoke their sufferings), though in her last novel, *The Wrongs of Woman*, she did move beyond her middle-class origins and began to imagine alliances between middle-class and working-class women.

Thus Wollstonecraft's originary 'Anglo-American feminism' considered many of the same questions – on class, race, national boundaries and the limits of liberal individualism – that modern, global feminism increasingly presses forward. That she did not (and could not) resolve the contradictions preoccupying her age should not obscure the fact that she did make these contradictions available to feminist inquiry. If we look to the historical moment in which so-called 'Anglo-American feminism' was forged, then, we see that it drew its immediate inspiration from the French Revolution, the tradition of sensibility popularized by Rousseau (certainly in the sexualized receptions of Wollstonecraft and Hays), the collectivist spirit of republican political reform (as opposed to Christian self-improvement), and in conjunction with the ongoing debates on slavery, literal and figural. Both the geographical boundaries of the term, and the intellectual and political qualities it supposedly encompasses, are ultimately inadequate for understanding Wollstonecraft and her 'founding text of Anglo-American feminism'. And equally important is the diversity of thought among Romantic-era feminists, especially regarding corporeality and sexuality: Hays, Williams and Robinson were far more positive about integrating traditionally 'feminine' qualities (for example sensibility and passion) into their feminism than was Wollstonecraft.[13] Similarly, Robinson's and Morgan's recuperations of the theatricality associated with aristocratic French femininity, both in their writings and public personas, suggest that it is a mistake to focus solely on

Wollstonecraft's brand of republicanism to the exclusion of the alternatives that revolutionary Frencophilia offered other women writers.

The 'Anglo-American' and 'French' feminist divide that preoccupied literary theorists until recently also continues to shape modern feminist philosophy, presenting yet another ironic legacy of 1790s Female Philosophers. Modern feminist philosophers have begun to inquire into the diverse traditions of philosophers and philosophical concerns excluded for a myriad of reasons – race, class, genre, gender – from canonical traditions. Thus, mystics like Mechthild of Magdeburg are now considered alongside materialists like Margaret Cavendish, and the Christian empiricism of Mary Astell alongside Heloise's Ciceronian 'philosophy of love'.[14] Wollstonecraft and Macaulay are consistent inclusions in these feminist reassessments of Western philosophy, their originally problematic status as 'female philosophers' taking on a new light, especially given renewed interest in the medieval Heloïse (instead of the Rousseauvian 'new Heloïse') as philosopher. Within current feminist philosophy, philosophy's relationship to and exclusion of the corporeal continues to generate heated debate, but here as with the Anglo-American/French dichotomy, the historical dimensions of this exclusion are often elided. For example, Claire Colebrook's helpful overview of current attempts to transcend the mind/body dichotomy associated with the competing feminist traditions of 'equality' and 'difference' relies on an ahistorical, if elegantly argued, formulation of that opposition. Colebrook reproduces the bogey of 'Anglo-American feminism' and its disembodied bourgeois individualism (77), in order to advance a more radical 'corporeal feminism' that is distinctively 'Australian'. 'Australian corporeal feminism', claiming a new specificity and corporeality, appears in fact as a free-floating set of ideas, adrift in time (yet 'contemporary') and space (yet 'Australian') (*ibid.* 89). Philosophy's disciplinary conventions partly explain this ahistorical move, and yet given the complex history of feminist writings on body and mind, difference, and equality, it is a pity to see this history elided, and thus ironically reproduced.

The internationalism, and indeed cosmopolitanism, of the origins of 'Anglo-American' feminism – in the works of Female Philosophers like Wollstonecraft, Hays, Macaulay, Robinson – resisted such national and geographic boundaries. Eurocentric but antinationalist in their approach to international politics, these Female Philosophers interrogated their Enlightenment and counterenlightenment inheritance. If theirs is an early, similarly problematic, instance of 'International Feminism' as analysed by Gayatri Spivak, then it too 'is defined within a Western European context', but one historically situated in such as way as to allow for its 'heterogeneity' to become 'manageable', or at the very least visible (164). The stubbornly 'Western European context' (as opposed to nationalist British context) of this Francophilic feminism that I have traced throughout *Citizens of the World* was intended and received as a radical challenge to the prevailing culture of xenophobia and Francophobia in revolution-era Britain. In this respect, Female Philosophers' 'Eurocentrism' in the 1790s (like Morgan's *'European* turn' two decades later) is markedly different from both earlier eighteenth-century and twenty-first-century Eurocentrisms. Earlier eighteenth-century cosmopolitanism had been a Eurocentric, elite, and almost universally masculine phenomenon, both in its radical Enlightenment and aristocratic manifestations. Only during the revolutionary wars did such cosmopolitanism (and especially Francophilia) become an acute threat to national security (and even to European racial distinctness, in Elizabeth Hamilton's case). As Female Philosophers, these Romantic-era feminists created from within and without this diverse cosmopolitan tradition new possibilities for intellectual, corporeal and political citizenship that looked beyond national, geographic and sexual boundaries.

The revolutionary cosmopolitanism of these earlier 'mobile women' was eventually eclipsed, both in Romantic-period and modern criticism, by the canonization of Jane Austen (Lynch 56). 'Such a turn was a repatriation', argues Deirdre Lynch, 'to, at the same time, England's green and pleasant land and a maternal bosom'. As a relieved *New Monthly Magazine* reviewer commented in 1820, 'we turn from the dazzling brilliancy of Lady Morgan's works to repose on the soft green of Miss Austen's sweet and unambitious creations'.[15] Today's critical reception of Austen is of course very different from such nineteenth-century readings of her as reassuringly provincial and unambitious, yet her singular status in canonical accounts of the British realist novel illustrates how and why predecessors like Smith, Robinson and Morgan were collectively put in their place. In poetry we find a similar 'repatriation': it is the Lake Poets who are 'the chief carriers ... in this era of the English nationalist aesthetics', turning 'from extreme Francophilism to equally extreme anti-Gallic patriotism' (Newman 241). In this nationalistic 'Reign of Virtue', to use Newman's term (241), it was Wordsworth in particular who eclipsed cosmopolitan and metropolitan contemporaries like Smith and Robinson. Their overtly politicized and cosmopolitan aesthetics, always in opposition to their age's intensifying nationalism and its domestication of women, found fewer allies as the revolutionary wars continued and women's influence was channelled along largely religious and moral lines. Women would increasingly play leading public roles in reform and philanthropic movements, but the fusion of 'the rights of woman' and revolutionary cosmopolitanism in the writings of Smith, Williams, Wollstonecraft and Robinson, and later Plumptre and Morgan, remains a remarkable accomplishment, unprecedented and unrepeated.

Notes

Introduction

1 There exists a large body of work on how traditional models of British Romanticism are unsustainable given the rediscovery of women writers; two of the earliest and most influential are Ross, *Contours of Masculine Desire* and Mellor, *Romanticism and Gender*. For women writers' impact specifically on canonical notions of (male) Romanticism's relationship to the Revolution, see Craciun and Lokke's Introduction to *Rebellious Hearts*.

2 See Eagles's *Francophilia* for the Whigs, and Lucas's *England and Englishness* on Tory cosmopolitanism; on the specifically Francophilic core of cosmopolitanism in eighteenth-century Britain, see Newman (1–48). On Montagu as citizen of the world, see Grundy (359).

3 Current critiques of Enlightenment cosmopolitanism are diverse and object to a number of characteristics that are arguably not essential to cosmopolitanism, for example: a teleological drive towards one world government (Toulmin); a guise for imperialism (Brennan); a 'comprehensive universalism' that is hostile to pluralism and multiculturalism (Guttman). Advocates of 'cosmopolitan democracy' include Habermas and Held.

4 It is important to distinguish that Colley's British nationalism is oppositional (against the French), while Newman's is focused on the self-generated English nationalist drive for self-recognition, internal colonization and, increasingly, opposition to French influence. I will generally refer to 'British nationalism', and less frequently to 'English nationalism', throughout this study for two reasons: first, because my focus is on the Francophobic elements of this oppositional nationalism, and conversely of the Francophilic aspects of radical cosmopolitanism in the 1790s, an approach more compatible with Colley's argument; second, because English Romantic-period nationalist writers like West and More generally used Britain and England interchangeably, partly a result of internal colonization, but also a sign of the fluidity of the usage amongst English writers.

5 Calhoun, 'Cosmopolitanism Is Not Enough' (2). Calhoun expanded this March 2001 plenary paper in several post-September 11 published essays: 'Class Consciousness' and 'Belonging'.

6 On Enlightenment cosmopolitanism see Schlereth's classic *Cosmopolitan Ideal*; on Enlightenment cosmopolitan historiography and economics, see O'Brien's excellent *Narratives of Enlightenment*.

7 Robbins, 'Introduction Part I', in Cheah and Robbins, *Cosmopolitics* (2). For examples of late eighteenth-century particularized cosmopolitanisms, see Kleingold.

8 More to Mrs Kennicott, 4 Feb. 1793, uncatalogued MS, William Andrews Clark Memorial Library, University of California, Los Angeles. In a previous letter to Kennicott, More recommended Fanny Burney as the public spokesperson for the Wilmot Committee, after declining the position herself, but could not even bring herself to utter Burney's new married name (she had married an émigré, d'Arblay): '*The Author of Evelina* (for I detest French names) will fill this place a thousand

times better' (18 Nov. 1793; William Andrews Clark Memorial Library, University of California, Los Angeles).

9 Along similar lines, Anne Mellor has recently argued regarding British women's writings on empire that they evoked an 'embodied cosmopolitanism' that crossed racial lines ("Embodied").

10 Rendall, 'Tacitus Engendered'.

11 See Trumpener and Ferris on bardic nationalism and the national tale, respectively. On British ethnic identities before the era of nationalism, see Colin Kidd.

12 Unfortunately, the British Museum's copy of this print is missing and can no longer be reproduced; see the *Catalogue of Prints and Drawings*, #7688.

13 In France, *poissardes* and privileged women writers (*précieuses*) shared an important historical connection (and marginalization) as female transgressors against the institutionalized 'correct style' of public address; see Hesse, chap. 1.

14 Macaulay also wrote in support of Corsican independence in her *Loose Remarks . . . In a Letter to Signor Paoli* (London: T. Davies, 1767).

15 The *British Critic's* review of *Sins* made this connection, dismissing *Sins* as 'perfectly French', filled with 'all the jargon of French republicanism' (v. 2 (1793): 81).

16 See however McCarthy's 'Why Anna Letitia Barbauld Refused', for an important corrective to the tradition of reading Barbauld as opposed to women and men receiving equal educations. On Barbauld's posthumous reception, determined in part by the discrediting of Dissent and by her family's selective republication of her work, see McCarthy's 'A High-Minded Christian Lady', in Behrendt and Linkin.

17 Marlon Ross has noted how Barbauld's poetry responded to *Village Politics*, but he does not discuss Barbauld's political prose. Ross positions More and Barbauld as dual 'transitional figures' whose writings span a wide rhetorical range, from sweetly feminine verse to 'agitated polemics' in verse (226), and thereby 'begin to establish, for the first time in British history, a discernible tradition in feminine poetry' (202).

1 Female Philosophers

1 While '"English Jacobins" is a wildly misleading description for British radicals in the 1790s', writes Mark Philp, the term does 'indicate an implicitly international dimension to the radical cause' (69).

2 See Warner and Duffy on the novel's early English reception.

3 In France, the establishment of the National Institute in 1795 institutionalized philosophy as a professional academic discipline for the first time. In order to curtail the explosion in commercialized print culture (including pornography) made possible by the 1789 lifting of press restrictions, according to Carla Hesse the Institute 'privileged analytical over narrative modes of philosophical enquiry' and thus 'excluded women from the new arenas where serious philosophical discourse was to take place' (111). In Britain, where far more women published before and during the revolutionary decade than in France (and which lacked a comparable institutionalization of philosophy), Female Philosophers similarly struggled with cultural authorities who sought to circumscribe their generic and political trespasses. As a counterrevolutionary weapon against such philosophical trespasses, 'Modern Philosophy' ironically circulated in the same popular genres as did Female Philosophers – the novel, conduct manual and political

pamphlet. In Britain, it was the Romantic-period professionalization of criticism that similarly sought to curtail women's unprecedented access to popular print (see Siskin).

4   See Wollstonecraft's reviews of Rousseau in her *Works* 7: 228–34, 362–3, 409.

5   As with the first editions of Wollstonecraft's and Macaulay's polemics, Barbauld's *Civic Sermons* and *Sins of Government* were initially published anonymously and identified as hers in subsequent editions.

6   Rendall, quoting *New Annual Register* (1794), in 'The grand causes': 161.

7   *Letters from the Mountains*, excerpted in Craciun, ed., *Routledge Literary Sourcebook*: 49.

8   Binhammer ('Persistence', 7). Watson also makes this point (46).

9   I made this argument in 'Violence Against Difference'; see also Binhammer's more recent essay, 'Thinking Gender'.

10 Robinson's *The False Friend* is also an extended dialogue with both Wollstonecraft and Godwin on philosophy's relationship to sensibility; Robinson's 1800 correspondence with Godwin also reflects this dialogue.

11 Qtd. in Kramnick, Introduction to Godwin's *Enquiry*: 12.

12 See Craciun, *Fatal Women*; Laqueur, *Making Sex*; Johnson's *Equivocal Beings* examines 1790s sexual difference as a crisis in sentimentality. Excerpts from these contemporary accounts of Wollstonecraft can be found in my *Routledge Literary Sourcebook*.

13 Hunt and Jacob, 'The Affective Revolution'; Wahrman, '*Percy's* Prologue: From Gender Play to Gender Panic'.

14 Hunt, quoting *Julie philosophe*, in 'Pornography': 327–9. Hunt outlines the important changes politicized pornography underwent in the 1790s.

15 Grant, *Letters from the Mountains*, excerpted in Craciun, *Routledge Literary Sourcebook* (49).

16 I discuss this feminist Satanism in detail in 'Romantic Satanism'. On the diversity of male-authored Satanism in the 1790s, see Schock.

17 Briefly, these self-reflexive Satanic references in Williams, Smith and Robinson are found in *Letters from France* (Williams), *The Emigrants* and *Elegiac Sonnets* (Smith), and Robinson's *Memoirs*, *Monody* and *Letter*, all discussed in Craciun, 'Romantic Satanism'.

18 Opie was a Dissenter and later became a Quaker; Hamilton was a Scottish Presbyterian/Episcopalian.

19 Qtd. in Grogan, 'Introduction', *Memoirs of Modern Philosophers* (24).

20 Grogan notes the similarity between Bridgetina's unkempt appearance and that of the female reader Sempronia in Vicesimus Knox's *Essays, Moral and Literary* (1778) (46).

21 Malchow argues that Frankenstein's creature is Africanized, while Mellor argues that he is distinctly Asian (*Frankenstein*).

22 On Perry and the *Argus*, see Werkmeister (340–75), as well as my chapter on Robinson.

23 Edgeworth, qtd. in Grogan, 'Introduction' to *Memoirs* (25). On Hamilton's reception, see Kelly.

24 Excerpted in Craciun, ed., *Routledge Literary Sourcebook*.

25 I am indebted to Carol Howard's argument that 'Savanna's family is sacrificed, so that Adeline's may remain intact' (368), and her overall conclusion that in Opie's novel 'The philanthropic gentry' and 'maternal authority...[remain] safely within the "private" realm' (368).

26   E.g., *Village Politics*: 'TOM. "I'm a friend of the people. I want reform". JACK. "Then the shortest way is to mend thyself". TOM. "But I want *general reform*". JACK. "Then let every one mend one"' (346).

27   Barbauld, *Remarks on Mr. Gilbert Wakefield's Enquiry into . . . Public or Social Worship* (J. Johnson, 1792), in *Works* 2: 446, 448.

28   On Barbauld, see poems such as 'Summer Evening's Meditation' and her comment regarding Unitarianism that her religion 'is set in the imagination and the passions, and it has its source in that relish for the sublime, the vast and the beautiful, by which we taste the charms of poetry and other compositions, that address our finer feelings' (qtd. in Adelaide Morris, 'Woman Speaking' 67).

2 Mary Robinson and Radical Politics

1   There is a growing body of work situating Robinson in relation to canonical male Romantics, especially Wordsworth; see: Pascoe, Curran, Vargo, Cross, McGann, and Craciun ('Mary Robinson'); on theatricality, see Pascoe especially, and Cullens, Setzer, Mellor ('Making an Exhibition'). In her PhD dissertation, Anne Close also argues that Robinson is more politically consistent in her novels than 'performative' readings imply, suggesting instead that we consider her more as a 'politician' with a distinct agenda.

2   Clark notes that 'there is little evidence that female friendly societies were mobilized in the 1790s for radical purposes' (147) but nevertheless cites the ephemeral meetings of an LCS 'society for female patriots' observed by a government spy (for details see Thale 43, 155, 83, 79).

3   Overviews of this sceptical tradition include Hilda Smith's *All Men and Both Sexes: Gender, Politics and the False Universal in England 1640–1832*, and Lloyd's *The Man of Reason*. Unfortunately, Smith omits any substantive discussion of the 1770s to 1830, despite her title, thus undermining her argument.

4   Maria Robinson to Cadell and Davies, June 17, 1804. Private Collection.

5   *Oracle*, 18 January 1794; signed 'M.R.' The 1806 version is slightly revised (*Poems* 1: 203).

6   For example, the 1806 version of the poem as 'The Birth-Day' revises the above-quoted stanza, lessening the conscious cruelty of the Duchess: 'All silver'd and embroider'd o'er,/ She neither knows nor pities pain;/ The Beggar freezing at her door/ She overlooks with nice disdain.' In its 1798 *Morning Post* incarnation as 'St. James Street. The Birth-Day,' the poem reads 'She neither knows nor pities pain,/ The beggar, freezing at her door,/ She views with insolent disdain.'

7   On the British Convention and trials for sedition and treason, see Goodwin, Barrell, and Wharam.

8   Transportation had become firmly established by the 1717 Transportation for Felony Act as an alternative to capital punishment, and prisoners had the right to appeal directly to the king for pardon (see Beattie 431–3).

9   'Tabitha Bramble', letter to Robert Dundas, 23 Jan. 1794 (Public Record Office, HO/102/10, f.121). I have compared this letter to signed letters in Robinson's hand, and conclude that the handwriting is hers. The letter does not include any postmarks, but in a different hand in the margin of the letter is written: 'in Lord Advocate's of the 27th Jany. 1794.' It is conceivable that she may have sent this letter to a newspaper intending to publish it as an open letter to Dundas, and that the paper forwarded the letter to the government.

10 I survey this range of British representations of Corday in 'The New Cordays.' Robinson, Williams, and Helen Craik are notable exceptions to counterrevolutionary British uses of Corday, because they maintain her republicanism, while most British accounts transformed her into a royalist.

11 For example, the Whig Friends of the People declined to join in the 1793 Convention, as well as the LCS's proposed second convention the following year, with both Fox and Grey repudiating universal male suffrage (see O'Gorman 165–7; Goodwin 280–1, 317).

12 Howell, *State Trials* 24 (558–9); also in Goodwin 308.

13 The hero/ine Sidney bears the name of the republican Sidney; Walsingham's mother was 'the descendant of an ancient, but ill-fated family: she was a great-granddaughter of Sir Sidney Waller, a gallant general who lost his life on that same day and with that same cause as the immortal Hampden' (*Walsingham* 1: 22–3).

14 See Craciun, 'The New Cordays'.

15 Godwin to Gerrald, rept. in *Caleb Williams*, 357.

16 Dated Dec. 30 1797 and published Jan, 1 1798 in the *Morning Post*, Robinson's poem was intended to preempt Pye's 'Ode for the New Year, 1798' (*Morning Post*, Jan, 18, 1798).

17 *Oracle*, Jan. 2 1794; *Oracle*, Jan. 18 1796; *Telegraph*, Jan. 18 1797. The radical *Telegraph* printed the Ode only to ridicule it in the adjoining editorial notes, among them: 'The LAUREAT's Ode. – Whatever may be said relative to the Invasion, it certainly has occasioned one great good – it has furnished Mr. PYE with *a new subject!'* (orig. emphasis).

18 M. Ray Adams's early essays on Robinson and Merry as political figures are rare exceptions to the often apolitical modern readings of both poets' sensibility, which have distorted Merry's impeccable radical credentials and perhaps forestalled investigations of Robinson's.

19 'Biographical Notice', 256.

20 Published in Paris, *Reflexions* was translated into French by Nicolas Madgett, an Irish member of the British Club, who in his later capacity as translator for the Committee of Public Safety would be particularly significant for Williams and Stone (see Chap. 3). In 1793 Madgett recommended to the French Minister of Foreign Affairs that, in response to British government plans to use a committee of émigrés to discover expatriate republicans, the National Convention establish in Paris a 'comité revolutionnaire Anglais' of twelve expatriate British and Irish republicans who could counter the influx of British spies, including Merry, Joel Barlow and Sampson Perry (Ministère des Affaires Étrangères, Corresp. Politique: Angleterre, vol. 587, f. 20, 43, 45).

21 Adams, ibid 32. The Godwin/Robinson correspondence is held at the Bodleian; one letter is reprinted in Robinson's *Selected Poems*, 367–70.

22 See *Courier* Nov. 28, 1794; *Telegraph*, Aug. 24 1795. Three Pittachio satires (the first definitely Merry's, the subsequent ones with unclear authorship) are reprinted by John Barrell in *Exhibition Extraordinary*, along with helpful critical commentary.

23 Humanitas, *War a System of Madness*, 58. George Miller is identified as the author in a subsequent publication. Behrendt also discusses this briefly (91).

24 The French were very interested in combating the British ministerial papers by funding their own paper; they were suspicious of Perry's political allegiance (as with many British radicals, e.g., Paine) but remained interested in the *Argus* as an independent (nonministerial) paper (see Ministère des Affaires Étrangères, Corresp. Politique: Angleterre, vol. 582, f. 157, 174, 246; vol. 585 f. 67).

25   There did appear in the winter of 1792 a paper printed by Stone's English Press at Paris, though this may be Stone's new paper, edited by Williams (discussed in Chap. 3): *The Magazine of Paris, or Gazette of the Republic of France* (Ministère des Affaires Étrangères, Corresp. Politique: Angleterre, vol. 582, f. 345).

26   On Perry and Stone, see Woodward (79). On Perry in the British Club, see Erdman 241–3.

27   Robinson to Godwin, Aug. 24, 1800 (*Selected Poems*, 368).

28   Robinson to Jane Taylor, 14 Oct. 1794. Folger Shakespeare Library, MS W.b.112.

29   See Favret, 'Telling Tales'.

30   Three extempore poems from 1794 identified as Robinson's bear a striking resemblance to Poeta Inter Minores' extempore poems; they are reprinted in the *Catalogue of the Collection of Autograph Letters*, by A. Morrison, ed. Thibaudeau (5: 286–8).

31   1797 saw the failure of several attempts to forge peace with France. On Oct. 31 1797, the *Morning Post* reported: 'Mrs. Robinson's Epic Poem, we understand, was written on the anticipation of PEACE; when it will now appear is uncertain; WAR may afford an affecting subject for her enlightened pen.' Like Tabitha Bramble, Poeta Inter Minores also targeted coquetry ('Advice to Miranda, On Her Coqueting,' 10 Nov. 1797) and sentimental conventions ('To Myra,' 1 Nov. 1797), alongside invasion paranoia ('Extempore. King's Bench Illumination,' 19 Oct. 1797).

32   See Setzer, Cullens, and Ty, *Empowering the Feminine*.

33   *Morning Post*, Dec. 21, 1797 (excerpting *Walsingham* 3: 253–4).

34   Philp notes how Godwin overtly addressed *Political Justice* to 'the philosophically alert intelligentsia rather than the revolutionary *sans culottes*' in part to avoid prosecution (*Godwin's Political Justice* 103–4).

35   On press restrictions see Werkmeister and Rea.

36   Godwin's defence of the 1794 treason trial victims, *Cursory Strictures* (1794), similarly appeared both as a pamphlet and in the pro-reform *Morning Chronicle* on 21 Oct. 1794 (see Chap. 5 in Philp, *Godwin's Political Justice*). A second excerpt from *Walsingham*, on the persecution of 'men of letters,' appeared in the *Morning Post*, 18 Dec. 1797.

37   I discuss Robinson's essay in 'Mary Robinson, the *Monthly Magazine*, and the Free Press'.

38   Judith Pascoe makes a related and significant point that here Robinson 'anticipate[s] and counter[s] Wordsworth's disparagement of German tragedies in the Preface to the *Lyrical Ballads*', by 'champion[ing] the theater's exhibition of "the most sublime efforts of the dramatic art"' (*Romantic Theatricality*, 139). I suggest that the overall tenor of 'Metropolis' is deliberately cosmopolitan, as well as theatrical, as Pascoe argues.

39   McGann notes the difference between these two writers' class sensibilities (*Poetics* 111).

40   Hesse 62, 49. But Hesse's argument is not convincing in its comparison to British women's access to print in this same revolutionary decade, as she bases her assessment on one outdated British statistic (39).

41   Robinson notes the exclusion of women 'from the auditory part of the British senate' (*Letter* 89). In her *Letter*, Robinson comes very close to Wollstonecraft's radical demand that women 'ought to have representatives' (*Rights of Woman* 147).

42 See for example Calhoun's *Habermas* collection; on the seventeenth-century public sphere, see DeJean.
43 *Selected Poems* 365; letter to Jane Taylor, Oct. 14, 1794 (Folger Library, MS W.b.112) orig. emphasis.

3 Virtue and Terror

1 There exists a vast literature on these female figures. See for example: Outram; Gutwirth; Hunt, *Family Romance*; Goodman's recent collection, *Marie-Antoinette*, includes many influential essays that have made Marie Antoinette a central figure in gendered critiques of the Revolution, especially its Jacobin phase.
2 See also Roe, *Wordsworth and Coleridge* and 'Imagining Robespierre,' and Liu.
3 As Roe has demonstrated, Coleridge and Southey use Robespierre to critique Pitt's own 'reign of terror' on British reformers through the treason trials, a radical critique voiced more overtly by John Thelwall's description of Pitt as 'that Minister who without the energy of Robespierre, has all his dictatorial ambition' (*The Tribune*, 28 May 1795, qtd. in Roe, 'Imagining Robespierre' 165).
4 Chris Jones also notes that 'Robespierre may be considered to be the historical original of many of the fictional villains of this period, such as Mr. Radcliffe's Schedoni, who similarly unites ambition, resentment and an icily rational homicidal logic' ('Helen Maria Williams,' 9).
5 I follow Carol Blum in using the French 'le people' instead of 'the people' because the French is singular and thus allows for more direct identification between an individual (for example Williams) and *le people*.
6 See for example Hunt, *Politics, Culture*; Carol Blum notes that particularly after the execution of Louis XVI, 'speeches and publications show an ever-shrinking vocabulary repeating, with hypnotic regularity, certain key words: virtue, people pure and mass, were contrasted with vice, enemies, corrupt and individuals' (*Rousseau* 195).
7 For more sympathetic views of Robespierre see Doyle's *Oxford History of the French Revolution* and Soboul's *Dictionnaire historique*.
8 Robespierre, reprinted in Bienvenu, *The Ninth of Thermidor*, 39.
9 Robespierre, reprinted in Bienvenu, *The Ninth of Thermidor*, 34–5, 38.
10 Furet, *Penser la Révolution*, as qtd. in Doyle and Haydon, 'Robespierre', 13; Linton, 51.
11 *Chronique of Paris*, Nov. 9 1792, qtd. in account of Robespierre by French historian Alphonse Aulard in *Robespierre*, ed. Rudé, 137.
12 Thiers, *The History of the French Revolution*, qtd. *Robespierre*, ed. Rudé 132.
13 Oct. 1792, in Thompson, ed., *English Witnesses*, 206.
14 Dubois de Crancé, excerpted in Rudé, ed., *Robespierre* 89.
15 See Bohls' good reading of this, 137.
16 Starobinski, qtd. in Blum, *Rousseau*, 218.
17 Robespierre, qtd. in Jordan, 28.
18 It is unfortunate that Dart relies on this abridged modern edition in his brief discussions of Williams, as this edition omits both the extract from the Supreme Being speech and Williams's commentary, as well as her responses to the Thermidorean trials discussed below.
19 On the significance of romance for revolutionary discourse, see Duff.
20 Letter from Riquetti, sister of Mirabeau, to Robespierre, 30 Germinal II, in *Robespierre*, ed Jacob,137.
21 Letter from Louise Jaquin to Robespierre, 13 Prairial II, in *Robespierre*, ed Jacob, 139.

22   Robespierre had recalled Carrier on Feb. 8 to account for the *noyades* at Nantes (see Thompson, *Robespierre*, 2:175). Williams concedes that the Convention did not authorize all 'the wanton acts of cruelty committed by the revolutionary army' in the provinces (2:3:136).

23   Huet, 'Performing Arts,' 141–2. Robespierre's distrust of representation is also evident in his policies, such as the Festival of the Supreme Being, which, unlike the earlier Festival of Reason, did not depict the supreme being literally; the law of 22 Prairial, eliminating the right to legal representation, also shares this 'same teleological concern' to transcend representation (Huet 142).

24   Williams's allusions to *Paradise Lost* are often noted by critics (e.g., Kelly 59).

25   See Rudé, *Robespierre: Portrait*, 52.

26   Qtd. in *Robespierre*, ed. Rudé, 103.

27   Qtd in Thompson, ed. *English Witnesses*, 206.

28   *Journal de Perlet*, 20 Thermidor 1794, qtd. in Baczko 12–13.

29   Robespierre's last speech to the Convention (8 Thermidor) disputed this rumour that he conspired to be tyrant.

30   Barras, *Memoires*, qtd. in Baczko 17.

31   Williams's romance with the married Stone, and her cohabitation with him after his divorce, generated unkind comments in England. Robinson's extramarital relationships with men like the Prince of Wales and Charles Fox made her a notorious figure whom 'respectable' women shunned. Burney's marriage to a French émigré in 1793 inspired a xenophobic reaction amongst the British elite. Craik's personal circumstances are the most remarkable of the four, which I discuss in 'The New Cordays'. Briefly, Craik was the daughter of a wealthy Scottish landowner, who probably had her working-class lover murdered, prompting her self-exile to England. There, Craik devoted her professional career as a novelist to dramatizing the dangers of paternal and sexual tyranny in feminist novels indebted to Robinson, Williams, and Radcliffe.

32   In the counterrevolutionary *Female Revolutionary Plutarch* (1808), a similar pornotopia is declared by a female Jacobin who declares a 'community of enjoyment' abolishing all private and sexual property (1: 267).

33   When Smith's daughter married an émigré in 1793, she wrote to Charles Burney for advice on how to make the marriage legal in France as well, as Fanny Burney had also recently married an émigré. Smith complained of the confusion regarding France's changing marriage laws: 'What the Laws of France *now* are I beleive [sic] nobody knows. Nor can it be guessed, I fear, what they will be' (*Collected Letters* 66).

34   Grant, *Letters from the Mountains*, excerpted in Craciun, *Routledge Literary Sourcebook*, 48–9.

35   See Williams's April 1794 letter to Ruth Barlow, in which she reflects on the uncertainty of her relationship to Stone and the possibility of 'a future state of celibacy', and which she signs 'M.S.', that is Maria Stone (Kurtz and Autrey, 45–7).

36   Nicolas Madgett, Dénonciation, 1 October 1794 (Ministère des Affaires Étrangères, Correspondance Politique: Angleterre vol. 588 f. 265). The divorce was registered 25 June 1794 (Archives de Paris, V10 E/11).

37   Williams notes in the section of *Letters* corresponding to this time the importance of obtaining foreign press to combat the Jacobin media (see 2:3:137–8).

38   Stone and Williams were naturalized in 1817 (Woodward 183), but in their Switzerland trip of 1794 Stone declared himself a French citizen, a status the

French officials in Switzerland debated in their correspondence regarding Stone and Williams (see fn. 41 below).

39 Nicolas Madgett, Dénonciation to Committee of Public Safety, 10 vendemiaire an 3 (1 October 1794); the document is stamped 'Approuvé' by the Committee (Affaires Étrangères, Corresp. Politique: Angleterre, vol. 588, f. 265). Madgett writes that 'La femme Stone qui lisait toutes les lettres de son mari, tant qu'elle a vecu avec lui, et qui peut etre en a soustrait quelques unes, connait l'objet de la mission de Jackson en irlande, et ses liaisons avec nos amis en angleterre, particulierement avec Stone de Londres qui était l'intermediaire de sa correspondence. La mechanieté naturelle de cette femme, jointe a la vengeance qui l'arrive contre un mari de qui elle est divorcée, la portera a son arivée en angleterre a devoiler à Pitt tout ce qu'elle sait, et a servir de temoin contre les deux detenus' [sic].

40 Jackson was a fellow British Club member, who was convicted of treason in 1795 and committed suicide while in custody. In the same volume of manuscripts as Madgett's dénonciation appears *A Full Report of the Trial of the Rev. William Jackson for High Treason* (London: GG and J Robinson, 1795), inscribed 'This copy belongs to Mr. Stone' (f. 377). Jackson was one of the names Madgett forwarded to the Committee of Public Safety in March 1793 for nomination to a 'comité revolutionnaire Anglais', which was also to include Robert Merry, Sampson Perry, Joel Barlow and John Oswald (see Affaires Étrangères, Corresp. politique: Angleterre, vol. 587, f. 20, f. 43, f. 45).

41 Rapport, 17 vendemiaire an 3, Committe of Public Safety (Affaires Étrangères, Corresp. Politique: Angleterre, vol. 588, f. 266). This *rapport* recommends that Coope be detained given that Stone is 'connu pour être attaché aux principes de notre révolution'. According to Woodward (183), Stone and Williams were not officially naturalized until 1817, but as early as his 1794 commission to the Committee of Public Safety, Stone declared himself a French citizen. Writing from Bále to the Commissaire des Relations Exterieures (Buchot), the French consul in Switzerland, Barthélemy, reported after a visit from Stone and Williams that 'Il m'a observé qu'il avoit entierement renoncé à son qualité de citoyen anglois, qu'il etoit devenu citoyen français & que je ne pouvoir moins que de le soutenir en [cette] qualité. Cette question est delicate. Peut-on renoncer à une qualité qu'on ficut de la nature? . . . . Il seroit peut etre convenable que j'eusse des instructions à cet egard. Je t'observe que Stone m'a dit qu'il avoit des commisions mercantiles du comité de salut public' (5 thermidor l'an 2ème; Affaires Étrangères, Corresp. Politique: Suisse (Barthélemy), vol. 448, f. 165–8). Transcribed with original errors.

42 Stone to Barthélemy (Affaires Étrangères, Corresp. Politique: Suisse (Barthélemy) vol. 447, f. 141; a French translation of this letter is in vol. 448, f. 257). Barthélemy's correspondence with Buchot regarding Stone and Williams's status in Switzerland discusses their nationalization status (lacking official proof, says Buchot (vol. 448, f. 439)) and mysterious mission (Affaires Étrangères, Corresp. Politique: Suisse (Barthélemy) vol. 447, f. 141, 146; vol. 448, f. 165–8, 257, 270, 354, 439).

43 Stern's essay on the Press untangles the complex provenance of these publications, noting also the Press's 'abiding interest . . . in writings by or about Americans' (358).

44 There exists an earlier magazine printed by the English Press: *The Magazine of Paris, or Gazette of the Republic of France* (Paris: Printed at the English Printing Office, [1792]) (Ministère des Affaires Étrangères, Corresp. Politique: Angleterre, vol. 582, f. 345).

45   Archives de Paris, D31U3 carton 3, #453, f. 2,4. Stern discusses this document (345–6). The *Acte* confirms that Williams was unmarried and living with Stone.

46   These titles are from the bankruptcy inventory of James Smith, the proprietor who succeeded Williams and Stone (Archives de Paris, D7U1/103).

4 Citizens of the World

1   Ministère des Affaires Étrangères, Contrôle des étrangers: Angleterre, 81 f. 80 (10–17 September 1791): 'Mad^e. Smyth. Mad^e Smyth anglaise est arivée icy [*sic*] depuis peu – et est descendue à L'hotel D'Yorek [*sic*] Rue Jacob. Cette dame viens de Londres. Elle compte rester quelques tems [*sic*] à Paris, et jra [*sic*] la suite voyager.' This record notes largely the arrivals of gentry and aristocracy, thus further narrowing the field to members of Smith's class. French records of this time often use variant spellings for Smith, including Smyth and Smythe, so this difference is probably insignificant. The Hotel d'York was a popular destination for English visitors at this time, and had been the site where the peace of 1783 was signed recognizing the independence of the United States. Smith's sister, Mrs Dorset confirms that in 1791 Smith lived both in Brighton and London, as Smith's letters also bear out, thus corresponding to the Contrôle des étrangers record of Mme Smyth's origin as London. There does exist another archival reference to a possible Charlotte Smith voyage to Paris, during the Peace of Amiens (1802–3), but as the age is so far off this must be a different woman: the Archives Nationales has a record of passports issued, including one for 'Smith (Charlotte) anglaise, âgée de 30 ans, allant à Paris' (*F/7/610, an IX). Smith had wanted to visit France during the 1802 Peace, but was too ill to travel (*Collected Letters* 384).
Smith's *Collected Letters* show a gap between 31 August and 27 November 1791 (the latter letter regarding William Wordsworth, who obtained from her a letter of introduction to Helen Maria Williams in Paris). On 8 June 1791, she wrote to the publisher Davies requesting a copy of Stewart's *Travels to the Most Interesting Parts of the Globe* (1789) and Williams's *A Farewell for Two Years to England* (1791), two good selections for someone preparing to travel (*Collected Letters* 34). *Desmond* incorporates two French pamphlets that would have been difficult to acquire in England (quoted p. 94 and 151). Blank and Todd suggest these may be fictitious, but I have identified them, both published in 1790: *Historie d'un malheureux vassal de Bretagne, écrite par lui même* (Paris, 1790); Taboureau de Montigny, *Lettre d'un démocrate partisan de la révolution, aux aristo-théocrates français* (Orléans: chez Jacob aîné, 1790). In *Desmond*, Geraldine Verney's account of her voyage from England to Paris in autumn 1791 may reflect Smith's own trip. Geraldine compares her impressions to those of her last French voyage in 1785 (when Smith returned from Normandy to England), and contrasts the actual French political situation to that which she was led to expect by émigrés to whom she had spoken in Brighton (323, 328).
In *Beachy Head*, Smith includes an enigmatic note regarding a Paris visit: 'I think I saw, in what is now called the National Museum at Paris, the very large bones of an elephant, which were found in North America' (*Poems* 234). The Jardin du Roi became the National Museum of Natural History in 1793, and in 1791 the Jardin did include displays from Richard's mission in North America, but I do not know if this included elephants (see Hamy). Smith's stay in a Normandy chateau in 1784–5 has been noted as a source of some of the Gothic French

settings of the earlier novels, but as far as we know she did not visit Paris on that trip (see Stanton's introduction to *Old Manor House*, xvii).

2 *Critical Review* n.s. 6 (Sept. 1792) 100; see Dorset's account in *Prose Works of Sir Walter Scott*, 49–50.

3 The British Club address is reprinted in Erdman's *Commerce des Lumières* and Alger's *Paris in 1789–94*. On the British Club see chap. 8 in Erdman and also Alger's 'The British Colony.'

4 Stanton's editorial note to this Nov. 1792 letter suggests that this proposed spring 1793 voyage to Paris is the one mentioned in *Desmond*'s Preface, but the June 1792 Preface referred to a previous voyage, that is the autumn 1791 trip that I suggest she probably made.

5 Starobinski 222.

6 Total figures are notoriously difficult to figure because of the incomplete records and the émigrés' mobility; these are Carpenter's figures (*Refugees*, 40–1), who, like Greer, also discusses the qualifications involved in the calculations. Most of Britain's émigrés returned home in 1802 (Carpenter, *Refugees*, 175).

7 Carpenter, 'London' 66 n.101. 'Total charitable relief' on behalf of all émigrés 'including the national church collection, amounts to £70,000' (Carpenter, *Refugees*, 48).

8 More to Mrs Kennicott, 18 Nov. 1793, William Andrews Clark Memorial Library, UCLA; orig. emphasis.

9 Qtd. in Keane, 'Anxiety,' 115–16.

10 More to Mrs Kennicott, 4 Feb. 1793, William Andrews Clark Memorial Library, UCLA. In *Considerations*, More repeated this sentence, but omitted the comment about the French being a 'cruel people' (7).

11 Greer, Appendix I.

12 Smith's perspective in the *Emigrants*, looking back after the execution of Louis XVI, echoes in significant ways Milton's post-revolutionary perspective on liberty in *Paradise Lost*; see Craciun, 'Romantic Satanism.'

13 On the 'Francocentrism' of this poem, see Bray.

14 Smith's cosmopolitanism is widely commented upon, especially in studies of her fiction: see Keane, *Women* 81–107; Bray; Lokke; Fletcher 219; Hilbish 467 (which catalogues the geographical diversity of Smith's settings).

15 Fletcher, citing Judith Stanton, also notes: 'As Stanton says, Charlotte's admittedly generalized hope for a universal brotherhood of man is symbolized by the success of international – and multilingual – relationships' (*Charlotte Smith* 219).

16 Robinson's doomed heroine in *The False Friend* (1799), Gertrude, learns that her mother's husband was a world traveller and 'citizen of the world' (4:281) who left his wife to go to India, leaving her open to seduction by Lord Denmore. Raised as an orphan, Gertrude falls in love with Lord Denmore, unaware that he is her biological father.

17 See Wohlgemut for this distinction between cosmopolitan and national heroines. Deirdre Lynch also reads *Corinne*, despite its lauded status as an origin of the national heroine, as more accurately a cosmopolitan 'fantasy of trans-nation, in which England and Italy overlap to form a space for feminine solidarities' (63). Lynch also notes how in Owenson's later work, perhaps as a result of *Corinne's* influence, 'national types like Glorvina are outnumbered by hybrid heroines' (70). *Corinne* is often read in terms of its culturally 'dialogic' or 'polyphonic' resistance to monological nationalism (see English Showalter, and John Isbell's Introduction to *Corinne*, respectively).

18   Qtd in Roe, *Wordsworth and Coleridge*, 114.
19   The most thorough account of the Gallipolis fiasco is Moreau-Zanelli's *Gallipolis: Histoire d'un mirage américain au XVIIIe siècle*. Previous American accounts like Belote's tend to exonerate Barlow too easily, despite the evidence that he knowingly sold land he knew the Scioto company did not yet own (see Belote, *The Scioto Company*). The *Prospectus* and *Avis* published by Barlow and Playfair in Paris in 1789 exaggerated the nature and cultivation of the land, in keeping with idealized accounts like Crèvecoeur's. It is not clear what happened to the hundreds of thousands of livres the Paris Compagnie de Scioto received from the émigrés, since these funds never reached the United States as promised (to buy the land from Congress), though it seems unlikely that Barlow himself pocketed it. William Playfair in Paris is often assumed to have taken the money as he was in charge of accounts, while William Duer ended up in debtor's prison in America, the scapegoat for the whole affair.
20   Volney, *View of the Climate and Soil of the United States of America . . . to which are annexed some accounts of . . . the French colony on the Scioto* (London: Joseph Johnson, 1804); qtd. in Hart 194.
21   In France in 1794, Crèvecoeur contacted 'his American acquaintances, Gilbert Imlay in Le Havre and Joel Barlow in Paris . . . apparently seeking some avenue of escape to the United States' (Philbrick 38). On these transatlantic commercial and political networks, see Verhoeven, 'Traveling Through Revolutions.'
22   On emigration debates in the first few decades of the nineteenth century, see Sussman.
23   Barlow to William Duer, 8 Dec. 1789, 29 Nov. 1789 (Belote, ed., 'Selections from the Gallipolis Papers' 61, 60); Belote reprints Barlow's Gallipolis correspondence. Like Stone and Williams, Barlow understood that the Revolution provided unparalleled financial opportunities. 'The great emigration which must be connected with such an event' as the Revolution, he wrote, 'promised much in favor of the sale of lands in America. I believed that the United States might be much benefited by turning this tide of emigration to that country' (Barlow to Benjamin Walker, 21 Dec. 179[1], in Belote, ed., 'Selections,' 72).
24   On Coleridge's resistance to seeing America as distinct from England, especially in terms of language and Pantisocracy, see Flynn.
25   April Alliston makes a compelling case, however, for the utopian island refuges found in the novels of Bernardin, Sand, and Brontë, often characterized by racial hybridization (142–3). I suggest that the immediate revolutionary context of the writings I discuss here made such utopian gestures impossible.
26   Crèvecoeur himself held slaves in his New York farm, Pine Hill. He contrasted his care of slaves as members of his family, with southern abuse of slaves, using a now notorious account of the 'Negro in the Cage'. The main opposition for the physiocratic Crèvecoeur was in fact between European (and New England) commercial society and the agricultural ideal possible only where land was available to all white men; see Jehlen.
27   According to Fletcher, Smith knew Edwards in 1784, and he encouraged her publishing (*Charlotte Smith* 64). While writing *The Young Philosopher*, Smith requested from her publisher copies of Edwards's *History* and Long's *History of Jamaica* (1774), both notorious proslavery accounts (*Collected Letters* 304).
28   Coleridge, qtd. in Coleman, *Maiden Voyages* 8. On the complex connections between race and gender in abolitionist writings, see Coleman's 'Conspicuous Consumption.'

29 On Smith's abusive husband, see Stanton, 'Mr. Monstroso'. In her letters, Smith often referred to herself as 'sold' to her odious husband by her father and his new wife (named Henrietta).
30 Rendall, *Origins* 73, 75.

Epilogue

1 Brightwell's (1854) *Memorials* of Opie also includes excerpts of Opie's journals during her three trips to France (also in 1829 and 1830); see *Maria Edgeworth in France* for Edgeworth's experiences, and vols. 5 and 6 of Burney's *Journals and Letters*. Charlotte Smith had wished to visit France during the Peace, but was too ill to travel (*Collected Letters* 384). Many British tourists during the Peace visited Williams's salon, including Fox, Erskine and the Opies, but Edgeworth chose not to (Woodward 45–7).
2 Archives Nationales *F/7/610 (an IX).
3 The novel was also published in London in 1796, as *Antoinette*. I quote from the 1800 Philadelphia edition.
4 Review of *Letters on the Genius and Dispositions of the French Government, by an American* (1810), *Anti-Jacobin Review*, 35 (April 1810): 337.
5 Plumptre to Mrs Morgan, dated 30 May at Paris, British Library Add. MS 78688, Evelyn Papers 4, vol. 3, f. 108.
6 See Bainbridge on canonical male authors' shifting opinions of Napoleon.
7 I quote from Staël's *Considerations on the French Revolution* and *On Literature* (both in *An Extraordinary Woman* 371, 206, 206).
8 See Plumptre, *Narrative* 1: 161; Morgan, *France* (1817) 2: 233–4, where she meets Mme de Genlis, who tells her that 'Buonaparte was extremely liberal to literary people'.
9 Byron, *Letters* 8: 189. On Byron and Staël, see Wilkes.
10 In contrast to these writers, Staël inherited her parents' strict sense of gendered spheres, and despite her critique of (distinctly British) patriarchal authority in *Corinne*, she praised British sexual mores in her nonfiction prose, for example in *On Literature*: 'If Frenchmen could give their wives all the virtues of English-women, including retiring habits and a taste for solitude, they would do very well to prefer such virtues to the gifts of brilliant wit' (*An Extraordinary Woman* 203). Her *Letters on Rousseau* (1788) had defended Rousseau's characterization of women in his most misogynist texts (*Emile* and the *Letter to D'Alembert*), inciting Wollstonecraft's critique in *Rights of Woman*.
11 On Wollstonecraft's diminishing Francophobia, see Wellington, 'Blurring the Borders'.
12 On the multitude of sins involved in this 'Anglo-American' creation of 'French Feminism', see Christine Delphy, 'The Invention of French Feminism'. The autumn 1993 issue of *Tulsa Studies in Women's Literature* was devoted to reassessing the 'Anglo-American feminist' tradition, and provides an excellent collective critique of this formulation.
13 On Hays in this regard, see Wallace; on Robinson and Wollstonecraft, see Craciun 'Violence Against Difference'.
14 See for example, Atherton and Tougas and Sara Ebenreck, *Presenting Women Philosophers*, which has a helpful essay on Heloïse's philosophy by Mary Ellen White. Catherine Villanueva Gardner looks in detail at how traditional ideas of

philosophic genre have been used to exclude women's contributions to Western philosophy, and discusses Macaulay, Wollstonecraft and George Eliot.

15 'On the Female Literature of the Present Age', *New Monthly Magazine,* 13 (1820): 637; I owe this reference to Lynch (64). See also Siskin, Johnson and Moretti on Austen's formative role in the critical fortunes of the Romantic novel.

Bibliography

Primary texts

Address Published by the London Corresponding Society at the General Meeting held at the Globe Tavern, Strand, on Monday the 20th day of January 1794. London, 1794.

Aikin, John, and Anna Barbauld. *Evenings at Home.* 6 vols. London: J. Johnson, 1792–96.

Barbauld, Anna Laetitia. *Civic Sermons to the People. Number I.* London: J. Johnson, 1792.

——. *Civic Sermons to the People. Number II.* London: J. Johnson, 1792.

——. *Reasons for National Penitence Recommended for the Fast Appointed on February 28, 1794.* London: J. Johnson, 1794.

——. *Remarks on Mr. Gilbert Wakefield's Enquiry into the Expediency and Propriety of Public or Social Worship.* London: J. Johnson, 1792.

——. *Selected Poetry and Prose.* Eds. William McCarthy and Elizabeth Kraft. Peterborough: Broadview, 2002.

——. *Sins of Government, Sins of the Nation; or, A Discourse for the Fast, Appointed on April 19, 1793. Selected Poetry and Prose.* Eds. McCarthy and Kraft. 297–320.

——. *Works of Anna Laetitia Barbauld. With a Memoir by Lucy Aikin.* 2 vols. 1825. Facsimile ed. with introduction by Caroline Franklin. London: Routledge/Thoemmes, 1996.

Barlow, Joel. *Political Writings of Joel Barlow.* New York: Mott and Lyon, 1796.

——. *Vision of Columbus. Works of Joel Barlow.* Vol. 2 of 2. Eds. William Bottorff and Arthur Ford. Gainsville: Scholars' Facsimiles and Reprints, 1970.

'Biographical Notice of Mr. Robert Merry.' *Monthly Magazine* (April 1799): 255–8.

Briquet, Fortunée. *Dictionnaire historique, littéraire et bibliographique des françaises et des étrangères naturalisées en France.* Paris: Gillé, 1804.

Burke, Edmund. *A Letter to a member of the National Assembly.* London, 1791.

——. *Reflections on the Revolution in France.* Ed. Thomas Mahoney. Indianapolis: Bobbs-Merrill, 1955.

——. *The Works of the Right Honourable Edmund Burke.* Ed. Judge Willis. 6 vols. London: Oxford UP, 1906.

Burney, Fanny. *Brief Reflexions Relative to the Emigrant French Clergy.* Introduction by Claudia Johnson. Rpt. with More's *Considerations.* Los Angeles: William Andrews Clark Library, 1990.

——. *Journals and Letters of Fanny Burney.* Ed. Joyce Hemlow. Oxford: Clarendon, 1972– .

——. *The Wanderer, or, Female Difficulties.* Introduction by Margaret Drabble. London: Pandora, 1988.

Byron, Lord. *Byron's Letters and Journals.* Ed. Leslie Marchand. 12 vols. Cambridge, Mass.: Belknap P of Harvard UP, 1973–82.

Coleridge, Samuel and Robert Southey. *The Fall of Robespierre.* Oxford: Woodstock 1991.

Craik, Helen. *Adelaide de Narbonne, with Memoirs of Charlotte de Cordet.* 4 vols. London: Minerva Press, 1800.

Crèvecoeur, J. Hector St. John de. *Letters from an American Farmer.* Ed. Manning. Oxford: Oxford UP, 1997.

Dacre, Charlotte. *The Passions.* 4 vols. New York: Arno Press, 1974.

Defauconpret, A. J. B. *Observations sur l'ouvrage intitulé La France, par Lady Morgan.* Paris: à la Librairie Stéréotype, 1817.

Dorothea; or, A Ray of the New Light. 2 vols. Dublin: Thomas Burnside, 1801.

Dorset, Catherine. 'Charlotte Smith.' *Biographical Memoirs.* Edinburgh: Robert Cadell, 1834. Vol. 4 of *The Miscellaneous Prose Works of Sir Walter Scott.* 20–70.

Edgeworth, Maria. *Maria Edgeworth in France and Switzerland: Selections from the Edgeworth Family Letters.* Ed. Christina Colvin. Oxford: Clarendon, 1979.

——. *Novels and Selected Works. Volume V: The Absentee, Madame de Fleury, Emilie de Coulanges.* Ed. Heidi Van de Veire, Kim Walker, Marilyn Butler. London: Pickering and Chatto, 1999.

The Emigrant in London, a Drama. By an Emigrant. London, 1794.

The Female Patriot. London, 1779.

The Female Revolutionary Plutarch. 3 vols. 3rd ed. London: J. Murray, 1808.

Genlis, Madame de. *The Young Exiles; or, Correspondence of Some Juvenile Emigrants.* London: J. Wright, 1799.

Godwin, William. *Enquiry Concerning Political Justice.* Ed. Isaac Kramnick. Harmondsworth: Penguin, 1976.

——. *Things As They Are; or, The Adventures of Caleb Williams.* Ed. Maurice Hindle. Harmondsworth: Penguin, 1988.

Grant, Anne. *Eighteen Hundred and Thirteen.* London: Longman, Hurst, Rees, Orme and Brown, 1814.

Hamilton, Elizabeth. *Memoirs of Modern Philosophers.* Ed. Claire Grogan. Peterborough: Broadview, 2000.

Hawkins, Laetitia Matilda. *Letters on the Female Mind, Its Powers and Pursuits; With Particular Reference to the Dangerous Opinions Contained in the Writings of Miss. H. M. Williams.* 2 vols. 2nd ed. London: J. and T. Carpenter, 1801.

Hays, Mary. *Letters and Essays, Moral and Miscellaneous.* 1793. Ed. Gina Luria. New York: Garland, 1974.

——. *Memoirs of Emma Courtney.* Ed. Eleanor Ty. Oxford: Oxford UP, 1996.

'Humanitas' [George Miller]. *War a System of Madness and Irreligion. To which is subjoined, by way of a conclusion, the Dawn of Universal Peace. Wrote on the late Fast Day, March 10ᵗʰ 1796.* Edinburgh, 1796.

Kant, Immanuel. *Perpetual Peace.* Trans. M. Campbell Smith. London: Allen & Unwin, 1917.

LaFontaine, August. *Clara Duplessis, and Clairant: The History of a Family of French Emigrants.* 3 vols. Trans. from the German. London: Longman, 1797.

Macaulay, Catherine. *Observations on the Reflections of the Right Hon. Edmund Burke, on the Revolution in France.* London: C. Dilly, 1790.

Memoirs of Female Philosophers. 2 vols. London, 1808.

Merry, Robert. *The Laurel of Liberty.* London: John Bell, 1790.

——. *Reflexions Politique sur La Nouvelle Constitution.* Paris: J. Reyner, 1792.

Moody, Elizabeth. 'Anna's Complaint; Or the Miseries of War.' In *War a System of Madness and Irreligion.* By 'Humanitas.' 63.

More, Hannah. *Coelebs in Search of a Wife.* 2 vols. 5th ed. London: T. Cadell & W. Davies, 1809.

——. *Considerations on Religion.* First American ed. 1794. Introduction by Claudia Johnson. Rpt. with Burney's *Brief Reflexions.* Los Angeles: William Andrews Clark Memorial Library, 1990.

——. *Strictures on Female Education: The Miscellaneous Works of Hannah More.* Vol. 1 of 2. London: Thomas Tegg, 1840.

——. *Tales for the Common People*. Ed. Clare MacDonald. Nottingham: Trent Editions, 2002.
——. *Village Politics*. In *Poems by Hannah More*. 1816. Facsimile ed. with introduction by Caroline Franklin. London: Routledge/Thoemmes, 1996.
Morgan, Lady (Sydney Owenson). *France*. [2 vols. in 1, but titlepage does not indicate this.] London: Henry Colburn, 1817.
——. *France*. 3rd. ed. 2 vols. London: Henry Colburn, 1818.
——. *The Wild Irish Girl*. Ed. Kathryn Kirkpatrick. Oxford: Oxford UP, 1999.
'On the Female Literature of the Present Age.' *New Monthly Magazine* 13 (1820) 633–8.
Opie, Amelia Alderson. *Adeline Mowbray*. Introduction by Jeanette Winterson. London: Pandora, 1986.
Paine, Thomas. *The Rights of Man*. Ed. H. Collins. Harmondsworth: Penguin, 1969.
Peacock, Lucy. *The Little Emigrant*. London: S. Low for the author, 1799.
Pigott, Charles. *Political Dictionary*. London: D. I. Eaton, 1795.
Pilkington, Mrs. [Mary]. *New Tales of the Castle; or, The Noble Emigrants, a Story of Modern Times*. London: Vernor and Hood, 1800.
Playfair, William. *France As It Is, Not Lady Morgan's France*. 2 vols. London: C. Chapple, 1819.
Plumptre, Anne. *Antoinette Percival. A Novel*. Philadelphia: Mathew Carey, 1800.
——. *A Narrative of a Three Years' Residence in France*. 3 vols. London, 1810.
The Political Testament of Maximil. Roberstpierre. London: F. and C. Rivington, 1796.
Polwhele, Richard. *The Unsex'd Females: A Poem*. London: Cadell and Davies, 1798.
Robinson, Mary. *Ainsi va Le Monde*. 2nd ed. London: John Bell, 1790.
——. *Angelina*. 3 vols. London: Hookham and Carpenter, 1796.
——. *The False Friend: A Domestic Story*. 4 vols. London: Longman & Rees, 1799.
——. *Hubert de Sevrac: A Romance of the Eighteenth Century*. 4 vols. London: Hookham, 1796.
——. *Impartial Reflections on the Present Situation of the Queen of France; by a Friend to Humanity*. London: John Bell, 1791.
——. *A Letter to the Women of England, on the Injustice of Mental Subordination. A Romantic Circles Hypertext Edition*. Ed. Adriana Craciun, Anne Close, Megan Musgrove, Orianne Smith. <www.rc.umd.edu/editions/robinson/cover.htm> Dec. 1998.
——. *Memoirs of the Late Mrs. Robinson*. 4 vols. London: Phillips, 1801.
——. *Monody to the Memory of the Late Queen of France*. London: T. Spilsbury and Son, 1793.
——. *The Natural Daughter*. Ed. Sharon Setzer. Peterborough: Broadview, 2003.
——. 'Present State of the Manners and Society of the Metropolis of England.' *PMLA* 119.1 (2004) 103–19.
——. *Selected Poems*. Ed. Judith Pascoe. Peterborough: Broadview, 2000.
——. *Walsingham; or, The Pupil of Nature*. Ed. Julie Shaffer. Peterborough: Broadview.
——. *The Widow, or A Picture of Modern Times*. 2 vols. London: Hookham and Carpenter, 1794.
Shelley, Mary. *Frankenstein*. Ed. Maurice Hindle. Harmondsworth: Penguin, 1992.
Smith, Charlotte. *The Banished Man*. London: Cadell & Davies, 1794.
——. *Collected Letters of Charlotte Smith*. Ed. Judith Stanton. Bloomington: Indiana UP, 2003.
——. *Desmond*. Eds. Antje Blank and Janet Todd. Peterborough: Broadview, 2001.
——. *Marchmont*. 4 vols. in 1. Facsimile ed. with introduction by Mary Anne Schofield. Delmar, NY: Scholars' Facsimiles and Reprints, 1989.
——. *The Old Manor House*. Ed. Anne Henry Ehrenpreis. Introduction by Judith Phillips Stanton. Oxford: Oxford UP, 1989.

——. *The Poems of Charlotte Smith*. Ed. Stuart Curran. Oxford: Oxford UP, 1993.

——. 'The Story of Henrietta.' *Letters of a Solitary Wanderer*. Vol. 2 of 3. London: Sampson Low, 1800.

——. *The Wanderings of Warwick*. London: J. Bell, 1794. Facsimile ed. with introduction by Caroline Franklin. London: Routledge/Thoemmes, 1992.

——. *The Young Philosopher*. Ed. Elizabeth Kraft. Lexington: UP of Kentucky, 1999.

Staël, Germaine de. *Corinne, or Italy*. Ed. and trans. Sylvia Raphael. Oxford: Oxford UP, 1998.

——. *An Extraordinary Woman: Selected Writings of Germaine de Staël*. Trans. Vivian Folkenflik. New York: Columbia UP, 1987.

Sterne, Laurence. *A Sentimental Journey Through France and Italy*. Ed. Ian Jack. Oxford: Oxford UP, 1968.

Tench, Watkin. *Letters from Revolutionary France*. Ed. Gavin Edwards. Cardiff: U of Wales P, 2001.

The Trial of Maurice Margarot. London: Printed for M. Margarot; London Corresponding Society; J. Ridgway, 1794.

Walker, George. *The Vagabond*. 2 vols. London: Printed for G. Walker, 1799.

West, Jane. *An Elegy on the Death of . . . Edmund Burke*. London: Longman, 1797.

——. *Letters to a Young Lady*. 3 vols. 4th ed. London: Longman, Hurst, Rees, Orme & Brown, 1811. Facsimile ed. as vol. 4–6 in *Female Education in the Age of Enlightenment*. London: Pickering, 1996.

——. *Poems and Plays*. 4 vols. London: Longman and Rees, 1799.

——. *A Tale of the Times*. 3 vols. London: Longman and Rees, 1799.

Williams, Helen Maria. *Letters from France*. 8 vols. in 2. Introduction by Janet Todd. Delmar, NY: Scholars' Fascimiles and Reprints, 1975.

——. *Memoirs of the Reign of Robespierre*. Ed. F. Funck-Brentano. New York: John Hamilton, 1929.

——. *Souvenirs de la Révolution Française*. Paris: Dondey-Dupré, 1827.

——. *A Tour in Switzerland*. 2 vols. London: G. G. and J. Robinson, 1798.

Wollstonecraft, Mary. *Collected Letters of Mary Wollstonecraft*. Ed. Ralph M. Wardle. Ithaca: Cornell UP, 1979.

——. *A Vindication of the Rights of Woman*. Ed. Carol Poston. New York: Norton, 1975.

——. *The Works of Mary Wollstonecraft*. Ed. Janet Todd and Marilyn Butler. 7 vols. London: Pickering, 1989.

Wood, Sally Sayward Barrell. *Julia, and the Illuminated Baron*. Portsmouth, New Hampshire: C. Peirce, 1800.

Young, Mary Julia. *Adelaide and Antonine: or The Emigrants*. London: J. P. Coghlan, 1793.

Secondary sources

Abrams, M. H. 'English Romanticism: The Spirit of the Age.' *Romanticism Reconsidered*. Ed. Northrop Frye. New York: Columbia UP, 1963.

Adams, M. Ray. 'Chapter IV: Mrs. Mary Robinson, a Study of Her Later Career.' *Studies in the Literary Backgrounds of English Radicalism*. Lancaster, PA: Franklin and Marshall College P, 1947. 104–29.

——. 'Robert Merry, Political Romanticist.' *PMLA* 2 (1967): 23–37.

——. 'Helen Maria Williams and the French Revolution.' *Wordsworth and Coleridge: Studies in Honor of George McLean Harper*. Ed. Earl Leslie Griggs. New York: Russell & Russell, 1962. 87–117.

Alger, John G. 'The British Colony in Paris, 1792–93.' *English Historical Review* 13 (1898): 672–94.

——. *Paris in 1789–94. Farewell letters of victims of the guillotine.* London: George Allen, 1902.

Alliston, April. 'Transnational Sympathies, Imaginary Communities.' *The Literary Channel.* Eds. Cohen and Dever. 133–48.

Anderson, Benedict. *Imagined Communities.* Rev. ed. London: Verso, 1983.

Atherton, Margaret, ed. *Women Philosophers of the Early Modern Period.* Indianapolis: Hackett, 1994.

Aulard, Alphonse. *Les Grands Orateurs de la Révolution: Mirabeau, Vergniaud, Danton, Robespierre.* Paris: F. Rieder et cie, 1914.

Baczko, Bronislaw. *Ending the Terror: The French Revolution after Robespierre.* Trans. Michel Petheram. Cambridge: Cambridge UP, 1994.

Bainbridge, Simon. *Napoleon and English Romanticism.* Cambridge: Cambridge UP.

Balayé, Simone. 'Staël and Liberty: An Overview.' *Germaine de Staël.* Ed. Gutwirth *et al.* 13–21.

Barrell, John. *Imagining the King's Death.* Oxford: Oxford UP, 2002.

Barrell, John, ed. *'Exhibition Extraordinary!!' Radical Broadsides of the mid 1790s.* Nottingham: Trent Editions, 2001.

Beattie, John. *Crime and the Courts in England, 1660–1800.* Oxford: Clarendon, 1986.

Behrendt, Stephen. 'British Women Poets and the Reverberations of Radicalism in the 1790s.' *Romanticism, Radicalism, and the Press.* Ed. Stephen Behrendt. Detroit: Wayne State UP, 1997. 83–102.

Behrendt, Stephen and Harriet Kramer Linkin, eds. *Romanticism and Women Poets: Opening the Doors of Reception.* Lexington: UP of Kentucky, 1999.

Belote, Theodore. *The Scioto Company and the French Settlement at Gallipolis.* Cincinnati: UP of Cincinnati, 1907.

Belote, Theodore, ed. 'Selections from the Gallipolis Papers.' *Quarterly Publication of the Historical and Philosophical Society of Ohio* 2.2 (April–June 1907): 41–92.

Berlanstein, Leonard. 'Women and Power in Eighteenth-Century France: Actresses at the Comédie-Française.' *Visions and Revisions of Eighteenth-Century France.* Eds. Christine Adams, Jack Censer, Lisa Jane Graham. University Park: Pennsylvania State UP, 1997. 155–90.

Bienvenu, Richard, ed. *The Ninth of Thermidor: The Fall of Robespierre.* New York: Oxford UP, 1968.

Binfield, Kevin. 'The French, "The long-wished-for Revolution," and the Just War in Joanna Southcott.' *Rebellious Hearts.* Eds. Craciun and Lokke. 135–59.

Binhammer, Katherine. 'The Persistence of Reading: Governing Female Novel-reading in *Memoirs of Emma Courtney* and *Memoirs of Modern Philosophers*.' *Eighteenth-Century Life* 27.2 (2003): 1–22.

——. 'Thinking Gender with Sexuality in 1790s Feminist Thought.' *Feminist Studies* 28.3 (2002): 667–90.

Blakemore, Steven. *Crisis in Representation: Thomas Paine, Mary Wollstonecraft, Helen Maria Williams.* Madison, New Jersey: Fairleigh Dickinson UP, 1997.

——. 'Revolution and the French Disease: Laetitia Matilda Hawkins's *Letters* to Helen Maria Williams.' *SEL* 36 (1996).

Blanc, Olivier, ed. *Last Letters: Prisons and Prisoners of the French Revolution, 1793–1794.* Trans. Alan Sheridan. New York: Farrar, Staus & Giroux, 1987.

Blum, Carol. 'Representing the Body Politic: Fictions of the State.' *Representing the French Revolution.* Ed. James Heffernan. Hanover, New Hampshire: UP of New England, 1992.

——. *Rousseau and the Republic of Virtue: The Language of Politics in the French Revolution.* Ithaca: Cornell UP, 1986.

Bohls, Elizabeth. *Women Travel Writers and the Language of Aesthetics, 1716–1818.* Cambridge: Cambridge UP, 1995.

Bray, Mathew. 'Removing the Anglo-Saxon Yoke: The Francocentric Vision of Charlotte Smith's Later Works.' *Wordsworth Circle* 24 (1993): 155–8.

Brennan, Timothy. *At Home in the World: Cosmopolitanism Now.* Cambridge, Massachusetts: Harvard UP, 1997.

Brightwell, Cecilia Lucy. *Memorials of the Life of Amelia Opie.* 2nd ed. Norwich: Fletcher and Alexander, 1854.

Brown, Laura. *The Ends of Empire.* Ithaca: Cornell UP, 1993.

Calhoun, Craig. ''Belonging' in the Cosmopolitan Imaginary.' *Ethnicities* 3.4 (2003): 531–68.

——. 'The Class Consciousness of Frequent Travelers: Towards a Critique of Actually Existing Cosmopolitanism.' *South Atlantic Quarterly* 101.4 (2002) 869–97.

——. 'Cosmopolitanism is Not Enough: Local Democracy in a Global Context.' Presented at the 'Local Democracy' Conference, March 2001, U of North Carolina, Chapel Hill.

Calhoun, Craig, ed. *Habermas and the Public Sphere.* Cambridge: MIT, 1992.

Campbell, Mary. *Lady Morgan: The Life and Times of Sydney Owenson.* London: Pandora, 1988.

Carnall, Geoffrey. 'The Monthly Magazine.' *Review of English Studies* ns 5 (1954): 158–64.

Carpenter, Kirsty. 'London: Capital of the Emigration.' *The French Émigrés.* Eds. Carpenter and Mansel. 43–67.

——. *Refugees of the French Revolution: Émigrés in London, 1789–1802.* Houndmills: Macmillan, 1999.

Carpenter, Kirsty, and Philip Mansel, eds. *The French Émigrés in Europe and the Struggle Against Revolution, 1789–1814.* Houndmills: Macmillan, 1999.

Catalogue of Prints and Drawings in the British Museum. Division 1. Political and Personal Satires. 11 vols. London, 1870–1954.

Cheah, Pheng, and Bruce Robbins, eds. *Cosmopolitics: Thinking and Feeling Beyond the Nation.* Minneapolis: U of Minnesota P, 1998.

Claeys, Gregory. 'The Origins of the Rights of Labor: Republicanism, Commerce and the Construction of Modern Social Theory in Britain, 1796–1805.' *Journal of Modern History* 66 (1994) 249–90.

Clark, Anna. *The Struggle for the Breeches: Gender and the Making of the British Working Class.* Berkeley: California UP, 1995.

Clayden, P. W. *Early Life of Samuel Rogers.* London, 1887.

Clifford, James. *Robert Merry: A Pre-Byronic Hero.* Manchester: Manchester UP, 1943.

Close, Anne. ''A Writer of Novels'': Mary Robinson and the Politics of Professional Authorship.' PhD. Diss. Loyola University Chicago. 2003.

Cohen, Margaret. 'Sentimental Communities.' *The Literary Channel.* Eds. Cohen and Dever. 106–32.

Cohen, Margaret, and Carolyn Dever, eds. *The Literary Channel: The Inter-National Invention of the Novel.* Princeton: Princeton UP, 2003.

Colebrook, Claire. 'From Radical Representations to Corporeal Becomings: The Feminist Philosophy of Lloyd, Grosz, and Gatens.' *Hypatia* 15.2 (2000): 76–93.

Coleman, Deirdre. 'Conspicuous Consumption: White Abolitionism and English Women's Protest Writing in the 1790s.' *ELH* 61.2 (1994): 341–62.

Coleman, Deirdre, ed. *Maiden Voyages: Two Women's Travel Narratives of the 1790s.* London: Leicester UP, 1999.

Colley, Linda. *Britons: Forging the Nation.* New Haven: Yale UP, 1992.

Cone, Carl. *The English Jacobins: Reformers in late 18th century England.* New York: Charles Scribner's Sons, 1968.

Conway, Alison. 'Nationalism, Revolution, and the Female Body: Charlotte Smith's *Desmond.*' *Women's Studies* 24 (1995): 395–409.

Cook, Malcolm. 'The Émigré Novel.' *The French Émigrés.* Eds. Carpenter and Mansel. 151–64.

Cookson, J. E. *The Friends of Peace: Anti-War Liberalism in England, 1793–1815.* Cambridge: Cambridge UP, 1982.

Craciun, Adriana. *Fatal Women of Romanticism.* Cambridge: Cambridge UP, 2003.

——. Introduction. Sophia King, *Waldorf, or the Dangers of Philosophy.* London: Pickering and Chatto, forthcoming.

——. Introduction. Mary Robinson, 'Present State of the Manners and Society of the Metropolis of England.' *PMLA* 119.1 (2004): 103–7.

——. 'Mary Robinson, the *Monthly Magazine*, and the Free Press.' *Prose Studies* 25.1 (2003): 19–40.

——. 'The New Cordays: Helen Craik and British Representations of Charlotte Corday, 1793–1800.' *Rebellious Hearts.* Eds. Craciun and Lokke. 193–232.

——. 'Romantic Satanism and the Rise of Nineteenth-Century Women's Poetry.' *New Literary History* 34 (2004): 699–721.

——. 'Violence against Difference: Mary Wollstonecraft and Mary Robinson.' *Making History: Textuality and the Forms of Eighteenth-Century Culture.* Ed. Greg Clingham. Lewisburg: Bucknell UP, 1998. 111–41.

Craciun, Adriana, ed. *A Routledge Literary Sourcebook for Mary Wollstonecraft's Vindication of the Rights of Woman.* London: Routledge, 2002.

Craciun, Adriana, and Kari Lokke. 'British Women Writers and the French Revolution, 1789–1815.' *Rebellious Hearts.* Eds. Craciun and Lokke. 3–32.

Craciun, Adriana, and Kari Lokke, eds. *Rebellious Hearts: British Women Writers and the French Revolution.* Albany: State University of New York P, 2001.

Cross, Ashley. 'From *Lyrical Ballads* to *Lyrical Tales*: Reputation and the Problem of Literary Debt.' *Studies in Romanticism* 40 (2001): 571–605.

Cullens, Chris. 'Mrs. Robinson and the Masquerade of Womanliness.' *Body and Text in the Eighteenth Century.* Eds. Veronica Kelly and Dorothea von Mucke. Stanford: Stanford UP, 1994. 266–89.

Curran, Stuart. 'Mary Robinson and the New Lyric.' *Women's Writing* 9.1 (2002): 9–23.

——. 'Mary Robinson's *Lyrical Tales* in Context.' *Re-visioning Romanticism: British Women Writers 1776–1837.* Eds. Carol Shiner-Wilson and Joel Haefner. Philadelphia: U of Pennsylvania P, 1994. 17–35.

Dart, Greg. *Rousseau, Robespierre and English Romanticism.* Cambridge: Cambridge UP, 1999.

Davis, David Brion. *The Problem of Slavery in the Age of Revolution.* Ithaca: Cornell UP, 1975.

DeJean, Joan. *Ancients Against Moderns: Culture Wars and the Making of a Fin de Siecle.* Chicago: Chicago UP, 1997.

Delphy, Christine. 'The Invention of French Feminism: An Essential Move.' *Yale French Studies* 87 (1995): 166–97.

Doyle, William. Introduction. *The French Émigrés.* Eds. Carpenter and Mansel. xv–xxii.

——. *The Oxford History of the French Revolution.* Oxford: Clarendon, 1989.

Doyle, William, and Colin Haydon. 'Robespierre: After Two Hundred Years.' *Robespierre*. Eds. Doyle and Haydon.

Doyle, William, and Colin Haydon, eds. *Robespierre*. Cambridge: Cambridge UP, 1999.

Duff, David. *Romance and Revolution: Shelley and the Politics of a Genre*. Cambridge: Cambridge UP, 1994.

Duffy, Edward. *Rousseau in England*. Berkeley: U of California P, 1979.

Eagles, Robin. *Francophilia in English Society, 1748–1815*. Basingstoke: Macmillan, 2000.

Eberle, Roxanne. 'Amelia Opie's *Adeline Mowbray*: Diverting the Libertine Gaze.' *Studies in the Novel* 26.2 (1994): 121–52.

Emsley, Clive. *British Society and the French Wars, 1793–1815*. Basingstoke: Macmillan, 1979.

Erdman, David V. *Commerce des lumières: John Oswald and the British in Paris, 1790–1793*. Columbia: U of Missouri P, 1986.

Eugenia, Sister. 'Coleridge's Scheme of Pantisocracy and American Travel Accounts.' *PMLA* 45 (1930): 1069–84.

Favret, Mary. 'Coming Home: The Public Spaces of Romantic War' *SiR* 33.4 (1994): 539–48.

——. *Romantic Correspondence: Women, Politics and the Fiction of Letters*. Cambridge: Cambridge UP, 1993.

——. 'Telling Tales About Genre: Poetry in the Romantic Novel.' *Studies in the Novel* 26 (1994): 153–72.

Fay, Elizabeth. *A Feminist Introduction to Romanticism*. Oxford: Blackwell, 1998.

Ferguson, Moira. *Colonialism and Gender Relations from Mary Wollstonecraft to Jamaica Kincaid: East Caribbean Connections*. New York: Columbia UP, 1993.

Ferris, Ina. *The Romantic National Tale and the Question of Ireland*. Cambridge: Cambridge UP, 2002.

Fletcher, Loraine. *Charlotte Smith: A Critical Biography*. Basingstoke: Macmillan, 1998.

Flynn, Christopher. 'Coleridge's American Dream: Natural Language, National Genius and the Sonnets of 1794–95.' *European Romantic Review* 13 (2002): 411–25.

Foucault, Michel. 'Of Other Spaces.' *Diacritics* 16.1 (1986): 22–27.

Fraistat, Neil. *The Poem and the Book: Interpreting Collections of Romantic Poetry*. Chapel Hill: U of North Caroline P, 1985.

Friedman, Susan Stanford. 'Relational Epistemology and the Question of Anglo-American Feminist Criticism.' *Tulsa Studies in Women's Literature* 12.2 (1993): 247–61.

Furet, François. *Penser la Révolution française*. Paris: Gallimard, 1979.

——. *La Révolution. De Turgot à Jules Ferry, 1770–1880*. Paris: Hachette, 1988.

Gardner, Catherine Villanueva. *Rediscovering Women Philosophers: Philosophical Genre and the Boundaries of Philosophy*. Boulder: Westview, 2000.

Gilman, Sander. 'Black Bodies, White Bodies.' *Critical Inquiry* 12 (1985): 204–42.

Gilmartin, Kevin. *Print Politics: The Press and Radical Opposition in Early Nineteenth-Century England*. Cambridge: Cambridge UP, 1996.

Goodman, Dena. *The Republic of Letters: A Cultural History of the French Enlightenment*. Ithaca: Cornell UP, 1994.

Goodman, Dena, ed. *Marie-Antoinette: Writings on the Body of a Queen*. London: Routledge, 2003.

Goodwin, Albert. *The Friends of Liberty*. London: Hutchinson, 1979.

Gray, W. Forbes. *The Poets Laureate of England*. London: Pitman & Sons, 1914.

Greer, Donald. *The Incidence of Emigration During the French Revolution*. Cambridge: Harvard UP, 1951.

Grenby, Mathew. *The Anti-Jacobin Novel*. Cambridge: Cambridge UP.

Griffin, Dustin. *Patriotism and Poetry in 18th Century Britain*. Cambridge: Cambridge UP, 2002.

Grundy, Isobel. *Lady Mary Wortley Montagu*. Oxford: Oxford UP, 1999.

Gueniffey, Patrice. 'Robespierre.' *Dictionnaire Critique de la Révolution française*. Eds. François Furet and Mona Ozouf. Paris: Flammarion, 1989.

Guest, Harriet. *Small Change: Women, Learning, Patriotism 1750–1810*. Chicago: Chicago UP, 2000.

Guttman, Amy. 'The Challenge of Multiculturalism in Political Ethics.' *Philosophy and Public Affairs* 22.3 (1993): 171–206.

Gutwirth, Madelyn, *et al*, ed. *Germanine De Staël: Crossing the Borders*. New Brunswick: Rutgers UP, 1991.

Habermas, Jürgen. 'Kant's Idea of Perpetual Peace, with the Benefit of Two Hundred Years' Hindsight.' *Perpetual Peace: Essays on Kant's Cosmopolitan Ideal*. Eds. James Bohman and Matthias Lutz-Bachman. Cambridge, Massachusetts: MIT, 1997. 113–53.

Hamy, E. T. *Les Derniers jours du Jardin du roi*. Paris, 1893.

Hart, R. Douglas. *The Ohio Frontier: Crucible of the Old Northwest, 1720–1830*. Bloomington: Indiana UP, 1996.

Harvey, David. 'Cosmopolitanism and the Banality of Geographical Evils.' *Public Culture* 12.2 (2000): 529–64.

Held, David. *Democracy and the Global Order*. Cambridge: Polity, 1995.

Hesse, Carla. *The Other Enlightenment: How French Women Became Modern*. Princeton: Princeton UP, 2001.

Hilbish, Florence. *Charlotte Smith, Poet and Novelist*. Philadelphia: Pennsylvania UP, 1941.

Hill, Bridget. *Republican Virago: The Life and Times of Catharine Macaulay, Historian*. Oxford: Clarendon, 1992.

Howard, Carol. '"The Story of the Pineapple": Sentimental Abolitionism and Moral Motherhood in Amelia Opie's *Adeline Mowbray*.' *Studies in the Novel* 30 (1998): 355–76.

Howell, Thomas Jones, comp. *A Complete Collection of State Trials*. Vol. 25. London: Longman, Hurst, Rees, Orme, and Brown, 1818.

Hudson, Nicholas. '"Britons Never Will be Slaves": National Myth, Conservatism, and the Beginnings of British Antislavery.' *Eighteenth-Century Studies* 34 (2001): 559–76.

Huet, Marie-Helene. 'Performing Arts: Theatricality and the Terror.' *Representing the French Revolution*. Ed. James Heffernan. Hanover, New Hampshire: UP of New England, 1992.

Hunt, Lynn. *The Family Romance of the French Revolution*. Berkeley: U of California P, 1992.

——. 'Male Virtue and Republican Motherhood.' *The Terror*. Ed. Keith Michael Baker. Oxford: Pergamon, 1994. Vol. 4 of *The French Revolution and the Creation of Modern Political Culture*. 195–208.

——. *Politics, Culture and Class in The French Revolution*. Berkeley: U of California P, 1984.

——. 'Pornography and the French Revolution.' *The Invention of Pornography*. Ed. Hunt. 301–39.

——. 'The Unstable Boundaries of the French Revolution.' *From the Fires of Revolution to the Great War*. Ed. Michelle Perrot. Cambridge, Massachusetts: Belknap Press, 1990. Vol. 4 of *A History of Private Life*. 13–45.

Hunt, Lynn, ed. *The Invention of Pornography*. New York: Zone, 1993.

Hunt, Lynn, and Margaret Jacob. 'The Affective Revolution in 1790s Britain.' *Eighteenth-Century Studies* 34.4 (2001): 491–521.

Jacob, Louis, ed. *Robespierre vu par ses Contemporains*. Paris: Armand Colin, 1938.

Jacob, Margaret. 'The Materialist World of Pornography.' *The Invention of Pornography*. Ed. Hunt. 157–202.

Jehlen, Myra. 'J. Hector St. John Crèvecoeur: A Monarcho-Anarchist in Revolutionary America.' *Readings at the Edge of Literature.* Chicago: U of Chicago P, 2002.

Jerinic, Maria. 'Challenging Englishness: Frances Burney's *The Wanderer.' Rebellious Hearts.* Eds. Craciun and Lokke.

Jewett, William. '*The Fall of Robespierre* and the Sublime Machinery of Agency.' *ELH* 63 (1996): 423–52.

Johnson, Claudia. *Equivocal Beings: Politics, Gender, and Sentimentality in the 1790s.* Chicago: Chicago UP, 1995.

Jones, Chris. 'Helen Maria Williams and Radical Sensibility.' *Prose Studies* 12 (1989): 3–24.

Jones, Vivien. 'Femininity, Nationalism, and Romanticism: The Politics of Gender in the Revolution Controversy.' *History of European Ideas* 16 (1993): 299–305.

——. 'Women Writing Revolution: Narratives of History and Sexuality in Wollstonecraft and Williams.' *Beyond Romanticism: New Approaches to Texts and Contexts, 1780–1832.* Eds. Stephen Copley and John Whale. London: Routledge, 1992. 178–99.

Jordan, David. 'The Robespierre Problem.' *Robespierre.* Eds. Doyle and Haydon.

Kadish, Doris. 'Narrating the French Revolution: The Example of *Corinne.' Germaine de Staël.* Ed. Gutwirth *et al.* 113–21.

Kaplan, Cora. *Sea Changes: Essays in Culture and Feminism.* London: Verso, 1986.

Keach, William. 'A Regency Prophecy and the End of Anna Barbauld's Career.' *Studies in Romanticism* 33.4 (Winter 1994): 569–77.

Keane, Angela. 'The Anxiety of (Feminine) Influence: Hannah More and Counter-revolution.' *Rebellious Hearts.* Eds. Craciun and Lokke. 109–134.

——. *Women Writers and the English Nation in the 1790s.* Cambridge: Cambridge UP, 2000.

Kelly, Gary. *Women, Writing, and Revolution, 1790–1827.* Oxford: Clarendon, 1993.

Kennedy, Deborah. *Helen Maria Williams and the Age of Revolution.* Lewisburg, PA: Bucknell UP, 2002.

——. 'The Spectacle of the Guillotine: Helen Maria Williams and the Reign of Terror.' *Philological Quarterly* 73 (1994): 95–113.

Kidd, Colin. *British Identities Before Nationalism.* Cambridge: Cambridge UP, 1999.

Klancher, Jon. *The Making of English Reading Audiences, 1790–1832.* Madison: U of Wisconsin P, 1987.

Kleingold, Pauline. 'Six Varieties of Cosmopolitanism in Late Eighteenth-Century Germany.' *Journal of the History of Ideas* 60.3 (1999) 505–24.

Kurtz, Benjamin and Carrie Autrey, eds. *New Letters of Mary Wollstonecraft and Helen Maria Williams.* Berkeley: U of California P, 1937.

Landes, Joan. *Women and the Public Sphere in the Age of the French Revolution.* Ithaca: Cornell UP, 1988.

Laqueur, Thomas. *Making Sex: Body and Gender from the Greeks to Freud.* Cambridge, MA: Harvard UP, 1990.

Leask, Nigel. Review of Helen Thomas, *Romanticism and Slave Narratives* (Cambridge: Cambridge UP, 2000). *Review of English Studies* 53 (Aug. 2002): 445–7.

LeBlanc, Jacqueline. 'Politics and Commercial Sensibility in Helen Maria Williams' *Letters from France.' Eighteenth-Century Life* 21.1 (1997): 26–44.

Linton, Marisa. 'Robespierre's Political Principles.' Doyle and Haydon, eds. 37–53.

Liu, Alan. *Wordsworth: The Sense of History.* Stanford: Stanford UP, 1989.

Lloyd, Genevieve. *The Man of Reason: 'Man' and 'Woman' in Western Philosophy.* 2nd ed. London: Routledge, 1993.

Lokke, Kari. '"The Mild Dominion of the Moon": Charlotte Smith and the Politics of Transcendence.' *Rebellious Hearts*. Eds. Craciun and Lokke. 85–108.

London, April. 'Clock Time and Utopia's Time in Novels of the 1790s.' *SEL* 40.3 (2000): 539–60.

Lucas, John. *England and Englishness: Ideas of Nationhood in English Poetry, 1688–1900*. London: Hogarth, 1990.

Lynch, Deirdre. 'Domesticating Fictions and Nationalizing Women: Edmund Burke, Property, and the Reproduction of Englishness.' *Romanticism, Race, and Imperial Culture 1780–1834*. Eds. Alan Richardson and Sonia Hofkosh. Bloomington: Indiana UP, 1996. 40–71.

Mahon, Penny. 'In Sermon and Story: Contrasting Anti-War Rhetoric in the Work of Anna Barbauld and Amelia Opie.' *Women's Writing* 7.1 (2000): 23–38.

———. '"Things by their right name": Peace Education in *Evenings at Home*.' *Children's Literature: Annual of the MLA Division on Children's Literature* 28 (2000): 164–174.

Malchow, H. L. *Gothic Images of Race in Nineteenth-Century Britain*. Stanford: Stanford UP, 1996.

Mandell, Laura. '"Those limbs disjointed of gigantic power": Barbauld's Personifications and the (Mis)attribution of Political Agency.' *Studies in Romanticism* 37:1 (1998): 27–41.

Maniquis, Robert. 'Holy Savagery and Wild Justice: English Romanticism and the Terror.' *Studies in Romanticism* 28 (1989): 365–395.

Marso, Lori Jo. *(Un)Manly Citizens: Jean-Jacques Rousseau's and Germaine de Staël's Subversive Women*. Baltimore: Johns Hopkins UP, 1999.

May, Gita. *Madame Roland and the Age of Revolution*. New York: Columbia UP, 1970.

McCalman, Iain. 'Newgate in Revolution; Radical Enthusiasm and Romantic Counterculture.' *Eighteenth-Century Life* 22.1 (1998): 95–110.

McCarthy, William. 'A "High-Minded Christian Lady": The Posthumous Reception of Anna Letitia Barbauld.' *Romanticism and Women Poets*. Eds. Behrendt and Linkin. 165–91.

———. 'Why Anna Letitia Barbauld Refused to Head a Women's College: New Facts, New Story.' *Nineteenth-Century Contexts* 23 (2001): 349–79.

McCarthy, William and Elizabeth Kraft. Introduction. Anna Laetitia Barbauld, *Selected Poetry and Prose*. Ed. William McCarthy and Elizabeth Kraft. Peterborough: Broadview, 2002. Introduction. Barbauld, *Selected Poetry and Prose*. 11–32.

McGann, Jerome. *The Poetics of Sensibility: A Revolution in Literary Style*. Oxford: Clarendon, 1996.

Mee, Jon. '"Reciprocal expressions of kindness": Robert Merry, Della Cruscanism and the limits of sociability.' *Romantic Sociability: Social Networks and Literary Culture in Britain, 1770–1840*. Ed. Gillian Russell and Clara Tuite. Cambridge: Cambridge UP, 2002. 104–22.

Mehta, Pratap Bhanu. 'Cosmopolitanism and the Circle of Reason.' *Political Theory* 28.5 (2000): 619–39.

Mellor, Anne. 'Embodied Cosmopolitanism and British Romantic Women Writers.' Paper presented at the 2003 MLA conference, San Diego, CA.

———. '*Frankenstein*, Racial Science, and the Yellow Peril.' *Nineteenth-Century Contexts* 23:1 (2001): 1–28.

———. 'Making an Exhibition of Herself: Mary "Perdita" Robinson and Nineteenth-Century Scripts of Female Sexuality.' *Nineteenth-Century Contexts* 22 (2000): 271–304.

——. *Mothers of the Nation.* Bloomington: Indiana UP, 2000.

——. *Romanticism and Gender.* London: Routledge, 1993.

Merians, Linda. ' "Hottentot": The Emergence of an Early Modern Racist Epithet.' *Shakespeare Studies* 26 (1998): 123–44.

Moreau-Zanelli, Jocelyne. *Gallipolis: Histoire d'un mirage américain au XVIIIe siècle.* Paris: L'Harmattan, 2000.

Moretti, Franco. *Atlas of the European Novel, 1800–1900.* London: Verso, 1998.

Mori, Jennifer. *Britain in the Age of the French Revolution, 1785–1820.* Harlow: Longman, 2000.

Morris, Adelaide. 'A Woman Speaking to Women: Retracing the Feminine in Anna Laetitia Barbauld.' *Women's Writing* 10.1 (2003): 47–72.

Morris, Marilyn. *The British Monarchy and the French Revolution.* New Haven: Yale UP, 1998.

Morrison, A. *Catalogue of the Collection of Autograph Letters.* Vol. 5 of 6. Ed. Alphonse Wyatt Thibaudeau, London, 1893–7.

Moskal, Jeanne. 'Gender, Nationality, and Textual Authority in Lady Morgan's Travel Books.' *Women Romantic Writers: Voices and Countervoices.* Ed. Paula Feldman and Theresa Kelley. Hanover: UP of New England, 1995. 171–93.

——. 'Napoleon, Nationalism, and the Politics of Religion in Mariana Starke's *Letters from Italy.*' Craciun and Lokke, eds., *Rebellious Hearts.* 161–90.

Newman, Gerald. *The Rise of English Nationalism.* London: St. Martin's, 1987.

Norberg, Kathryn. 'The Libertine Whore: Prostitution in French Pornography from Margot to Juliette.' *The Invention of Pornography.* Ed. Hunt. 225–52.

Nussbaum, Felicity. *Torrid Zones: Maternity, Sexuality and Empire in Eighteenth-Century English Narratives.* Baltimore: Johns Hopkins UP, 1995.

——. '(White) Anglo-American Feminism in Non-US/Non-us Space.' *Tulsa Studies in Women's Literature* 12.2 (1993): 263–70.

O'Brien, Conor Cruise. *The Great Melody: A Thematic Biography and Commented Anthology of Edmund Burke.* London: Sinclair-Stevenson, 1992.

O'Brien, Karen. *Narratives of Enlightenment: Cosmopolitan History from Voltaire to Gibbon.* Cambridge: Cambridge UP, 1997.

O'Gorman, F. *The Whig Party and the French Revolution.* London: Macmillan/St. Martin's, 1967.

Outram, Dorinda. *The Body and the French Revolution.* New Haven: Yale UP.

Pascoe, Judith. *Romantic Theatricality: Gender, Poetry and Spectatorship.* Ithaca: Cornell UP, 1997.

Philbrick, Thomas. *St. John de Crevecoeur.* New York: Twayne, 1970.

Philp, Mark. 'English Republicanism in the 1790s.' *Journal of Political Philosophy* 6.3 (1998) 235–62.

——. 'The Fragmented Ideology of Reform.' *The French Revolution and British Popular Politics.* Ed. Mark Philp. Cambridge: Cambridge UP, 1991. 50–77.

——. *Godwin's Political Justice.* London: Duckworth, 1986.

Plongeron, Bernard. Introduction. *L'abbé Grégoire et la République des savants.* Paris: Éditions du Comité des travaux historiques et scientifiques, 2001.

Priestman, Martin. *Romantic Atheism: Poetry and Freethought, 1780–1830.* Cambridge: Cambridge UP, 1999.

Rapport, Michael. *Nationality and citizenship in revolutionary France: the treatment of foreigners 1789–1799.* Oxford: Clarendon, 2000.

Rea, Robert. ' "The Liberty of the Press" as an Issue in English Politics, 1792–1793.' *The Historian* 24 (1961): 26–43.

Rendall, Jane. '"The grand causes which combine to carry mankind forward": Wollstonecraft, History, and Revolution.' *Women's Writing* 4.2 (1997): 155–72.

——. *The Origins of Modern Feminism*. Basingstoke: Macmillan, 1985.

——. 'Tacitus Engendered: "Gothic feminism" and British Histories c. 1750–1800.' *Imagining Nations*. Ed. Geoffrey Cubitt. Manchester: Manchester UP, 1998. 57–74.

Rigney, Ann.'Icon and Symbol: The Historical Figure Called Robespierre.' *Representing the French Revolution*. Ed. James Heffernan. Hanover, NH: UP of New England, 1992.

Robbins, Bruce. 'Introduction Part I.' *Cosmopolitics*. Eds. Cheah and Robbins. 1–19.

Roe, Nicholas. 'Imagining Robespierre.' *Coleridge's Imagination: Essays in Memory of Pete Laver*. Eds. Richard Gravil, Lucy Newlyn, Nicholas Roe. Cambridge : Cambridge UP, 1985.

——. *The Politics of Nature*. Basingstoke: Macmillan, 1992.

——. *Wordsworth and Coleridge: The Radical Years*. Oxford: Clarendon, 1988.

Rogers, Katharine. 'The View from England.' *French Women and the Age of Enlightenment*. Ed. Samia Spencer. Bloomington: Indiana UP, 1984. 357–368.

Ross, Marlon B. 'Configurations of Feminine Reform: The Woman Writer and the Tradition of Dissent.' *Re-Visioning Romanticism British Women Writers, 1776–1837*. Eds. Carol Shiner Wilson and Joel Haefner. Philadelphia: U of Pennsylvania P, 1994. 91–110.

——. *The Contours of Masculine Desire: Romanticism and the Rise of Women's Poetry*. New York: Oxford UP, 1989.

Rudé, George. *Robespierre: Portrait of a Revolutionary Democrat*. New York: Viking, 1975.

Rudé, George, ed. *Robespierre*. Englewood Cliffs, New Jersey: Prentice-Hall, 1967.

Schlereth, Thomas. *The Cosmopolitan Ideal in Englightenment Thought*. Notre Dame: U of Note Dame P, 1977.

Schock, Peter. '*The Marriage of Heaven and Hell*: Blake's Myth of Satan and its Cultural Matrix.' *ELH* 60 (1993): 441–70.

Setzer, Sharon. 'The Dying Game: Crossdressing in Mary Robinson's *Walsingham*.' *Nineteenth-Century Contexts* 22 (2000): 305–28.

——. 'Romancing the Reign of Terror: Sexual Politics in Mary Robinson's *Natural Daughter*.' *Criticism* 34 (1997): 531–55.

Showalter, English. 'Corinne as an Autonomous Heroine.' *Germaine de Staël: Crossing the Borders*. Eds. Madelyn Gutwirth, Avriel Goldberger and Katryna Szmurlo. New Brunswick: Rutgers UP, 1991. 188–92.

Simpson, David. *Romanticism, Nationalism, and the Revolt Against Theory*. Chicago: Chicago UP, 1993. Siskin, Clifford. *The Work of Writing: Literature and Social Change in Britain 1700–1830*. Baltimore: Johns Hopkins UP, 1998.

Smith, Hilda. *All Men and Both Sexes: Gender, Politics and the False Universal in England, 1640–1832*. University Park: Pennsylvania State UP, 2002.

Smith, Olivia. *The Politics of Language, 1791–1819*. Oxford: Oxford UP, 1984.

Soboul, Albert, ed. *Dictionnaire historique de la Révolution française*. Paris: PUF, 1989.

Spivak, Gayatri Chakravorty. 'French Feminism in an International Frame.' *Yale French Studies* 62 (1981) 154–84.

Stanton, Judith. 'Charlotte Smith and "Mr. Monstroso": An Eighteenth-Century Marriage in Life and Fiction.' *Women's Writing* 7 (2000): 7–22.

Stern, Madeleine. 'The English Press in Paris and Its Successors, 1793–1852.' *Papers of the Bibliographical Society of America* 74 (1980): 307–59.

Starobinski, Jean. 'The Political Thought of Jean-Jacques Rousseau.' Rousseau, *Political Writings* 221–32.

Sussman, Charlotte. '"Islanded in the World": Cultural Memory and Human Mobility in *The Last Man*.' *PMLA* 118 (2003): 286–301.

Sutherland, Kathryn. 'Hannah More's Counter-revolutionary Feminism.' *Revolution in Writing: British Literary Responses to the French Revolution.* Ed. Kelvin Everest. Buckingham: Open UP, 1991. 27–63.

Thale, Mary, ed. *Selections from the Papers of the London Corresponding Society, 1792–1799.* Cambridge: Cambridge UP, 1983.

Thomas, Helen. *Romanticism and Slave Narratives.* Cambridge: Cambridge UP, 2000.

Thompson, James Mathew, ed. *English Witnesses of the French Revolution.* Oxford: Basil Blackwell, 1938.

——. *Robsepierre.* 2 vols. Oxford: Basil Blackwell, 1935.

Tougas, Cecile, and Sara Ebenreck, eds. *Presenting Women Philosophers.* Philadelphia: Temple UP, 2000.

Toulmin, Stephen. *Cosmopolis: The Hidden Agenda of Modernity.* Chicago: U of Chicago P, 1992.

Trouille, Mary Seidman. *Sexual Politics in the Enlightenment: Women Writers Read Rousseau.* Albany, New York: State U of New York P, 1997.

Trumpener, Katie. *Bardic Nationalism: The Romantic Novel and the British Empire.* Princeton: Princeton UP, 1997.

Ty, Eleanor. *Empowering the Feminine: The Narratives of Mary Robinson, Jane West, and Amelia Opie.* Toronto: Toronto UP, 1998.

——. *Unsex'd Revolutionaries: Five Women Novelists of the 1790s.* Toronto: Toronto UP, 1993.

Vargo, Lisa. 'Tabitha Bramble and the *Lyrical Tales.*' *Women's Writing* 9 (2002): 37–52.

Verhoeven, Wil. 'Land-jobbing in the Western Territories: Radicalism, Transatlantic Emigration, and the 1790s American Travel Narrative.' *Romantic Geographies: Discourses of Travel, 1775–1844.* Ed. Amanda Gilroy. Manchester: Manchester UP, 2000. 184–203.

——. 'Traveling Through Revolutions: Chastellux, Barlow, and Transatlantic Political Cultures, 1776–1812.' *Revolutionary Histories: Transatlantic Cultural Nationalism, 1775–1815.* Ed. Wil Verhoeven. Basingstoke: Palgrave, 2002. 10–20.

Wahrman, Dror. '*Percy's* Prologue: From Gender Play to Gender Panic in Eighteenth-Century England.' *Past and Present* 159 (May 1998): 113–60.

Wallace, Miriam. 'Mary Hays's "Female Philosopher": Constructing Revolutionary Subjects.' *Rebellious Hearts.* Eds. Craciun and Lokke. 233–60.

Warner, James. 'Eighteenth-Century English Reactions to the *Nouvelle Héloïse.*' *PMLA* 52.3 (1937): 803–19.

Watson, Nicola J. *Revolution and the Form of the English Novel, 1790–1825: Intercepted Letters, Interrupted Seductions.* Oxford: Clarendon, 1994.

Wellington, Jan. 'Blurring the Borders of Nation and Gender: Mary Wollstonecraft's Character (R)evolution.' *Rebellious Hearts.* Eds. Craciun and Lokke. 33–61.

Werkmeister, Lucyle. *The London Daily Press, 1772–1792.* Lincoln: U of Nebraska P, 1963.

Wharam, Alan. *The Treason Trials, 1794.* Leicester: Leicester UP, 1992.

Wohlgemut, Esther. 'What do you do with that at home?': The Cosmopolitan Heroine and the National Tale.' *European Romantic Review* 13.2 (2002): 191–7.

Woodress, James Leslie. *A Yankee's Odyssey: The Life of Joel Barlow.* New York: Greenwood P, 1968.

Woodward, Lionel, *Une anglaise amie de la Révolution Française: Hélène Maria Williams et ses amis.* Paris: Honoré Champion, 1930.

Index